SECRETS OF WYCLIFFE MANOR

GRAVESYDE PRIORY MYSTERY, #1

PATRICIA RICE

PLEASE JOIN MY READER LIST

PLEASE CONSIDER JOINING MY NEWSLETTER FOR EXCLUSIVE CONTENT AND NEWS OF upcoming releases. Be the first to know about special sales, freebies, stories from my writer life, and other fun information. You'll even receive a thank-you gift. Join me on my writing adventures!

<u>JOIN HERE</u>

ONE

Cairo, 1809

"Two piasters, miss, only one English shilling!" The Egyptian merchant shoved an armful of beaded bracelets into nineteen-year-old Clarissa Knightley's face, forcing her to halt in the narrow, crowded alley.

Colorful fabrics and birds in cages hung overhead. The heady scent of spices mixed with the stench of smoke and dung. Baubles and trinkets and shawls distracted the eye. . .

"Stop looking, birdwit," Beatrice snapped, forcing past the merchant to yank Clare away and proceeding through the cacophonous bazaar like Napoleon through. . . well, Egypt.

A ship through the current? Not original enough. Her sister was a force of nature. A hurricane through an island?

"Two piasters, miss!" Another young man cried, waving a shawl in her face. "I have wife, children, only two piasters!"

"Look, we could take one to mama. They're so pretty and cheap, Bea. . ." Clare tried to glimpse the offerings as her sister dragged her past aromatic spice barrels and tables of glittering jewelry.

"Like pretty faces, pretty trinkets are cheap, but once they drag you in, they won't let go until they empty your pockets."

Pretty faces empty pockets. . . Did that mean people with pretty faces were poor or made other people poor?

Pondering the grammar, Clare shook her hand free to defiantly examine a shawl. Bea sailed on without her.

The explosion shattered Clare's complacence. In an instant, a screaming maelstrom of running soldiers, musket fire, and blood engulfed the colorful bazaar. She froze in shock at the splatters on her white gown. Their bodyguard abruptly flung her backward, into the arms of a stranger in smelly robes. "Run, missy, run!"

More soldiers firing weapons shoved past, propelling her backward into the escaping mob.

Surrounded by a barrage of noise, shoved heedlessly from one malodorous stranger to another, spectacles lost in the melee, Clare lost consciousness—and Bea.

∾

LONDON, FEBRUARY 1815

ADDING MARMALADE TO HER TOAST, CLARE THOUGHT OF HER LATE SISTER'S warning as she contemplated the fiasco of last night's entertainment. *Pretty faces empty pockets.* Perhaps if she had a pretty face or a plumper pocket, she might learn what that meant.

After paying to have her first novel published, her pocket was considerably leaner.

She handed the toast under the tablecloth for small fingers to grab.

"How did you fare at the soirée last night?" Meera Abrams, companion, best friend, and trusted apothecary, sorted through the morning's post.

"Not well." Clare sighed at the embarrassing memory. "A gentleman asked if I liked Wellingtons, and I told him the general was a brilliant man, but I was glad the war was over. When everyone giggled and the conversation returned to discussing boots, I realized they were talking fashion, not politics. I fear I had been watching a maid tuck a crumpet into her apron and imagining a scene of a girl starving in the attic who must serve in this opulence."

Meera laughed. "It is all fodder for your novel, so good came of it. And there will always be another chance."

Clare shrugged. "Unlikely. I cannot go without a companion, and my aunt is only here for the week. Since you will not accompany me, and I cannot afford a new gown for every event, my matchmaking opportunities are limited to bookstores."

"Where you have your head in a book, when you are not keeping track of Oliver and how many pennies you have left. You don't even notice men."

"I think I am meant to be an old maid. Being a wallflower is amusing." Inured to her lack of social skills, Clare poured a second cup of tea. "Last night I heard that all society believes Oliver is heir to a fortune but lacking in the upper story."

That was a lie, but she saw no reason to correct idiocy. Another wit had whispered that Bea had been a termagant who had followed her soldier husband to Egypt, where they'd got themselves killed, which apparently made the entire family odd.

That *on dit* was painful, but closer to the truth, although malaria and dysentery had killed her brother-in-law, not the bomb. But admittedly, her family, although descended from a respectable line of noble, if eccentric, earls, had never been normal. Clare and Oliver were perfect examples.

"Your father's sister means well," Meera said sympathetically. "She is trying to see you receive the attention your mother's illness and death denied."

"She is trying to steer me to a better set of acquaintances," Clare said dryly, donning her spectacles to study the morning newssheet. "She does not approve of you or our bluestocking friends."

Aunt Martha had terrified her into attending the soiree by warning that her father's family was considering removing Oliver from her care. They thought he needed a man in his life. Horribly, Clare feared they might be right.

She and her nephew had already lost all they loved. She couldn't let relative strangers take him away. Only, marriage simply didn't seem to be in her cards.

So, she'd settled on finding a male tutor to be the man Oliver needed, if she could find one she could afford. She feared she'd been foolish in risking the household budget to have a book published in hopes of earning a little bit more.

Should her family learn about her scandalous occupation. . . Her male pseudonym prevented that. She simply must wait to see if her risk provided a future.

It had been a year since her mother's death. Her family was right that she needed to enter society again. Well, not exactly again. Between her father's death, her sister's marriage, and her mother's illness, she never really had been presented. These days, she'd rather not be. After Egypt, she preferred to keep her distance from men and crowds. Even the masculine scent of sandalwood induced a need to flee.

Clare didn't explain to her bold friend that she had been relieved that no one had asked her to dance. Men inhabited her worst nightmares. She had spent a week in perspiring anxiety, fearing that the soiree would be a crush. She'd rather become a hermit then spend another evening attempting small talk with large, noisy males.

A smashing, splintering *bang* disrupted her reflections. Clare shrieked and dropped her teacup. Clasping the table so as not to drop under it, she waited for blood-curdling screams.

Meera sensibly checked the street behind the draperies.

"A carriage collided with the night cart. Messy, but no one's hurt." She returned to her seat. As an apothecary, she would have run outside to assist if anyone had been injured.

No blood. No foul-smelling strangers.

Clare gritted her teeth and mentally repeated her mantra. She could do this. Her house was safe. No one bombed the streets of London. Thugs would not enter her gracious parlor.

Meera mopped up Clare's spilled tea. Oliver darted from beneath the table to watch the commotion outside. Clare closed her eyes until the din settled and her heart stopped racing. She was fine. She was more than fine.

Hand shaking, she raised a piece of toast to her lips and focused on the newssheet.

Napoleon had escaped his prison!

No, no, she would not borrow trouble. Napoleon would not be sailing the channel with his army. . . No muskets and uniforms in the streets of London.

Her imagination might be the death of her one day. Conflict was easier to control in fiction.

"Does the post bring any replies to your search for a tutor?" Meera asked, attempting to distract her.

As a distraction, it worked well. Her nephew had a brilliant mind, but like the rest of the family. . . he was not normal. Finding not only a *suitable* teacher, but a male one who would work for a female with little money. . . Complicated.

Hoping for a reply to her application to the employment agency, Clare flipped through the rest of the post until she reached an official-looking missive from *Wycliffe Manor*. What on earth? Had that not been sold eons ago?

She slit the seal, then raised her cup for a sip while skimming the stilted composition. . . and spluttered hot tea across the linen. Coughing, unable to speak, she waved the missive until Meera took the letter and put toast in her hand.

Short, round, and dark compared to Clare's tall, thin, and pale, Meera possessed the logical mind that Clare did not. "Bad news?" she asked worriedly, because Meera's life, like Clare's, had been a string of bad news. They had that much in common. Her friend read the letter at Clare's wave of permission. "Wycliffe Manor? In Gravesyde Priory? How gothic. What is this about?"

Methodically chewing cold toast to cool her burned tongue and gather her thoughts, Clare shook her head, not immediately answering. Surprises were generally bad news. When she'd recovered sufficiently, she took the letter back and read it more carefully.

"My great-grandfather was the Earl of Wycliffe." She frowned at the elegant writing. "The original estate dated back to a priory destroyed in the 1500s. The village still bears the name. The first earl rebuilt and renamed the property Wycliffe Manor. I've never seen it. The last earl sold everything when it became clear the line of succession had died out."

"Is that allowed?" Meera asked in suspicion. The daughter of a Jewish apothecary and an India-born Hindu, she had only incidental knowledge of British nobility.

Clare struggled to find any hint of fraud, but the letter was quite plain, once her boiling brain accepted the impossible. She wasn't quite there yet. "I'm not a solicitor. I don't know the laws. I just know what I was told—the earl sold everything and divided it up between his sisters and daughters. My grandmother invested her share in this house and a trust fund to maintain it." So, the money belonged equally to Clare and Oliver, despite the gossip.

"But the letter says you also own a share of *Wycliffe Manor*. How is that possible?" Meera attacked her boiled egg as if it had personally offended her. Meera had a few anger problems, for excellent reasons.

A niggling possibility blossomed in Clare's wild imagination . . .

"It's *not* conceivable, if the manor had been sold, as I assumed. The earl owned vast estates and wealth. There were coffers of jewels inherited over the centuries. My grandmother's sapphire was a gift from that collection. I suppose Wycliffe Manor may have been entailed and couldn't be sold? But then, I wouldn't inherit a share of it. Women normally don't, which is why the earl sold everything. His only relations were female."

Meera waved her fork. "None of that makes sense. Take it to your solicitor. He will find out."

After years of death and disaster, Clare was afraid to allow even a glimmer of anticipation. But just this once, could she hope something good had fallen on their doorstep? "If this is really true, if I have a second home. . ."

Meera looked at her questioningly. "A second home?"

"It says I own a share of a *manor*. What if we could rent out this town-house for the Season? The extra income. . ."

A gleam of understanding reached Meera's eyes. "We could go elsewhere these next months? We could escape Jacob?"

After her father's death, Meera had mistakenly believed his assistant's attention meant he would marry her. She'd dreamed of sharing the apothecary shop with a husband who respected her knowledge.

Unfortunately, he had shown his true character when Meera had told him of their impending parenthood. Instead of doing what was right, he had made a deal with her father's landlord and locked her out of the shop.

Clare clutched the paper as if it were diamonds and gold. "If this is true, I can not only earn the money I need for a tutor, but you can lose Jacob and his threats until your child is born."

As her seven-year-old nephew settled at the table to finish his breakfast, she added, "Do you think a tutor might be more agreeable to working for a woman and teaching Oliver if we are living on an estate with servants?"

"Even a derelict castle with a dozen unknown cousins is healthier than a summer in London with Jacob at the door, but let's be cautious," Meera advised.

"For a change?" Clare added, because caution had never been a family trait as far as she was aware.

TWO

Captain Alastair Huntley, late of the U.S. Army Corps of Engineers, lifted his eye patch and attempted to focus on the hieroglyphics the family solicitor had sent. Just the light of the oil lamp sent a shard of pain straight through his wounded eye socket and into his skull.

He lowered the patch, finished his brandy, and ripped another page out of an ancient ledger to wad up and feed to the coal fire. His damned arm still couldn't toss it far enough to hit the hearth.

Grinding his molars, he set the letter aside and picked up a dart from the abandoned billiard room. He chose a name outlined in blue on the bizarre embroidered tapestry on the wall, took aim, and hurled. The dart at least reached the wall, but it hit a pink block in a different century and family than his target. Arm and aim not improving.

"Good thing you're an engineer and not an artillery man," Walker said discouragingly. "I don't recommend wagering on any dart games in the near future."

Daniel Walker was far more than his right-hand man, but Hunt hadn't found a title that encompassed trusted sergeant, steward, secretary, physician. . . The list was endless.

Nuisance would do for now. Hunt ripped out another page, wadded it, and flung it at his nagging friend. The paper fell far short. Walker knew to stay out of range. "Want to try surveying with your dominant eye closed?" Hunt snarled.

He swung and tossed another dart at the enormous tapestry containing his family tree, a tree that rightfully didn't contain him. He aimed at his so-called grandfather's name, the man who hadn't lived long enough to claim his title and thus lost a kingdom. Family trait, it seemed.

The dart hit another damned female.

"Symbolic," he declared, rewarding himself by pouring another fine snifter of brandy. If nothing else came of this insane trip through his grand-mother's home, he had the pleasure of emptying an excellent wine cellar— the part which hadn't turned to vinegar, at least. When he was drunk enough, he slept through the pain.

"Don' have no fancy eddycation," his assistant mocked.

Which was a lie. Walker had been raised in Philadelphia, the grandson of emancipated slaves who had educated themselves. His parents had taught a school for non-white children. When his parents died of influenza, a white professor and a schoolteacher adopted him. He was probably better educated than Hunt, even if he wasn't allowed in the university.

"What symbolism?" Walker returned to poring over ancient account books.

Everything in this meandering walled village ridiculously called a manor house was ancient. The building itself, as far as Hunt could discern, had started with an abandoned monastery in the sixteenth century and been added onto by every earl since. Gauging from the worm-eaten furniture, the earls moved in and moved on. Like termites.

"Everywhere I look on this ostentatious ode to bad choices," he gestured at the family tapestry, "it comes up female. Females are useless. They cannot possibly set this cesspool to rights again."

"Which is why the estate solicitors hunted you down. The women had the sense to marry well and flee." Having heard all this in one version or another over this past month since their arrival, Walker continued his research.

"My mother didn't marry wealth. Everyone on here descended from women. The solicitors could have looked for other male descendants closer to home." Except there didn't seem to be any.

It had been his damned mother who'd insisted he seize this opportunity while he convalesced. Her quest seemed fictitious, but damaged as he was, he'd had no other purpose at the time. Still didn't.

He flung another dart. Hit another pink square.

"Your aim isn't improving," Walker noted, inciting another paper wad. "We've done the research. The males in your family lead short lives."

Hunt snorted. Only good surgeons had prevented him from being another family casualty. "We're obviously ferocious warriors," he agreed dryly.

As an engineer, he'd only been a casualty of war for being in the wrong place when the Brits had arrogantly sailed into New Orleans, a month after the peace treaty had been signed. Irony everywhere. He'd simply been building a defensive blockade.

From all he could determine, his mother's deceased male relations had been of similar ilk, drowning while navigating flooded rivers or inventing contraptions that exploded or being shot by poachers, in Africa. He did not come from a line of bankers.

He didn't come from a line of earls either. His father had been a surveyor and—despite the tapestry's claim otherwise—his maternal grandfather was *not* the earl's son. The mystery was why he was poking around, trying to translate tomes that, when read with one eye, looked like chicken scratches.

"Your family lacks a sense of self-preservation." Walker intruded on Hunt's cogitations.

"Fine one to talk." Spotting the damned bat flittering near the ceiling that he'd not been able to catch, Hunt picked up his pistol and blew another hole in the crumbling plaster. The bat fled. Walker snorted disapproval.

Walker had been with him at the time the Brits fired—a distinct lack of self preservation for a free black man in a slave state. Stupidity was a generic trait, it seemed, not inherited.

Anyway, the tapestry lacked accuracy. Huntley knew his mother's story. The earl's son had not fathered her. So, he was a Reid in name only.

He hadn't tried to explain that to the solicitors desperate for a male heir. Having Walker read him the English laws of inheritance as it applied to the apparently abnormal Wycliffe estate had occupied months of convalescence from injury and infection. He was an engineer, not a lawyer. But unable to practice his profession with one eye and a bum knee, he had to occupy himself somehow. The fresh sea air of his journey from Philadelphia to England had given him time to heal and the opportunity to grasp the legalities involved.

His eye might never recover. If he kept exercising, his arm would eventually improve. He still had hopes for his knee but none for his career. Engineers needed to be able to read and walk. He'd see this damned place settled on some deserving relation, then vanish into his misery. Only curiosity had prevented him from jumping off the side of the ship on the way over. The return journey offered more opportunity if it became clear his eye was truly lost. He did not want to end up the impoverished uncle drinking himself to death in his sister's small home.

He dreaded meeting his aristocratic relations in his current condition. Men who thought themselves better than others caused his non-noble blood to boil on a normal day. A sneer at his scarred visage would drive him to retaliation—not at all a good idea if he wanted to dump this hellhole on the idiots.

Worse yet, it seemed he had to face *female* heirs, who might simply faint at his appearance. That should give cause for amusement.

He'd spent the better part of his life in male company through school and career. As an officer, he was accustomed to shouting orders and men jumping to obey. He couldn't be the simpering fop an earl's family, especially if they were female, expected.

He prayed the women he'd written had sense enough to bring male family members with them.

"Lack of self-preservation is apparently a well-known family trait." Hunt continued his brandy-addled train of thought. "Doubt that my privileged ancestor would have dropped the entail elsewhere."

"Sign of intelligence." Walker shelved one ancient ledger in exchange for another. "If your tapestry is correct, the last earl inherited when he was only twelve, after his father died. His brothers died young, leaving him the only male progeny. So, the earl dutifully married and produced an heir, who carelessly died before begetting more than girls. The women would suffer if the land reverted to the Crown with the title. What else could he do?"

"Sell this relic, as he did everything else," Hunt replied in disgruntlement, exercising his torn muscle by ripping out another page and heaving it at the fire. It bounced off the hearth. Again.

"The old man had to live somewhere," Walker reminded him.

A pounding echoed down the enormous corridor. Hunt couldn't climb stairs, so he'd taken up residence on the public ground floor. Good thing, since the elderly caretakers seldom toddled out of the kitchen. Although answering the door to anyone insane enough to travel to this isolated crypt at this hour required armaments. Perhaps he'd set up cannon on the porch.

Walker stoically opened the armory hidden behind bookshelves, stuck a pistol under his coat, and headed for the door. Hunt re-loaded his weapon and placed it on top of the desk. He couldn't hit the wall if he tried, but with his scars and eye patch, he could scare Hades out of the most hardened criminal.

Walker returned with a male fashion plate Hunt recalled having met once in the solicitor's office. In his current state of drunkenness, he couldn't immediately recall the visitor's name, but he remembered his profession —*banker*. Hunt squinted at the fancy caped coat and top hat and waited for the fellow to doff them. The fop appeared to be looking around for someone to. . . help him take off his own coat?

Hunt hid his grin as Walker gestured at a straight chair, set his pistol back on a shelf, and returned to his comfortable wing chair by the fire. Hunt paid Walker for his brains, and brought him here as his invaluable friend, not to act as a fancified African servant. Walker sipped his brandy and perused another ledger. Even though he didn't look up, Hunt knew they both waited for the banker's reaction.

The visitor—Bosworth?—frowned, figured out how to pry off his fancy outerwear, revealing an expensively tailored jacket and barbered blond hair. He looked puzzled as to what to do with the garments he'd removed. Hunt was just drunk enough to enjoy the farce. "Have a seat, sir. We're informal here. What disaster has brought you out on this gloomy night?"

Since he couldn't properly remember the banker's name, he didn't attempt introductions.

"N-no disaster, n-not at all," the banker stammered, finally laying his coat over the back of the only free chair. "On my way to Birmingham and thought to check in with you, see how you fared." Instead of meeting Hunt's eyes, he studied the book-lined study with an odd air of. . . possessiveness?

The high-ceilinged, wood-paneled walls, old leather tomes, and great stone hearth created one of the most comfortable rooms in the rambling manor. Hunt didn't like the man's greedy gaze.

He took down a clean snifter and gestured to ask if their visitor would like some.

Since Bosworth seemed unable to look Hunt in his. . . one. . . eye, he didn't immediately catch the gesture. When he did, he shook his head. "No, thank you, I do not partake."

Hunt didn't trust anyone who didn't partake. What did the man drink, water? That would kill him faster than alcohol. He shrugged and set the glass back. "Is there a problem with the accounts we sent you last month? I followed Latham's instructions as far as I'm aware."

"N-no, no, not at all. The fund has the wherewithal to expend a great deal more than that. Latham tells me you have invited all the rest of the family. I cannot say the fund will support so many. There was never any thought to that, I believe. The viscountess lived simply and the funds grew, but they are just for basic maintenance, one realizes." He shifted uncomfortably in the chair, crossing his doeskin-clad legs, revealing his high-topped riding boots.

He glared balefully at the deep leather wing chair Walker occupied by the fire.

"I understand the family is wealthy. I do not expect them to desire the support of a maintenance fund," Hunt said dryly. "We can increase our staff once we find suitable labor. But as long as it is just the two of us, we'll save expenditures while we determine what condition the old place is in."

"Yes, yes, very wise. I'm glad you're sensible. But these letters Latham said you sent. . . You invited all the family to share in the ownership? That can be complicated, very complicated indeed." The banker seemed unaccountably nervous.

Hunt leaned back in his chair and focused his one eye on the shivering dandy, wondering why he was really here. "We have read the documents. Latham agrees. The manor belongs to all the old earl's heirs, not just me. I cannot sign estate papers without their knowledge. If that is complicated, blame it on my great-grandfather. Is there anything else I should be aware of?"

"N-no, no, not at all. My father sends his regards. We are proud to serve Wycliffe Manor and the family in any way we can. He was quite close with the viscountess but isn't up to traveling the distance any longer, you understand. I simply wanted to personally extend my offer of assistance and assure you that the manor is in good hands should you wish to return to your own home at any time."

Hunt was not a suspicious man by nature, but groveling bankers were a new experience. Knowing neither the solicitor nor banker had actually expected him to sail the seas to overlook his property raised his suspicion higher. He chose not to reveal that he had every intention of dumping the manor on family and bolting back home. "That's very good of you, sir. I will take that into account in any future decisions. May I offer you a room for the night after you've had the courtesy to ride all this way?"

The banker glanced around the high-ceilinged study with dark shadows dancing in the firelight and sighed in satisfaction. "Yes, that would be most pleasing, thank you."

Hunt had the distinct notion that the banker coveted this gloomy mausoleum.

THREE

London, March 1815

"Why are we sneaking out before dawn?" Clare asked again as Meera ushered them into the hired carriage.

The driver tied their trunks on back while Meera held a sleepy Oliver until Clare climbed in and could take him. Meera had insisted on using her own meager savings to hire their transportation, so Clare really could not complain about setting out at this hour.

"Because some men need to be taught lessons the hard way." Not exhibiting any of Clare's agitation, Meera pulled up her skirts and climbed in.

"Oh dear." Clare worried at her bottom lip and scanned the almost empty residential street for villains. Her house was old, but the neighborhood was quiet and respectable. "What have you done?"

Meera had every right to be furious at Jacob for driving her from her own home, but she was nothing if not sensible. Clare hadn't been worried —until now.

"He *never* wanted me. All he wants is my father's formulas!" Meera crossed her arms and stared stubbornly ahead—even as shouts suddenly rang out from down the silent street.

"The formulas? He courted you for the formulas?" *Pretty faces, empty*

14

pockets. . . Oh, double dear. Jacob had a pretty face and Meera had a pocket of valuable recipes. More than a pocket. Her father had made an extremely comfortable living on the formulas he'd improved with Meera's help.

"He offered to marry me in name only if I gave him my father's book of pharmaceuticals. I refused. He already has my shop!"

Behind them, angry shouts contained crude epithets like *whore* and threats of retaliation.

A sound like a shot had Clare ducking, covering Oliver, and swallowing a scream. "You did more than refuse, didn't you?"

Meera signaled the driver to hurry and peered behind the carriage as the horses picked up speed. "He's ripping off his clothes and scratching like a madman." She sat back, smiling in satisfaction.

Attempting to steady her nerves, Clare sat up again. "Itching powder?"

Meera nodded. "Stupid bugger didn't change *all* the locks. He'll have to throw out his linen. I may have unleashed a few bedbugs and fleas as well."

Concentrating on not shaking, Clare refrained from repeating the adage about what happened when one lies down with dogs. But Jacob was the dog and Meera had caught a child, not fleas. Aphorisms weren't always useful.

Well, if she had second thoughts about this adventure, it was too late to turn back now. Clare prayed Wycliffe Manor came with baying hounds and massive butlers and footmen at every door. Her solicitor knew where they were. So did her servants. Jacob would know soon.

"Don't all apothecaries have formula books? Why does he want your father's?" A good mystery always entertained. Perhaps she could write a short story.

"Jacob worked with my father enough to know he improved formulas from my mother's family as well as his own. No one else possesses those recipes. At least my father had the decency to marry my mother for her books." Meera sounded only slightly indignant. "Together, we spent our lives perfecting his medicines. That was the reason he was so successful. Because I'm a woman and cannot obtain the new apothecary license, Jacob simply thought the formulas ought to go to him."

"Just because you don't have an apothecary license doesn't mean you can't work as a druggist! And what about your experiments? I know you were carrying on your father's work. What happens now?"

"I have my father's books and my notes. I will continue experimenting. The new apothecary law will prevent me from following my father, but I'm more interested in being a druggist anyway. I have no wish to go into sick-rooms and physick patients as he did."

Clare pondered that as the carriage clattered away, leaving Jacob in its dust. "I suppose women have dispensed drugs as herbals for centuries. You would be quite good at it."

Meera shrugged. "Not in the wilderness. What do you think the manor will be like?"

"Enormous. Ancient. My solicitor has researched. He claims it has been maintained by a skeleton staff. I expect drafty corridors, closed-up, musty rooms, and perhaps a quaint village nearby. I pray for a library, but I will not hold out hope for more than moldering volumes of religion. There is an old tome on poisons I cannot find anywhere. That might be asking too much."

"But there will be room for my laboratory and possibly a place to buy supplies?" Meera sounded more anxious about this than the angry man she left behind.

"Probably entire deteriorating wings of space, but supplies. . . I understand Birmingham is growing rapidly. We'll hope the estate has a carriage and horse so you may go shopping." Of course, if the estate had been abandoned by all but caretakers for years. . .

Clare glanced up as her nephew finally climbed to his knees to look out. Before long, he was hallooing passersby as if he were an approaching mail coach driver.

What would be best for all was a welcoming family and a staff of understanding servants to keep out Jacob and tolerate Oliver's eccentric behavior. That she knew better than to expect.

~

As the hired carriage rolled up a heavily forested drive late the following evening, Clare fretted at her lower lip and gripped her reticule. They had seen no village. *Gravesyde Priory* might not exist as more than an ominous address.

The turrets of Wycliffe Manor rose above the trees, silhouetted against a hazy moon. She had a writer's imagination and real-world experience with disaster. . . And this gothic horror was cut off from civilization by a steep drive and a deep brook that was practically a moat.

"How can we make a castle into a home?" Clare checked to be certain her nephew still slept. He'd have nightmares of a certainty if he saw this looming structure at night.

Perhaps she could quell her own nightmares by knowing soldiers couldn't approach without giving the manor's inhabitants plenty of time to hide.

"It won't be forever," Meera reminded her, although she sounded a little more worried now that the thrill of revenge had worn off.

"It probably has dungeons filled with bones and ax murderers in the attic." Sometimes, Clare's imagination was a little too much of a good thing. The journey here, worrying about what would meet them at the end, had given her time to picture beasts and caverns and laughing madmen with scythes. She'd had quite enough of mad beasts, and men in general, if she were to be honest.

The carriage jostled them up a rutted drive that didn't promise wealth and comfort.

"They're your family. Do you have killers on the family tree?" Meera attempted to peer out the window.

The forest made visibility difficult, but the manor's silhouette against the moonlit sky was imposingly enormous. "No, just a lot of inept, would-be scientists and adventurers who can't hold onto their money as far as I'm aware. One wonders what the first earl did to warrant a kingdom."

"Poisoned the king's enemies?" Meera asked dryly. "Accidentally."

That actually sounded quite likely. A mad scientist in the dungeon was not impossible. Although she was pretty certain this was a faux castle and wouldn't have real dungeons, but the overall gloom excited every possible fantasy.

The carriage rattled up to a tower entrance. No footman greeted them. No lamp lit the way.

"We should have waited until morning. The inhabitants are no doubt doddering off to sleep after an excess of wine at dinner." Meera was not only practical but cynical.

Clare was *tired* of being practical. More than tired. Exhausted. She wanted someone to share her burdens. She wanted a fantasy world where she could write and finish her next book in peace. She had dreamed of sunny skies and huge windows overlooking cows and wheat fields. She had hoped for the welcoming arms of distant family. She feared her fantasies had led her astray, but there was no turning back now.

"Waiting until morning meant we would have had to waste coins on another night at an inn, for no good reason if we have beds waiting for us here." Not necessarily more optimistic than her friend, Clare simply preferred fairy tales to reality.

The last ten of her twenty-five years had made her very practiced at fantasy. Magic beanstalks were entirely possible. Letters from strangers declaring she owned a share in a country manor. . . why not?

It was the hungry giant who might eat her that had her praying this storybook had a happy ending.

~

THE GAP-TOOTHED CRONE OF A HOUSEKEEPER HUNT HAD INHERITED WITH THE manor scratched at the open study door and resentfully held out a tarnished silver salver containing two white rectangular pieces of cardboard. "The lady has arrived, my lord."

Helga hadn't liked being told that guests were expected, and she should stay upstairs.

Weary of explaining that he wasn't a lord, Hunt swung his chair back to the desk and took the cards. *Two* visitors? Did he dare hope the lady who'd written had brought a husband or brother? He might steel himself for one aristocratic lady wilting into a faint at his scarred visage—if she came accompanied by someone useful. He squinted with his one eye in the feeble light but couldn't read the names. The excess of brandy didn't help. "Show them in."

The tall, skinny crone performed her disappearing act.

"I'll add bodyguard to your list of duties," Hunt said to Walker as he held up the cards to the oil lamp. "Helga only cackles and nags at me when you're not around."

"Better than being told to clean the lamps." Which was what the butler had told Walker to do when they'd arrived.

His over-educated steward glanced over Hunt's shoulder to verify the name of the brave female who had dared the journey to nowhere. "Miss Clarissa Knightley and *Mrs. Meera Abrams*?"

Not a man, then, damn it. Hunt emptied his glass and poured another. "Who the devil is Meera Abrams?" Hunt knew the tapestry up and down. No Abrams appeared on his invitation list.

Now he had to deal with the distinct possibility of fake heirs slipping past his early warning system. Ripping another page from an ancient ledger, he wadded and cast it at the fire. His arm was growing stronger. His aim was not.

The damned bat fluttered across the ceiling. Ladies didn't like flying rodents. He took aim.

~

After the carriage driver deposited their trunks inside the entry, Clare gazed around Wycliffe Manor's imposingly grim, semi-circular foyer with trepidation. "It's not the gateway to hell," she assured herself.

"Not hell," Meera agreed. "No grate. Icicles in the winter."

"An entire forest on the doorstep for fuel," Clare concluded. Pragmatism occasionally countered her overactive imagination. "I didn't think England had any more forests. One must wonder how the trees survived the ax. Perhaps they are an experiment in how to grow a fortress."

In the dim light of a single oil lamp, the portraits of ancient ancestors in wigs and billowing fabric glared down disapprovingly from the dark panels separating the foyer from the rest of the manor. A leaded transom over the creaky, massive, front doors might tease hell's inhabitants with a glimmer of light during the day. Not even moonlight illuminated the gloom at this hour.

Her fear etched the scene vividly to transcribe into her journal later. "Can we make a castle into a home?" she murmured after the servant vanished through a door preventing them from entering the main hall.

"It's just for the next six months," Meera repeated her mantra.

Clare nervously watched Oliver drift to a head-high statue of a lion and lean against it. His blond hair tousled from his nap, his clothes wrinkled and filthy from crawling all over the carriage, inside and out, he appeared a ragamuffin from the streets. Blessedly, no trap doors opened and dumped him into the cellar.

Anything so plebian as interior stairs were apparently hidden behind the two-story paneling directly ahead, the one adorned with paintings of men in perukes and horses and hunting parties in gilded frames. Shadows prevented seeing higher.

Oliver returned to cling to her hand, almost twisting his head like a little owl trying to take it all in.

She did not fare well in male company, and she could not hope the captain who had signed the curt invitation would be a welcoming father figure. Her own father hadn't been particularly warm. Her brother-in-law had been a right solid ass.

She'd learned to stay out of the way. In a place this large, surely that was easily done.

The manor's solicitor in Stratford had assured her that she was, indeed, one of the heirs to Wycliffe Manor, so that part of the letter wasn't a complete fantasy. She simply couldn't imagine why anyone in their right mind would *welcome* a poor female relation—and her imagination was quite good.

They simply needed beds for the night. She would be strong, like Bea—in the morning. Right now, if a ghost shouted *Boo!* she'd flee into the night.

A shot reverberated from the other side of the panel. Shrieking, Clare instinctively grabbed Oliver to run. Before she could lift him, the unflustered housekeeper returned and gestured for them to follow.

Frozen and shaking, Clare inhaled and fought for reason. This wasn't a bazaar. It contained no shouting mobs, no smoking gunpowder. She shouldn't fear—

A flurry of wings flew over her head, aiming for the transom window. Shrieking again, Clare ducked.

Meera simply watched their flight. "Bats. There's a hole in the glass."

Bats, of course.

And pistol shots, naturally, not exploding shells. She remembered her brother-in-law's men shooting at anything that moved. Madmen. All males were quite mad. Scientists should study the problem.

Fighting for control, she clenched her lips and clutched her reticule. The housekeeper hadn't even flinched. Gray-haired, thin, and stooped, she was no doubt half deaf. So much for warm arms and welcoming family. Clare couldn't wait to meet the rest of the staff. They might all be as old as the manor. Maybe they were actually spirits of servants long past. The madman may have shot them.

Clare finally appeased her terror by noting this was exactly the atmosphere she needed to inspire her work. If she could just keep critiquing the setting. . .

The housekeeper held open the heavy door into the unlit interior.

The paneled entry was merely an anteroom to the marble splendor on the other side, what she could see of it in the dark. Overwhelmed, Clare strained her neck trying to gaze up the stairs that spiraled out of sight. An enormous Oriental vase filled with barren branches adorned the bottom curve of the stairs. She had to hang onto Oliver's hand to prevent him from dashing into the shadows.

With only the light of a single lamp, the housekeeper led them past closed doors and the stairs. About midway down the corridor, a hint of firelight danced along the floor and wall. The housekeeper gestured for them to enter.

Oliver didn't want to. Meera took his hand, and they waited for Clare to precede them into the dragon's lair. Telling herself that soldiers faced worse fears every day, lying to herself that madmen did not write polite letters, Clare stepped into what appeared to be a study.

Against a roaring fire in a stone fireplace, the massive beast of her worst nightmares rose from behind a mahogany desk—wearing a uniform coat and holding a pistol. Dark hair escaping an old-fashioned queue, he loomed over her like a terrifying pirate. His massive shoulders spread as wide as the embroidered wall-hanging behind him. He stank of alcohol.

Courage vanishing, Clare reminded herself that this immense mansion was part hers, clasped her reticule as if it were a weapon and not fragile cloth, and shakily nodded acknowledgment of his non-greeting. Rather than terrify herself more, she studied the dim cavern.

In the far corner, an African man dressed in high collar and vest sat in a leather chair, taking notes. A pirate's assistant? He did not look up with curiosity or anything else, as if they were both no more than part of the furniture. She clenched her molars to prevent their chattering.

The setting was exceedingly gothic—and not the least welcoming. Beasts were not welcoming family.

Inhaling again to steady her fractured nerves, Clare returned to the massive figure she assumed to be Captain Alistair Huntley—a distant cousin, according to the solicitor. In the shadow he cast, she could discern what appeared to be an old-fashioned cravat that he'd tugged and disarranged. His dark uniform coat was certainly not tailored by London's finest but strained at broad shoulders and chest. He could break her in two. He at least set aside his pistol, although the stench of gunpowder lingered.

Gulping, she finally dared lift her gaze to study a stubbornly square chin, high cheekbones, and a jaw ravaged by pain.

That was definitely a black eyepatch covering the right side of the beast's face, but she didn't need his eyes to know. . . *He was not any relation to the earl.*

In shock, she wondered what disaster she had led them into.

When she said nothing, her host crumpled a ledger sheet in his huge fist. Her horror magnified as he flung the page into the fire. Around the hearth lay scattered the wads of torn book pages. She might resist judging a person by his appearance, but only a *real* madman desecrated books!

"First, you shoot up our home and then burn the books? Who are you and what are you *doing*?" she cried, diving to retrieve the pages before they caught fire.

FOUR

THE LADY HAD TAKEN ONE LOOK AT HIS RAVAGED VISAGE AND DIVED FOR *PAPER* rather than meet his—one—eye.

Hunt reined in his temper and a thirst for another fortifying brandy and watched his elegantly attired visitor scoop up crumpled trash. In this light, with his vision, he couldn't discern more than a fancy bonnet and slim form as she smoothed out the faded, useless accounting columns in her gloved fingers.

"Miss Knightley." Hunt determinedly summoned manners he'd abandoned years ago—while attempting to prevent his tongue from falling out once the firelight revealed her.

Good Lord in Heaven, thy name isn't hallowed if this was His idea of a good joke.

This was the *unprepossessing spinster* the solicitor had sent? He'd expected a sour-faced old maid, not a beribboned maiden who dropped a fistful of papers on his desk like an angry—fairy—goddess. She appeared little more than spun sugar and gold.

Was she a fraud after all?

"These are valuable documents," she announced in terse, rounded vowels, not bothering with a modicum of the manners or decorum he strained to present.

Haughtily straight in that elegant traveling apparel, she backed away with the disdain of every stiff-necked British aristocrat he'd ever despised.

22

Even though he couldn't see her face beneath the ridiculous hat brim, her posture was *not* drab and her ridiculous allegation was not *unassuming*. Perhaps the Brits defined the word differently. Irate fairy, he drunkenly decided.

Fearless. The females of the earl's family were as fearless and stupid as the males.

Maybe if he could see beneath that rigid bonnet. . . A pale ringlet dangled from beneath the ugly brown brim. Her rounded, lofty—angry—tones spoke volumes—an aristocratic lady accustomed to having her way, not a grateful spinster. *Damn*. She wouldn't stay. His brain sloshed inside his skull while he attempted to sort out impossible impressions.

"The ledgers are ancient trash under which this decrepit edifice is sinking," he retorted, less than politely. "Who needs to know the price of turnips in 1763?"

"Future historians!" she countered. "These could be precisely the research information I require." She continued smoothing papers as if they were precious silk—and avoiding looking at him, which irritated more.

He wanted to yank back her hat brim and shout that the here and now mattered more than the past and gone, just to make her look at him, but her companions eased in behind her.

They both belatedly recalled their manners. He straightened. She stiffly offered her gloved hand. "Mr. Huntley, I presume? I am Clarissa Knightley."

Hunt stared at the glove. Did he shake it? Kiss it? He'd been a soldier for far too long. Well, hell. Their guest had behaved rudely first, so what did it matter?

Determined to be proper, he took Miss Knightley's fingertips and attempted a bow, grateful he didn't fall flat on his face. The desk would catch him, but he'd prefer not to appear a complete ass.

When had he last cared how he appeared to anyone?

"Was the journey difficult?" he asked, his drunken wits barely recovered after she'd shaken him out of them. "Please, take a seat."

Of course, there weren't any. Wait, should he introduce himself to. . . He peered at the exotic observer and the boy. Her maid? Her. . . son? Could there really be a boy left in the family? The solicitor had definitely said *spinster*.

The lady glanced around, presumably for the missing seats, then gestured the child toward the spare straight chair.

Using his cane, Hunt poked Walker—who was no better than he, practically gaping at the maid or whoever the colorful parrot was assisting the boy into the seat. Jolted out of the solitude of his enormous brain, Walker leaped up to present his wing chair to the lady.

"No, please." Miss Knightley waved away the offer. "We do not wish to disturb you, Mr. . . ."

She turned back to Hunt, waiting expectantly for an introduction. Or she turned her bonnet in his direction anyway. He assumed she was waiting on him. "My apologies, Miss Knightley, this is my friend, Daniel Walker. He is assisting me in learning the estate books."

"The ones you are destroying." She dug her dart deeper.

Before Hunt could respond in kind, the blond boy intruded. "He's black."

Hunt expected an uncomfortable silence.

The indomitable Miss Knightley didn't skip a beat. "And you're pink and white, and Captain Huntley is nearly brown. Personal comments are not polite, dear." She offered her hand to Walker. "Pleased to meet you, sir. Is there a library or has he destroyed that too?"

Whoosh, in two seconds flat, she'd erected a bridge over the bloody great chasm of race and class that Hunt had gone down fighting over more than once. So, that's why etiquette existed. Good to know.

"Through there." Walker gestured at a door behind him. "Hasn't been added to in half a century, I fear. Probably only good for fuel." Raised by schoolteachers, Walker spoke the King's English as well as Hunt, possibly better, since he tried harder. He had also hung around Hunt too long and was dangerously sharp of tongue.

The lady froze. Hunt could swear she stood taller, like a hound that scents a fox.

Her tone was as icy as expected. "Half a century is perfect for those of us who appreciate history, thank you."

Continuing the introductions, she gestured for the colorful parrot to step forward. "My good friend and companion, Mrs. Meera Abrams. We will try not to bother you further this evening, if you would call the housekeeper to direct us to our rooms?"

Eager to have her disturbing presence removed, Hunt bowed again and reached for the bell pull they'd installed as soon as he'd arrived, almost tripping over his cane in his haste. "A room has been prepared. Have you dined? We are informal. You can ask Helga to bring up tea and whatever is in the kitchen."

Crude, Hunt, crude. But once he'd found what his mother sought, he'd be gone. What did it matter?

Except he needed someone to stay and take over the place, and so far, if she was legitimate, she was it. He doubted she would last the night.

The boy abruptly scrambled out of the chair. "Turret." He dashed out.

Turret? The child knew the word turret?

The parrot bobbed a curtsy and ran after the boy.

"My sister's son," the lady said in apparent apology for his abruptness. "He has. . . a speech problem. He is quite exceptionally bright, just not a good communicator."

"And you have been left with his care?" He had no idea if leaving a child with an aging spinster was unusual in this society. He'd think grandparents would have been more suitable than an unmarried maiden with no resources. He needed to study the chart.

"Yes," was all she replied. She glanced at the library door but reluctantly bobbed a curtsy. "I do thank you for this invitation, captain, and look forward to a proper conversation in the morning."

"As do I, Miss Knightley . We have much to discuss." Standing, he clung to the knob of his cane as Helga entered.

Their guest strode off, spine straight, skirts swaying around her *unprepossessing* stature.

Walker whistled.

In relief, Hunt dropped into his chair. "What the hell was that?"

"Battle lines drawn, I'd say. Want to fight the war all over again?"

"Hell, no." Hunt reached for his brandy. "We may have won this last one, but I've never fought a female general."

One who wouldn't even look at him—because he was so horrible to look upon or too plebian to acknowledge? Probably both.

"HE'S AMERICAN," MEERA WHISPERED AS THE HOUSEKEEPER STOMPED UP THE grandiose marble staircase, lit only by a single lantern. "And very large."

At the top, two narrow halls ran off to either side, and a wide hall led straight down the middle of the manor—over the study where a madman shot bats?

"And very drunk." Clare cringed at the possibility of living with a soldier who shot up the roof over their heads—or the floor beneath their feet.

She suspected the captain must once have been a handsome man. Now, he was simply terrifying. Well, in her inexperience, most men were terrifying —or, at very best, dangerous to her wellbeing, especially when drunk.

The lamplight cast towering shadows over bare walls that stretched an eternity toward the back of the house. Ghosts and monsters might leap out of doorways. They hurried to catch Oliver as he raced down the hall, opening any door that wasn't locked.

A low moan whispered from the shadows.

Clare clutched Meera's arm. "What was that?"

"The old earl's ghost," the housekeeper said in disgruntlement. "Every so often, he comes around."

"A loose flue," her weary friend countered, increasing her pace.

Yes, yes, of course. Old houses made odd noises. Still, she had to ask, "Did the earl die here?"

"A'course, and his son a'fore him, and the viscountess after, all gone to the worms."

Charming, simply charming. Helga appeared old enough to have killed them all.

The housekeeper opened a door to show them a room halfway down the hall from the stairs, but Oliver ran on.

Clare and Meera followed Oliver.

"If the captain was injured in battle against our soldiers, might that mean he hates the British and will throw us off the parapets?" Clare murmured another of many entertaining possibilities as she darted looks through doorways Oliver opened.

"No parapets here, miss," the skinny housekeeper said, reluctantly following. "Anyways, the captain can't climb stairs and sleeps below."

Clare supposed that was reassuring—as long as he didn't spend his time shooting up the ceiling. If this really was her home, she had a battle on her hands. She loathed the idea. She simply wanted a little peace to write her book. And a place for Meera to hide until the child was born. And then they would determine what to do from there.

Was that another moan?

Oliver shouted from the gloom at the far end of the hall and vanished.

"That's an old tower," the housekeeper said with a sniff. "'Tain't fit nor safe. I can make him up a nice trundle right in here." She gestured at a small guest bedroom with no more than an armoire, an unadorned bed, and a night table. Easy enough to clean but. . .

"Let us see what Oliver has discovered." Clare hurried after her nephew. Forget flues and moans and mad Americans. She was part owner of an earl's *manor*. In all its gloomy gothic glory, this was *her* house. She might have little experience with men, but domestic matters had ruled her life since her father's death and her mother's subsequent illness.

Of course, choosing a chamber furthest from the stairs was an inconvenience. . .

Appropriating the oil lamp, she glanced into the sparse rooms her nephew had opened in his journey. "I assume staff is limited," she said. "We are capable of taking care of ourselves if you'll show us the linen cupboard and the kitchen stairs. We do not wish to impose."

Until they learned more, at least. The solicitor hadn't been as forthcoming as she would have liked. No doubt he didn't wish for her to worry her pretty little head.

Said head had kept them fed for over a decade now. The beast below might terrify her, but so did wolves at the door.

The housekeeper reluctantly followed. "It's just meself and himself to see to the gentlemen. There's daft Betsy in the village. She can fetch and carry if you like."

That definitely did not sound promising. Perhaps the estate was as house poor as she. It seemed likely, given the size of this colossal edifice. "We will speak with the captain in the morning to see what can be done. For now, we are accustomed to doing for ourselves."

They found Oliver only by dint of knowing his habits. At the end of the main corridor, the faux turret room—not a tower—was heavily draped in moldering velvet. A big tester bed with no covers showed no sign of a little boy. Clare lifted draperies until she found Oliver curled up on pillows in a window seat, already sound asleep.

"He's like a little dormouse," Meera said, lips curling with fondness.

"He'll fall out those old windows, he will," the housekeeper exclaimed in alarm.

"No, he'll just get chilled and drop to the floor. If we put a blanket and some pillows nearby, he'll be right as rain. If it wouldn't encourage mice, I'd leave him a bit of bread and cheese. He'll be up before the rest of us, hunting his breakfast." Clare searched through the armoire until she found a worn blanket in a bottom drawer. She shook it and when no dead bugs fell out, wrapped it over his shoulders. She took cushions from the other seats and laid them on the floor next to him.

Straightening, she glanced around, rejected the turret room—Oliver liked to be alone—and followed Meera back to the hall. They'd apparently reached the back of the main block. Past Oliver's chamber, double doors presumably led to one of the wings they'd barely glimpsed as they drove up. She deliberately closed off images of madwomen locked away. . .

Across the corridor was a large turret room with windows, a dressing room, and a fine mahogany tester bed.

"Excellent, this will do. Let us find the linens." Clare returned to the hall, the housekeeper protesting all the way.

While Meera unerringly aimed for the cupboard, Clare pinned the surly housekeeper with her best officious stare. "Helga? Do you have a proper name you wish to be called? I understand the captain is an American and hasn't quite learned our ways."

"Helga Gaither, my lady," she muttered under a frown. "The captain said as I was to give you the warm rooms, near the chimneys."

"Well, Mrs. Gaither, that was exceptionally thoughtful of him." And blatant male presumption since she had every right to choose her own room, but she was still being polite. "I think we might manage not to freeze, especially on a lovely spring night like this. Now, if you will show us to the kitchen, we'll prepare a little tray to hold us until morning."

The inn had packed a hamper, and they'd eaten on the road, but it was early enough to be peckish.

"The captain said I was to—"

Servants needed training. Clare could see this might not be as easy as it had been at home, where no male orders countermanded hers. Another point to discuss in the morning, when she might summon more courage to face the beast.

"Mrs. Gaither." She used the authoritative voice she'd been forced to learn at a very young age. "I have papers showing I am entitled to a share of the estate equal to the captain's. If I am to be your employer, then you will need to take orders from me as well. I will have a word with him in the morning."

Mrs. G's gums flapped but nothing emerged.

Meera returned with linens and pillows, and chuckled. "Why don't you and Mrs. Gaither make the beds while I see what's in the kitchen? If I'm to do any cooking, I need to explore."

"Cook? In *my* kitchen?" Mrs. Gaither could barely contain herself. "That Gypsy in my kitchen?"

"Mrs. Abrams is quite British, you know." Accustomed to this reaction, Clare didn't bother explaining Meera's unusual background. Or habits. Clare had to give her a place in the household that the servants understood, especially once the child started showing. "Mrs. Abrams is my companion and secretary. Please treat her with the same respect as you do me." Which wasn't much at all—yet. These things took time—and stretching the truth.

"Like that African," Mrs. G said grumpily. "At least, this one is proper English. I'll fetch a tray."

Having worked out everyone's position in relation to herself, the house-keeper departed without helping with the linens.

"Does that mean she'll bring us water to wash in, or that you're allowed in her domain?" Clare asked, joining Meera in making up the bed.

"We can manage without her, if necessary," Meera said. "I want to explore. I've not found any evidence of mice up here, but perhaps I will in the kitchen. I wonder if they have a servant's hall where I might sleep?"

"You have your choice of rooms, as always, my weird friend. If you prefer sleeping with the mice and the ancient ones, I shall make it happen."

Making no pretense of being a lady, Meera snorted. "If I were not here, you'd starve, Oliver would become a hermit in the attic, and we'd never see the two of you again. I'll run down to the kitchen and fetch the water. It will give me an excuse to study what we're up against."

Clare would not let Oliver remain as ignorant and helpless as she. One way or another, she intended for her nephew to have the education she had never obtained. If she must face a beast to find a tutor, she'd do it.

Somehow.

FIVE

THE ACHE IN HIS HEAD MATCHING THE ONE IN HIS KNEE, HUNT PACED THE marble gallery. If he were to guess, he'd say the gothic cathedral windows were originally in the main chapel of the priory. The remains had been converted into one long, wide salon.

Unfortunately, the windows overlooked a veritable forest. At dawn, the evergreens encased the manor in shadow, but the gray light through the tall, drapery-less panes was more than sufficient to illuminate the obstacles of faded chairs and gilded tables. Once the weather warmed, he'd take his aching bones outdoors and practice on less stable ground. Surveying required a great deal of climbing over rough terrain. If he worked hard enough, he might beg a surveying position somewhere with Walker as his eyes. The West was opening up and needed engineers. He'd never be able to return to the military.

As it was, his knee threatened to buckle far too often for him to lose the walking stick. In frustration at another stumble, he pounded an upholstered chair, sending up a cloud of dust. He sneezed.

A smaller sneeze echoed from above. He exercised in here every morning and didn't remember an echo. He sneezed again. The second sound produced no response.

Carefully balancing on his ebony cane, Hunt studied the second-story railed gallery traversing the length of this room. With a wall lined in immense oil paintings, the walkway led to a small minstrel's balcony. He wondered if this waste of space had been used since kings roamed the land expecting entertainment.

He scanned the railing until he caught a flash of blue. He'd been a small boy once. He recognized the temptation to explore unencumbered by adults and caution.

Unfortunately, he had no reason to believe the worm-ridden railing was stable. He'd not been able to climb up there to test.

"Boy," he called after the rascal, who'd hidden in shadows. "The railing isn't safe."

The boy, of course, didn't stir.

He and Walker had established their own meal preferences when they'd provisioned the larder upon arrival. The Gaithers had welcomed the full pantry, if not the extra work. Food and small boys generally went hand in hand.

Worried that he might lose the only chance he'd found so far to unload this rubbish heap, Hunt turned around. "Breakfast is this way. I hope you like bugs and butterflies. We might have some witch's brew. I'm partial to rat tongue."

He hoped that was the scuttle of small feet following. The door to the upper gallery was in this direction. The only stairs the boy could take down, however, were the marble ones.

The tap of his cane hid any further sound as he took the side hall to the main corridor so he could see the stairs. A child might become lost in this maze, but he rather thought this one would not. A long line of explorers and adventurers needed a solid sense of direction.

Sure enough, by the time Hunt had hauled his limping carcass to the breakfast room, hasty inroads had been made in the eggs and toast on the sideboard. Judging by the scattering of crumbs and curds, they hadn't been made by the ladies.

Where had the brat gone? Really, there was only one good hiding place.

"Do you like rat's tongue?" he asked, adding bacon to his plate. "I'm partial to witch's brew, but you probably prefer vulture milk." He poured coffee for himself and a glass of milk, just in case.

When had the kitchen started serving milk? And where had they obtained it?

"Vulture milk, please," a small voice said from beneath the tablecloth.

Hunt took his usual seat and held the glass under the table. The breakfast room was tiled. If the milk spilled, so be it.

The glass was taken with a small "thank you."

Now he had to wonder if they had enough milk for a growing boy. He knew for fact they didn't own a cow.

The breakfast room had sufficient light that he could read last week's news sheets by squinting his one eye. He'd objected to Gaither ironing the paper when it arrived. After a week of traveling by mail coach, farm cart, and apparently peddler's sack, creases were the least of the paper's problem.

The patter of feminine boots warned his comfortable silence—and the boy's hiding place—were about to be assaulted. Folding the paper, he fortified himself with a stiff gulp of the black brew Helga had yet to learn to make properly.

"What an *amazing* library we have," the lady exclaimed, sailing into the room with a musty tome clutched to her small, not *amazing* bosom. At least, this morning, she seemed more forthcoming.

In the early morning light, he finally had full sight of his distant not-exactly-a-cousin. She didn't have three heads, at least. She still wasn't unprepossessing, although she was daintier than her attire last night had led him to assume.

In her plain muslin, she looked satisfyingly more like a spinster: pale cheeks, hair in shades of flaxen raked into a bun, and gold-rimmed spectacles concealing her eyes. Primly posed lips and a small, sharp nose completed the image. Not a flaming beauty, but pleasant, almost scholarly. The library had apparently melted the termagant of the prior evening.

She still wouldn't look at him directly. With mechanical precision, she helped herself to the buffet and set out her plate and her silverware at the far end of the oval table. He doubted that she was aware of how her wispy gown shifted over slim curves with her motion.

He finally remembered to grunt a "Good morning."

She smiled tightly, and—his gaze froze on pink, moist, delectably puffy...

She used that perfect mouth to bite into a corner of toast and cast him an expectant sideways glance. "Captain? Did your injury affect your hearing?"

His hearing? Possibly his mind, but he hadn't noticed a problem hearing. It was a wonder, he supposed, given the extent of his injuries. "Wool-gathering?" he suggested, realizing she'd asked a question. "I apologize. You were saying?"

She handed a piece of bacon under the table. "Nothing of importance. Were you injured in the war?"

Apparently, she didn't mind *speaking* to him—just looking at him. And sitting near him. Annoying but tolerable, he supposed.

"Yes, cannon shell. Walker saved my life. Not entirely certain why. Was your room satisfactory?" He'd vowed to remember he was civilized today. This wasn't a tavern or soldiers' mess. No dart throwing, pistol shooting, or paper wadding. No desecrating of useless ledgers.

He squinted but couldn't read the title of the tome she'd placed by her plate.

"Very satisfactory, thank you. I fear we are understaffed, however." She chose her words cautiously. "If you have invited the rest of the family, as I gather from your invitation, we will need more than two caretakers who really should have been pensioned off long ago."

She kept saying *we*, as if she'd already accepted ownership and responsibility. That's what he wanted, wasn't it? He just wasn't accustomed to sharing leadership with a *woman*. Were all British females this overbearing?

"I've been informed there is no local labor to draw from." He sounded stiff, even to himself. "It seems the priory village is almost gone. I was hoping guests might bring their own servants."

She lifted her head in his direction and raised a delicate eyebrow from behind her teacup. He thought perhaps her eyes behind the spectacles were blue-gray. They regarded him with suspicion.

"England has been at war for decades. Fortunes are declining. Able men have been lost or incapacitated. Farms are neglected. The chances of anyone who accepts your invitation still possessing servants willing to travel to this outpost is miniscule." She picked up her toast and pointed it at him. "And you apparently have not noticed the consequences of being descended from a line of adventurers and scientists who spend more than they ever earn."

He sipped his bitter brew while he processed that declaration. No money? "I was told that the estate consisted of an exceptionally large trust fund dispensed equally among all the earl's immediate heirs. I realize he died nearly half a century ago, but surely all the lands he sold to fund the trust. . ."

"Were dowered to *women*, who married men remarkably similar to their brothers and fathers." She thought about that a moment. "Possibly because they were the only men to whom they were introduced."

"I see." Perhaps a little too clearly. He'd rushed to judgment. "And none of these women thought to marry solicitors or bankers or investors who might manage their funds?"

"Not profitably. One funds what one knows—scientific expeditions to South America, steam engines in Scotland, and in one exceptional act of brilliance, a shipyard in the Americas, I heard." She sipped her tea.

"Steam engines may be viable in the future. Shipyards should be profitable." Although if they were in America. . . He winced. They might be blown to kingdom come. "I don't remember noticing any of them on the list of trust investments I've been given."

Mostly, he'd looked at pounds and shillings compared to the maintenance of this monstrosity. Walker had assured him that the funds were adequate to maintain the status quo, unless a roof fell in. The manor needed income to protect against disaster or make major improvements—like replacing crumbling ceilings the Gaithers apparently didn't notice.

Hunt had hoped to put the estate into production to ensure an income, but he wasn't a farmer. So far, he hadn't determined if the land beyond the woods was even arable. But a cow and chickens might help the food budget. They had to buy feed for horses anyway.

Miss Knightley handed a napkin under the table. A moment later, the napkin returned and a small figure darted out to the hall.

In her prim voice, she continued, "The original trust was divided between all the earl's daughters, sisters, and grandchildren quite some time ago. Each family had its own funds to waste. I gather you're a direct descendant of the earl's only son. My grandmother was the earl's youngest daughter. Her dower purchased my home and established a maintenance trust in perpetuity. I like to think she saw what happened to her older sisters and sensibly made sure we had a roof over our heads."

Hunt tried to think of something pleasant to encourage her to continue talking so he might learn more of his mother's family. He only managed, "Intelligent woman."

She folded her spectacles and slipped them into a pocket. "She married a man who used the rest of her dowry to fund archeological expeditions and had a daughter who married a man who collected ancient artifacts. Which is how my sister met and married a soldier who preferred Egyptian tombs to fighting. Money easily acquired is equally easy to spend."

Hell and damnation. Hunt tore off a hunk of bacon and contemplated the demise of a fortune once greater than the king's, according to his mother's tales. "I'd hoped anyone choosing to claim occupancy here would also be able to donate sufficient funds to invest in returning the fields to production."

She shrugged. "Find the lost family jewels, and you won't need us."

∼

FEARING THIS OPPORTUNITY TO SAVE FUNDS FOR OLIVER'S TUTOR MIGHT evaporate, Clare recklessly threw the family's ill-kept secret into the pot. If the solicitors believed Captain Huntley was an heir—despite his distinct lack of family features—then he deserved the information. Perhaps an army man would know how to search. The estate solicitors certainly hadn't been helpful. They'd insisted the jewels were a myth—which they very well could be.

She had summoned all her courage to confront the beast, but the possibility that she'd have to use her own limited funds to support this gothic monstrosity had raised her hackles. She had already leased her modest townhome, hoping to save the expense of upkeep, while earning rent money to hire a tutor. She wasn't prepared to pay servants and upkeep of a *castle*.

She definitely meant to hunt for jewels if that was the case.

Meera and Mr. Walker chose that fraught moment to enter the breakfast room, arguing.

"We *do* educate the poor, sir," Meera exclaimed vehemently. "We simply do not force school down the throats of people who can barely scrape together food for the table."

"Which is why government must provide schools and basic necessities or you do no more than breed slums and slavery!" At the captain's throat-clearing, Walker glanced up, noticed they had an audience, and shut up.

"Tea?" Clare asked politely into the silence, lifting the teapot she'd carried to the table. She'd have to ask later how Meera had managed to dive into a political discussion before breakfast.

The table had not been set. Meera defiantly filled a plate at the buffet and sat down across from Clare. Walker shoveled a mound of food onto his plate and took a place at the captain's right.

She could almost feel the pair waiting for Clare or the captain to object to their presence. Employees, Hindus, and Africans did not normally sit with their so-called betters in society. Meera had been sitting at Clare's table since they were twenty. Apparently, Mr. Walker had been sitting at the captain's. She saw no reason to change now.

Captain Beast didn't even notice. He picked up his newspaper, nodded, and pushed himself to his feet with his walking stick. "Miss Knightley, at your convenience, we should discuss these matters in my study."

"Even if you are my third or fourth cousin, that would not be seemly. Meera is my companion and my friend. She will accompany me." Not looking in his direction, Clare kept her tone just this side of frosty. In her limited experience, men kept their distance when she spoke to them that way. She held her breath to see if the dragon breathed fire.

He scowled and limped out.

"Has he always been surly or is this attitude a result of his injuries?" she inquired solicitously after he was gone.

"He's a soldier accustomed to ordering folks about," Walker said. "You'll grow used to it."

"I very much doubt it." Setting aside her napkin, Clare left the table to the political combatants and went in search of Oliver.

She found him hidden behind a wing chair in the library, an enormous book of bird illustrations in his lap. She'd taught him to read, but most of the descriptions were in Latin. She'd learned French from a governess while her father was still alive, but her education had ended with his death when she was fifteen.

She'd explored the magnificent library this morning. The part directly off the corridor had no windows, only shelves. But at the far end, the room formed an L. That part ran along the outside wall and was brighter than the captain's windowless study.

Clare had examined the shelves, reveling in the depth and breadth of the knowledge at her fingertips, even if it was half a century old. The mahogany shelves soaring to the high ceiling might be a bit dusty, but they were sound and filled with bound volumes, with some of the pages still uncut.

Her explorations revealed it had once been managed by a librarian who had created a system of filing and left a list of titles under each subject. Clare had already found the textbook section. She pulled one down on simple mathematics and laid it on the long table. "We should hunt for hiding places for the jewels. If you'll sit here and practice your sums for half an hour, I will help you look."

The bird book was nearly as large as Oliver, but he hauled it to the table, climbed up on a chair, and deposited it next to the textbook. "Two robins lay three eggs twice a year. That is six robins in one year. Those six robins lay more eggs the next year. Why are there not more robins?"

Oliver didn't exactly have a speech problem so much as a social one. He disliked strangers.

"Numbers subtract as well as add." She found paper and a pencil in a drawer. "If crows eat two of the eggs, then there is only one robin in the nest. Let's put the numbers on paper, shall we?"

Teaching Oliver was a challenge. She couldn't rap his fingers the way her governess had when she tried to ask questions. He'd only clam up and slide under the table. Or vanish entirely. It had taken them an entire day to locate him the time her banker had visited and spoken sharply. Clare had found another banker. That one had been looking at her as a possible investment anyway.

She was dying to take the book of medieval poisons she'd discovered to her room and complete the pages waiting for her research, but Oliver was more important than her novels.

And then, of course, the captain was waiting for her. How did one speak to a beast? Had the captain been a slender dandy of a banker, she might have managed. But he was huge and intimidating and glared like a pirate. . . .

When the clock struck the hour, Oliver looked up eagerly. "Now?"

"You have an excellent grasp of today's lessons, sir. I will show you the basics of hidden panels, but if Meera is done with her breakfast, I must speak with the captain. We'll have plenty of time to physically search rooms later. First, we research."

She led him to the open index. "I know this is difficult to read, but you will learn it little by little. Here is the section on architecture—which is about buildings and might contain plans for the manor. The index tells us what side of the room, what bookcase, and which shelf. Can you read that?"

Oliver studied the notations. "Center?" he asked tentatively. "Number three?"

Clare went to the large center wall and counted three bookcases over. "I learned it starts with the entrance and counts clockwise. Which shelf?"

"Five?"

Clare counted from the bottom to a shelf over her head. "We'll need the stepstool. Can I trust you to climb up and take down only one book at a time? And then when you have them all on the table, I'll be back to help you read them."

Returning her spectacles to her pocket, she held her breath as he rolled the stool over and nimbly climbed up. From the moment he'd learned to walk, Oliver had been an explorer. She couldn't keep him off stairs or ladders or from the top of furniture. All she could do was direct his energy and hope she kept him safely busy.

She adored her nephew as if he were her own, which to all intents and purposes, he was. Given his parents' adventuring tendencies, Clare had the care of him from birth. After tending an infant, it had only seemed natural to step into the role of nursing her mother in her illness.

Flirting with gentlemen had never been an option. She hoped Captain Huntley understood that her timidity didn't mean she was stupid or helpless. If he meant to hunt for the family jewels, he couldn't dictate the hows and wherefores.

Should the treasure ever be found. . . then they could bring in the lawyers.

SIX

"Now, Miss Knightley, let us discuss the formalities first." Hunt hoped a business-like approach would work with a female who roamed his study knocking on the panels dividing it from the library. His head pounded abominably, and she wasn't helping. "If you would take a seat?"

She did not. He had feared his visage might be appalling to a genteel lady but was she actually *afraid* of him? Or did aristocrats simply not listen to mere soldiers?

He'd learned to make generals listen. He could do this—but he wasn't standing here like a booby if she refused to sit. He returned to his chair, tapped his fingers, and waited for her to obey.

"Certainly, we must talk." She removed a section of ledgers to knock on the wall behind them. "My solicitors assure me that you are, indeed, who you say you are—a distant American relation. And that you're a soldier, not an ax murderer."

An ax murderer? Wonderful.

She continued. "They have looked over the papers you sent that prove the earl's descendants, male *and* female, share the property and concur with your assessment. I do not exactly understand why we were not told of this sooner."

All the ladies he'd ever met had flirted, hid behind fans, and whispered among themselves. If they had questions, they deferred to their male companions. He'd become accustomed to thinking of them as empty-headed, feathered nodcocks.

This one spoke crisply like a man, while refusing to look at him, leaving him bumfuzzled, a state with which he was not familiar.

Her companion yawned in apparent boredom. Today, the foreign lady wore garish pinks and reds, although he assumed the gown was fashionable since it resembled Miss Knightley's white, sprigged one. At least the companion did not try to speak like a banker.

Employing his limited patience, he spread the paperwork he'd accumulated across the desk for reference. In this poor light, he couldn't actually read them clearly. "I suspect the estate's hide-bound solicitors of forgetting the earl's terms over the years of pursuing a male heir."

"They did not search very hard," she said dryly. "If descendants through the female line are not a concern, then Oliver is no secret. I do not know most of my relations. For the most part, they did not visit the city. But one assumes there are other males not old enough to have killed themselves yet."

He grimaced at this way of stating it. "My assumption is that the estate's solicitors stuck with tradition and preferred looking for descendants of the earl's son."

The companion finally spoke with a worldly cynicism not normally employed by young women. "Our assumption is that the manor trust is the solicitors' largest account, and they did not wish to have women overseeing it."

Miss Knightley continued searching the shelves, not objecting to this impertinence.

Uncomfortable discussing laws and trusts with ladies, Hunt appreciated the solicitors' reluctance. Female minds did not think linearly. He adjusted his aching knee and attempted to adjust his attitude. If he wanted to leave the estate in hands other than his own, he'd better learn their abilities.

"The thought that they did not want supervision had occurred, Mrs. Abrams," he acknowledged. "I have Mr. Walker discreetly looking into our affairs. I am not entirely certain when the search for an heir began."

Miss Knightley pointed at the packet of papers she'd dropped on his desk. "Perhaps give those to Mr. Walker. When he was alive, my father moved all our trust funds from the earl's solicitors to a London firm. I had them look into the people handling Wycliffe Manor's holdings. Latham and Sons tend to invest the funds in their own clients. Did they assure you they could continue taking care of the estate if you wished to return to your home?" She slid the last ledger back in place with a solid thump. No hollow hiding places there.

"They actually told me there was no need in my coming at all, that they simply needed my approval on some paperwork for everything to continue as it was. Which made me suspicious." And since he had nothing better to do. . . He didn't expound. He had an irrational fear that the firm had waited until he was incapacitated to notify him. In which case, one must wonder what else they'd hidden.

"So, the property has been sitting here, moldering, while a few local men played with the attached trust? Charming." Miss Knightley fished spectacles out of her hidden pocket, donned them, and studied the fireplace next.

"We have found no evidence of fraud. The funds are legitimately invested. The accounts grew over time. Trust expenses were disbursed for caretakers and maintenance as directed. Walker assures me all is in order." Except no one attempted to create income from a substantial property, which to Hunt's practical mind, was a criminal offense.

"So, you decided to do the task of the estate's lax solicitors and find additional heirs to oversee the estate in order for you to return home? Otherwise, you could have simply settled in here, claimed it for your own, and no one would have been the wiser." Leaning over to examine the hearth, revealing a shapely posterior, Miss Knightley began systematically pushing each brick of the hearth.

"Precisely. I'm an engineer. I build bridges and roads. I do not gad about society or play politics and have no interest in farming. I thought perhaps to meet my mother's family and see if any had interest in acquiring the place, since it is not entailed in any way. And then, after studying all the papers, I learned the earl had obtained dispensation to allow lands to descend through his daughters and sisters, and the daughters of his deceased brothers. I suppose had any of his nephews survived, they might have saved the day, but they didn't."

Hunt swung his chair to gaze at the tapestry instead of the lady's form. "Apparently some female understood this oddity enough to establish the family tree up to roughly 1800. I've had to research to find everyone."

Mrs. Abrams rose to examine the work. "No one has lived here for the last fifteen years?"

Hunt used his cane to point at one of the few names in blue. "I was told the earl gave this property to Lord and Lady Reid, his only son and his wife, as a life estate. Then after his son's early demise, and that of his brothers and various nephews, the earl gave up hoping for an heir and sold off his more valuable estates. This was the last one, so he lived here until his death."

The lady gave up her inspection of the fireplace to examine the tapestry, coming close enough for him to detect a scent of lilies. He'd been celibate for far too long if just a scent aroused him. Hunt pushed his chair away, leaving her room to look. He'd already studied the dates up one side and down the other until he knew them by heart.

"The earl died almost half a century ago. The solicitors tell me that my grandmother, Lady Reid, moved in then. She had the life estate and two daughters in Reid's name and every right to do so. And here's why I am not laying any claim to legitimacy. . . According to my mother, my grandmother, the viscountess, left Lord Reid and fled to France, leaving him and their daughter behind. She only returned after Reid died, and she did so with my mother, who is obviously *not* his child."

Miss Knightley nodded knowingly and returned to fireplace searching. "That explains a great deal. Although marriage makes you legitimate in the eyes of the law, you do not resemble the family in any way. I assume your mother did not bear our rather distinctive traits and people noticed. She grew up under the lash of malicious tongues. I cannot imagine how her older sister must have taken her appearance. Consequently, she fled to the Americas at the first opportunity. Her mother retired here to the country to hide her sorrow and shame and did her best to keep up with the family who scorned her by creating the tapestry."

"Spoken like a novelist," Hunt said in scorn, reacting to her fantasy and not questioning family traits. They definitely did not look alike. He was a great dark beast, and she was a slender fair lady. Given their non-relationship, that was to be expected.

She sent him a sharp look. "What makes you say that?"

"Your tale is pure romance. The viscountess was a selfish woman who abandoned her family. When it suited her to return, she surrounded herself with all the wealth and leisure the masses dream of and did nothing with them. And if it is *her* jewels you are searching for, she could have had the decency to tell the earl's descendants where she hid them, since they were most likely part of the funds that should have been distributed."

"The solicitors claim no knowledge of them," the lady admitted. "But I know that my grandmother received a pearl or a sapphire on every birthday until the earl's death, as did the earl's other daughters. We were given to understand he inherited centuries of family jewels. Once he declined the entailment, he gradually distributed them as gifts. We were told he did not sell them. Have you examined some of the portraits in the gallery?"

When he bit back a disgruntled reply, she glanced in his direction. "Oh, my apologies, they're on the next floor." She returned to fireplace vandalism. "The women in the paintings are all adorned in diamonds and rubies and other rare gems. I shall try to relate them to the tapestry. I assume the portraits represent the earl's immediate relations. One must wonder if the earl spent his life in bed to avoid the fate of the other men in the family."

Hunt had speculated about that as well. He assumed the earl didn't have to make his way in the world as the others did, hence their tendency to wander off adventuring. "I would have to go back to the original inventory of the estate at the time of the earl's demise to know if jewels were included. It's quite possible each woman simply kept her own." Hunt's leg ached. He needed to stand and stretch it.

He preferred keeping his distance from the lady, but she was going about her search all wrong. He removed a measuring stick from the desk drawer, pulled himself upright, and began gauging the depth of the fireplace.

"But Lady Reid, your grandmother, would have received a considerable number of jewels upon marriage and the birth of children and so forth. And if the earl lived here prior to his death, he could have hidden any remaining jewels." Miss Knightley shrugged and allowed him to measure while she moved on to tapping walls.

"He could have sold them all. This is no doubt a fruitless waste of time." He continued calculating anyway because he was bored, this was something he knew how to do, and he needed to find the diaries his mother wanted. Walker was systematically working through a million years of estate ledgers and journals but had yet to find any personal papers.

"It occurs to me," the lady said with a frown, glancing at the tapestry, "that a lot of people have died in this isolated manor, all at unexpectedly early ages. Are the jewels cursed?"

Mrs. Abrams stood in a flutter of colorful shawls. "This is not Egypt, Clare. Englishmen do not curse jewels. If you do not mind, I will catalogue the portraits and their gems and match them to the tapestry. It will give me something to do."

"And I should see what occupies Oliver. You might teach him the measuring trick so he can practice his mathematics on the upstairs fire-places." Miss Knightley turned to follow her friend.

Hunt was surprised to discover he was disappointed at their departure.

He ought to be relieved. "Does this mean you will be staying?" he asked before the lady could escape.

"Yes, I believe we will, although staffing is a concern. How does one post a letter from here?" She removed her spectacles to polish them—revealing large, long-lashed blue eyes to accompany those lush lips.

Jarring himself from lascivious thoughts, he replied, "There is a small walking path through the woods to Priory Common about a mile away. Walker can take a letter when he goes in for supplies."

"A mile? Capital! We can take a walk after lunch." She sailed off in search of her nephew.

Leaving Hunt frustrated in more ways than one.

"THE CAPTAIN IS HONEST," CLARE ADMITTED TO HER COMPANION. "I DID NOT expect that."

She hadn't expected him to be imposing, either. Or intelligent. The few men she generally met tended to be weak-minded clerks and officious, elderly bankers. Although she supposed that was preferable to her terrifying time in Egypt when she'd been surrounded by thieves, madmen, and reckless adventurers like her brother-in-law. Presumably, Captain Hunt was of the mad or reckless sort, but injured, he was limited to shooting ceilings and drunkenness.

With a sigh, she gazed at the portrait of the earl at the head of the gallery. The last Earl of Wycliffe's hair color could not be discerned beneath his wig, but the fair-haired boy on his knee displayed all of the family traits. He'd even been staged to show how his thumb curved backward and that his ear lobes attached at an angle unusual to anyone outside the family.

Captain Huntley displayed none of these oddities, nor the dimples or widow's peak of the boy in the portrait. If he resembled his mother, that lady had been honest. Nicholas, Viscount Reid, was not the captain's grandfather, and the captain was not an heir of the blood, only by marriage.

She wondered what had driven Huntley's grandmother to flee wealth and family for the unknown of French society. That sounded much like an act of desperation. Clare was rather familiar with that feeling. The memory of those minutes after her sister's death when she'd had to fight her way from a bloodthirsty mob, and the weeks attempting to take her infant nephew home to safety, had not faded with time. She never wanted to feel that level of fear again.

If the viscount had died very young in this ancient manor, as well as the earl and the viscountess, were they safe here? Surely the manor's secrets were too old to be dangerous.

Having a soldier around, even an injured one, added a layer of defense, she supposed. Although she wasn't entirely certain pistols were preferable to itching powder and bedbugs. Just the sound of firearms returned nightmares.

As if her thoughts had come to life, a muted thud behind the wall of paintings caused her to jump backward.

Meera dismissed it. "Not a ghost. Mrs. Gaither is just old and clumsy."

Eyeing the wall warily, Clare steadied her nerves and continued, "It's a nice day. I would like to walk into the village to post my letter to the solicitors telling them we are staying and asking about hiring staff. Do you wish to remain here or come with me?"

She had promised her nephew a romp in the woods, but Meera was a city girl.

"I need to find a source of rodents for my experiments, but I am not at all familiar with woodland creatures." Meera made a moue of distaste. Her interesting condition had yet to slow her down.

A clatter startled them. Pulse leaping, Clare waited, but the sound did not repeat. After the moaning walls last night. . . "You might want to explore the empty rooms for your rodents. We may have rats."

Deciding she'd had enough of the haunted gallery, she headed for the stairs. Her ancestors could wait for a rainy day.

Meera hastened to follow. "If Mr. Walker is going with you, then I suppose I should accompany you. Give me time to don boots. I assume you asked your solicitors to forward correspondence from my clients as well?"

That was a concern. Now that Clare understood Jacob's danger, she must ask her solicitors not to reveal Meera's presence. "Of course. You are certain Wycliffe will suit your needs?"

"Look at this place." Meera gestured at the huge corridor they traversed. "I could set up a thousand experiments and a dozen laboratories and no one would even know! I will put this time to most excellent use, I assure you. Except for the kitchen, laundry, and servants' hall underneath one of the new wings, the cellars are mostly unused. I think I will start there."

Shutting out her overactive imagination and visions of ghosts and rats in ancient priory foundations, Clare waited as Meera rummaged in search of footwear in the chamber she'd taken for herself. Then, donning pelisses, bonnets, and scarves, they rounded up Oliver, dusted him off, wrapped him up, and met Mr. Walker at the front entrance.

"You are certain you do not wish to take the pony cart?" he offered. "The road is a much longer route because a vehicle requires a bridge, but it will save your boots and hems from mud."

He was elegantly attired in polished knee boots, beaver hat, and crisp linen, as if prepared to spend the day on St. James.

Clare studied his attire and glanced down at her old woolen walking gown. "Perhaps you would prefer to ride? We are prepared for mud."

He adjusted his cravat as if it might be too tight. "I am fine, thank you. The locals do not quite know what to do with me, so I have to dress the part I wish to establish."

Meera waved a dismissive hand. "Who cares what they think? As long as you behave as a gentleman, that's all that matters."

Said the brown-skinned woman with the overlarge nose, Clare thought with a mental grin. Meera's forceful character had provided the strength Clare had desperately needed when she'd returned from Egypt with an infant, to find her mother dying. She'd consulted her as an apothecary but didn't think she'd have survived without Meera as her friend.

She picked up her old skirt and stepped outside to the broad entrance stairs.

They'd arrived in the gloom of night. They hadn't had time to admire the exterior in daylight. Oliver dashed down the immense front steps, then walked backwards to study the towering manor. "Not real turrets," he said in disappointment.

They stood in the drive to study the manor sprawling across what had to be more than two city blocks. The gray stone Gothic front section contained some of the original ornamentation, including gargoyles and cathedral windows. Even the attic windows were large and multi-paned.

Was that a shadow crossing the attic window beyond the gallery? Probably a trick of light. Who would live in that cold empty garret when there was a city of proper bedchambers below?

The faux tower at the entrance was duplicated in the corners. Clare assumed they held staircases to the various halls in this front portion.

They had to stroll down the drive to study one of the wings off the back. The façade was obviously fake, to match the original. Still, the square stones and arched windows were impressive.

"How many rooms, do you know?" Clare asked, setting off down the drive.

"Can't count them all. Hard to say if a gallery and a balcony are rooms. Attics are a labyrinth. Really haven't explored the wings. Cellars have storage areas with only partial doors. Do they count? I should imagine the place could hold the population of an entire village just as if it were a castle." Walker pointed out a walking path into the woods.

"So, all the earl's extended family could have lived here and presumably chose not to. That's rather sad." Clare knew nothing of gardens, but the shrubs that must have once lined this path had evidently expired. Occasional green twigs poked up through the dead branches and debris. Daffodils brightened the layers of leaves with their golden faces. "I wonder if Lady Reid enjoyed gardening? This must have been lovely once upon a time."

Walker shrugged. "The captain's mother gardens, but it is mostly vegetables. There is a kitchen garden in back that Helga maintains when she has time. The place needs gardeners."

"I can look after the kitchen plot," Meera claimed, poking among the dead leaves for green sprouts. "Herbs are my specialty, but carrots and potatoes and the like are easy enough. I'll need them anyway, so I may as well be useful."

"I suppose the more we do for ourselves, the fewer servants we require. Is there a general mercantile, at least?"

"If that is what you wish to call it. There is one old man who sits behind a counter, takes the post, sells bits and pieces. An old lady sets up a cart in front with vegetables she grows herself. I think they sit there and gossip all day. It's not much of a village. I'm not sure why anyone would live here, to be honest." Walker helped Oliver down from a limb he'd climbed upon in search of a pinecone.

"I would guess it was a place the earl came to hunt and fish and that sort of thing. He may have leased a townhome in London when the Lords were in session. I assume his son's widow simply preferred solitude. What matters now is what's to become of it. It's too large and too isolated for a charity like an orphanage or a hospital. I cannot imagine any of the family having sufficient resources to improve it or the desire to do so."

"I believe the captain is hoping your family will stay and maintain it," Walker said warily. "There seem to be enough of you."

"Sell it," Clare said callously. "We can always use money."

"Who would buy it? It's outdated, isolated, and of no advantage to anyone." Meera added a few more greens to the assortment she gathered in a basket. "Besides, imagine the nightmare of dividing up any proceeds between a million distant relations. What if some didn't wish to sell? How would you prove all the claims? Removing the entail created chaos."

"If the trees were cleared, perhaps it could be farmed." Walker didn't seem particularly concerned.

After scrambling over a rain-swollen stream, they entered the village of Gravesyde Priory without reaching any conclusions. Clare gazed in dismay at the collection of thatched cottages in various stages of disrepair. Ragged flower and vegetable gardens indicated a few inhabitants remained. A lone sheep wandered the barren common. "It does not look as if it's been lived in since Shakespeare's time."

"The populace may have been some of his contemporaries," Walker said dryly, leading the way to a long, low medieval building of vertical timbers and white-washed wattle walls. Smoke curled from its leaning chimney.

Clare supposed they must look like an exotic circus to the town's residents. Walker left them at the mercantile so he might take a look at the abandoned blacksmith's shop. His departure didn't stop the shopkeeper from staring as they entered.

Oliver dashed about, oblivious, exploring the shop's meager contents.

Clare introduced herself to the merchant behind the counter, asked to post her letter, and inquired about buttons for a gown she wished to mend.

He spoke around his pipe, nodding at a shelf where Oliver poked through items. "Got buckles. Bit of thread."

Buckles? Unless one counted men's court dress, no one had worn buckles —since the earl's time.

"Do you have anyone here who might *make* a simple button?" she asked.

"Peddler carries them when he comes." He looked over at the old woman. "He gave them molds to Betsy, didn't he? Reckon she did anything with 'em?"

"He couldn't sell what she made, so she couldn't pay him for more materials. Don' know what she did wit 'em." The wizened old woman with frail wisps of white hair held up a handful of withered potatoes. "Got good tatties for your soup."

"I imagine Mrs. Gaither could use those, thank you. How much?" Clare dove into her small store of coins. She had riches compared to these people. "Where might we find Betsy? Mrs. Gaither mentioned she might be useful up at the manor for fetching and carrying."

"She's a bit nicked in the nob," the old man warned. "But reckon she could fetch and carry well enough. Her mam has the second house to the right, one with all the jumble in the yard."

After paying for their purchases, including a piece of horehound for Oliver, they returned to the street to find Betsy's house. The yard with all the "jumble" was easily located. Clare gazed in amazement at the whimsical home-made ornaments hiding among the flowers—pinwheels and gnomes made of clay and bits of fluff and colorful wooden birds carved out of old wood and painted.

"Nicked in the nob?" Meera said cynically.

"Creative, at least." Clare marched up to the front door.

SEVEN

HAVING SEARCHED THE STUDY AND LIBRARY AND FOUND NOTHING OF THE DIARIES his mother wanted, Hunt carried his frustration to the next level. He forced his unbending knee up the staircase to the art gallery. The women in the paintings did indeed wear copious jewels. He wrote down names and dates to match to his tapestry, along with the types of jewels they displayed.

Apparently, there was an order to the exhibit—with the earl at the head of the gallery, his younger siblings next, all bejeweled, even the boys. Then the earl's heir as a young man with his viscountess and their first daughter. Hunt's grandmother looked content enough at this point, and there was no clue to her unhappy future. He knew his mother was curious about her older half-sister in the portrait, but there had been no communication as far as he was aware.

That painting was followed by likenesses of the earl's daughters in their finest court gowns. After that, the family penchant for portraits deteriorated, or they kept them in their own homes. There were a few with women holding babies. One proud mama held up a baby boy, so females weren't the only progeny.

Then, remembering the remark about not resembling his family, he limped back the length of the gallery, examining each portrait for tell-tale traits. The more recent ones had blond-streaked hair similar to Miss Knightley's. They were given to showing off high brows and widow's peaks and fancy earrings in their delicate lobes. The older ones wore wigs which disguised these traits. They all looked very pale and English compared to his swarthier complexion. He didn't know what else to look for. He should ask. If any impostors were to show up, he might have a warning.

He hoped more family would arrive, accompanied by husbands, sons, and men who would know how to handle the property. He had the notion that Miss Knightley had no intention of staying. She was a citified lady giving her nephew a summer in the country. She'd said her other relations didn't live in the city. Country people were far more likely to remain in his estimation.

Overhead, a squirrel must be running loose. Hunt glared at the ceiling, but after a loud thump, the noise stopped. He wasn't up to traversing more stairs. They needed servants living up there.

He was back in the study, sipping brandy and comparing his notes to the tapestry when the walking party returned, chattering and carrying in the scent of rain and cold air. It had been a long time since he'd enjoyed the familiarity of family and home. He didn't fool himself into believing he had them here.

The excited babble drifted away as they returned to their respective rooms to dispense with coats and boots. The old butler apparently did not waste his silver-polishing time on greeting them. They needed a young foot-man, Hunt supposed. He'd ask the solicitors if they knew of a hiring firm to which they might apply. Ladies could not be expected to fend for themselves as he and Walker had been doing.

He was feeling a trifle homesick when Miss Knightley entered in a whisper of petticoats and delicate scents. His neglected cock reacted to her femininity before his head, and he refrained from standing as he knew he ought.

"We have brought back Betsy to fetch and carry so poor Mrs. Gaither needn't wear herself out. We think she might be useful at needle and thread as well, if you have any mending. And we have learned peddlers come through once a week, so if you need any notions, start making a list." She roamed around the room, wearing her spectacles to examine any tomes she'd missed in her earlier search.

The dratted female never sat still. She still avoided looking at him.

"If I had any notion what a notion is, I would." Grudgingly, he watched her catch and release boring tomes on agriculture. She still wore the sturdy walking gown she'd donned after lunch, but he could see enough of her shape to acknowledge that she wasn't a child. If he could move past her rounded vowels and haughty chin. . .

But neither of them meant to stay. Why bother?

"Needles, thread, buttons, combs and such for us. Nails and tools, sometimes remedies—although once she has her supplies, Meera can make up most anything we need in that way. Her father was a chemist and apothecary. Mostly, I think, peddlers carry things they've picked up at market fairs, so it might be toys or an excess of onions or whatever. You can ask him to bring something particular the next time he comes, hence, the list." She opened one of the books and seemed immersed.

"I have visited the portrait gallery," he admitted when she did not look up.

She glanced at him in alarm. "You did not injure your knee by doing so?"

Her unexpected concern gave him a moment's pang, but he waved it away. "I cannot spend the rest of my life not climbing stairs. It was time I made the attempt." And paid the price, but he didn't mention that.

She looked dubious but nodded. "Did you discover anything interesting?"

"I could not see family resemblances other than hair color and widow's peaks on the more recent portraits. The jewels are excessive, especially on the older portrayals. I'll inquire about the inventory of the earl's estate. My mother has a single ruby pendant, but I noticed the portrait of my grandmother as a young wife shows an entire filigree necklace made of gems with a similar pendant."

"The jewelry may have been dismantled and the gems sold. But an inventory really should have been maintained." She gave up on her search of the shelves. "One would think the study an ideal hiding place. Jewelry should be kept in a vault. Do you have a preferred time for dinner?"

It took a second to follow her leap-frogging thoughts, especially now that she faced him, and he could admire her delicate bosom. She concealed the decolletage with a gauzy scarf, but she wasn't entirely bereft of necessary curves.

He dragged himself from the prurient. "Yes, a vault, of course. Not many houses have them. Tell Helga any hour you prefer. I'm not particular."

"Since we all seem to be following country hours and eat an early breakfast, and Mrs. Gaither lays out a nice cold luncheon, I think six will suit. It will be awkward running a household where everyone has a say."

She fled before he could register that impossibility. *Someone* had to be in command or there would be anarchy.

Well, if he meant to leave the place, it was their problem, not his. Just thinking of a dozen people commanding a meager staff had his head in a spin. The old earl had most likely been mad to write that will.

The lady's question about all the early deaths had him wondering if the earl had deliberately left no one as heir to prevent an heir from killing him. He shook his head at his own idiocy. Men died. The end.

Hunt put on a fresh shirt and cravat for dinner, but without his uniform coat, his wardrobe was limited. And without any current income, he wouldn't be expanding it.

Not earning his way fretted at him. The army had provided food and shelter and pay in return for his services. He couldn't afford a life of leisure.

He discovered the party gathered in the small parlor between the gallery salon and the formal dining room. They seemed to be watching the new hire with bemusement.

Hunt assumed Helga had given the new maid the ancient black gown, white apron, and mob cap she wore. At least the housekeeper hadn't put the stout female in a wig. Kinky brown curls escaped the cap, and she'd already spilled wine on the apron.

"Captain Huntley, this is Betsy Green. She'll be helping Mrs. Gaither. Would you like a brandy?" Miss Knightley had changed into a frothy frock of ruffles and lace. Without her spectacles, her eyes matched the blue of her gown.

The gown skimmed curves he shouldn't be noticing. He reached for the decanter.

"No, sir, that's me duty." Sturdy Betsy yanked the decanter from his grip and sloshed brandy into a wine glass. "There ye be, captain, sir."

Training servants had not been part of his education. He took the meager glass and sipped. The brandy really was fine, even without the snifter.

"Have we developed a plan of attack?" he asked, deliberately avoiding the enticing Miss Knightley and addressing Walker.

"Attack?" The maid asked in alarm.

"He's American, Betsy. He speaks a different language. You may go and help Mrs. Gaither. We can fend for ourselves now." The lady dismissed her new hire with patience.

Once the maid was gone, Hunt inquired, "I thought she was to fetch and carry? Isn't it a waste of time having her do what we can do ourselves?"

"Her mother insisted that she be trained for above stairs." Mrs. Abrams sipped and grimaced at the sherry. "Her mother is ill and fears Betsy cannot support herself after she's gone."

Hunt gave that a thought. "Makes sense, I suppose. But someone has to train staff."

"And since we have no staff to do so. . ." Miss Knightley allowed that thought to dangle.

They all winced at a crash from the dining room.

"I trust you were not too attached to the china?" Mrs. Abrams asked dryly.

"The Sevres is locked up. Mrs. Gaither is only allowing us heathens to use the Staffordshire." Miss Knightley turned to Hunt. "But we have learned something of interest from hiring our new maid."

He raised his eyebrows and waited.

"Betsy's mother says the lady who was here before always wore ropes of white beads when she rode through the village in her carriage. I assume she meant pearls."

CLARE HAD NOT BEEN GIVEN AN OPPORTUNITY TO APPROVE THE DINNER MENU. IT consisted of a fine potato soup and lamb, so she would not complain. Her eccentric friend had given up food prohibitions long ago, after Meera's mother died, and she took up her father's science. Clare only had to worry over Oliver's pickiness. Mushy suited him, so he'd consented to eat the soup and rolls and try a few stewed carrots.

The formal dining table had seats sufficient for two dozen. The four of them, plus Oliver, made an awkward seating arrangement.

She concentrated on the food and not the company. The captain had taken the head of the table and glowered like Zeus over the heavens. She couldn't decide if he made her uncomfortable because she was unaccustomed to a man at her table or because of this particular man. She rather thought she'd prefer a skinny dandy so she did not feel so. . . weak and female. Of course, even a skinny dandy could be mad and shoot someone.

"According to the estate ledgers, the manor's trust paid for the last inhabitant's personal maid, a housekeeper, footman, maid, cook, and driver." Walker gave her something better to think about. "I should think if wages have not changed too much, we could hire more staff."

"If we can find them," Clare reminded him, relieved to have her errant thoughts diverted. "I can write to the registry in London, but I cannot imagine anyone of good character and reference would respond. There might be a hiring fair in May, but that's over a month away."

"I'll ask the solicitors about local staffing agencies," the captain offered. "Although I believe I need to go into Stratford and visit their office when I request the estate inventory. I don't wish the request to be ignored."

A distant clangor interrupted any further discussion.

"The door." Walker pushed back from the table. "Helga won't hear it downstairs. And I'm concerned that Gaither *can't* hear."

"You may be right," Meera said as he headed out. "I tried asking him about the cellars, and he told me his smeller was just fine."

Grinning, Walker left to answer the bell.

"How many people did you invite, captain?" Clare dabbed at her lips and rang to call Betsy. A house party might be entertaining, but not if it interfered with finishing her book. Worse, Oliver was averse to strangers. He might never be found again.

But if they were family. . . They might stand as another line of defense should Jacob arrive. As fortune-hunters. . . Well, that remained to be seen.

"Twenty or thirty, I daresay," the captain replied. "Every time I uncovered a new direction, I whipped off an invitation. But I asked all of them to consult with the solicitor's office first, so I did not have to separate wheat from chaff. I did not give out directions. I don't know how anyone could find their way to this outpost without help."

At the sound of voices echoing down the corridor, he pushed up from his seat.

They waited expectantly, until a languid, feminine voice drawled, "An African servant, I declare! How exotic and very American."

Even Oliver stared as the speaker flounced in with an assault of lavender scent and a rustle of petticoats.

Clare swallowed at sight of the elegant creature posing in the doorway. The lavender beribboned travel gown must have come from the latest French fashion plate. Her matching boots had no doubt never experienced a muddy street. Her bonnet—Clare could only eye the purple confection of feathers and roses in awe.

Walker had to ease around her. "May I present Miss Lavender Marlowe, the late earl's great-granddaughter, and. . ." He glanced down the hall and waited for an ancient granny to dodder up. "Mrs. Ingraham, her companion."

Wearing bombazine so old it had a sheen, the elderly companion bobbed her plain black bonnet and didn't speak.

"Miss Marlowe," the captain said coldly, not bowing. "I expressly told the solicitors to notify me of claimants. We are unprepared."

Clare winced as the young beauty's eyes teared up. The child could be no more than sixteen or seventeen. What in all the heavens had brought her here? It couldn't be good.

"I am so sorry," the newcomer almost wept. "We came from the north, and Stratford seemed so far out of the way, and we asked directions. . ."

That was really quite clever of her, Clare had to admit. Pretty faces and youth shouldn't have that degree of courage. Stupidity now. . . Ignorance could be a factor.

Pretty faces empty pockets. . . Surely not from one so young.

The captain remained unforgiving. "The solicitor's office documents claimants to the estate. I'm afraid I will have to ask you to continue on to Stratford. I'm sure you understand we cannot simply accept every stranger as. . ."

The beauty dabbed a handkerchief at her eyes, and her boldness disintegrated into tears.

Shaking her head at his density, Clare threw down her napkin. "Oh, for pity's sake, captain, look at her. Use your eyes and your wits. Miss Marlowe, of the Cheshire Marlowes?" At the girl's terrified nod, Clare continued. "I am Clarissa Knightley, of London." She continued the introductions around the table.

Meera had already sent Betsy after the housekeeper. Mrs. Gaither arrived, wiping her hands on her apron and narrowing her eyes in suspicion.

"Mrs. Gaither, would you be so kind as to show Miss Marlowe and her companion to a prepared chamber?" Clare turned to the newcomer. "We have no one to deliver dinner to your rooms, I fear, but there is enough for all if you'd care to join us."

She steeled herself to ignore the intimidating captain's glower. She had learned he wouldn't bite off her head, and he legally could not heave her out.

It seemed she could stand up to a half-blind cripple. Interesting.

The girl bobbed and thanked them and hurried off after the housekeeper. Clare hoped she had a carriage driver to carry in luggage. The butler never seemed to leave the cellar.

Once they were out of hearing, Captain Huntley returned to his chair and took a large sip of his wine before speaking. "They could be *anyone*. You cannot accept tears as passport."

"Well, I could, I suppose." Clare carefully cut a piece of lamb, knowing she ought to curb her unruly tongue. But she had spent a lifetime behaving as society dictated, and it had taken her nowhere. "If this is my house as well as yours, I should be able to invite anyone I wish."

He growled. She was quite certain he *growled*. But she had made her point, and he had not bitten off her head. Or shot her. She wondered if that was a possibility.

She continued, unrepentant. "But Miss Marlowe has the family hair, widow's peak, and her thumb bends backward, did you not notice? She is most certainly a relation of some sort. And you will recall there is a Marlowe married to one of the earl's daughters on the tapestry. . ."

He grimaced and took a large gulp of wine. "I was looking for people who can run an estate, not dependents!"

"Really, captain, are you sure your injury did not cause your wits to leak?" Clare had run her own household for too long to accept the whims of others, madman or not. "If you are a descendant of the earl's *eldest* child, then the viscount quite likely married and had children well before all his sisters. Consult the marriage dates on the tapestry. Even if the last generation has not been included, it is obvious that you are most likely older than any of your cousins, unless you expect our aunts and great-aunts to step up and take your place."

He definitely growled, glared, and shoved a roll between his teeth.

Clare thought she might be enjoying herself rather more than she'd expected. A tiny little fern frond of hope unfurled in her tensely knotted insides.

EIGHT

Unable to trust his leg on horseback, Hunt hadn't been able to ride the property as he ought. The next morning, frustrated by his limitations, he harnessed the horse to the two-seater cart they'd brought with them. It was useless for riding fields, but it would take him to Stratford.

Whatever vehicle had brought the weepy young lady last evening had taken itself off by morning. It would have been nice if at least one of his non-relations would arrive with something useful like a real carriage and horses. Not that they had stable hands to care for them.

"I should be back by evening," he told Walker. "If not, you'll have to do the locking up. It seems we are not quite as invisible as I'd believed."

"Not if schoolgirls can find us," Walker agreed. "Although I'd be tempted to hand thieves anything they desire. Most of it is good for nothing but a bonfire."

"Don't let the ladies hear that. They'd no doubt have hysterics." In an excess of civility, Hunt had refrained from sending any more moldering ledgers to perdition. Not his problem, he kept telling himself.

The realization that only impoverished, unmarried females would be desperate enough to make this journey chilled him to the bone.

If he was imaginative enough, he'd say the men of this family were hexed. He should look into how the last heir died.

As Hunt took the carriage out, Walker admonished, "Don't break the other knee."

Now there was another cheerful thought.

When Hunt returned later after dark, drenched from a persistent drizzle, he wasn't any happier. It was late. The meager bridge crossing the normally small stream had been hazardous in the rising water. The meat pie he'd brought to eat along the way had worn off. His knee ached. And the reason for his lateness continued to slow the exhausting trip to a crawl.

No light welcomed them. He drove around to the stable. The boy followed on his weary pony. The cow tied to the back trudged in their wake.

Hunt swung his stiff leg from the cart and unharnessed the horse. The silent boy did the same for the pony, then unhitched the cow. He waited for orders.

How he'd come to acquire a deaf-mute servant he'd explain to himself another time. For now, he gestured at a stall he and Walker had filled with feed. One of the things one learned in the field was to forage and prepare.

The boy nodded, and together, they settled the cattle in for the night. Now what the devil did he do with him?

Hunt almost wished for the managing Miss Knightley.

They took the side entrance into the darkened house.

To his utter surprise, the butler greeted them. No doubt pushing eighty, with wispy gray hair covering the edges of his pate, Gaither was stout but seemingly hale. Hunt was fairly certain the deaf old man hadn't heard him arrive. Had he been waiting?

"This is Ned." Hunt spoke loudly and gestured at the gangly adolescent. "Feed him and find him a room below, will you?" He wasn't in a humor to explain a deaf mute to a deaf senior.

Not unintelligent, Gaither bowed and gestured for the boy to follow.

Now that he was inside, Hunt could hear distant voices. Doffing his wet gear, wondering if he should take himself to the kitchen for whatever the cook might have on hand, Hunt went in search of company first. A fire to dry out his aching knee would be welcome.

He found the women gathered in the family parlor. Walker had intelligently absented himself. Still garbed in purple, but not weeping, the adolescent worked a needlepoint while Miss Knightley had set a small desk so the firelight fell across the pages she was scribbling. The elderly companion was nowhere in sight, but the Hindu female studied an ancient volume while measuring ingredients into an array of jars.

Facing the door, Miss Knightley noticed him first. She hastily tucked her papers into a painted box and locked it. "Captain, welcome back. I've instructed Mrs. Gaither to leave stew warming. You look fair drenched."

He rubbed his damp hair, but his hat had taken the brunt of the rain. "Just dampish. If I ring, will Betsy bring a stew or must I hunt it?"

"Did Mr. Gaither meet you? If he didn't doze off, he should be sending up Betsy with a supper. Come sit by the fire and dry off. Did you learn anything interesting today?"

He warmed himself over the fire and attempted to imagine this as an evening in the tavern with his men. Colorful gauze and feminine scents were as foreign to him as India, and he didn't know how to properly address a skittish lady about business. If he pretended they were men and not just bedwarmers. . .

"The solicitors have shown me the estate inventory at the time of the earl's death in 1780, and it contained no mention of jewels. There were lists of artworks, so I know someone performed a proper audit." He'd asked for a copy, but it might take weeks. "If there ever were any, he gave them away, and all trace has been lost."

Miss Knightley wrinkled her long, aristocratic nose. He almost decided it was cute instead of haughty. Obviously, exhaustion addled his brain.

"It is never easy, is it?" she commiserated. "It's obvious from the paintings that the jewels once existed, but as you say, he may have given them away. You must be chilled through. Pull a chair closer to the fire. Miss Marlowe, if you'd be so kind as to move a table. . . ?"

Hunt nearly snorted as the eager adolescent jumped up to do the lady's bidding. Miss Knightley had the soul of a general, even if his eyepatch put her off.

He waited until Betsy set down a tray of steaming stew, hot bread, and a mug of ale before continuing. "I asked about a servants' registry and was told there was none in Stratford. I might have to apply to Birmingham."

All three ladies appeared more disappointed at this news than at the loss of a fortune in gems.

"But we do have the wherewithal to pay staff, if we find them?" Miss Knightley asked.

"It all comes out of the household budget. If we want to dine on wine and caviar, we cannot afford staff to serve it. I made the assumption that you would prefer additional help to eating fish eggs and found a boy who might be trained as needed." He'd decided if she could hire a maid, he should be entitled to someone who could be the butler's feet, if not his ears.

"A boy? How old? Where is he? I do hope the Gaithers are caring for him after that long journey! What did you have in mind for him to do?" Miss Knightley finally addressed him directly.

Tonight, her eyes were a translucent blue. He didn't see any fear or disgust there. The skin beneath his patch itched, but while he actually had her attention, he refrained from scratching.

"They tell me his name is Ned, and he's about fifteen. He's strong enough to handle the cow I purchased. He has his own pony. A farmer was attempting to teach him to hoe and plant, but the boy can't hear and thus didn't take instruction well. The farmer was not patient, and the vicar objected to his treatment and took Ned in. You said you might train servants. . ." He let the sentence dangle as the women all talked at once.

FRIDAY MORNING, THEY ALL TRAIPSED OUT TO ADMIRE THE MIRACLE THAT WAS A cow. Clare thought it might give her next book verisimilitude if she knew how a cow worked, but squeamish, she backed away as the first squirt hit the pail.

Ned, the new boy, seemed to have a fine grasp of the mechanics, and Oliver was fascinated. Clare left them under the supervision of Miss Marlowe's companion, who seemed to know more of country ways than a genteel lady's companion should.

Miss Marlowe had not been very forthcoming when discretely questioned.

Clare knew she should be copying a final draft of her new novel if she were to meet her deadline. But the sun was out, and exploring the grounds couldn't be a bad thing. Meera abandoned the cow to follow her to the court-yard that may once have been the priory's cloister. It was now protected by the manor's wings. Instead of an extensive formal garden, the parterre appeared to contain herbs and vegetables.

Meera clucked approvingly. "Look, this section is medicinal. The one over here is savories for cooking. This appears to be the potato and onion plot. Some are already sprouting. The walls form a barrier against the weather, and they have afternoon sun. Someone knew what they were doing."

In knee-high boots, leather trousers, and a rough broadcloth jacket, the captain limped from the house. "I heard you were all enjoying a milking exhibition."

No longer startled by the captain's rough presence, Clare wrinkled her nose and studied the greens. "Not exactly refined, is it? How does one communicate with young Ned?"

"Gestures, mostly. He's a quick student and follows by example, the vicar said."

"Does anyone know his parentage? Should we be assuring someone he's well taken care of?" A bit daunted by a gentleman in partial dishabille, Clare kept her eyes averted from the captain's cravat-and waistcoat-less chest. His very broad and solid chest.

She now had to wonder who did the laundry and ironed shirts. Walker didn't seem likely. No wonder the housekeeper seemed resentful of their presence. Adding laundry to all she had to do was beyond reasonable.

"Ned was left at an orphanage years ago. We have no knowledge of his family."

"Poor lad. Do you think he might be trained as a footman since Gaither is not very useful above stairs?" Clare wasn't entirely certain of the etiquette of parceling out duties in their strange household.

"I imagine he's more comfortable outside until he adjusts. He can mind the cattle, dig the garden, carry loads, that sort of thing. Scrub pots in the evening perhaps? Should we leave that to Helga?" It almost sounded as if it hurt him to ask.

Clare bobbed a curtsy and dared a smile of approval. She swore he took two steps back and appeared ready to flee. But he held his ground, standing stiff and stern and awaiting her decision.

She needed to learn to do the same. "It is not what is normally done but seems practical. Thank you for rescuing him."

Before he could escape, she consulted him on a different issue. "Have you noticed that food disappears from the buffet before Mrs. Gaither clears the platters? She says we have a ghost."

It was difficult to discern his expression behind the eye patch, but he sounded baffled. "A ghost that eats? Unlikely. Are you certain Oliver does not return to clean up? Young boys are always hungry."

"Not Oliver. He is a very picky eater. He tells me Mr. Ghost has *slippers*. I am not clear on the distinction. Do ghosts wear shoes? You and Mr. Walker wear boots."

That was definitely a frown creasing the visible part of his brow. "I'll talk to the Gaithers. They may be hiding a family member and fear being sacked. I'll reassure them that there's food for all."

With a nod of gratitude, she lifted her skirts and abandoned Meera to her gardening.

Outside the servants' entrance at the rear of the east wing, she found Betsy doing the laundry. Well, that relieved Mrs. Gaither of some of her burden. The clumsy maid had suds all over the flagstones and was now endeavoring to hang barely wrung sheets from a line too high for her stumpy limbs to reach. Clare glanced around, found an old wooden stool surely intended for the purpose, and hauled it over to the line. "You wash, I'll hang."

She'd never hung laundry in her privileged life, unless hanging her unmentionables counted. But she liked clean linen, and this was a good day to air sheets.

Not long after, Mrs. Ingraham hurried from the direction of the barn, clucking. "No need for 'e to do 'at, Miss, it's not for ladies." She tugged the soaked sheet from Clare's hands.

Taken aback, Clare didn't argue. She was too startled by the woman's speech. Where on earth had Miss Marlowe found a companion who spoke so poorly? Certainly not in the city, where she'd be scorned and an object of ridicule. The fashionable Miss Marlowe with her boarding school manners would never accept ridicule. What could her family be thinking?

Given a new mystery to explore, Clare left the two country women to the chore and hied herself back into the house—where she apparently belonged.

NINE

With everyone outside enjoying the day, Hunt continued his search for the letters and diaries his mother insisted the viscountess had kept. He imagined his grandmother would have burned them, but he, too, was curious about his French grandfather. And he supposed, now that the war had ended, he should learn how any family he had there had fared.

He had to assume his mother's half-sister, his aunt, had inherited a trust as the rest of his family, excluding his mother, had. The earl had been petty in ignoring a child obviously not his son's, but Hunt supposed it was understandable.

He'd not encountered any vaults or hiding places in his search of the ground floor. But he originally hadn't been looking for one. The ground floor of the main block of the house, along with the usual common rooms, contained a library, a study, and an estate office littered with books and papers that would make good fire fodder. He'd searched those first.

Before he dragged his knee through the multitude of rooms in the wings or upstairs to the endless maze of bedchambers and private suites, he'd run a second search on the main floor for concealed vaults. Removing all the books in the immense library and tapping walls, as Miss Knightley had done in the study, seemed futile. He started with measuring walls.

He was surprised to discover someone had laid out ancient volumes on the library table—although he shouldn't be. Miss Knightley seemed inordinately fond of decrepit tomes.

He studied the pages she'd left open—architectural treatises? What the devil. . . ?

Despite himself, he was squinting at the drawings when a scurrying scuttle made him aware he was no longer alone. Feeling sure the women or Walker would have made themselves known, he refrained from checking under the table for the silent boy.

He felt some kinship with the only other male in a family of females.

The boy's excellent surveillance position gave him an advantage in determining the safety of his surroundings and to notice an intruder with *slippers*. The Gaithers still claimed no knowledge of a real person and insisted the ghost of the late viscount visited regularly to be certain they took care of his property. Hunt didn't believe in protective spirits, although he was starting to wonder what had killed his grandfather-by-name-only for him to have died so young. He saw no evidence that the viscount had done more than drink his way through barrels of brandy.

He really needed his knee to work again so he could climb the stairs and solve a few of these mysteries. Walker preferred account books to attics.

"I don't think the manor is old enough for a priest's hiding hole," Hunt said to the air. The page on how such places were hidden had been left open.

A small figure scampered from beneath the table and to the hearth.

Hunt glanced from the book, over to the massive stone and timber fireplace. "True, there is sufficient room for a concealed door."

Wishing he'd brought his surveying equipment, he produced the large measuring stick he'd marked up. "Write down these numbers, will you?"

The boy knew exactly where to find pen and paper. Amazingly, he could also write his numbers.

They were deep in calculations of depth when Miss Knightley appeared in search of her lost charge. "Oh, you've found the book, excellent! From what little I can tell, an architect used it to renovate several rooms, including the library."

"He tried, anyway," Hunt said dryly. "But it seems appearance weighed more than accuracy or stability in his choices. I'm amazed the chimneys do not fall on our heads."

"Surely they are not quite so bad," she said in alarm, tugging Oliver away from the grate. "Any modifications of this old block must have lasted a century or two."

Hunt set aside his stick and pushed at the mantel where he'd discerned an anomaly. "Modern methods are more reliable." As if to prove his point, the mantel clicked, and the panel beside the hearth opened.

The boy crowed in excitement, until learning the small cupboard revealed still another book, with room for nothing more.

They all peered at the ancient leather-bound tome and the brown and withered lady's glove.

"Perhaps it is a clue? It smells vaguely of. . . jasmine?" Miss Knightley touched the glove. When it didn't crumble, she lifted it to read the book's title. The perfume intensified. "A Church of England prayer book."

Hunt hoped it might reveal the location of his grandmother's diaries or papers, but his one eye had difficulty focusing on fine print. "Did you wish to peruse it or shall I have Walker take a look?"

She gingerly flipped a few pages and shrugged. "I will study it after he does, but it appears a child's hiding place."

Hunt had to agree. Awkwardly, he addressed the disappointed boy huddled in his aunt's skirts. "You make an excellent apprentice, sir. I will need your aid in investigating the rest of the manor."

The shy child nodded.

"Mrs. Gaither has laid out luncheon. Go wash, and I'll meet you in the breakfast room." She detached the child from her skirts and sent him off. "I do thank you, sir, in allowing him to help. He needs to feel useful, but there is little he can do to help Meera or me. I've told him he must help us search for treasure."

She diverted her gaze to the book and glove rather than look at him.

He was not normally a vain man, but she made him feel like an ogre. He considered the withered glove again and froze. Maybe she didn't avoid him, but studied the. . . blood-stained glove.

"Perhaps the spots are mold or soot," she murmured.

Hunt didn't think so. He returned the glove to the cupboard. "Until we know more, best to leave it here. The architect responsible for this hearth did not build the hiding place in your book. Other hearths might differ also. We'd have to inspect each one—if you really wish to continue."

He now had doubts about uncovering the manor's secrets.

"There are rather a lot of hearths." She wrinkled her nose in distaste. "Even if we want to know more, we'd need an army to search."

"I *am* Army," he said with a smirk he couldn't resist. "I can do it, once my knee accepts orders. It is a pity our latest guest is not so useful as your nephew."

Not that he imagined any woman capable of climbing through fireplaces and making calculations and. . . hunting for more bloody gloves? He just didn't know how else to introduce the topic of their schoolgirl intruder.

Miss Knightley was quick. "Have you found Lavender's connection in your papers? I see on the tapestry that one of the earl's daughters married a Marlowe and had two boys, but it does not extend far into our generation."

Hunt wanted to rest his leg, but she seemed prepared to flit at any sudden move. She was the only sensible choice for discussing the family aberrations, and he didn't want to scare her off. "My research has not located any marriage lines for either of the sons, only death notices to show they died in their early twenties."

The family really did have a run of rotten luck.

"Oh, dear." She looked a trifle bemused, an unusual state for the lady. "Really, I don't think so many family traits can be denied. She even has the dimples, when she is not weeping. But. . ."

Hunt waited to see how she excused the child's lack of documentation. *Dimples* hardly counted, but now he had to wonder if Miss Knightley had them. She never smiled in his direction.

"Mrs. Ingraham is not a refined companion or even a lady's maid," she continued. "No proper family would have hired her for their young daughter—not to travel here alone, of a certainty. I fear we must question her."

Hunt almost fell over in astonishment. She admitted she might be wrong?

And then remembering how the miss had wept at the first sign of trouble. . .

"Perhaps you and Mrs. Abrams might question her?" he suggested, reluctantly.

Her smile was almost laughing as she glanced up at him. And there were the dimples. His insides did a backflip of a sort he'd not known since adolescence.

"The soldier quakes at a few tears? Certainly, sir. We will be your first line of defense."

Hunt was unaccustomed to being laughed at. Instead of being taken aback, her laughter warmed him in ridiculous ways. Apparently, he enjoyed impertinence.

A BLOODY GLOVE! CLARE'S IMAGINATION SPUN WILDLY. SHE'D BE SEEING AX murderers around every corner if she did not rein in her notions—but a medieval mystery! Well, perhaps, just an eighteenth century one.

For many reasons, Clare wrote under a male pseudonym. Walking a fine line of respectability was one of them. Under different circumstances, her nephew might have been a viscount—on both sides of his family. His place in Debrett's would open doors and gain him respect despite his oddities. And Clare was all he had to maintain that recognition. As a spinster living alone, preserving her position as a lady for his sake had not been easy.

Meera had been her first act of defiance. Writing novels had been next.

The manor might be another, but the eccentric inhabitants were a welcome relief from the tension of living in London's close-knit society. How much of her prim lady role could she set aside under these circumstances? Did she dare reveal her unseemly curiosity about the glove and the prayer book? And a ghost that wore shoes and ate breakfast?

First, she needed to interrogate Miss Marlowe.

Mindful of the missing food and ghostly reports, Clare first lingered near the dining room until Betsy cleared the luncheon platters. Not catching anyone sneaking about, she then sought out Miss Marlowe to ask if she'd like to examine the family portrait gallery. Apparently bored, the girl eagerly acquiesced.

"This place is even larger than my school," Miss Marlowe confided as she gazed from the upper galley to the lower. "Just imagine the balls one could have!"

Clare would rather not. The idea of so many strange gentlemen in one place— She shuddered. Meera's condition was a painful lesson in what happened when one flirted with charming men.

"It does seem a shame to waste so much space," Clare agreed evasively. Young girls deserved their dreams. "Are your parents planning on giving you a Season now that you have finished school?"

They strolled slowly, admiring the portraits in the gray light from the windows. A scraping noise above caused her to hesitate, but the captain had mentioned squirrels in the attic. She shivered and continued on.

"I did not exactly finish," Miss Marlowe said with a sigh. "I was not much of a student, and it seemed a foolish waste of funds learning to be a lady. So, when we heard about the manor. . . I thought it might be fun to live in a fine house."

Hmm, whoever her parents were, they did not own a "fine" house. Clare wondered what constituted "fine." More than a cottage? More than a townhouse?

"Manors are an immense amount of work. Did your school teach you how to run a household? I didn't attend school and had to learn from my mother." Clare halted in front of the portrait of the earl's daughter holding up her baby son, who had apparently died as a young man. If nothing else, she was learning about her hitherto little-known family.

"I learned needlepoint and drawing and piano and how a proper dinner table should be set and very many foolish things. I thought housekeepers ran households." The girl showed little interest in the portrait that might be of her Grandmother Marlowe.

"Ladies tell housekeepers and cooks what to do." Clare indicated the elegant lady wearing a fortune in emeralds and diamonds. "I never knew my grandmother. I was too young when she died. Did you know yours?"

"That old besom? She's the one who sent me to school so I did not dirty her doorstep." The child lost her air of insouciance to glare at the portrait. "I suppose that is my father. He was the eldest son."

Well, let it not be said that Miss Marlowe was a slowtop.

"I suppose she must be my great-aunt. I did not even know I had uncles," Clare said encouragingly. "They must not live in London."

"My grandmother lives near Manchester, on one of the properties the earl once owned. My father died in a duel before I was born," Miss Marlowe said with a touch of scorn. "You would have still been in the schoolroom. His younger brother died in a naval battle. We are not a fortunate family, are we?" She strolled on as if discussing dinner.

A duel? Clare caught a glimmer of understanding and attempted deeper examination. "I am so sorry about your father. That must have been tragic for your mother. I hope she had family to help her through a terrible time."

Miss Marlowe shrugged. "His family gave her a stipend that kept a roof over our heads, I've been told. I was too young to remember. Is your father still alive?"

Clare allowed the momentary diversion. "We lost him when I was fifteen. He was considerably older than my mother and was taken by an apoplexy after his investments suffered financial reversals. As you say, we're not a fortunate family. Is your mother still alive?"

Miss Marlowe pretended interest in a portrait of two young girls wearing flowers and ribbons in their hair. "I have not heard otherwise. Who do you think these children might be?"

"One of the family with more wealth than ours," Clare said dryly. "My sister and I never had our portraits sketched, much less immortalized in oil."

"Your nephew says he is hunting for treasure. Do you think the manor might really conceal jewels? If so, we could all have our portraits done."

Oh, dear. Had Miss Marlowe heard the tales before she arrived and thought to include herself among the heirs?

Because Clare was fairly certain that Lavender Marlowe's parents had not married, which would explain why the girl knew so very little of her relations and the captain had found no trace of her existence.

TEN

Meera stirred camphor and eucalyptus oil into the menthol unguent and capped the jar. Now came the hard part.

Men did not accept female druggists.

She knew she possessed her father's formulas and experience. She'd worked with him since she was able to toddle, after all.

The only person beyond Clare who had accepted Meera's expertise had taken advantage of her romantic inclinations to obtain the formulas—probably one good reason women should not work outside the home. Although, if she'd had more experience, she might have known Jacob was rotten. How did one gain experience without being hurt?

Oliver had joined her to explore the medieval cellar where she'd set up her compounds. If they meant to stay a while, she'd like to order jars. She felt awkward asking for funds from the household budget unless she was providing useful services.

"What if there are hiding places in the floor?" she asked the boy, offering him a broom to clean her workspace and better search the stones.

A single oil lamp lit the table. The cellar had no windows, which helped maintain the even temperature that better preserved her medicinal ingredients.

Oliver swept a patch of stone floor clean and sat down to pry at mortar. He shook his head when nothing loosened.

The light from a swinging lantern threw a beam down the corridor beyond her half door. Meera prepared a label for her unguent before they were interrupted.

A moment later, the rather dashing Mr. Walker held up his lantern to take in her workshop. "I came to tell you dinner will be ready in half an hour. You need more light in here."

"I did not wish to waste candles or oil. I can prepare this compound practically in the dark." She cradled the jar and her hopes in her palm. "Might I ask a favor, sir?"

"Don't be 'sirring' me. I'm Walker. What favor?" He held out his hand to draw Oliver from under the worktable.

Oliver actually accepted it. Meera took that as a sign the gentleman could be trusted.

"Then I should be Meera. I don't think I wish to be called Abrams. Although, perhaps, if I had a man's name, it might be easier to sell my medicine." She held out the jar. "Could you persuade the captain to use this on his knee? It should relieve the pain, which would encourage him to bend it more."

Walker held up the lantern and read the jar. "Every morning and evening?" He opened and sniffed and grimaced. "Smells strong enough to work."

Meera breathed a sigh of relief. "I have no other way of earning my way in this household. I like to be useful."

She thought that behind his carefully neutral expression she saw a modicum of interest. Not laughing at her was sufficient to smooth her fractured pride a trifle.

"Have you asked Helga about her arthritis?" He actually held out his arm for her to take as Oliver scampered ahead of them.

"I don't think she approves of me," Meera murmured as they passed the kitchen. She'd had a lifetime to learn that her brown skin was a barrier between her and the general population. "I thought perhaps Clare might mention it. I wanted to have enough jars prepared first."

"British folk aren't any more open-minded than American, then? I thought since they banished the slave trade. . ."

Meera sniffed. "That affected no one on this island except the traders, who were evil people anyway. You did not see us invite any Africans to move here or see us abolish slavery in the colonies, did you? And we did not fight a war with Americans to force them to stop their dreadful practice."

Walker chuckled. "Instead, we fought it to prevent your Navy from enslaving our sailors. The world is an odd place."

"And until we can vote, we have no say in it, so we must do what our conscience dictates while surviving as we can. It's not as if women or poor people of any sort can expect better."

"You are too cynical for your age and gender—*Meera*. I will take this to the captain and see you at dinner." He bowed when they reached the ground floor and departed down the hall.

Oliver was already flying up the marble stairs, neatly avoiding the floor vase.

Meera followed more slowly. She'd never met an African before. Until her father's death, hers had necessarily been a sheltered life.

Knowledge was a good thing, she decided. If she'd been more experienced with men, one wouldn't have taken advantage of her. She was well aware that prejudice came from ignorance, and she did not wish to be one of the ignorant. She might have been wary of this alien rural manor, but she would use the experience to learn.

That decision lasted just long enough for her to discern a cloaked shadow slipping down the dark, unused bedroom corridor to the right of the stairs.

She screamed.

HUNT WAS DONNING HIS WAISTCOAT WHEN HE THOUGHT HE HEARD A SCREAM.

He never wanted to hear screaming again. This was no war zone—

Excited voices echoed down the hall to this small utility room he'd claimed for himself.

Twitching his cravat into place, Walker stopped in the doorway, listening.

"I'm not hearing things then?" Hunt couldn't dash anywhere, but he yanked his leg along in the direction of the commotion.

The unguent Walker had suggested stank too badly to stomach before dinner, so he simply endured the pain for now.

The screams had quieted by the time they reached the shoulder-sized vase by the marble stairs, but the women's voices were still elevated. Ladies did not generally speak loudly, he'd learned. Something was wrong.

While Walker took the stairs two at a time, Hunt swung his stiff leg awkwardly, using the damned stick to propel him.

By the time he reached the top, Miss Knightley and her intrepid nephew were nowhere in sight. He could have sworn he'd heard her voice, but only a terrified Mrs. Abrams and Miss Marlowe remained.

The marble stairs led to a wide main corridor, presumably where the ladies had their chambers. Walker was striding down a narrow hall to the right, along the gallery side of the manor.

Uncomfortably, Hunt addressed the two women he preferred to avoid. "Explain."

"Ghosts!" The teary adolescent wept. "Meera saw ghosts."

They were on a first name basis already? Fine. "What precisely did you see, Mrs. Abrams?"

"A shadow, wearing a cloak." Mrs. Abrams straightened her short, stout figure. "It surprised me."

"Understandably." He tried to sound reassuring. "Has Miss Knightley gone ghost-hunting then?"

That brought a small smile. At least she did not have difficulty looking on him. "More likely, she's chasing after Oliver."

Which confirmed Hunt's impression that the timid scholar defended her nephew like a lioness. "Would you mind accompanying me to the approximate area where you saw this figure? Did he vanish when you screamed?"

Miss Marlow clung to Mrs. Abrams, looking more eager than terrified.

The lady thought about it. "I think he moved very quickly before vanishing. I came up the stairs. Our rooms are straight down the main hall. I'm not at all sure why I happened to glance down this narrow one. A sound, perhaps?"

"Or a smell? Are you sensitive to smells?" Because Hunt was noticing a distinct odor of. . . fried potatoes?

He limped down the narrow hall behind the gallery and saw Oliver emerging from a doorway. There were doors only on one side, and Walker stalked from one to the next, throwing them open. The place was a nightmare of interlocking chambers. They'd never find anyone that way.

"Now that you mention it. . ." Mrs. Abrams delicately sniffed the air. "Perhaps Oliver has been raiding the kitchen?"

"Or we have a ghost that smells of hot grease. Keep your doors locked at night, ladies, but I do not think this ghost wishes to meet you anymore than you do it." Hunt limped after the intrepid explorers.

Miss Knightley popped out of another chamber holding a fire iron and looking exasperated. "We need a floor plan of this maze."

Interesting. She would confront ghosts and not him?

"Exactly my thought. I believe there may be a partial drawing in the estate office. Call off your troops and let us eat dinner and plan our campaign like intelligent officers." He knew he sounded gruff but his damned knee hurt, and he was frustrated at not being able to hunt down the culprit who caused it.

At thirty, he was starting to feel old and decrepit already.

Miss Knightley actually glanced up at him. No one had a lantern. Perhaps he didn't look so fearsome in the dark. "Definitely, let us plan. Hunting shadows requires illumination."

Even though she carried a lethal weapon, she did not sound terrified—of him or the ghost. A lioness definitely lurked behind the timid miss disguise.

The women left for their separate rooms to finish dressing. Already in his dandy clothes, Walker offered to guard the corridor until the ladies descended for dinner.

"I'll start wearing all black and fade into the shadows," Walker said wryly, holding up his dark hand against the gloom.

"Or wear a cloak," Hunt suggested. He could barely make out his own pale skin.

Walker took his meaning. "Easy enough to slip about in this gloom wearing a dark cloak. I'll watch for movement and the odor of cooking."

"A place this large needs gas lighting." Hunt limped off, examining the high ceiling for a good means of installing pipe.

Once they were gathered in the small family parlor for sherry before dinner, Hunt managed to corner Miss Knightley. Impatient with small talk, he dived into a more immediate concern than ghosts. "Did you learn anything from our questionable Miss Marlowe?"

"Her father died in a duel before she was born. His family paid for a roof over her mother's head. Said mother does not seem to play a presence currently. And grandmother is a besom who sent her to boarding school. You may reach your own conclusion." She sipped her sherry and watched as the others discussed ghost searches.

"I'm impressed by your interrogation skills," he admitted, annoyed that she wouldn't look at him again. "A duel? Of all the . . ." He cut off his epithet. If his appearance offended the lady, his crude opinion would more so. "Age old story? Anticipated marriage vows but not death?"

"And the mother was most likely not considered suitable or had no family or they'd have done better by her. Although, I must say, she's not gone hungry, which is the usual fate of such a misalliance."

They watched the fashionable Miss Marlowe laugh and flutter her fan and otherwise sparkle among the dull older company.

"She would do very well in the marriage mart if she had a dowry and someone who would shade her background just a wee bit." For a shy spinster, Miss Knightley spoke with worldly cynicism. The woman was not unintelligent.

"Why did you never seek marriage?" he had to ask.

"No money, no sponsor, and a houseful of responsibility. Everyone died, and I spent my youth in mourning," she said flatly. "My sister had hoped she and her husband could make their fortune and see me take London by storm, but then they died. Not that I would have, mind you. I am quiet and scarcely a diamond of the first water. But at a younger age I might have enjoyed the grand ballrooms and having a flirtation or two."

"I am not at all certain what a diamond of the first water might be, but I should think you would compare favorably to other misses better than yon flirt." He'd far rather talk to a sensible miss anyway.

"I suspect marriage is highly overrated," she said dismissively. "How about you? Why have you not married?"

Her quiet outward appearance concealed an unexpectedly sharp mind. Women were a mystery—one he lacked patience to explore. He simply wanted information. He supposed it was only fair to offer answers in return. "I was betrothed before the war. I'm not rich and couldn't risk leaving her a poor widow when I marched off to battle, so we postponed the nuptials. She found someone else while I was gone."

She frowned at her sherry glass. "What was she like?"

Hunt hadn't given it much thought recently. "Fair-haired, pleasant. Her father was a lawyer. It would have been a good match."

She made a distinctly unladylike noise. "How romantic. No wonder she looked elsewhere. Marriage wouldn't suit you."

That stung, but she wasn't wrong. "There are some delights a marriage allows that cannot easily be found elsewhere." Hunt knew he overstepped boundaries, but he was a soldier and a man. Romance held no interest, but he could not deny physical pleasure.

He thought she grew pink. He hoped that was an indication that she was not entirely ignorant, although why it should matter was beyond his feeble understanding. He wasn't a rake who seduced innocents.

"My sister enjoyed the wedded state, but she was the sort who enjoyed society and adventure. Marriage allowed her freedom. And that is all I have to say about that."

She took his arm to go into dinner when Betsy announced it. It seemed Gaither was too old to carry out any of his duties.

Fried potatoes were one of the dishes set out for their delectation, he noted.

He seated Miss Knightley at his right so she could not flee. He really did not wish to suffer Miss Marlowe's foolish schoolgirl tales. "What happened to your sister?"

"Her husband was a soldier who believed he could bring back Egyptian treasure. They thought themselves invulnerable to injury and disease." She spoke curtly.

Hunt couldn't tell if she hid grief or disapproval, no doubt both given the outcome. "I am sorry. I see why a large family might be a blessing. At least some might survive to care for the next generation. But watching so many die— Your nephew is fortunate to have you."

They watched Oliver slip beneath the table with his chicken on a roll.

"I'm not so certain I am what he needs. I hope to find a tutor who will understand him."

And there was the reason he must keep his distance. He would be returning to his home and what remained of his career in a few months. Her future was here, with a child who needed security.

Hunt sipped his wine and pondered gas lighting instead of Miss Knightley's enticing scent—still lilies, he thought.

A small hand tugged at his trouser leg. He slipped more chicken and a roll under the cloth.

Miss Knightley chuckled, and any thought of gas lighting fled as he felt the sensation clear to his groin.

Obviously, he was an oaf unsuitable for civilized society.

ELEVEN

Once Captain Huntley and Mr. Walker agreed to take rooms in the front upper hall where the ghost had been seen, Clare breathed a sigh of relief. Jacob had seemed mad enough to follow Meera. If he was sneaking around, looking for the formula book. . . She preferred the devils she was coming to know.

Sitting close to the captain at dinner, breathing in his shaving lotion, having his boots bump her slippers under the table, had been a lesson in courage. Men were normally repellant creatures who stank of sweat or talked too loudly or caused her to feel insignificant. Or shot bats and other living creatures.

Captain Huntley shot bats, but he smelled of sandalwood and leather. He barely spoke at all, but he listened when she did, and he didn't bring his pistol to the dinner table. She was all about in her head to be aware of a gentleman simply because he knew how to be considerate. It was proximity, she was certain. Not an entirely bad thing, perhaps.

At the moment though, opening the unused upper chambers was her concern. She couldn't ask the elderly Mrs. Gaither to both cook and clean. And Miss Marlowe might have an education in running a household, but she obviously had no experience, which left Clare to delegate tasks.

Despite his stiff knee, the captain insisted on joining them while they made up his new rooms. Together, they all beat mattresses, dusted, located linens, and rearranged furniture, instead of spending the evening on separate floors.

"You are certain the shadow you saw was not Ned or Oliver?" Walker asked, flinging a mattress on a bed. "Boys explore."

"Oliver and Ned are small. The ghost was not," Meera insisted, shaking out a sheet. "And Ned was scrubbing pots in the kitchen. Oliver would break his neck on a cloak."

"It is very good of you both to change rooms for our sakes," Clare said, placating the argument. If Meera did not mention Jacob, she could not. He was just the sort to wear a cloak and hide.

She tried not to admire how the captain shoved a wardrobe back in place single-handedly, despite his lame knee and weak arm. He'd removed his frock coat so as not to filthy it on the furniture as he moved it about. Muscles bulged beneath his shirt and—when he bent over—they bulged beneath his trousers. She gulped and looked away. She'd not ever seen a man without his coat. No wonder they wore them!

"We're accustomed to camping on hard ground," the captain pointed out, straightening and looking for something else to do. "You did not need go to this trouble."

"Ladies should not 'ave to," Mrs. Ingraham agreed, although her accent was thick enough to misjudge her words. "Thee needs more staff."

Dressed all in black, the older lady probably had a cloak. . .

"This is fun, gr—" Miss Marlowe cut off whatever she was about to say. "And we can search for treasure while we're at it!"

Clare tried not to be too suspicious of Miss Marlowe and her odd companion.

"No treasure in these rooms," the captain said in disgust, wiping the filth off his newly cleaned waistcoat. "The insides of these wardrobes haven't been touched in a century."

"If there are no fingerprints in the dust, then we know no one has looked inside them, at least." Clare tugged a counterpane into place and thought about it. "I wonder how long it has been since this side hall was dusted? Has there been enough time for dust to gather?"

"Walker and I haven't explored the upper floors until today," the captain said, apparently following her thoughts.

"We're not trackers," his friend reminded him. "If the ghost has left a trail in the dust, he's no doubt walked it many times, in any number of directions."

By now, everyone had caught on. There was a general bustle as lamps and candles were located and lit. Even Mrs. Ingraham trailed in their wake as they crept down the hall where the mysterious figure had vanished.

Old carpets had been removed, leaving century old or older wood exposed. It should have been waxed annually, but that was a task for an enormous staff. Dust had collected along the walls, but to Clare's disgust, the center was well trampled.

"We ruined it. We've left trails everywhere in our earlier search."

The captain held up his lamp to examine a dark chamber. "Let us go back to our original idea of examining the architectural drawings first. Let's not trample any more possible paths until we work out a scheme."

The party looked reluctant to give up the game. Clare held Oliver's hand to prevent him from creeping away. "If a ghost is lingering to search for treasure, then he hasn't found it, has he? We may have two very different searches, one for treasure, one for ghosts."

"Can we block the halls so no one can pass?" Meera suggested worriedly.

"Stairs all over," Walker said. "Won't work."

That wasn't reassuring at all. Giving up any hope of copying fresh pages this evening, Clare hurried back to the marble staircase, then hesitated. "Should we perhaps use one of these upper salons for gathering in the evenings? Mr. Walker, do you think you could find the floor plans the captain mentioned?"

"I am not an invalid," Captain Huntley objected. "I am perfectly capable of descending to the parlor."

"Yes, but I need to put Oliver to bed, and if there is any chance we have an intruder—" She let that thought dangle.

Now that dinner was done, Mrs. Gaither had belatedly joined them, looking sour at this disturbance to her evening hours. Reluctantly, she pointed down the wide main corridor to their bedchambers. "Lady Reid liked the blue salon for entertaining. The flue was cleaned last fall."

"You knew Lady Reid?" Clare asked.

The tall, stooped housekeeper unlocked a door into a salon covered in Holland linen. "I worked for Wycliffe Manor most of my life."

"Who did she entertain all the way out here?" Intrigued, Clare stripped one of the linens from a sofa.

The others fanned out to do the same, revealing a delicate blue and gold suite of Chippendale sofas, chairs, and tables. Not all the manor looked like an abandoned hunting lodge, then.

Walker left to look for the drawings. Oliver crawled under furniture, hunting for heaven's knew what. The captain started work on the fire.

"Family," Mrs. Gaither said with a shrug. "A few friends, the vicar once in a while."

The housekeeper had known the earl and viscountess in their later years —and maybe even the viscount earlier? Although she would have been quite young and probably worked below stairs. Clare made a mental note to ask some time when they weren't quite so busy.

Anticipation built once Walker returned with a rolled-up scroll of paper. Would it reveal hiding places for ghosts or treasure? An Aladdin's vault for jewels. . . She'd much rather consider treasure than madmen.

Once the men had anchored the scroll on the long sofa table they'd hauled to the room's center, they all gathered to study it—except Oliver, who'd fallen asleep on a settee by the window.

"I cannot read it," Miss Marlowe cried in frustration. "It might be in Egyptian for all I can tell."

Privately, Clare agreed. Thousands of tiny lines and print covered the paper, all of them meaningless to her. Dreams of Aladdin's cavern crashed.

Mrs. Gaither and Mrs. Ingraham didn't even look. They wandered off, having formed a bond over linens. More odd behavior for a genteel companion but not one Clare intended to question given her choice of a druggist for company.

"Here's this salon." Using a magnifying glass, the captain placed his finger on a tiny rectangle. "This plan is just for the original manor, not the wings, which must have been added later."

Meera made a face. "And only one floor?"

"No, here is a drawing of the cellars under the main block." Walker traced the lines. "I believe the current kitchen is actually under the new east wing because this doesn't show the entrance in the courtyard. The original kitchen before the wings were added would have been under the main block, possibly under the dining area."

Clare surrendered. "I'd rather track dust."

"If we could find the old cellar entrance, we could build a retort down there for gas, run the piping for lights through—" The captain lost her entirely at that point.

"We didn't come here for treasure anyway," she whispered to Meera. "I'd like to write a few pages before bed. I'll take Oliver. Stay, if you wish."

Meera glanced at the men and Miss Marlowe. "Her companion left. I think I'll stay, keep her company, and see what I can learn."

Clare would like to stay just to watch the captain at work, which was why she would leave. He had his career. She had hers.

Except the instant she crouched down to lift Oliver, the captain was there to take him from her arms.

"He's too heavy for you to lug around," he murmured, letting her lead the way.

"I have been doing so since his infancy. It's hard accepting he's no longer small." She wasn't entirely certain what she would do with herself should her nephew ever go off to school. Daringly, she voiced her main concern to this man who knew more of the world than she. "Do you think I am holding him back?"

"I think we all grow and learn at our own pace. He will let you know when he feels safe enough to be on his own. Keeping his distance under tables may well be his way of easing from you."

"You give me hope, at least. I fear I coddle him, but he's never been. . . I don't have the words."

"I knew a young man in school who preferred his own chambers to the company of his fellows. Others tried to bully him, but he'd walk away with a book to his face. That man is now a very respected lawyer." He laid Oliver in his bed, after Clare pulled down the covers.

She'd wanted to avoid the intimacy of being alone with the captain. That they could discuss such things with familiarity. . . made her heart yearn for what she could not have. It was too easy to see how Meera had fallen under the spell of a partner who understood her interests.

"I thank you, captain, and will let you return to your battle plans. We'll see you in the morning." She firmly led him to the door and offered her hand in parting.

He bowed over it and held it a moment too long. "Good evening, Miss Knightley. And I do wish you'd call me Huntley as others do. I should rather forget the designation of a position I can no longer fill."

He limped off, leaving her a trifle stunned.

Would a man as formidable as he not be able to continue his career due to his eye?

She had very selfishly been considering only her own problems. His might be even greater.

TWELVE

Despite his new room being closer to the roof where he could hear the odd pops and creaks of the house settling, Hunt had to admit the large bed upstairs suited better than the trundle he'd been using on the ground floor. He'd not had a good night's rest since resisting laudanum after his first weeks of misery. Last night, the larger bed and the smelly unguent had kept his knee from waking him.

That didn't mean it was any easier descending to the breakfast parlor. Who in hell had ever thought a house this size would be a good idea? The answer, of course—someone with more money than sense. Give him a good army tent any day.

Once he was up and running again, he'd be off and someone else could deal with ghosts and moldering, drafty halls. Although, maybe aristocrats weren't quite as stuffy as he'd feared.

When Hunt arrived at the table, Oliver popped out from beneath to point out a subtle rearranging of the beans and bacon—apparently items the boy had not touched.

"I don't think ghosts eat real food," Hunt said, filling his plate. "Are you sure no one else has eaten?" Ghosts and bloody gloves. . . What the hell had he got himself into? They'd have him believing spirits moaned in the attic and creaks were footsteps.

"Saw Betsy set it out." Oliver grabbed toast and slid back under the table. "Saw man shoes right after."

"Very interesting. Perhaps we might set a trap." Before Hunt could sit down, Walker and the little druggist entered, arguing over. . . the slave trade?

He needed to ask Walker if he'd perused the prayer book yet, but the damned ghost had distracted everyone.

"Our visitor has returned," Hunt said, to point their attention to the food. "I don't know if he prefers beans and bacon or if he simply thought it would be easier to disguise the missing bits."

"And what did he do for food before we arrived? Or was he not here then?" Walker examined the various platters before helping himself.

"Mrs. Gaither said the viscount's ghost regularly stops in to see that his house is being maintained. Can we assume some visitor passes through?" Mrs. Abrams settled on oatmeal and toast.

"In which case, what did he do before we arrived? Forage in Mrs. Gaither's pantry? Not exactly difficult given the maze down there." Walker set his plate across from the lady. "The pantry isn't near where the Gaithers have set up housekeeping."

Oliver popped out for more toast, wrapping it around a sausage. Mrs. Abrams handed him a napkin laden with raisins and other dried fruit. The women definitely encouraged the boy's bad habits, but Hunt could see that scolding wasn't a solution. In a house this size, Oliver would simply vanish —like the ghost.

Miss Knightley finally arrived, wearing a faded yellow gown adorned in green ribbons that matched one she'd threaded through her hair. She was too slim to be called *stately,* but she still had a. . . comportment of dignity. Hunt remembered their earlier conversation about his former fiancée and decided his intended had been young and. . . unprepossessing. Miss Knightley, however, imposed her presence even when she donned spectacles and refused to look at him.

"It makes logical sense that the intruder occupies the third floor," she announced. "We cannot possibly catch him by surprise even if we have floor plans and track him through the dust." She added eggs and toast to her plate and sat down next to Mrs. Abrams at the center of the oval table.

Hunt thought he needed to see if the table had leaves that might be removed so she was closer.

"We were discussing setting a trap." Hunt sipped the unpalatable brew Mrs. Gaither called coffee and waited for his co-general's opinion. If he didn't find her interference so damned annoying, he'd be amused at her dictatorship.

"Yes, a trap was my conclusion. He cannot keep up with us any better than we can find him." She poured a cup of tea and concentrated on her food.

"A dog," piped a small voice from beneath the table.

Over the rim of his cup, Hunt noted they all froze. Just hearing Oliver suggest a viable solution was sufficient to cause a pause. The notion of a dog. . . was actually quite good.

"I like that," he said in approval. "I'm not certain where we'd obtain one."

Miss Knightley looked as if she might object, but her nephew had her flummoxed.

"Stable," Walker said with an exaggerated sigh, stabbing his sausage. "There's a stray Ned has been feeding in the stable."

"Of course." Hunt cursed his knee, then vowed to get about more so he knew what was happening in his own damned house. Well, not his house. . .

Miss Marlowe drifted in without her companion. She didn't look so fresh and dewy this morning. There were circles under her eyes. She offered a faint smile and helped herself to tea and toast.

Given what little he'd learned of the lady. . . "What kind of dog is in the stable?"

Miss Marlowe's head of dangling curls jerked up, and her eyes widened.

"Small, dirty, lots of hair," Walker said with indifference. "Not much of a guard dog."

"Guinevere is a very good guard dog," Miss Marlowe said defensively. "She barks and bites ankles and would scare off any old ghost."

"And presumably, everyone else?" Walker added without expression.

"She likes me." Sullenly, the adolescent sipped her tea, her composure a little less haughty than it had been.

Miss Knightley glanced at him. If they were to be co-generals, it was good that they understood one another. Hunt nodded and let her manage the children. Women were good at that sort of thing.

"Oliver, might you and Ned give Guinevere a bath this morning and bring her inside? Perhaps she can be trained to only bite intruders." Miss Knightley nibbled at her toast without giving any indication that she noticed or cared about the reaction of others.

Interesting. It wasn't just him that she ignored.

Oliver burst from beneath the table and ran off shouting for Ned. Miss Marlowe stood a little more slowly, glancing nervously at each of them. "You won't mind? You won't throw me out?"

"Is the dog the reason you left school?" Miss Knightley inquired politely.

"I found her," the girl said defensively. "She's mine. She loves me."

When no one else does was the unfinished part of that sentence even Hunt recognized. If Miss Knightley was correct—the girl was essentially an orphan whose family wanted nothing to do with her.

He'd had no idea what an enormous pie he'd bitten into when he'd sent those invitations.

"Then you will need to care for her the same way you would one you love," he said. "Responsibility is not easy. Just ask Miss Knightley."

"I can do it." The girl held up her chin. "I took care of the kittens until they took them away from me." She stalked off, leaving her meager food on the table.

Miss Knightley sighed. "I had best find a tutor for Oliver before he reaches that age. I really do not think I can manage alone."

"I believe you will manage better than whoever raised Miss Marlowe. And since this is beginning to feel as if we really are family of sorts, might we address each other more informally? If I'm to scold the child when the dog piddles on the floor, I really cannot continue calling her Miss Marlowe." Hunt sipped his black brew in resignation.

The others quickly chimed their agreement. So, family, they were.

~

"THE PEDDLER IS HERE, MISS, THE PEDDLER'S COMING UP THE DRIVE!" BETSY shouted breathlessly, rushing into the family parlor where Clare searched the furniture for concealed drawers.

She'd discreetly inquired of Walker concerning the prayer book, but dedicated professional that he was, he was comparing the text word for word with a newer version and had found nothing of interest.

Convinced her search was fruitless, she was willing to be distracted by Betsy's news. "I'll fetch my shawl and be out directly. Should we offer him ale or cheese?"

"I'll do that, miss." Betsy bobbed, then proudly displayed an enormous thread-covered button she'd sewed to her gown. "I made these. I could make more."

Clare nodded absently. Big buttons were no longer popular. She needed dainty shell ones for her linens. Fabric ones to match her gown. . . She hurried off to fetch her shawl and Oliver. He might enjoy inspecting a peddler's cart.

By the time she and Oliver reached the drive, the peddler was talking to Betsy, Lavender, and Meera while sipping ale, munching bread and cheese, and displaying his wares. The newly scrubbed Guinevere ran in circles, yapping. Fortunately, the dog bit no ankles in its excitement.

Clare froze when she realized the peddler was a dark-haired young man who teased and flirted with his customers. She let Oliver run ahead while she studied the situation. There was something disturbingly familiar about him. . .

Captain Huntley—Hunt—limped out to join her. "Did you not wish to purchase a few baubles?"

"I am not at all certain it's proper," she murmured, watching. "I try to set a good example, but I am out of my milieu. Do I send the servants to purchase buttons? Should I keep Lavender from flirting with him? It does not seem appropriate."

She waited for him to comment on the peddler's familiarity, but he did not. So, it must be just her. She had little experience to draw on. Perhaps all men looked alike. But the broad shoulders, wide brow—even the muscular build—did not seem very peddler-like. Perhaps he'd been one of Wellington's soldiers.

That gave her a little more confidence when Hunt scoffed and offered his arm.

"You can lead by example. I suspect Lavender will do as you do, but only to the extent that suits her needs."

"Ah, the lady of the house," the peddler exclaimed as they approached, winking at the captain. "I am Henri. It is a delight and pleasure to serve you."

Henri had an accent, not terrifically strong but just enough to identify him as French. After all the years of war and fear of French spies—Clare did not know how to respond. Napoleon was free again. . . What might French spies do in the rural countryside?

"The lady would like to see buttons." Hunt spoke for her.

"Ah, *oui*, I have samples of beautiful buttons. Choose the one you like, and next week I will return with them." He brought out a wooden box filled with sample cards.

Mrs. Gaither chose some spices and pickled condiments while Clare studied the buttons. "Why do you only carry samples? Surely keeping orders must be difficult?"

"The suppliers, they cannot manufacture quickly. Gentlemen want the fancy silver and pewter, and the ladies like wool thread and horn and shell, and it must all be made by hand. So, they prefer to have orders. Are these not exquisitely done?" He showed her a card of threaded buttons.

"I could do that," Betsy said stoutly. "And paint them kind." She pointed out a plain metal.

The peddler nodded warily. "If you can fulfil orders, I can bring the materials and molds and pay you by the card when you are done. But the materials will cost you."

Betsy looked crestfallen. "I only got this much." She held out two copper coins.

This was something Clare knew how to do. She'd haggled with shopkeepers after her father's death and with Arabs in Egyptian markets—once out of her sister's sight, anyway. Her meager budget had never allowed anything else.

The others picked through fabrics, thread, and books while Clare and Henri agreed on a price Betsy might afford with an advance on her wages.

His promise to return next week with the materials left the maid so ecstatic, she engulfed Clare in a hug. "Thank ye, milady, thank ye! You'll see. I make the best buttons! You'll want to buy them all."

Clare thought that unlikely unless she made a new gown.

Still, she couldn't remember the last time she'd been hugged—perhaps her sister had before she died, but Bea wasn't much of a hugger. She couldn't decide if she liked it but disengaged with a smile. "We'll see what Henri brings, shall we?"

She found a pretty pincushion to replace her old one and added that to her button order. Oliver brought her a book and looked longingly at the sweets the peddler waved beneath his nose.

"Allow me." Hunt took the basket of candies and ordered half a pound to be shared by all.

Oliver grabbed his favorite and made his thank you with his mouth full.

Clare hated to be grateful to the captain for anything, but that he noticed Oliver's silent plea raised him another notch above bat-slaying, book-hating monster.

"You'll be staying awhile then, my lord?" the peddler asked, taking his coins. "I can bring any candies you like."

Clare still had a very uneasy feeling. Perhaps it was Meera's unpleasant experience that made her wary of charming young men. *Pretty faces empty pockets. . .* But it felt like more than that—as if Henri was seeking information —spying? But she supposed it was a long trek out here, and he'd like to know his customers.

"Likely for the summer," Hunt said agreeably. "If you'll bring some linen handkerchiefs next time, I'd appreciate it."

"I can hem handkerchiefs, Captain Hunt!" Lavender cried. "I can even embroider your initials. He has some pretty linen. You just need to choose what you like."

Clare supposed she could have offered to help sew instead of feeling an ugly twitch that the captain turned his attention to the girl. She really didn't need male attention. She had a book to finish, while Lavender was at loose ends. Feeling defiantly independent, Clare requested pen nibs and ink for the next trip.

"I am happy to see folk occupying the manor once again," Henri said after they'd settled all their purchases, and he was back in the wagon seat.

"How did you know we were here?" Clare had the sense to ask.

Henri waved in the direction of town. "Old Mr. Oswald, the postmaster, told me." He tipped his hat. "It's been a pleasure."

Clare held Meera back as the cart rattled off. "Did he not seem familiar to you?"

Meera wrinkled her nose. "A little, perhaps? Why?"

"Because he very much resembles the captain when he frowns. And did Hunt not say his mother is half French?"

Meera watched the wagon roll down the drive. "You think. . . ? Why?"

"Treasure," Clare said grimly. "If he's related, he may know of the jewels."

THIRTEEN

HUNT STUDIED THE BREAKFAST ROOM WHERE HELGA—*MRS. GAITHER*—LAID OUT breakfast and lunch buffets. A buffet was easy to filch from. Depredations into serving dishes and plates on a dinner table would be more difficult. He suspected the fellow must steal from the kitchen in the evening.

Oliver slipped in to see if the luncheon buffet was out. How did the interloper know when it was served if the boy didn't? Their housekeeper wasn't exactly a timely sort. Hunt refused to believe in a ghost that spied through walls.

Just as he was concluding he didn't have sufficient troops or places of concealment to create a good trap, Miss—*Clare*—drifted in. Juggling informality with ladies and formality with servants addled his mind.

"I daresay these old walls have hidden passages and doors we've yet to uncover. Or we really do have a hungry ghost." Studying the room, she spoke as if he were one of the walls.

She handed a bell to Oliver and shooed him under the table.

The female general had been making plans without him again. Hunt considered tearing up a ledger and throwing paper wads to attract her attention, but he wasn't drunk at this hour.

Today, she wore a sensible blue garment in a fabric that flowed around her figure as she moved, providing a tantalizing glimpse of rounded hips. A shawl concealed her bosom. Studying Clarissa Knightley had become an unhealthy fascination.

With his ugly visage, he might never be able to do more than ponder women unless he paid for them. One more depressing notion to add to his treasure chest.

"Who do you expect to come running if Oliver rings the bell?" He was bitterly aware that a tortoise would escape before he limped after it. And his shooting at an intruder would more likely involve putting bullets in the ceiling or innocent bystanders.

"If he's a smart ghost, after our search yesterday, he will avoid us for a few days," Clare predicted, studying the room. "But just in case. . . Lavender has agreed to hide behind the drapery and discover how he's entering. Oliver's bell is for ringing as the ghost flees. Meera thought to hide behind the door. The hall is a conundrum."

Well, even if she wouldn't look at him, she acknowledged his existence. Hunt showed her a hidden servant's door. "Another escape route. Walker will hide in here. That leaves us to seek concealment in the hall."

"Then what do we do, tackle him?" She checked behind the drapery. "We can only hope to learn bolt holes and maybe scare him off."

Hunt resented that he could not halt a thief in his own damned home. How could he offer his mother's relations a safe harbor if any vagrant could take up residence in these vast spaces?

But they all hid themselves as planned. Mrs. Gaither and Betsy carried platters of meat, cheese, and bread to the sideboard in the seemingly empty room. They waited some more.

And as Clare predicted, the thief did not appear.

Oliver was the first to call it quits, crawling from under the table to wrap bread around a handful of ham, then crawling back under. As the clock gonged the half hour, they all emerged in discouragement.

"He is no doubt laughing at us." Walker bit into a wizened apple from the cellar. "What if we set trip wires?"

"That was next, but I need to find the tools. That's a lot of screws and wire." And crawling on a bad knee and focusing with one eye. But Hunt refused to give up what he knew best.

"We should have ordered them from Henri," Lavender said cheerfully. "Wasn't he just the handsomest creature you've ever seen?" She fed a piece of meat under the table to the puffball that followed her in.

A guard dog barely half a foot high was no dog at all. Hunt wanted a good hound.

He noted Clare was amazingly silent on the subject of the peddler's looks. Given his own appearance, he didn't think it his place to comment on another's. He was relieved when the dour Mrs. Abrams spoke.

"Handsome is as handsome does, in my experience. You would do well to set your sights on a hardworking young man who sees you and only you. Attractive flirts only lead to trouble."

"Or develop your own skills and forget men entirely. They are seldom to be relied on," Clare added without inflection.

The lady didn't like men? Interesting. "That's just a bit biased," Hunt objected. "We're not all alike."

She darted him a quick look, then returned to studying her plate. "I am sure there are very many hardworking reliable men. The problem is that they give no consideration to what a woman thinks or wishes and will not allow us the freedom to go our own way."

He'd given Abigail her freedom, and she'd left. Hunt didn't feel compelled to point out his failure. "You only say that because all the men in the family tend to go their own way and die as a result. That does not mean they weren't reliable. If women had the opportunity, they would most likely do the same."

"Women have more sense," Clare said curtly.

"I shall live here and raise dogs," Lavender declared, not exactly proving women had more sense.

"Cheaper than horses," Walker acknowledged. "You should at least raise hounds that you might sell."

"Sell?" Lavender's dismay was so clear that a round of coughing afflicted the table's occupants.

Hunt didn't have the heart to remind the child that the solicitor had yet to review her claim to be family. What would he do if she was illegitimate, as Clare assumed?

∿

WITH MRS. GAITHER'S PERMISSION, MEERA HAPPILY DUG IN THE KITCHEN garden. She'd never had much room in her city plots for anything larger than herbs and onions and the like. Here, she could have fresh greens, along with the root vegetables the housekeeper grew. Cucumbers for pickling, perhaps.

Her child might grow up a lot healthier here—if she could make a place for herself.

Charting the various plots, she wasn't aware of Walker's presence until he was beside her.

"Is there anything I can do to help?" he asked. "I'm not accustomed to spending every day buried in books."

She looked up at his nattily-attired figure and shook her head. "You will dirty your pretty clothes. Did you not bring anything old?"

"If you were traveling, would you bring old clothes? I had not planned on digging gardens." He took her hoe and tested it on one of the parterres. "It will need compost to break it up."

"You've started a nice manure pile already, thank you. I'm a little afraid of teaching Mrs. Gaither about kitchen scraps, although she may already know." She went back to separating potatoes.

"How did you learn about planting if you lived in the city?" He plied the hoe with ease.

"Druggists need a reliable supply of plants. I've brought some seeds with me and ordered more from Henri. I thought I'd contribute to the household before growing my more esoteric plants. My knowledge of vegetables is limited, but some things are basic."

"I used to help in my mother's garden. I can be your beast of burden and start breaking up the dirt." He took off his restrictive coat and carefully folded it over a bench. His bright yellow waistcoat fit snugly on his broad chest. He might not be large like the captain, but he was muscular.

She really shouldn't be noticing. She debated mentioning that her "interesting" condition might prevent her working much longer, but she wasn't prepared to discuss it. They'd had many stimulating intellectual discussions, but that did not mean they were close enough for intimacies. "That will be extremely helpful, thank you. What are you hoping to find in the estate books?"

"At first, I was looking for what crops they raised, how much they earned, that sort of thing. But it's become apparent the only thing anyone planted here in decades is trees. There is apparently an orchard of nut and fruit trees on a protected hill. I've kept an eye out for blossoms, but it's early yet."

"Interesting. We should take an expeditionary tour to learn more of the estate if we're to stay here all summer. Oliver would enjoy that, I believe." Fruit and nut trees— Meera recalled her father's fond memories of their family home in warmer climes, before his family had been forced to flee. "An orchard explains why Mrs. Gaither has such a good larder of dried and pickled fruits."

"As the captain said, we're not farmers." He whacked the hard ground, breaking it into clumps. "But it looks like this estate might support the village if we were. I know they're saying crops aren't profitable, and I assume that's why they're not renting out the land, but it's still odd that the estate was abandoned. I suppose I'm hoping to discover why. Is the place haunted by bad memories of previous inhabitants? How did they die? I've always enjoyed a good puzzle."

"You do puzzles. I like to experiment," she declared boldly. She'd had to leave all her work behind when they'd fled. But if they were actually able to stay until fall—she'd like to return to her experiments with mice. Ghosts didn't interest her.

"So does the captain, but he's limited these days. He wants to build a retort for coal, run pipes, and use the gas for lighting. What do you blow up?" He tossed dirt clods as if digging for treasure.

She chuckled. "I try to make mice healthier in hopes of finding compounds that will help people. My science does not include explosives. How did you and the captain meet?" She was taught not to ask personal questions, but digging a garden plot together encouraged small talk.

"My stepparents were teachers at the school we both attended. Hunt beat up bullies who picked on me. I helped him with the papers he hated writing."

His tone was matter-of-fact, but Meera found the Americans fascinating. "So, you went to engineering school and joined the army together?"

He snorted. "I had an education because my stepparents taught school, but even they couldn't get me into a university. Hunt did that."

"I don't understand." She understood prejudice. She couldn't attend university because she was a woman. She assumed Walker couldn't attend because he wasn't white. How did one overcome that?

Walker chuckled. "He told them I was his servant. I studied the same books he did. Read his class notes. Helped him write his papers. He's whip smart, but he'd rather be doing than reading. I'd rather be reading than blowing up things. I didn't want to be an engineer, but I learned all the mathematical calculations and how to use them. When he became an officer, he put me on the payroll as a clerk. We just kind of kept learning together."

"And now that he's no longer employed with the army?" she couldn't resist asking.

"He'll work something out. He always does. I have skills I can hire out because of him. I'll not abandon him when he needs me."

That was a commendable attitude, Meera thought, but she didn't dare say anything that personal. Yet.

Watching him dig stirred physical sensations that had brought her nothing but trouble. Learning more of his integrity. . .

She couldn't set a bad example for Clare and Lavender. She returned to studying her garden plot.

Speak of the devil. . . The girl traipsed out to join them. "What are Captain Huntley's initials so I may embroider them?"

"Alastair Reid Huntley," Walker answered. "You could have asked him. He won't bite off your head."

"I was afraid he might. He's tying string all over and cursing awfully. And Guinevere does *not* piddle on floors," she added indignantly. "Betsy spilled mop water. I wonder where a ghost piddles?" She flounced off on her own mission.

Meera looked at Walker, who'd already drifted into thought at a child's casual question.

Indeed, where would a ghost relieve himself? The manor had a few washrooms adjacent to the newer wings, but the water was very noisy. Did the ghost carry a chamber pot down three flights of stairs to the privy and wash outdoors?

"I'm not standing guard on an outhouse," Walker declared, as if following her thoughts.

"We should tell the captain," Meera suggested.

"And have him curse more?" In resignation, Walker laid down the hoe and picked up his coat. "I vote we leave the intruder alone, but I'd better go in and finish his floor crawling before he chews up our meager staff."

"Did the unguent help at all?" she asked anxiously.

"Possibly, but it's not as if he'll admit it. Hunt is a good man, but an irascible curmudgeon when he's in pain."

Meera picked up her gardening tools. "And Clare is shy of men, but she'll murder him if he endangers her family. I'm not sure cursing is a danger, but with Oliver within hearing. . ."

"We'd better save them from themselves." Walker took her implements and offered his arm.

Unaccustomed to being treated as a lady, Meera feared she was in serious danger of liking this man too well. And of enjoying this rural retreat that could never be hers. . .

FOURTEEN

"It's possible our intruder has already fled," Clare called from the estate office as she explored old tomes that afternoon. "And all you're doing is setting us up for a literal fall."

The men were crawling around outside her door debating likely spots of catching a fleeing thief. They grunted and ignored her observation. She was unsurprised.

"At least look for hiding places while you're down there," she daringly suggested, feeling brave in what should be her own home. She probably teased an angry bear. She'd like to think they'd taken this ghost business a little far, but if there were any chance Jacob was here, hunting for Meera's book. . . Her imagination would turn her raving mad.

"How would an intruder escape the grounds?" Meera asked, joining the party late. She'd changed out of her gardening clothes into the only gown she owned for dinner.

That was a most excellent question. He'd have to steal a horse. Clare assumed he would have done so by now if he feared being caught. Giving up on the futile search of the estate office, she closed the ledger she held. She had barely begun to scour journals and ledgers dating back a hundred years. Worse, she had no idea what she was looking for.

Should she ask about the prayer book? They hadn't told Meera or Lavender about it, so perhaps not just now.

Meera's lack of attire presented a different concern for Clare to address.

"I wonder if any of the wardrobes contain clothes? With no modistes or fabric shops in the village, how does one replace old clothes?"

"Clothes!" Lavender perked up. She'd been reluctantly tapping walls and looking in drawers, but they'd finally found a subject she knew. "I love sewing."

"Do you make your own gowns?" Clare hated sewing, couldn't afford fashionable modistes, and had no lady's maid to care for delicate fabrics, so her wardrobe leaned toward the functional and unadorned. They would need to hire a laundress if they started wearing fancy dress.

The girl picked up her dog and took time to form a reply. "I like to add trim. I modified old styles for the other girls, and they'd give me their leftovers so I could do mine."

Meera caught Clare's attention with a meaningful glance and gestured at her waist. "Older fashions had excess fabric and adjustable laces. I could use a few new gowns."

Of course, she could. Clare winced at her selfishness. Meera couldn't disguise her condition much longer. She would need to let out bodice seams. Less revealing fabrics and laces would be useful.

"Let us forget treasure and ghost hunts and go on a fashion hunt!" She slammed the last ledger into place and stepped into the hall.

Captain Huntley sat on the floor, wrapping wire around a screw in the woodwork. If his expression could be determined behind the concealing eyepatch, she'd say he appeared disgruntled. She thought the tight line around his mouth might be pain. He interested her a little too much.

"We plan to traipse through dust," she warned him. "If you wish to check for footsteps first, you had best lead the expedition." Encountering mad Jacob, thieves, or ghosts might make a thrilling scene in a novel, but she'd rather not experience it alone.

Hunt tightened his wire, tested it, and reached for his cane. "I'm about out of wire. Let's see if we can learn to avoid the traps." He signaled Ned, who hovered in a doorway. Using gestures they'd developed, he pointed at the wire, then down, and sent the boy to warn the Gaithers.

"You'll need lamps and candles." Wincing, he pushed to his feet.

Clare had a nearly irresistible urge to tell him that massaging weak muscles sometimes helped. She'd eased her mother's leg cramps that way. But the idea of touching his leg. . . She had to turn away to hide her blush.

"If the viscountess used the blue salon, may we assume her chamber was near it? That would be the most likely place to find old clothes." Meera eagerly picked up a lamp from the hall.

"We've already trampled that corridor. How much dust can be left? We need keys. A lot of the doors are locked." Lavender ducked into the dining room. Setting her fluffball dog down, she brought out a brace of candles. The puppy sniffed along at her heels.

"Have we tested the doors off the gallery hall?" Walker traveled reluctantly after them.

"Oliver may have. Let me see if he's in the library." Keeping up with her nephew in this sprawling palace once he grew brave enough to explore would be a challenge. A tutor had become even more essential.

Once they'd dragged him upstairs, Oliver happily pointed out his scuff marks in the dust of the unlocked suites he'd explored. The wardrobes were all empty.

"One of us should descend to the kitchen and ask Mrs. Gaither where to look," Walker grumbled.

"We need a butler who comes when called," Clare countered. "It is not our place to invade her territory." Or she would have gone down and asked the elusive caretakers more questions.

The main corridor where their bedrooms and blue salon were located was so trampled with footsteps there was no hope of tracking a ghost.

"Young Ned can't hear the bell. Apparently, neither can our butler. We'll have to hope the peddler will pass word that we're hiring." Hunt sorted through a ring of keys for the locked door next to the salon.

"Mr. Henri will have to bring any new hires with him. It's not as if we're providing transportation from the nearest coaching inn." Clare followed Hunt inside once he found the key.

The viscountess's bedchamber was also adorned in blue to match her salon. Clare studied the damask hangings on the tester bed, but they were too heavy and faded to be of much use.

Meera opened the wardrobe. "Here we go. It's not much."

Lavender swooped in to embrace the last-century gowns. "Velvet! Just look at this. . . We can cut around the moth holes. This wine color will look fabulous on you Mrs. Abrams! And the satin. . ." She sighed longingly. "Look at this lace!"

"Velvet will be lovely in the fall. We should keep looking." Leaving Meera and Lavender removing the gowns, and an ecstatic Guinevere chasing dust balls, Clare followed the men down the main corridor as they opened locked doors.

She'd never in her life imagined she'd follow men. Instead of familiarity breeding contempt, perhaps it eased anxiety. And curiosity had a tendency to overrule wariness. . .

Now that Meera and Lavender had their lace and velvet, Clare pursued other interests—like ghostly thieves and jewels and history. She'd like to know more about the previous inhabitants.

Oliver raced ahead.

"You should search these chambers for letters or journals!" she called to the men, dying to find out more about her ancestors.

"Later. I'm looking for ways of running piping into this windowless corridor. It's blamed dark even in the day." Hunt held up his lantern to examine the ceiling and walls.

Of course, it was dark. And with one eye, presumably even darker. She understood, but pipes were not interesting. Clare followed Oliver into a succession of unlocked bedchambers. Walker did the same. The linens, draperies, and covers had been stripped from the beds, leaving only bare wood and the occasional mattress. She examined the window draperies. "Maintenance must be excellent. No sign of damp, and these windows are ancient."

"An engineering ancestor, perhaps," Walker said dryly, running his hand over the old wood. "Can all this cloth be used for something besides covering windows?"

Clare wrinkled her nose. "Brocade is not fashionable. Given the enormous expense of draperies, we'd do better to ask Henri to bring us fabrics on his next visit." She might manage a little on her pin money.

She opened the drawers in the wardrobe and discovered a few men's pantaloons and some well-worn linen shirts. Her exclamation brought Walker over.

"Do you think these were the earl's? They'd have to be over half a century old!" Clare drew them out. "Good wool and leather. He must have been a tall man."

"Might fit the captain, although breeches. . ." Walker shook his head, holding them up against himself. They nearly reached his ankle and were twice his waist. "They might suit for working in."

Clare didn't have the same difficulty studying Walker as she did the captain. Perhaps size made the difference? He was less intimidating. "And the linen is of excellent quality. Lavender might work with it."

She opened another drawer and discovered yellowing linen so old she feared it might disintegrate if she touched it. Unable to resist curiosity, she lifted it. . . and gasped. Her ever-creative mind leaped to the worst scenario. "We really should learn how the viscount died."

~

At Clare's faint cry, Hunt pocketed his measuring tools, found Walker signaling him from two doors down, and limped to join them.

His co-general held an armful of yellowing linen and wore a horrified frown. Walker indicated the open drawer at the bottom of an ancient armoire.

He peered in the drawer and grimaced. "Flintlock cavalry pistol," he responded without thinking. "French design." He lifted it out and checked the chamber. "Empty."

His grandmother had lived in France. Had this been hers? Clare's continued silence finally registered. He shook his head at her expression of horror. "Men keep weapons. It would be very odd not to find firearms in a hunting lodge. There is an entire armory in the study. I own a pistol. It's not useful for game but shoots rats just fine."

"And I would much rather you didn't." She looked at the bundle of rags in her hands. "It was hidden under shirts that haven't been touched in. . . Do we know how the viscount died?" she asked again.

"No." Hunt stuffed the pistol in his trouser band. "And we will not ask. I have no interest in learning if his ghost haunts the place. I want to find the intruder stealing food."

Refusing to speculate, he marched back to the corridor. Walker followed, carrying a load of male clothing. Meera pounced on it, showing it to Lavender. "What about cutting the breeches to fit Walker? He needs work clothes."

Leaving them to a discussion of seams and hems, Hunt gave up on noting dimensions in his notebook and set out for the unexplored gallery corridor before they conjured any more mysteries.

Clare followed on his heels. "Firearms should be locked away. Oliver has an active mind. He could find shells!"

"And gunpowder? Fine, I'll lock it up." Her fears would have him wondering if one of his French ancestors had swum the Channel to shoot a viscount.

He traipsed down the corridor, unlocking doors to check the dust, although how a ghost would trample dust in a locked room was beyond his comprehension.

The only footprints they found were in the hall where the entire party had trampled up and down in earlier searches. The rooms across from the gallery were smaller, with single beds. For single guests?

Clare searched empty armoires. "Has the prayer book shed any clues?"

He assumed the prayer book was too old to lead him to his grandmother's diaries, so it was of little interest to him. "Some of the passages are underlined. If there's a code, we haven't deciphered it."

The lady actually turned to look at him, her jaw set stubbornly. "May I study it? I could copy out those passages. They could be clues to murder or treasure."

So, she could look at him when she wanted something. He stopped to test a crumbling plaster wall. "They're likely passages someone wished to emphasize or memorize. Walker can mark up a newer book for you to study. I prefer more practical pursuits. I think I can run piping into this corridor for gas lighting."

She sighed, probably in irritation at his refusal to offer conspiracy theories. "You said you needed some sort of furnace to burn the coal?"

A sensible topic, at last. "A retort, yes, to trap the gas and send it through the pipes. I'll have to go to Birmingham for the parts. They ought to come under maintenance expense, and the trust should pay for it. We'll have to find out how often coal deliveries can be had out here."

Holding Lavender's puppy to keep it out of mischief, Meera hurried after them. "We should open one of the new wings. We've gathered everything we can find in the suites."

"We'll test the dust first. No one should have trampled the wings yet." Hunt limped down the gallery corridor to the corner of the damned bloody huge manor.

Once they all stood outside the double doors to the east wing, Walker held a lantern while Hunt worked through his key ring. He was aware of the women all but holding their breaths, as if anticipating Aladdin's cave.

The door creaked open on unused hinges. Hunt held up his arm to prevent them from rushing through.

With all the doors closed and the only window at the far end, the corridor on the other side was nearly pitch black. Hunt's one eye couldn't discern a damned thing.

Gritting his teeth, he tested lifting his patch, aware that Clare surreptitiously watched.

Nothing. He could tell nothing in the dark. He refused to register disappointment. His companion breathed a little sigh of what might be dashed hopes. She even daringly brushed his sleeve with slender fingers in what he thought might be a gesture of sympathy. He didn't want pity.

He'd had months to accept that he was half-alive. He had a lifetime to see what he could make of it.

Must and mold overwhelmed the olfactory senses. Hunt sneezed. The ladies coughed and drew out their scented handkerchiefs. He held his lantern so the light spilled over the dusty floor until he could determine a difference in pattern. *Footprints.*

He held up his hand for quiet and gestured for Walker to take the ladies back to the safety of their chambers.

His insolent friend snorted. Hunt was an officer, accustomed to having his orders followed. Not one of this motley army retreated. He grimaced and considered locking the door again. They needed silence to catch the culprit—

His domestic co-general caught him by surprise when she pointed at a narrow servants' door barely visible in the dark. She raised a questioning brow.

Right, the culprit most likely hid above and used the uninhabited corridor for ingress and egress. The kitchens were under this wing. The door could very well lead there as well as the attic.

Hunt gestured for Walker to guard the corridor while he eased open the staircase door. It didn't squeak. Someone had oiled it.

They all glared as he gestured for them to retreat, but he wasn't forfeiting this round. He might be a half-blind cripple, but he was twice the size of everyone present and had nothing to lose if he encountered a thief.

Unfortunately, he couldn't climb swiftly or quietly. To Hunt's startlement, Oliver slipped around him and ran soft as a mouse on sock feet, vanishing into the darkness above.

The ladies gasped. Clare looked as if she might faint. Walker had his grim face on. No choice now. Hunt dragged his wretched knee up the stairs in a one-legged gait that would warn entire armies.

The stairs led to an attic over the main block of the manor and a door into the new wing. The new wing's corridor housed dozens of doors, presumably rooms for guests or servants. The door into the old attic led to a maze of beds and discarded furniture. Any of the servants could have accessed it.

Oliver had disappeared. Hunt held up his lantern to study the well-trampled dust. Someone was living here.

From beyond the old attic wall, a deep baritone cried cheerfully, "Well met, monsieur! You have fairly trapped me, and I surrender."

Hunt barely had time to follow Oliver's dusty path through the storage area before everyone swarmed up the stairs. Damned good thing he was giving up the army as a career. Apparently, no one obeyed disabled officers. Including dogs. The hairy mutt scampered ahead to join the lad.

Hunt studied the path down which Oliver had disappeared and decided the gallery might be directly below. It hadn't been a ghost moaning and creaking.

Crossing the crowded storage room, he entered still another corridor, locating Oliver in a square of light from still another door, arms and legs akimbo and looking fierce. The boy wasn't timid, by any means. Hunt clasped a hand on the boy's skinny shoulders and inserted his own bulk in the doorway just enough to cause the intruder second thoughts about fleeing.

A wall of windows opened on a long studio.

Clare inserted herself behind Hunt to peer in. "Mr. Henri?" she murmured in puzzlement, pulling Oliver backward against her skirts.

The peddler? Hunt studied the intruder, but even with his one eye he could see differences. The man was older, bigger, with pain etched into his features.

"Arnaud, not Henri." Despite his shirtsleeve attire, the stranger swept a gallant bow.

That's when Hunt noticed he held an artist's paint brush in a hand with only four fingers. "French? That's bold, sir, living on enemy soil."

The Frenchman matched his glare. "You are fine one to talk, then, eh?"

Hunt shrugged. "Fair point. Do you have another name? Is Henri a relation?"

Clare huffed impatiently. "Could we not discuss this over a nice cup of tea? It's icy up here."

"As mademoiselle wishes." The Frenchman made a gallant bow. "You must allow me to dress more properly for a salon."

Hunt growled, and giving up on glaring, pointed a finger back the way they'd come. "All of you, down. Go fuss over tea. I need a word with Monsieur Arnaud alone."

The supposedly shy spinster cast him a piercing glare and ushered her charges through the attic. Walker studied the situation, shrugged, and followed. At least one person in this household understood females needed protection, even if the damned women didn't.

FIFTEEN

Claire disliked being barked at, but she disliked even more the proximity of so many large men in a dark, icy attic. She might *write* medieval mysteries. She didn't wish to live them.

Modern, civilized behavior required tea and a warm family parlor.

"What if he's a French spy?" Lavender whispered as she arranged the tea table according to some prescribed pattern learned at school. "He will cut our throats in our beds!"

"Guinevere will save you," Clare said dryly, trimming Mrs. Gaither's thick country crusts and cutting the sandwiches into proper triangles.

"We're not at war anymore," Meera replied more pragmatically. "One must wonder if the viscountess was a spy though."

"Great-Aunt Gabrielle?" Arnaud asked, appearing in the doorway looking more respectable, if decidedly shabby. "Is laughable! She despised Napoleon. He took our lands, killed Maman. . . He is a terror."

Hunt followed him. In the light of a fire and oil lamps, the resemblance between the men was more visible, especially in height and breadth. Clare wanted to retreat behind the draperies with Oliver. But she took a deep breath and settled on the loveseat behind the tea tray. "Introductions and lineages over tea, gentlemen. Let us pretend we are cultivated."

"Ah, my brother told me the lady was proper and would disapprove of my trespass. My apologies, mademoiselle." Arnaud bowed, nearly toppled, and righted himself before settling where Clare indicated.

That's when she realized—that despite his size—the man was half-starved. Had he been moaning in hunger in the attic? Or in pain? They should have searched sooner. She poured tea and noticed he reached for the cup with a hand missing the small finger.

She gestured at Betsy. "Tell Mrs. Gaither there will be one more for dinner." At second thought, she glanced at the men, more concerned about health than shyness. "Or is Henri about? Should we make that two?"

"He will be back on his usual day, my lady. There is just me, although I might eat his portion, given opportunity." The visitor grimaced self-deprecatingly.

"Tell Mrs. Gaither that a relation of the viscountess is visiting and prepare her best meal," Hunt ordered, sending Betsy into a dither as she rushed off.

Their visitor had taken a large wingback chair. Hunt took a similar one. Both men dwarfed the stout frames. Meera settled next to Clare to help pass cups. Walker and Lavender chose gilded chairs more easily shifted closer to their repast.

Claire hoped Oliver and the dog were nearby. She kept one eye on the drapery. A steady rain beat against the panes. "Once you have your tea and take the edge off your hunger, might someone begin explanations?"

Hunt left his tea to cool and cleared his plate in a few swallows—an army man, first and last. "I've explained that my grandmother, the viscountess, left for France, and my mother was born there. My mother never knew her real father, and she asked me to find diaries in hopes of learning more of her family. She feared they may have suffered in the revolution."

"Rather likely given the years of warfare." A war which had begun again. Clare only took a small triangle and pushed the tray closer to the men. If she thought of them as small, hungry boys. . .

The Frenchman chewed his sandwich and let his host do the talking.

Hunt grimaced at his tea, then continued. "Apparently, if you still wish to consider us *family*, we have acquired a few more from my distaff side. Henri and Arnaud Lavigne are unrelated to the earl and heirs, but as relations to the viscountess, they should be granted visiting privileges, agreed?" He dared defiance to his edict with a lifted, undamaged brow.

If he'd had the use of both eyes, Clare might have cowered under the chair at his commanding glare. For her sake, it was better he hid behind the patch.

"You have proof of that relation?" Walker asked with his usual cynicism.

Arnaud shrugged. "We have our documentation of French citizenship. But as to the relation to our great-aunt. . ."

"We will need the diaries, I imagine." Hunt seemed unconcerned. "But if we can accept Lavender based on appearances. . ."

Clare had to laugh. "As Monsieur Lavigne says, fair point. The resemblance is almost uncanny. Do you resemble your mother, Captain?"

"I do, in fact, although she is much prettier. I will have to write her of our discovery. She owes me a lifetime of apple pies." Hunt bit into a pastry in satisfaction.

It was the first time Clare had seen the captain appear anywhere close to happy. It looked good on him.

"I'm not sure I understand," Lavender said tentatively. "Captain Hunt is *French*, he is not related to the earl? Does that mean he is. . ." She frowned and whispered, "Baseborn?"

Clare exchanged a glance with Hunt, who nodded at her to explain. Given what they suspected of the child's heritage, she tried to do so circumspectly. "The captain's parents are married. He is quite legitimate. His mother's parents were married, so she is legitimate in the eyes of the law. However, that does not mean the earl is his grandfather by blood. I am gathering the captain's true grandfather is French."

She left Lavender puzzling over that and frowned at their visitor. "Why did you not simply introduce yourself when we arrived?"

Arnaud shrugged his wide shoulders. "The house has been empty. I am a trespasser, a homeless vagrant. I did not know you. Henri was to find out more."

Hunt scarfed down another sandwich and gestured. "So, explain the relationship."

Arnaud followed his example and finished off the sandwiches before taking a cake. "Captain Huntley's grandmother, the viscountess, is my Great-Aunt Gabrielle, my grandmother's sister. Our estates are in France. Lord Reid met her on his tour of Europe, married her, and brought her home as one of his trophies."

"That was well before the late hostilities," Hunt clarified.

Arnaud shrugged. "*Oui*, although French, English, they always war. But our families visited over those years." He glanced at Lavender and modified whatever he meant to say. "The viscountess was unhappy here and returned to her home. In France, she fell in love with a cousin of my father's. The affair did not end well. After Lord Reid's death, she returned to England for her eldest daughter. She took with her the child born of her affair."

"And raised her two daughters in London," Hunt added. "The

viscountess did not return to Wycliffe Manor, her marital home, until after the death of her father-in-law, the earl."

"This is like a novel." Meera turned up her nose in disapproval. "The French relations return to the manor but the English ones do not. Except Clare and Oliver, of course."

"The English have wealth and no need of a roof over their heads," Arnaud said dryly. "All Henri and I have was lost—family, land, title, all worthless now. We came away with our lives only. This is not our ancestral home, but in her last years, our aunt made us welcome here."

"Your clothes and pistol in the wardrobe?" Walker asked.

Arnaud nodded. "Brought in my younger days."

"Perhaps instead of Wycliffe Manor, we should rename the place Wycliffe Haven, Home for the Displaced. But we should consider our growing need to fill the pantry. As I understand it, one does not hunt for rabbit or quail in spring." Clare was only joshing, but a small cry from the draperies caused her to wince.

"No rabbit stew," Hunt said loudly. "I had enough of that in the army. I daresay we won't starve just yet."

"I paint toys for manufacturers in Birmingham, and Henri occasionally sells my small oil paintings. I can contribute my earnings," Arnaud offered. "I had no way of refilling the larder for the items I stole while I was invisible."

How long had the poor man been starving in the attic? She had so many questions. . . And ideas for her next book.

As the rest of the party discussed financial practicalities, Clare noticed no one mentioned the missing jewels. Was she the only one who believed the viscountess had returned to this lonely outpost for a reason?

A woman whose family and lands were threatened in France had very good cause to live in oblivion if it meant she might help her loved ones.

LATER THAT EVENING, AFTER PUTTING OLIVER TO BED, CLARE LEFT THE REST OF the party to their own pursuits. She had used the book of poisons from the library to finish her draft. She only need start copying to fresh pages and send her second novel to the publisher. She had the idea for a Gothic mystery for the third. She simply required time to think and write.

She'd left the door to her sitting room ajar so she could hear if Oliver sneaked out across the hall. She heard Hunt's limp as he accompanied his cousin upstairs. They should probably install Arnaud on this floor instead of leaving him in the unheated attic.

She had anticipated meeting aunts and cousins, other share owners in the manor. This family of strangers. . . was almost as peculiar as visiting Egypt. Almost.

Hunt's familiar limp in the hall did not frighten her nearly as much as a foreign vendor grabbing her arm. She supposed, practically speaking, she could outrun him, if necessary, but he was twice her size and strength. She ought to be wary. . . but she wasn't. It wasn't as if he were a pretty face prepared to empty her nearly empty pockets. She had to grow a spine and reach out.

If she couldn't trust Hunt, then they were already in trouble.

Still, she hid the case containing her novel before daringly traversing the corridor. "Do you have a moment?"

He looked tired. His injuries had probably drained him more than he realized. But he didn't brush her off. He waited expectantly.

That gave her a little courage. "Would you like to sit by the fire while I explain my theory?"

Amazingly, he followed her without hesitation. Americans were far too informal, but she enjoyed the difference, particularly the part where he listened. She gestured at the comfortable chair by her warm grate. He settled in and stretched his bad leg toward the heat.

First, she showed him her prayer book. "I don't know if we are in a position to restore the village, but it's a pity we have no church on Sunday."

He nodded. "I'm sure there must be more prayer books in the library. We should set them out tomorrow and hold a small service. It would take a fortune in jewels to restore the village to the point where a vicar is needed. I keep hoping we'll find someone who will know how to return the land to use. With income, the estate might build a bridge over the river so visitors can more easily reach us from the highway. I doubt that comes under maintenance."

She pondered what he said. "It does seem manufacturing is more likely to provide income if even your cousin is painting for the factories. I just hate to see this place abandoned."

She didn't know why she said that since she'd only intended to spend the summer here. But she seemed to be growing attached to the creaky old halls.

"As do I. I thought installing lighting might make it more attractive to buyers. It doesn't seem like the family cares what happens to it."

Oh well, she dreamed of making this a home. He wanted to sell it. It was a miracle men and women spoke the same language.

"You said you had a theory?" He focused his one eye in her direction.

"About your grandmother," she said, a trifle nervously. She didn't think he'd laugh at her, but she didn't want him to think she was a silly chit either. "Lady Reid returned to the manor after the earl died, correct? Some time in the 1780s?"

He thought on it. "My mother left for the States after the war with the British ended. I was born there in 1785. She knows of the manor but never mentioned visiting. I imagine my grandmother would not have left London until both her daughters were well situated."

"If the tapestry is correct, your grandmother must have been in her forties then, a rather young age to almost bury herself alive in this place when she could so easily remarry. It's sad that she died only fifteen years later, so young and alone." Clare waited to see if he followed her thoughts, but he was a man and reasonably ignorant about women.

"As you said, she probably hid from society in shame, just as my mother left England for the same reason." He waited expectantly, as if she might actually have more to add.

"Maybe that was a tiny part. Remember, the viscountess was French, at a time when France was in turmoil. She might not have been welcome in society for that reason as well. It's also possible the earl's death left her without an allowance, although one would expect her eldest daughter to have provided support." Clare tried to cover all possibilities before she launched into her fantasy.

"The same eldest daughter who has yet to reply to my invitation," he added dryly. "The sister who never wrote to my mother, even though they were raised together after the viscount's death."

"I looked your aunt up in Debrett's," she admitted. "Elaine, Marchioness of Spalding. She married in 1782. Marrying her daughter to a marquess was quite a feat for Lady Reid to accomplish. She was no outcast in society." She let him ponder that a moment.

"My mother has told me next to nothing of her aristocratic upbringing. I cannot imagine she was much interested in marrying lords. She works with the church, teaches school, and putters in her garden, and seems completely content with the life of a surveyor's wife." He frowned in thought.

"How old are your cousins?" she asked.

"Henri and Arnaud? Henri is younger than I am. Arnaud is older. What has this to do with anything?" He looked confused.

"They both speak very good English. Ask them if they went to school here." This was drifting from her point, but Clare liked all her historical facts in order.

"Even if they did, they would have been infants in the 1780s. If the viscountess left London after her daughter's grand marriage, what has that to do with them?"

"Puzzle pieces," she admitted. "I needed to talk this through because the theory only just occurred to me. Giving her eldest daughter a season that snared a marquess would have been extremely expensive. Your grandmother may have used up all her assets and simply retired here because she could afford no more. But she had family in an increasingly dangerous France."

"This is coming back to the jewels, isn't it?" His thin lips lifted in an almost-smile. "You think she was searching for the earl's treasure chest."

"Very good." She straightened and boldly looked him in the eye. "She had pearls. We don't know what became of them after her death. She had to have known what was in the earl's vault because her husband would have allowed her to use the family jewels while he was alive. She had family in a country on the brink of revolution. She *needed* those jewels."

"We need the diaries my mother says she kept," he said flatly. "This is all speculation without the diaries."

"They may have been burned," she warned. "She may never have found the jewels. And we don't as yet know what the prayer book and bloody glove represent. Do we know how she died?"

He shoved himself out of the seat. "For all that matters, do we know how the viscount or the earl died? I leave you to the speculation. I must stay with the practical. The manor needs lighting. We need to determine if any of the land is arable. And my time here is limited, so it must be done over these next months. If my wealthy, titled relations have no interest, I may turn the place back to the solicitors and tell them to sell."

The unimaginative beast stalked out. Feeling bereft, Clare fought an irrational urge to fling pillows at him. She would never solve these mysteries on her own.

SIXTEEN

On Sunday, while Clare led a prayer service in the drafty gallery that had most likely once been the priory chapel, Hunt left her to it and appropriated the library table. Feeling vaguely guilty that Clare had to perform his duty because he couldn't easily read the elaborately scripted prayer book, he rolled out an old draft of the main portion of the manor. He hoped he might use it for sketching gas pipes.

For the millionth time, he cursed his game leg and blind eye. Even with all the draperies open and lamps sitting on the table, the lines and fine print on the drawing blurred. And climbing up and down the stairs to determine which cellar supported which room was asking for permanent damage to his knee.

He'd meant to prove that he could still be useful. He seemed to be accomplishing the exact opposite. He'd spent his entire life working toward a career that would allow him to make the world a better place, and he couldn't even install a single gas line.

Walker apparently took Hunt's curses as invitation to carry in the prayer books he'd been working on. "I've duplicated all the passages, but I see no correlation to a treasure hunt or a murder."

"The lady who owned the glove probably pricked her finger. Let us not allow Clare to lead us down stray alleys with her rather active imagination. The only thing peculiar about the glove and prayer book was the fact that they were hidden. And that could just be a child's guilt for marking up pages they shouldn't have." Hunt was in no humor to be optimistic.

Last night, in the lady's room, she'd woven a spell of possibility around him. In the bright light of day, he didn't even know why he cared what had happened to the jewels. Or this damned manor, for all that mattered. They didn't belong to him. He'd be gone by fall. He didn't think any of his so-called relations would starve if no jewels were found. His French cousins were no relation to the earl and had no more claim on them than he did.

But he couldn't sit idle. After Walker left, while the rest of the household prayed, he hunted down magnifying glasses, ripped out the ghost traps, and found a better use for the wire. He used it to tie the magnifying glasses to lamps so he might read the architectural drawing.

By the time the prayer service broke up, his head ached abominably, but he had a plan. Now, he just needed the parts for construction—and labor to drill through floors and walls. First, he'd apply to the trust for funds to begin the work.

And to pay him and Walker for their labors.

When Clare appeared in the library a little later, Hunt pointed out the prayer book. "Walker used an almost identical book to underline the passages. He says he can find no correlation to murder or treasure. He's looking for codes now."

This morning she wore a slightly frillier gown than usual. It had ruffles on the hem and neckline that whispered enticingly over small, firm mounds as she lifted the book to study it. He might only have one eye, but it could see her exceedingly well. She'd curled her fair hair around her face so it dangled over delicate ears adorned with small gold baubles. The rest of the silver-gold mass she'd confined in ribbons and pins. He assumed this was her Sunday best. It led to more lascivious thoughts than her modest daily attire.

Perhaps *he* should be reading the prayer book.

She frowned as she flipped the pages. "I don't think there's a code here. She's underlined the lessons about sin and wicked men. I didn't notice that the original book had a name inside. Prayer books often do. Did Walker find a name anywhere?"

Hunt lay down his pencil and took the book from her. "He didn't mention a name. This version is blank in front. Wicked men? You think whoever owned the book might have been abused in some manner?"

"If a woman owned it, possibly. Given the lady's bloody glove, I would assume so. This book is a general one from the library, not a personal one.

Personal ones are more likely to have the owner's name and the date it was received. But I suppose that's too easy." She sighed and set the book down. "Meera is laying out a light luncheon. I gave Mrs. Gaither the day off."

"Then let us partake. We'll find Walker wherever there is food." He offered his arm, and after a moment's hesitation, she accepted it. He felt as if he were taming a feral kitten.

She shrank back against him when they entered the small breakfast parlor and Arnaud was already there, loading his plate with everything in sight. His cousin was little more than a skeleton. Hunt had heard a little of his story last night. It hadn't been fit for a lady's ears. Aristocrats did not fare well in revolutionary France.

"He's an artist," Hunt whispered in her lovely ear. "He carries no weapons."

"Unlike you," she retorted, inhaling and straightening her slim shoulders.

She was learning boldness. He chuckled. "Unlike me. Except he can see to aim them, and I cannot."

She made a dismissive noise. "Neither of you need weapons to bring down most assailants, especially if your opponent is female. There's Walker. Let me talk to him."

If their opponents were *female*? What kind of men did she associate with? Hunt loaded up his plate and kept his ear tuned to the conversation.

"Not on the cover or title page, but there are initials on a blank page inside," Walker confirmed. "G comma VW and the date 1761."

"Gabrielle, Viscountess Wycliffe!" Clare said without hesitation. "And 1761, was that not the date of her marriage according to the tapestry?"

Not bothering to take a seat, Arnaud finished chewing a mouthful before adding, "My great-aunt was Catholic. She would not have owned an English prayer book."

"Not before she married. But if the viscount insisted they attend the Anglican church, then she may have acquired one at the time they wed— which is the date in the book." She added bread, cheese, and a pickle to her plate and took a seat across from Meera.

"You must have known her." Hunt glared at his scarecrow cousin. "Did she never say she was unhappy? Aside from running away to France and taking a lover, anyway."

Arnaud added more bread and pickled onions to his plate and took a seat next to Walker. "I wasn't born when she was in France. I came here as a schoolboy in 1791, after the peasants rose in revolt and my parents feared for our lives. The viscountess was living in this outpost and seemed perfectly content. I do not know what arrangements she and my parents made for the school they sent us to. She did not have many servants and did not live richly."

"One assumes that means she had not found the jewels and lived off the trust, as we do." Clare made a moue of dissatisfaction and nibbled at her bread and cheese.

"We need the diaries. Speculation is useless." Hunt put an end to what could only be a distressing conversation. "I have to go into Birmingham to buy parts and look for labor. Everyone should make a list of things they need —although the trust only provides maintenance, not clothing." He deflated Lavender's eager expression.

Clare looked torn. "I have funds for fabrics, but it would not be at all proper to travel with you without Meera."

Traveling with Clare all day, bumping hips. . . improper and unwise. "The cart is too small for three. I'll inquire if the trust provides for transportation in the interest of maintenance. Every household must have some means of fetching servants and food. Seems reasonable to me." Although it might cut into his piping budget. He'd set Walker to looking at the funds.

"If I am also an owner, might I also write the trustees?" Clare inquired, a trifle defiantly.

"About clothing budgets when we need lighting?" Hunt countered.

Walker chuckled. "You need a third party to settle disputes. I'll write all your fellow shareholders again."

"Excellent idea." Hunt shoved back from the table.

There was a reason chain of commands existed—but he couldn't demote the one person who had actually agreed to take on some responsibility, even if she put people before practical matters.

LATER THAT AFTERNOON, WITH THE STEADY PATTER OF RAIN AGAINST THE PANES, Clare sat beside the fire in the shabby family parlor. She supposed in the earl's time, it might have been the withdrawing room, since it was between the ballroom and the formal dining room. But if Wycliffe Manor had once been a medieval priory, this area most likely had been the monks' outer parlor. Since they did not use the gallery as a ballroom, and they did not entertain, she preferred the older term. She nibbled at her pen as she edited her final pages.

Oliver studied a picture book he'd found in the library. While her puppy slept at her feet, Lavender worked on the gowns they'd appropriated from the wardrobes. Meera was helping hem since Mrs. Ingraham was gossiping with Mrs. Gaither in the kitchen. Clare rather enjoyed the cozy family gathering. She'd not known anything so comforting in a long while.

Lavender was the first to glance up worriedly. "Do I hear horses?"

Guinevere leaped up and dashed for the door, yapping.

Oliver was already on his feet. Meera set aside her sewing and ominously picked up scissors. Who else but Jacob would ride through a storm to this isolated abode on a Sunday? Shivering, Clare hunted in the desk drawer for a letter opener and wished for a burly footman.

Apparently, Arnaud had appointed himself to that duty. She could hear his heavy tread on the stairs. Hunt couldn't move that fast and Walker had a lighter step.

Peering through a window with a view of the drive, Oliver excitedly cried, "Henri!" and they all relaxed.

"I didn't think he was due until next week." Lavender set aside her sewing. "Do you think he brought my threads?"

Returning the letter knife to the drawer, Clare pondered how one treated an itinerant peddler related to one of the owners of the manor. She supposed they needed to invite him inside. So many decisions she really hadn't been taught to handle. . .

She followed the others to the back hall. Henri didn't know his heritage had been exposed. He was still pretending to be a peddler. Well, he *was* a peddler, but he was also a relation to Hunt. It was all very perplexing.

Apparently, the men had decided on the appropriate etiquette. They had invited Henri in at the portico entrance between the gallery and the parlor. When Clare arrived, he was divesting himself of wet cloak and hat and pounding Arnaud on the back. That decided that. They would add peddler to the family.

"Bring him in by the fire," she called. "Where is Ned? Have him bring up tea."

"Better, I have coffee in the wagon," Henri called. "Good afternoon, beautiful mademoiselle! I will fetch your parcels and the coffee as soon as I speak to my brother, *mais oui*?"

"Coffee? You have decent coffee?" Hunt was already donning his coat. "I'll unload while you and Arnaud talk. I hope it is not bad news."

The brothers exchanged glances. Of course, it was bad news. Refraining from rolling her eyes, Clare dispatched Oliver and Lavender to the kitchens and Walker to aid Hunt.

Once the wagon was unloaded and all four men gathered in the study, their excited shouting and arguing could be heard down the hall, setting Clare's nerves on edge.

"What news can a peddler bring that has them so upset?" Meera asked worriedly. "Henri cannot know our personal business. Would he bring news from France?"

Cuddling her pet, Lavender all but hid in a corner—exceedingly unusual. Oliver had retreated behind the draperies. The men were terrifying them, not protecting them by keeping them ignorant. Clare preferred to avoid conflict, but not if it meant she must sit silent and frightened.

When Betsy finally appeared in the corridor bearing trays of cups and a coffee pot, Clare intervened, steering her from the study to the parlor. "By the fire, please." She addressed the drapery. "Oliver, will you tell the captain that coffee will be served in here?"

Ned arrived with a tea tray and cakes, and she had him fetch another table. They were settled comfortably by the time the men erupted from the study in search of their dreadful black muck.

Following behind the others, Hunt observed her arrangement with a glint in his eye. "I'm glad you're *my* co-general," he murmured, leaning over to confiscate a cake. "Being outmaneuvered by a female would be most embarrassing."

"You were terrifying us," she said primly. "Has the king died? Are we at war again? What is happening?"

"The news arrives here rather late. I'll have Henri show you the news sheet. It concerns them more than us." He finished his cake and joined the other men in pouring coffee.

With a few words, Hunt had Henri apologizing and handing over the post as well as the news sheet. "Since this is Sunday, I have left your new maid with her grandparents in the village. They sent me out here with your post." Henri bowed and relinquished the letters.

Aware the others watched expectantly, Clare didn't ask about the maid but opened the news sheet. It took a moment to find the right headline, but here it was. . .

"Napoleon has an *army* already? They have overthrown the new king?" No wonder the men were upset. "What does this mean to your family?"

"More war," Arnaud said grimly. "More armies. And the people will starve, again."

SEVENTEEN

"Your cousins will not try to return to France, will they?" Clare asked anxiously, finding Hunt in the library directly after breakfast on Monday.

He had hoped the women would be content with the new maid and the *notions* Henri had brought. He should have known Clare would not be selfishly satisfied with the provisions but would look at the whole picture, like any good officer. Impending war affected them even here in an outpost of nowhere.

"They have family, friends, lands there. I cannot stop them if they choose to fight Napoleon." Tyrants needed to be stopped, but Hunt was not in a position to volunteer. Being helpless chafed.

"They are not soldiers," she said in a frustration to match his own. "Like you, they need to be building, not destroying. It would be far more useful if they could earn money and send it home to help their family. Perhaps we could start a business with all this grandeur and employ them." She flung her arm in a disparaging gesture indicating the enormous L-shaped library.

Building instead of fighting was a unique outlet for frustration.

"What business would we start in this outpost when there isn't even enough population to provide the labor?" He had to be practical. Dreamers like Clare had no idea of the work needed to produce their vision.

"It can be done, one person at a time." She opened her hand to reveal half a dozen exquisitely painted buttons. "Betsy spent all night painting these.

Henri thinks he can sell them to the factory for twice what we paid. It's a tiny amount, perhaps, but for Betsy, it's a new pair of church shoes. If we had a church, that is," she added wryly.

"You should be talking to Walker. He's the bookkeeper among us. I have no purpose in your dream world." He moved his lamp/magnifier down the page to add another line to his drawing.

She smacked his sore arm. The little chemist's unguent had eased some of the ache, but the muscles still hurt from disuse. He winced and glared. "What?"

"Betsy will go blind trying to paint these things in the dark. The factories in Birmingham have installed gas lighting to increase production hours. We could do the same. Factories need engineers as well as bookkeepers and workers." She stood there in her baggy muslin gown, wrapped in shawls, and still managed to look and sound like an indignant general. *Unprepossessing*, his foot and eye.

"You want to start a *factory*?" Astounded, he stared at the draft with its tiny lines and let her enormous dream wash over him. He wanted to say she was insane, but there was just a kernel of possibility. . .

"They have to start somehow." She yanked her shawl in place and looked more thoughtful than indignant now. "We have all this space. . ." She threw her arm out again, giving him a glimpse of cleavage when the shawl fell back. "If we could start by lighting one room sufficiently for several people to work in comfort. . . Betsy with her buttons, Lavender with her sewing, Arnaud with his painting. . ."

"We would not need the approval of all the owners if we only lit and heated a room." Attention grabbed by her revealing gestures as much as her words, he caught on quickly. "We could not convert the entire manor without seeking permission, but a workroom is reasonable."

"Henri could be our salesman and distributor or whatever one calls him. He has a gift for talking that's far better than being grabbed by the arm and having a scarf waved in one's face." She grimaced as if she spoke from experience.

"I still plan to write all the known owners," he warned. "We should not build dreams if neither of us plans to stay. They may all wish to sell."

She sighed. "Which may be best. Someone flush with funds could have a hunting lodge to sit here empty year after year until it deteriorates, and the village turns to dust and people go hungry or work as slaves from dawn to dusk in the city."

"That's what the manor was designed for," he reminded her. "I still think anything else is a creative fantasy, but there is no reason we can't try, especially if it keeps Arnaud and Henri occupied. I don't think either of them would survive war. Arnaud has tried once and barely made it out alive. Henri has lived here so long, he is barely French."

She nodded in relief, and her smile brought out the family dimples. "I'll help you write our relations. Perhaps they will recognize my name and be more likely to respond. I would like Lavender's grandmother to know where she is, and it should be most enlightening to hear from a marchioness, if we can reach your aunt."

The people were becoming more than names on a tapestry. Hunt wasn't at all certain he wanted to know the individuals behind the names now that he'd been ignored, but he supposed it wouldn't hurt to try once more—especially if he had a partner who might add a more personal touch.

"Before we start our campaign. . ." Hunt held up his hand before she could dash off for pen and paper. "We should hold a family meeting. We are making plans for them without their approval."

She stuck out a plump bottom lip, apparently feeling bold, indeed. "We can't be dictators?"

Hunt couldn't help it, he grinned. It felt good to relax again, if only for a spare moment. "That's Napoleon's method. Do you have an army?"

There were the dimples again. "Our family is our army, and we're the co-generals, remember? But to avoid a revolt, I suppose we can insist that everyone arrive on time for dinner this evening and hold our meeting then."

"*Before* dinner. You will need to include Betsy," he reminded her. Although how anyone as clumsy as the maid could make those delicate buttons was beyond his limited imagination.

"It is a formula for strengthening the blood," Meera murmured, setting a bottle of elixir on Walker's desk. Since the servants' stairs down to her workshop weren't far from his estate office at the back of the house, she had taken to stopping there when she emerged at the end of her workday. Today, Oliver was on the floor, testing boards and panels. "If you could give it to Monsieur Arnaud and tell him to take a spoonful in the morning and before bed, please."

"You could give it to him yourself," Walker suggested, setting aside his pen and rising from his chair as if she were a lady. "The captain is appreciative of your unguent. It seems to help."

She shook her head. "I am not an apothecary. I am not licensed to go to patients and diagnose them. I am overstepping as it is. But I cannot watch people suffer when I know my compounds help."

"I fear I don't see the difference, but I will make certain Arnaud receives this. Do you have a list of supplies you need? I believe the captain intends to head for the city tomorrow."

She beamed. "I will bring my list to dinner, thank you! Why do you think the captain and Clare have called a family gathering?"

The usually amiable Walker frowned and shook his head. "I don't know, but I fear I may have bad news to add. Tell them I may be a little late. I need to study these books more to be certain of what I've found."

Meera glanced at the stack of ledgers. "Not jewels, I gather?"

"The opposite, I think. Perhaps I should wait until another day and talk to the captain alone." He remained standing while she dithered in the doorway.

"No, it is better to share bad news. Sometimes, it is not so bad that way." She thought. Maybe. "I will see you at dinner, then."

She hurried off, fretting at her lip. She was enjoying the safety of this enormous manor and the company of men who might prevent Jacob from harming her or the babe. If they had to leave. . .

They had nowhere to go. That couldn't happen.

Now that the moment had arrived, Clare nervously clenched and unclenched her hands. She couldn't believe she was doing this, committing to a future she might never see come to fruition. Worse, she must do so in front of men—large, intimidating men. Arnaud and Henri entered the parlor, already arguing heatedly. Why would they listen to a feeble female? Hunt thought she was creating fantasies. Walker. . . scarcely recognized her existence.

She bolstered her courage by reminding herself that others mattered more than her fears.

Betsy was creative and could do better for herself than servant. At the moment, she was bossing around the new maid Henri had brought, a nervous slip of a woman with a sharp nose and thinning hair, who might also have dreams.

Looking lonely, Lavender cuddled her puppy while her companion rocked and knitted. The child was talented and apparently needed to make her own way in the world. Mrs. Ingraham seemed more comfortable in the kitchen with the Gaithers. Did an old woman have dreams?

Meera and Walker arrived late, arguing, as always. For two people who agreed on almost nothing, they seemed to be together a lot. She knew both of them had talents wasted here. Would it be better for them to move on to an uncertain future or remain here?

Why would anyone listen to a timid spinster?

Hunt had poured his own brandy before Betsy arrived and cradled the snifter now, standing by the hearth with his coat undone and his neckcloth loose, looking imperious and just a bit piratical. He didn't make her shake in her shoes any longer, but her daring did.

Grumbling as always, Mrs. Gaither had produced ratafia so the ladies could partake. Betsy managed to fill the glasses without spilling too much.

"I believe we're all here, Miss Knightley." Hunt bowed formally in her direction. "Betsy, we need you to linger as well. Marie, if you will help Mrs. Gaither in the kitchen, Betsy can catch you up later."

Marie, the new maid, bobbed a curtsy and departed. Betsy hovered near the exit. Everyone else took seats, except Oliver, who sat on the floor with a book. Heads swiveled back and forth expectantly. Hunt nodded at Clare to begin.

She grimaced and gathered her limited courage. "I am not very good at speaking. This seemed much simpler when I explained it to the captain earlier. But, I think, the simplest place to start is that we have this enormous manor no one seems to want. Yet it provides a haven for those who occasionally have need of it."

A head or two bobbed but no one seemed eager to leap in.

She took a deep breath and tried again. "The manor might possibly be sold for some low sum as a hunting lodge, and the funds distributed to whatever heirs are found. But that would mean the people like Betsy who live here will eventually have to leave their homes for the city. And it just seemed to me. . ."

She saw no way to say it except bluntly. "Most of the heirs don't need funds. The village does. Some of us do. Some of us need an occupation and a home. And here is this enormous manor where we can be safe while we learn and develop our. . ." She couldn't say *business*. That seemed so. . . mercenary. She closed her eyes and sighed at the hopelessness of explaining.

Meera, however, brightened. "I could be a druggist, but I need customers. If we had a village, I would have customers."

Even Lavender seemed to consider this. "I could sew for ladies, but there are no ladies."

Betsy grinned. "I make buttons. Henri says he can sell my buttons. I can buy Mama a new pot." She frowned. "I made a hole in the old one."

Arnaud frowned ferociously, while Henri watched him with hope. Clare thought she understood some part of the argument there. Arnaud, as the eldest, felt compelled to return and fight. Henri didn't want him to go. She crossed her fingers and prayed.

Hunt finally joined in. "If we had someone who knew farming, we might be able to feed a village. But it's hard to attract a good steward when there is nothing here for him."

"Except a roof over his head," Arnaud pointed out, reluctantly. "That can be very valuable to the right person."

Clare wondered if Arnaud had experience in farming. The revolution had torn apart the great estates decades ago.

Walker cleared his throat uncomfortably. The chatter that had started after Arnaud's comment died down. Clare waited for bad news. Over the last ten years, she had only known bad news. Well, she'd published a novel and the publisher wanted a second, but that was relatively meaningless in the overall scheme of things. She owed more than she earned thus far, and the occupation was hazardous to Oliver's future.

Walker stood up. "I have been examining the estate books. They ended in 1800, upon the death of the viscountess, so I may be missing a great deal from the last fifteen years. I've not had time to do a thorough search, but I thought I might warn you before you make too many plans." He glanced nervously at Hunt. "I didn't have time to tell you first."

Hunt sipped his brandy and nodded. "We're all in this together. Go ahead."

"The viscountess deposited a large sum in her account once a year, in December. Then she turned around and paid a similar sum to the bank that holds your trust assets. I have done some preliminary searches. The deposit came from a London jeweler." He smoothed out a collection of receipts and laid them on the table.

"You think she sold her jewels to add to the maintenance fund?" Hunt asked, frowning. He picked up one of the receipts. "This is for a single pearl."

Walker handed him the bundle. "Each one is for a single pearl. I had no idea they were worth that much. The receipts go back to the year the old earl died."

Having sold her own mother's jewelry, except for the sapphire pendant she kept for Oliver's Oxford education, Clare understood the implication. "She was paying a debt with her pearls."

Walker looked relieved that she understood. "I fear so. I don't know what the debt is, but I must assume if it exists, it hasn't been paid these last fifteen years. Since the property is not entailed, there may be a lien against the manor of which we're not aware."

EIGHTEEN

By Tuesday morning, Hunt had had the entire night to work up a good fury. When he reached his study to find the prim Miss Knightley waiting with her draft letter to their relations, he unleashed his pent-up wrath.

He stormed up and down the room, oblivious to the pain in his knee. "That bloody banker *knows* about the debt! He could have told us at any time. I could have just heaved the manor back in his lap and told him what to do with it."

"You have not verified there *is* a debt yet," the very prepossessing Miss Knightley argued. This morning she had tucked a pencil in her golden ringlets and left off her spectacles. "You are needlessly terrifying the household just when I had them interested and hopeful."

"She did not sell her pearls to pay the servants!" he shouted. "That was no small sum."

"It may have been a personal debt. I do not understand why there should be any mortgage at all," she countered, looking anxious but determined. "The earl was exceedingly wealthy. He had no need to borrow. Perhaps your grandmother paid off her debt. You need to write the banker and solicitor."

"And say what? Please, tell us if we owe money? Are you planning on foreclosing on the property after we make it habitable? Do you really think they'll tell us the truth?" He reached for the brandy decanter, but it was early morning. He'd emptied it last night when he'd locked himself in with Walker and the books. So, he had a headache as well as a bum knee.

"You cannot go off half cocked and storm about like a. . . a. . ." She stumbled over a metaphor—just as he stumbled over the damned rug.

He grabbed a shelf to steady himself and nearly yanked it down. "I can storm all I damned well please. I despise being played the fool. I'll have to go into Stratford and confront the bastards."

She flinched at his bad language. "Blasphemy will land you in prison. Choose your words carefully."

"Hell and damnation," he growled, flinging crumpled paper at the fire.

Ignoring his temper, she valiantly continued, "Our intent is to keep your cousins occupied. Have Arnaud look around the grounds to see if he thinks there is any arable land. Perhaps he'll recognize the nut and fruit trees that Walker says were planted. And Henri can still take his cart into the city and bring back more buttons for Betsy and fabric for Lavender. You could give him a list of what you need for lighting. If it is coming out of the trust, there is no reason we shouldn't spend it while we can."

"Tell them yourselves! Why should I be the idiot who raises their hopes?" They had agreed this was a temporary situation. She was being reasonable. He was not.

He just kept seeing that smirking fop in that chair telling him everything was fine—*while admiring the study he meant to make his own.* And come to think of it, the banker had been assessing the crystal and china in the buffet when he'd come down for breakfast the next morning. Hunt had sensed something awry then, but he'd allowed the stuttering English dandy to fool him.

He didn't mind so much for himself, but he'd invited his entire damned family, raised hopes that shouldn't be raised, and was about to humiliate himself as an easily gulled American.

"Ladies do not tell gentlemen what to do," she said stiffly. "I thought, if you and I are family. . ." She let the thought dangle.

"You could tell *me* what to do?" He snorted. He'd never understand women. Or English society.

There were dozens of reasons why he shouldn't allow her to continue with her insane fantasy. But the golden fairy stood there in all her frail frippery looking as if she'd blow away in the wind—and for once, *she didn't display an ounce of fear.* He growled and roared and glared at her like a beastly pirate—and she flinched at his language and fearlessly ordered him about.

He'd created a monster.

"Why aren't you fleeing my presence in terror?" he demanded, irascibly.

She wrinkled her nose in puzzlement. "Do you intend to shoot me for arguing?"

"I made the damned banker nervous with silence. I roar at you, and you *argue!*" He wanted to ask where the polite miss who shivered in his presence had gone—but that same polite miss had ignored his orders and gone her own way since arriving.

She was a chameleon, a skinny spinster with the soul of a fire-spewing dragon. A skinny spinster with spun gold hair and blistering blue eyes and cheeks that turned rosy with anger.

"Someone must argue with you," she pointed out, her cheeks pinkening. "You pay Walker, so he won't. Did you want Lavender to come in and burst into tears? I believe she's crying in the parlor at the moment. And Betsy can barely hold a water pail, she's so upset. And your cousins are packing their bags."

Hunt flung a ledger at the damned tapestry. He'd have to rip off heads just for upsetting her. "Fine. I'll go to Stratford. Henri should go into Birmingham and fling money at button and toy manufacturers. I'll tell Arnaud to get his. . . backside. . . outdoors and have a look at fruits and nuts. And you, you go buzz around someone else."

"Well, I don't plan on leaving until my townhouse is empty again. So, I will start arranging a workroom. And writing all our family." She bobbed a curtsy and started out.

"Tell them to bring their jewels," he shouted after her. "They may need to sell them if they wish to flush money down this worthless privy!"

He could cover the distance to Stratford in half the time if he could ride a damned horse. The pain to his knee would be almost worth it, if he thought he could stay in the saddle. Far better to take his rage out on the men who caused it than on a flighty fairy who thought she could change the world with dreams and magic.

While he was there, he would determine if Lavender was an impostor, although what the hell he would do about it, he couldn't say. Amazing that he'd once commanded men to build bridges under cannon fire but couldn't command a few weeping females.

He had managed to pull on his riding boots without curling up in agony and was shrugging into his greatcoat when the little druggist arrived in the corridor through the servants' stairs. She carried a paper packet she diffidently held out.

"Powders for the pain. If you take them with ale, it will help numb the ache for a while. Take too many, and you will over-exert yourself and be sorry tomorrow." She stepped away the instant he took the packet and examined the contents.

Had she been a man, he'd have told her what she could do with her damned pain powders. But she so seldom spoke to him. . . And her unguent did seem to help. He refrained from barking. "Thank you, Meera." He sounded gruff. He knew he did. But riding out with a hangover, in a cold March wind, to talk to treacherous vipers did not improve his humor.

"Clare may be a dreamer, but her ingenuity has allowed her to survive more disasters than you realize. Please don't make the mistake of dismissing her suggestions." Without waiting for a reply, the little druggist lifted her colorful skirt and departed.

Well, anyone left standing at the end of the day was a survivor, he supposed. Not chastised, he strode off, determined to ride to Stratford and back in a day.

~

WALKER SHOWED CLARE THE ORIGINAL DRAFT OF THE LETTER HUNT HAD dictated to the family. She remembered it well—a formal declaration of ownership and not in the least welcoming. She sat at the desk in the study and improved the draft she'd try to show the dratted man, hoping she wrote a more interesting invitation. Walker, at least, made a few practical suggestions.

And then they sat down with the list of relations Hunt had compiled and began writing. Clare added more personal notes to Lady Lavinia about Lavender, as well as to family she'd met and who might remember her. She dithered over what she should add to Hunt's aunt, the marchioness. Finally, she settled on a note saying Hunt's mother sent her best wishes and hoped she was in good health.

They folded the letters and waxed them with an old coat-of-arms seal they found in the desk.

"A pity the earl isn't here to frank them. Half the letters may be refused for the cost alone." She received so few letters, that she gladly paid for them. Surely her relations weren't poor.

"If they can't afford postage, they can't afford to travel here," Walker said pragmatically. "We ought to make it a great heavy letter that costs a fortune so only the wealthy read it."

She flung a discarded draft at him. "We want the ones who *need* a roof over their heads."

"That's foolish. If the place is in debt, wealth is more useful." Walker gathered up the letters to take down to the village.

"Are you wealthy?" she asked. "Do you think you are useless?"

He shoved the letters in his coat pocket and considered that. "I am not useless to the right people. But to society as a whole. . . I am worthless as anything but a paid laborer. I own nothing. I have no wealthy connections. It's only you, with your rich family, who can possibly make anything happen."

She flung another discarded page at him. "I cannot vote. I cannot own anything. But I am not stupid or helpless. My rich family, as you call them, could very well be stupid and helpless. In which case, *we* are better than *they* are. We have power in our brains and skills."

"The captain's right. You *are* naïve. But dream worlds are fun to live in for a while. After I return from the village, I'll start hunting for mortgage documents." He walked out.

Clare grimaced. Did that mean he liked what she'd said or that he simply thought she was all about in her head and was just placating her as one did a child?

Speaking of children. . . Oliver had sneaked in to read an old book he'd found. It didn't appear to have pictures, so she didn't know how he could read it. She had written several employment agencies about tutors but had no response. It had only been a week, so she supposed she shouldn't be disappointed yet.

Oliver really needed a man to whom he could relate and not another female in his life. But so far, her searches had determined that men didn't want to work for a woman. . .

She sighed and wondered how one found employment agencies in Birmingham. One of the problems of being displaced was learning her new surroundings. Perhaps Henri could find out.

She gave Oliver a geography book with lovely maps—probably a hundred years out of date but that didn't matter. He'd learned his letters and numbers at an early age. He was learning to read big words all on his own and pictures helped. He had an amazing memory. He happily set the tattered older book aside.

She tracked down Arnaud in the gallery, where he and Lavender were cleaning the lower part of the towering windows to let in the meager sunshine. The mirrors on the opposite wall reflected the light so the immense space was the brightest in the house. Overhead, dusty crystal chandeliers simply looked sad, but with candles. . . She could see the appeal. She still needed another shawl to keep from shivering.

The floor was marble tile, which didn't help to warm the space. "We'd need to burn an entire forest to make this place comfortable," she warned.

Lavender gestured at the trees blocking the sun. "We can start there. We had a landscape teacher last year who said the grounds around a house should be limited to low-lying gardens, not trees." She stood inside the towering fireplace and gazed up the chimney. "Although we might need a chimney sweeper."

"It is not any colder than the attics," Arnaud said dismissively, studying the play of light the trees created. "Although I agree, the pines should probably come down. They may be a wind barrier in winter, but this room is meant for light."

"When the priory was rebuilt, I'm sure the first earl intended this as both ballroom and a place to walk in winter when it is too cold to go outside. I don't believe it was meant to be heated all day. We could ask in the village about chimney sweeps, I suppose." Clare tested one of the Queen Anne sofas. The cushion sank and the silk upholstery separated a little more. The scattering of graceful furniture with cabriole legs and shell carvings had to be a century old—possibly a redecoration when the newly married Lord and Lady Reid moved in?

She gazed up at the portrait gallery railing on the upper floor. "I wish the paintings could speak and reveal the manor's secrets."

"Those old biddies would natter about their children and their gowns and tell us nothing useful." Lavender retreated from the hearth and spun around as if dancing. "A ball would be so lovely. Musicians in the minstrel's gallery, glittering candles. . ."

Clare couldn't blame her for the fantasy. The ballroom scene with crystal chandeliers reflected in the dark windows and mirrors, with hundreds of couples dancing in glorious gowns, already played in her head, except the guests would be in medieval gowns. She may as well imagine monks chanting.

With a sigh, she gave up the dream and returned to the practical. "We should all hunt for the orchards Walker says were planted during the viscountess's time. Do nut and fruit trees last for twenty or thirty years?"

"Mrs. Gaither will know." Lavender lifted her hem and glided across the room like a perfect lady. "Grand. . . Mrs. Ingraham used to make jams and jellies. If there is enough, we could sell the extras!"

It took a moment after she left before Clare realized she was alone with

Arnaud. She remembered quaking in her shoes the night she'd met Hunt, but she must be growing used to large, terrifying men. She tilted her head back and dared to ask, "Do you know aught of farming?"

He shrugged. "As a boy, I followed my father around. I cannot say I remember much of it. He had men who knew the soil and crops."

"Then you might know how to hire the men we need to farm whatever is out there. Should we all go tramping about after lunch and see what we can find?" Clare tried not to hope too much. It shouldn't matter if this stranger rode off to war. She'd only just met him after all.

But anyone would want to feed and comfort a starving animal. It was human nature. A man of his stature shouldn't look like a haunted skeleton.

NINETEEN

Hunt returned to the manor well after dinner, feeling as if he'd been run over by an army and left for dead. He had no one to blame but himself, which didn't make him any less grumpy.

Ned waited to take care of the horse, thank all that was holy. Hunt leaned heavily on his walking stick just to reach the portico entrance. He was too tired and furious to be hungry. He simply wanted to beat up a few fools and go to bed.

Except the fools weren't here. The manor held good people here at his invitation. Why they thought a one-eyed crippled would be of any use to them was beyond understanding. He'd have to tell them all to go away.

The doddering butler met him as before, although Hunt discerned the strong smell of gin this time. Still, if it meant supper was in the offing. . .

He'd rather have it sent to his room, but he knew everyone waited anxiously. Captain Huntley never missed a duty call, no matter how unpleasant. At least no one was dead this time. Yet.

He shrugged off his coat. Remembering the last of the pain powder in his pocket, he poured it on his tongue and swallowed the bitterness. The relief didn't last long, but it might get him upstairs and through the interrogation.

Stupid young fool that he'd been when he'd proposed to Abigail, he hadn't considered the enormous responsibility a family represented. At the time, he'd only been thinking of a warm bed and a willing woman of his own. She'd done him a favor by leaving. The army hadn't taught him what to do with a family.

To his surprise, everyone was gathered around a table upstairs in the blue salon, studying what appeared to be a crude sketch. The supposedly shy spinster beamed at him and gestured at an empty chair by the fire where his brandy waited. Blessedly, she didn't question but let him heat his weary bones.

Lavender removed her dog from a footstool and put the stool where he could reach it. Meera produced another packet of pain powder and glanced at him questioningly. He slipped them in his pocket for later. He'd have to ask her about the ingredients. They didn't knock him out like laudanum but had provided a little relief.

"You have several orchards," Arnaud announced, carrying the sketch over to Hunt's chair. "I'll have to draw this larger so you can see, but they're down the side of the hill, protected from the prevailing wind."

Hunt sipped his brandy and tried to study the sketch, but it was useless. "Walker verifies they're within the manor's boundaries?"

Hunt was the surveyor, but Walker had learned enough to look for boundary markers.

"According to the markers and a survey we found, the manor's land extends over the brook in the east. The bottom land probably floods but might take some crop. The village is on manor property to the south. The land to the west is wind blown and rocky and of little use except for hunting and dangerous even for that. The grounds to the north appear to be mostly forested hillside, possibly fit for sheep or goats if cleared."

The woods would contain deer and rabbits, but Hunt wouldn't mention that in front of squeamish ladies. Oliver, at least, had apparently been put to bed.

The new maid carried up his meal. He'd thought himself too tired to eat, but the smell of stew and hot bread had him ravenous. Perhaps he could simply not tell them the bad news. They were all excited by their explorations, even Arnaud. Henri wasn't present, so he must have gone to the city.

"What condition are the orchards in?" he asked, delaying the inevitable.

"A lot of dead wood needing pruning. They could benefit from a good application of manure and blood meal and perhaps a pine mulch, but they have new leaves. I've been reading up on them in your library. There are conflicting recommendations. It would require some experimentation." Arnaud settled on the sofa and held up a book.

His cousin might stay if he thought he had a purpose here.

Clare watched Hunt anxiously. She hadn't forgotten his reason for going to Stratford. He didn't meet her eye but concentrated on his stew.

"We measured the long gallery," Lavender said tentatively.

And there was another subject to be avoided—Lavender. Unpleasant news everywhere he looked. He merely raised his eyebrows and waited.

"The gallery is the room with the most light, but we don't know if you can install your gas pipes there. Or if the chimney draws." The girl lifted her chin defiantly, as if fearful of being dismissed.

Damn it all, he shouldn't be encouraging fantasies. Maybe he could leave before it all fell apart. They had nine months, after all, anything could happen.

"All the chimneys should be inspected," he agreed. That was neutral enough. "I've meant to look for an entrance to the priory cellar to see if piping is possible."

Walker and Arnaud discussed fishing in the stream while Hunt ate. The manor did have bountiful grounds to support a family with only a little effort. But one couldn't earn an income on fish and nuts. Even if they had complete access to the trust, the funds would eventually dry up without replenishment.

"Did you bring back any more servants?" The little apothecary—druggist —asked. One of these days, he'd learn the distinction.

"I have left word with the solicitors that we are hiring. They tell me that, except for the Gaithers, most of my grandmother's staff either retired to the village or moved on to the city. The estate used to earn rents from the shops and cottages, but none has been paid in years."

"Given the lack of maintenance, that is only fair," Clare said dryly, apparently giving up on waiting for him to answer her unspoken questions. "It's a bit of a chicken/egg situation. Why would anyone pay rent in a moribund town, so why fix up houses for which no rent is earned?"

If even Clare was feeling discouraged—that did not bode well. But he was oddly reluctant to dampen their dreams.

"It all takes time. Let us see what the future brings." It had disaster written all over it from his perspective.

Clare's eyes lit with what he feared was mischief. "I have written all our relations. If they all show up, we'll have a population large enough to make a village!"

Hunt hid his wince.

~

WEDNESDAY MORNING, CLARE PACKAGED UP HER NEWLY COMPLETED, FRESHLY transcribed manuscript, determined to walk into the village and post it, after it stopped raining.

In the meantime, she needed to question the curmudgeon. She knew Hunt was hiding from her for a reason. Given his grumpiness last night, she very much feared they'd be out of the manor soon.

That was pessimistic, she knew. She'd simply lived with disaster for so long, that she had come to expect it.

Hunt wasn't in any of the usual places. No fire heated the study or library. Walker worked alone in his office at the back of the house. Henri hadn't returned yet. She followed voices and found Lavender and Arnaud had set up an easel and a work table in the gallery, although they weren't present. It wasn't any warmer here than in the attic, but she supposed it was less isolated.

Lavender had provided a blanket for her dog to curl up in. Guinevere looked up when Clare entered but had the sense to stay where she was warm.

The voices came from above. She glanced up and found the pair studying ancestral portraits. "Are they worth anything if sold?" she called up, feeling particularly out of sorts.

"No Rembrandts," Arnaud called back. "No artist I recognize. But we did discover an anomaly."

"Someone has doctored the paintings!" Lavender called cheerfully.

"Doctored?" Clare wanted to find Hunt, not examine ancient oils. Which was ridiculous. She should just march into town. "Do I need to come up and see?"

"Not much to see," Arnaud admitted. "There are patches of paint in odd places that don't belong to the original. It is the same color in each painting, as if they only had one powder to use, and they dabbed it on as close a color as they could find. So, if the paintings had been worth anything, they're worth less now."

"Vandalism?" she asked, puzzled.

"That would be foolish. Do you think I might bring one of these down to work on, see if I can discover what is beneath the glob?" Arnaud leaned over the railing.

A loud hammering echoed from beneath her feet. Clare nearly jumped.

The last noises they'd heard in here had been Arnaud's footsteps in the attic, but he was standing in the gallery this time.

"That's Hunt," Arnaud explained. "He found an entrance to the foundation under these rooms."

"Of course." She muttered *dratted beast* under her breath but nodded politely. "I see no reason you shouldn't examine the paintings if you're so inclined. I daresay they need cleaning."

She left them choosing a painting to desecrate. Perhaps a maid wouldn't be too nosy about her package. She didn't want to walk into the village alone.

What she *wanted* was to locate the old cellar and chew off the captain's ear. But she was a *lady*. Ladies did not do that sort of thing, she was quite certain. Besides, cellars were dark and nasty and probably contained bones and rats and spiders.

Which was exactly why he was hiding down there, despite his bad leg.

Clare ended up recruiting the new maid, Marie, to accompany her. If they were accosted by villains in the forest, Hunt had their kidnapping and murder on his conscience.

Or drowning. With all the rain, the brook was running high over the stepping stones. Clare was glad of her pattens. If the men wanted to fish, it would have to be from further up the bank.

She learned that Mr. Oswald, the postmaster, was Marie's grandfather. He beamed like a proud parent when they arrived to mail the parcel. "Aye, it's good to see the old place opening up. We sent to our Tom to let the others know as you be hiring."

"I don't suppose you know of anyone who worked in the orchards or with the grounds?" Clare had no idea who Tom might be, but she hoped that meant word was spreading.

"Aye, Tom will tell them. Folk don't much like working in them factories. Good fresh air and sunshine is what a body needs. They'll be knockin' at the door soon enough." He took her coins. "Reckon I should carry some of them notions the peddler sells?"

"Not just yet," Clare advised. "Let us see who shows up. If we hire more staff, they may need a few things to spend their coins on. Marie, what would you suggest?"

Clare couldn't gauge the maid's age, perhaps a little older than Betsy, closer to forty. Her hands were calloused from hard work and lines already marred her weathered face, but she broke into a lovely smile.

"Toffee and threads and maybe some nice linen. It's been ages since I had new things." She held out her gown disparagingly.

Clare knew by *linen*, she meant underclothes. "We need a seamstress! Lavender can do fine work, but we need someone to sew durable clothes for the servants. Perhaps, Mr. Oswald, you could order some good, sturdy fabric so it's on hand as needed."

She knew she was being horrible. If Hunt had discovered a mortgage they couldn't pay—which she had to assume since he wasn't speaking to her —then this was all for naught. But if the house went to the bank, what happened to the maintenance trust? Would it be divided between the heirs who didn't really need it?

Why not provide poor people with a small share of those riches first?

She'd never had a lot of money and had always been frugal. She was rather enjoying playing Lady Bountiful, if even for a few months.

Horrible people and events might hover outside her little fantasy world, but for now, she'd wave a magic wand and make a bubble of happiness happen.

Hunt would no doubt kill her.

TWENTY

ONE MORE DAMNED THING. . . HE OUGHT TO JUST BOOK PASSAGE HOME.

Hunt had to bathe off layers of filth and spiderwebs, leaving him far too much time to think about the blanket-wrapped infant bones he'd discovered. The foundation under the original hall where he'd found them might be a thousand years old for all he knew.

Telling the over-imaginative Miss Knightley about baby bones would only create havoc they didn't really need—especially if they were losing the house anyway. But he didn't want to tell anyone that either. He needed time to work out a sensible plan—without hysteria.

Not wanting to face his too perceptive co-general, he debated going hungry rather than go down to dinner but decided that was the act of a coward.

When he showed up late in the formal dining room, he realized his tactical error—the troop that arrived first claimed the most favorable battle position. Clare had placed Lavender at his right, her antique companion at his left.

The not-so-shy spinster had taken the seat of hostess at the far end of the long table, placing Arnaud on her right. Had Henri been here, he would no doubt be on her left. At it was, Walker and Meera had taken the center, across from each other, where they could pursue their argumentative courtship. There would be no talking through them.

Hunt raised a glass in disgruntlement to the lady's tactics. Clare didn't deign to notice.

Fine then, he hadn't wanted to talk to her anyway.

He barely grasped any of the adolescent's incessant chatter until he caught mention of the earl's painting. He turned his one-eyed glare on the chit, who was too self-involved to flinch. "You did what to a valuable painting?"

"Cleaned it," she said brightly, not having the sense to be wary. "There was a repair patch with tiny numbers and letters scratched into it. Arnaud says we must clean them all if we wish to discover what the numbers mean."

Arnaud was at the far end of the table, probably regaling Clare with a more comprehensible version of the tale.

The child had already gone on to cutting down pines and cleaning chimneys before he'd worked through her revelation of hidden figures in oil. It seemed they'd had a busy day while he'd been below, risking life and limb in spiders and mud to find the support structure to the gallery. And discovering a graveyard. Or a crypt.

He wanted to know about hidden letters, damn it. That sounded much more hopeful than bones.

The nattering grandmother on his left—*grandmother*, that was it. He'd wager Mrs. Ingraham was no paid companion but some relation to the illegitimate child chattering on his right. She was going on about laces and uniforms, and he thought he'd take leave of his senses if he did not escape.

Picking up his plate and glass, Hunt stood. Without a word, he carried his meal into the small breakfast parlor with its oval table. He set his dinnerware on the sideboard, ripped off the tablecloth, found the table spacers, and removed them. The boards didn't go easily. He whacked them hard until they shifted, then tore them out, flinging them to the far wall.

By this time, he'd gained the attention of the other diners. Loyal, unquestioning Walker, who understood him better than most, joined him in shoving the table top back together, into a much smaller, more intimate table. In satisfaction, Hunt skipped the cloth he'd flung aside, set his plate on the battered walnut surface, and took a chair.

To Hunt's shame, Oliver crept in, examined the new arrangement disapprovingly, and returned to the main dining room where table linen provided a hiding place. He could hear Clare talking to her nephew as the others carried in their plates to join Hunt, looking puzzled, worried, and otherwise entertained.

"I gather you have something to say?" Arnaud asked, not masking his amusement.

Hunt growled and sipped his brandy, waiting to see who else would brave his ill humor.

Walker, of course. Meera followed warily, leading Lavender and her companion. To Hunt's satisfaction, they left a chair open beside him. Clare turned the table by leading Oliver in by the hand and sitting him in the empty chair, placing a small plate in front of him. Oliver sent Hunt a disgruntled look that probably matched his own, then dug into his potatoes.

Walker and Meera hastily stood up, rearranged their chairs, and added a chair next to Oliver for Clare. She carried in her half-finished meal and settled in without looking at him.

"Rude," she muttered.

"Grumpy," Oliver added.

"Brave," Hunt retorted.

Oliver sent him a wary look, probably trying to determine who was brave. Hunt nodded at the child's plate. "You're eating dragon fodder."

The boy considered the potatoes, nodded, and dug into beans he'd squashed into soup. "Pig swill."

Hunt almost folded up in laughter. Instead, he lifted his glass in toast. "To pig swill."

They all stared as if he'd lost his mind. Perhaps he had. But for one tiny moment of time, he was back in charge and life was almost normal. "Arnaud, what is this about damaged artwork?"

He ignored Clare, who ignored him in return. Fine.

Arnaud wrinkled his broad brow in thought. "I think you may need to find Aunt Gabrielle's diaries to understand what the markings mean. They are both numbers and letters. They were applied after the last painting was done, which was of the viscount as a young man, so presumably any time after that, which was what, the last fifty years? We've only cleaned a couple of paintings, so we don't have all of them yet."

Sound, sensible words that could be processed into action. Plus, the diaries might provide the information he sought without disturbing anyone with his grisly discovery. Hunt nodded approval. "Not the work of vandals or children, then? Sounds like a code. We need to develop a more systematic approach to our search for the diaries."

Unlike his optimistic co-general, he didn't believe the diaries led to jewels. He would just hope it led to a sensible explanation of the medieval cellar's content. Besides, he appreciated an intriguing challenge.

Betsy wandered in, looking bewildered at the rearrangement of tables. She set down a platter with a roll of something sugar-covered. "Will that be all? Shall I clear the. . . other. . . table?"

"Coffee and tea, please," Hunt ordered. "We're taking our drinks in here this evening."

"Spotted Dick," Oliver crowed, shoving aside his beans and potatoes.

Clare pushed his plate back in front of him. "Finish up your pig swill while Betsy fetches plates."

Spotted Dick, good Lord, no wonder the child favored pig swill and dragon fodder. They were mild in comparison. Hunt handed the lad a dinner roll to use for pushing food onto unfamiliar utensils. Oliver knew how to use them. He simply didn't.

"What systematic approach do you suggest?" Walker asked, eyeing the pudding roll and intelligently wincing at the notion of cutting into a *Dick* of any sort.

"We either enlist an army, or tackle one floor and one wing at a time. We've pretty well covered the most obvious, the public floor of the original manor. The new wings are shorter and shouldn't take long. We'll search their ground floors first."

"I doubt your grandmother hid diaries in the billiard room." Clare finally spoke, revealing she'd already explored some portion of the unused, unheated wings. "Unless you think the earl hid a journal."

At least she wasn't questioning him about the mortgage—probably because she'd already surmised he wouldn't be calling for this search if the manor wasn't in debt.

"The men can explore the billiard wing, the women can poke around the sewing room and whatnot in the other wing." Hunt had walked through the dusty, unlit east rooms once and had only the vaguest notion of what was there. "If you think it will help, we can switch later."

She frowned but nodded. "We approach our searches differently, so switching is wise. We might set Oliver to looking at every book in the library for anything handwritten."

The boy was more interested in the clean plates Betsy was setting on the table, signaling it was time for pudding.

"First thing after breakfast then." Trusting he wasn't raising unjustifiable hopes, Hunt sliced off a piece of pudding and placed it on Oliver's plate.

Then he took coffee instead of brandy in anticipation of a clear head in the morning.

WEDNESDAY MORNING, KNOWING THE NEW WINGS HAD NOT BEEN USED IN decades, Clare wore her oldest, darkest gown for searching. She felt like a scullery maid by the time she'd worked her way through Holland covers and months of neglect. Maybe years. The Gaithers might have run dustmops and dusters so the cobwebs did not multiply, but the draperies had not been touched and the carpets were moth-riddled. All the windows needed a good scrubbing. One simply could not abandon a house this long without consequences.

Meera had dirt smeared on her cheek from crawling around baseboards with Oliver. Clare hadn't wanted her friend climbing ladders in her condition. So, Lavender had been the one to look under drapery boxes and in upper cabinets and pound on paneling and mantels. Clare had systematically searched all closets, cabinets, and desks—the interiors of which presumably had not been dusted since the death of the viscountess, maybe longer.

"We should have brought dusters and mops," she said wearily, collapsing on one of the delicate gilded sofas in a ladies' salon. Since the wings were at the back of the manor, they were intended for private use of the family, not public display like the gallery and great hall and formal dining room.

"Then we would never have completed the search today, and we would have run out of clean mops hours ago." Meera took a slender chair by the cold hearth and wiped another dirt smear over her forehead. "I had hoped to find just a sapphire or two, at the very least. Decoding books is too much work."

Which meant either Walker had told her that they needed mortgage money, or she was making the same assumption as Clare. It really shouldn't matter to either of them. They had a home in London. It was just currently an unpleasant place to be. But Lavender and the Lavignes needed a home. And the people in the village needed employment.

Lavender held up some table linen she'd found in a dresser. "I found a lovely damask. Do you think it's too heavy for a gown?"

"It would have to be a dinner gown," Clare said wearily. "It's a lovely fabric, though. I suppose it was used for the ladies' tea table. Did they do tea in hunting lodges? How many ladies would actually have visited here?"

"The viscount and his wife evidently lived here when they first married, but I don't know that tea was popular then. Maybe they had drinking parties," Meera said cynically, examining the fabric Lavender held out for her. "But this is much too light a color for me, for any reason."

They all hid their disappointment at not turning up papers or diaries of any sort, just a few edifying tomes and a French novel. Clare glanced around to ask Oliver what he'd found, but she didn't see him—or Guinevere. "Where's Oliver?"

"Last I saw, he was in the office with the escritoire and the wicker dress form. I found a few scraps of fabric there but nothing large enough for use." Lavender headed for the doorway.

"Do you think she'd know a book if she saw one?" Clare whispered as the girl departed.

"She does seem to be fashion obsessed." Meera put her feet up on a tapestried stool. "Would any of this furniture be worth anything if sold?"

Clare shrugged. "It may have been grand once, but it doesn't appear anyone has redecorated for a century or so. I cannot imagine they did anything more than unload unwanted artifacts from the earl's other houses."

"Might you sell off everything if the bank claims the property?" Meera gazed around with interest. "I've never owned anything quite so fine. I might start my own establishment."

"There's my penny-pinching friend," Clare said with a grin. "We should probably start selling it off now, or we'll drown the market if we do it all at once."

Meera actually nodded as if she were taking the advice seriously. "Some of this appears to be French and might fetch a good price. We would need a wagon. Perhaps we might start a used furniture shop in Birmingham."

Clare wanted to remind her that the funds would go to the heirs and after dividing up would hardly be worth the effort, but Guinevere raced yapping into the room, followed by Lavender and Oliver, looking a trifle excited and bewildered. Conversation halted and they waited expectantly.

"I think Oliver may have found something." They both held slim, moldering tomes that appeared ready for the fire.

TWENTY-ONE

Hunt studied the window seat Oliver had pried open. He was reasonably certain the lock had not been part of the original construction. It was artfully concealed in scrollwork that had been added later, making it look like one solid piece. He'd not have thought to pry it open.

But when you were only three feet tall and crawling, window seats were at eye level. Applying a nutpick to the lock was brilliant. He patted Oliver's shoulder. "Well done, son, well done."

Oddly, both the hiding place and the books exuded the same floral fragrance of the glove they'd located. He ran his finger over a fine layer of dust in the box and held it to his nose. What had Clare called the scent, jasmine? The viscountess must have added sachet powder.

The ladies had already removed the musty tomes from their damp hiding place. An outside wall was not the best place for books. Clare had insisted on lighting the big hearth in the library so she might lay the books in front of it in hopes of drying them out. Meera was concocting some powder to sprinkle between the pages to reduce the stench of mold. She had Lavender cutting herbs to dry in Mrs. Gaither's oven to freshen the paper once the stench was absorbed.

Hunt couldn't read the hen scratching in the volumes, but they were obviously hand-written and dated like diaries. They might simply say "I visited my mother today," but it was more than they had discovered so far. His mother should be thrilled.

He and Oliver searched the east wing from window to window, looking for more seats with locks, finding none. They only found the open ones Clare had already searched, which contained nothing more than moldering pillows and the occasional trinket or gewgaw—no hidden spaces.

"It must be time for lunch." Hunt shrugged on his coat over his dust-smeared linen and steered the boy toward the old hall. "We should wash up first."

By the time they reached the oval table in the breakfast room, the women already had their plates filled and were studying a few of the diaries. No formal dining here. They had taken time to clean up and straighten their hair, but their gowns were still as dusty as his shirt and waistcoat.

"Her writing is atrocious, and it's almost all in French," Clare reported in disgust, cleaning her spectacles. "My French may be as bad as her writing."

Lavender wrinkled her nose. "They smell and makes me sneeze. And my French is not very good."

"I know Latin, not French." Meera closed her book and handed it to Arnaud, who hadn't picked up any of the tomes. He looked at it warily and didn't comment.

"I know French but cannot read the writing." Hunt filled Oliver's plate, then his own. He pointed the boy to the chair at his side so he'd sit at the table instead of under it. "Arnaud, you and Henri are the French experts."

His cousin shrugged, ignoring the book beside him. "I do not wish to invade our aunt's privacy. It seems a sin."

Hunt glared at his cousin. He might argue later, in private, and find out what really bothered him. But Arnaud wasn't an heir dependent on finding jewels to save the manor. Maybe he should confide in his cousin about the skeleton. . . Nah, Arnaud was still stiff and too uncomfortable with his circumstances.

"There may be some English in later volumes. We just started at the beginning." Clare opened to the first page and read the French aloud. "I believe that is saying *This is my diary and no one but me is authorized to read it.*"

"Basic schoolgirl. How old was the viscountess when she married?" Hunt sipped his ale and dug into a cold meat pie.

"If we believe the tapestry, in 1761, when she was only fifteen. This is dated January of that year, and it sounds as if she might have been given a blank book as a gift." Clare flipped to the end. "This last page is July of that year. If I'm reading the scribbles correctly, she is enraptured by the beautiful, golden Englishman."

Arnaud snorted and dug into his food as if starving, which technically, he probably was.

"Should we start with a later date? If you read the difficult passages aloud, I can try to translate." Hunt would rather box them all up, pack his bags, and head home, but he was in over his thick head now. By thinking he was generously offering his family a luxurious home, he'd merely embroiled himself in mysteries and complications. And now he had skeletons to contend with.

"I'm almost afraid of what we'll find," Clare admitted, echoing his dire thoughts. She took the tome Arnaud had abandoned to flip the pages.

Hunt winced. Even if the infant skeleton was medieval, they might discover his grandmother had shot the viscount and fled for France—except the viscount had lived after her departure. Did he really want to know what had driven her to flee? He understood some of Arnaud's reticence.

"If our goal is the jewels, what if we begin with the earl's death?" Meera suggested. "Or when she returns to Wycliffe Manor? Wouldn't that be more appropriate to our search?"

"I like that. The dates don't need much translation so we can all hunt for the ones starting in the 1780s, after the earl died." Satisfied, Clare dug into her food, like the good general she was.

Hunt spent the rest of the meal wondering what it would be like to kiss those smug lips. It was more entertaining than wondering what dire secrets the manor concealed.

THEY SPENT THE AFTERNOON LINING THE DIARIES UP IN ORDER. THEY DISCOVERED the ones from Lady Reid's time in France weren't in the collection. Arnaud was somewhat happier about that. They set the more recent ones closest to the library fire and sprinkled them with Meera's concoctions.

That evening, Clare carried the London volumes from after the earl's death to the blue upstairs salon. Except for Arnaud, even the men gathered to hear her read the entries in her rusty accent. She started where the viscountess planned her eldest daughter's introduction to society.

Unlike any other man she'd known, Hunt listened attentively and translated where needed. Only, after a few pages, they both went silent.

Arnaud had been right not to participate. The diary was incredibly personal and not meant for public consumption.

"She left her home and lover in France after the viscount's death so she might raise her eldest daughter, yet even after all those years, the relationship still seems so very... strained," Meera murmured. "I suppose all mothers and daughters harbor some tension during adolescence, but these sound like royal battles."

"I gather that's the reason Elaine attended boarding school—to avoid her mother." Clare tried to imagine such a hostile relationship, but her own mother had been a passive force in her life.

The volatile viscountess apparently met her match in her haughty eldest daughter, who treated her as if she were the French trash gossip made her out to be. The viscountess unleashed her frustration and tears on the diary's pages. Had she been so temperamental in real life?

Clare sighed unhappily. "Well, when one does not have access to an earl's fortune because of a youthful mistake, it is difficult to provide the luxury expected of their station. All the rest of the earl's grandchildren had grand balls and gowns, but the viscountess had to sell pearls just to pay for a modest wardrobe."

"The part where she replaces the ropes of beautiful pearls with fakes is interesting." Lavender studied the volume Clare had set aside. "She must have had a treasure trove of pearls to sell."

"Skip to the year she left London and moved to Wycliffe Manor," Walker suggested.

"Skipping her triumph at finding a future marquess for Elaine but watching her other daughter sail away? More passion and tears." Clare glanced questioningly to Hunt. "Do you know when your mother left for the Americas?"

He shifted uncomfortably in the wing chair. "Probably around 1783. She married my father here, but they left soon after the wedding, as I understand it."

"So, Lady Reid didn't move into the manor until roughly two years after the earl's death," Clare calculated. "I wonder if staff stayed on or if she arrived to an empty household. I'll have to go down and sort through the other volumes."

She'd changed into a clean gown for dinner. Brushing it down, she rose from her warm, fireside seat to brave the chilly dark.

To her surprise, Hunt rose with her, apparently intent on escorting her downstairs.

"You don't have to do that," she told him. He'd been limping badly again after all their crawling about. "I can take a lamp."

"Let me pretend I'm useful," he said gruffly. "I can carry books."

"So can I," she said dryly but didn't argue more. If nothing else came of this adventure, she had learned that male pride was a beast not easily tamed. She no longer dared ask him about the mortgage, an obvious thorn in his paw.

They both carried lamps to cut through the shadows of the dark corridor. A light gleamed under Arnaud's door. He was an oddity but not her concern, other than trying to feed him, anyway.

At the top of the stairs, Hunt halted and caught her arm. "Do you hear a horse?"

"Henri has returned?" His peddler humor might lighten the heavy atmosphere.

Hunt shook his head. "Too fast for a cart. Fetch Walker while I disturb Arnaud. I want people at the door."

She'd been so absorbed in the manor's mysteries that she'd forgotten the outside world was full of danger. Heart in throat, she lifted her skirts and ran back to the salon while Hunt limped on to Arnaud's room.

At her warning, Walker hurried for the staircase.

Oliver had been put to bed. Clare didn't want to leave him unprotected, but she was dying of curiosity. Who would be out there at this hour? She grabbed a poker from the hearth. Meera seized another of the sturdy iron instruments. Lavender tucked Guinevere under her arm as if she might unleash her to bite ankles.

They eased into the hall. Hunt's lamp swung down the stairs. The door knocker rapped.

"Not a burglar then," Meera whispered in relief.

A burglar might be preferable. He'd get lost in the maze of rooms and probably starve to death before becoming any danger to anyone but himself. Clare tucked that idea aside to pursue later when she sat down to write her new novel. The manor really was an inspiration.

Below, Hunt and Walker stopped at the study, presumably to retrieve their pistols. That made her hesitate. She considered fleeing, but surely, the weapons were just a precaution?

Arnaud waited in front of the vestibule, holding what appeared to be a fire iron from his own room. Once the men were gathered, they vanished through the massive door that cut off the entrance from the hall.

Clare thought evil thoughts about that horrible entry preventing her from seeing or hearing anything inside the house. And then she realized a back-up army could guard the inner doors. She dashed down the stairs to position herself. Meera and Lavender joined her, clutching their chosen weapons. Clare almost giggled at the sight they made.

The voices from the vestibule were muffled, but one sounded louder and angrier than the others.

"Jacob!" Meera gasped in horror. Without further warning, she hefted her fire iron and flung open the double doors.

"Oh dear." Clare hesitated. With three large men in there, Jacob wasn't a danger to anyone except himself. But they had pistols. . . She shuddered in terror and glanced longingly back to the safety of the stairs.

She couldn't abandon Meera. Gritting her teeth, she turned to Lavender. "Go upstairs and keep an eye on Oliver, will you please? This is a domestic issue. The rest of us are in no danger."

Wide-eyed, Lavender glanced at the entry, at Clare's still upraised weapon, and then back to the stairs. "It's dark," she whispered.

"Take my lamp." Once she handed it over, Clare steeled her shaky nerves and slipped into the chilly entry like a shadow.

The vestibule was lit only by Hunt's lantern. Still, it wasn't difficult to discern the occupants. Meera ranted like a fishwife, spewing creative obscenities and waving her long tongs. The three men stood guard, their size alone an intimidation. Why didn't they fling Jacob out the door?

Because Jacob was pointing a pistol at Meera.

Jacob had a *pistol*! Large men. Dangerous weapons. Enclosed space.

Clare struggled with the irrational images rising in her head. *Men. Weapons. Explosions. Blood.* . . Hysteria compressed her lungs, and she fought to breathe.

Apparently sensing her struggle, Hunt pulled her protectively against him. She wanted to protest but instead, buried her face in the familiar scent of his coat and fought her inner demons. She knew he had a pistol under that coat, which frightened her more.

Physically, Jacob wasn't intimidating, but his was the only weapon visible. He waved it menacingly. "A wife belongs with her husband!" he shouted. "Fetch your things. We're going home."

Apparently, Jacob counted on the lie convincing others that he had the right to order his spouse about. Legally, if they'd been married, he had every right to force her home.

Too furious to be rational, Meera shouted, "I am not your bloody wife you maggot-pated, caw-handed cod's head! You will be fortunate to escape with both your balls!" She jabbed her tongs at his lower regions.

Jacob darted back, leaving Meera to stumble and right herself. Apparently conscious he had only one shot against five people, he held his pistol only on Meera. "You're hysterical. If I shoot you now, I have witnesses that it's self defense. Now fetch your bags, and we'll not bother these fine folk more."

That jarred Clare back to rationality. Jacob must be under the mistaken impression that these *fine folk* didn't care what happened to Meera.

Shuddering but too appalled to abandon her best friend, Clare forced herself to speak sensibly. "You would have her ride pillion all the way to London?"

Meera had not announced her condition. Clare couldn't mention how riding pillion would be dangerous to the babe. Perhaps that was his intent. Despite that shocking thought, she didn't dare swing her weapon while Jacob's pistol was focused on Meera. She was frozen in the protective shelter of Hunt's arm—

Until Jacob gripped Meera's arm and flung her weapon aside.

Flashing images of being seized and tossed while screams and blood choked her senses. . .

She'd frozen then, but this time, rage rose up to heat her. While caring, healing Meera stumbled at the hands of a mad toad, Clare abandoned Hunt's side and swung her poker.

As if waiting for that move, Hunt wrapped his big fist around her weapon, adding force and direction. With his strength, the iron struck Jacob's elbow so hard he staggered and his arm flew up. His pistol fired, shooting the ceiling, scattering chittering bats out the broken transom.

Clare shrieked, but rather than cower, she dropped to her knees to hover over Meera, watching in fear as Arnaud grabbed the empty pistol.

Disarmed, Jacob bent double and clutched his elbow in agony. "You broke my arm!"

"Better that than your testicles, one assumes?" Calmly, Hunt flung open the front door.

With grim satisfaction, Walker grabbed Jacob by the back of his coat and booted him out. Holding the lantern and appearing vaguely bemused, Arnaud slammed and bolted the door.

Clare almost collapsed in relief.

Meera was the one who fainted.

TWENTY-TWO

Waking the next morning, Meera grimaced at the sight of Clare in the chair at her bedside. "You did not need to lose sleep over me."

Clare handed her a glass of water. "I added the powders you've been taking. Is that all right?"

"They're just to give me extra strength." She sipped obediently, hiding her utter humiliation. The household now knew she was a fallen woman and a harpy of the worst sort.

"Everyone has stopped to check on you. We're keeping your breakfast warm. Shall I ask Marie to bring it up?" Clare didn't leave her chair but watched Meera swallow her concoction.

"Can I sneak to the cellar and never come out again?" she asked bitterly.

"Punish you because Jacob is insane? Why?" Clare asked in genuine puzzlement.

"Well, I'm the one who didn't realize he was insane. Although he's not really. He's unbalanced by greed and selfishness. But not realizing his character shows how stupid I am. And then, last night. . . I behaved horribly."

"You didn't shoot him. That might have been a mistake," Clare said thoughtfully.

Meera giggled, then started to cry. Hastily, she wiped her eyes. "I was enjoying the company of people who treated me like a genuine lady. I have ruined it all."

"Do you think they'd all be asking after your health if they no longer respected you? I, for one, am exceedingly impressed by your vulgar vocabulary, but that's neither here nor there." Clare waved a slender hand. "Walker seems unusually concerned. You should probably talk to him."

"Walker?" Her pulse increased. Stupid hearts, they had no brains.

"Imperturbable Walker is extremely perturbed. He's been by several times." Clare stood. "Let me help you dress. Then you shall languish in front of the fire in the blue salon while I summon your breakfast and tea. I will send him up with it."

"Don't you dare!" Meera protested in alarm.

"I dare. And then, you will help me build a list of those entertaining epithets so I may find ways of using them." Clare opened the wardrobe and pulled out Meera's only good gown. "You and Walker are useless at reading the diaries anyway. Keep him busy while I work with Hunt."

Man-shy Clare and the formidable captain? Intrigued, Meera dragged herself from her bed of humiliation. Talking to Walker. . . That remained to be seen. First, she needed to hide her formula book, as the viscountess had hidden her diaries.

Jacob would return, and he was mad enough to bring reinforcements.

HUNT RODE OUT BEFORE BREAKFAST TO BE CERTAIN THE THREATENING JACKASS from last night wasn't lying in wait on the grounds. The spring day was brisk but sunny, and it felt almost normal to be out and about again. A man could get used to riding his own property, overseeing its welfare.

But the property wouldn't be his after December, so he tried not to indulge fantasies of ownership. He needed to learn what he could and could not do with one eye and a bum knee.

He hadn't dared aim his pistol last night for fear he'd miss the intruder and hit others.

It was becoming increasingly obvious that his eye would not recover. That was probably the reason he was indulging his eccentric *family's* search for jewels that did not exist.

Although they *had* turned up the diaries. For that, his mother would be grateful, so he could be generous in giving his vastly available time. From the sounds of it, his volatile grandmother would never have entered an abandoned cellar, so he had no hope of solving the skeleton's mystery. He suspected it was the remains of the old priory crypt down there. The bones could be medieval, for all he knew.

Once he'd decided Jacob was gone, he returned, curried the horse, and let himself in the side door to the mouth-watering scent of bacon. He ought to change out of his riding clothes, but he hated wasting his knee on climbing stairs for the sake of propriety.

And after last night, what exactly was propriety? He'd thought English ladies were polite, genteel creatures who would faint at such an exhibition. . . Well, Meera *had* fainted, but he suspected it hadn't been from an excess of terror.

Apparently, he was late to the repast. Only Arnaud lingered, finishing his coffee. His cousin had insisted on teaching the cook how to brew it properly —or perhaps one of the maids had learned. For that, Hunt was grateful.

"After seeing us in action, do you miss your noble family?" Hunt asked, emptying the remains of the breakfast platters on his plate. Mrs. G might be a plain cook, but she provided bountifully.

Arnaud snorted. "What is left of them tear at each other's throats over politics and money. Last night was no comparison. There is something to be said for a hermit's life."

"Boring. Is that what you will do if we cannot keep this place, become a hermit?" Hunt nudged his cousin into considering the future.

"Then there is a chance that you will lose it?" Arnaud asked cautiously.

"Unless we can catch the bank in fraud or Clare finds jewels, conceivably, yes. It's hard to imagine earning enough income painting buttons to pay what is owed." There, he'd said it. Hunt stretched his legs beneath the table. "I'd like to see a cottage industry develop, if only for the sake of the village, but it won't help the manor."

"You have yet to meet the other heirs. Might they help?"

Hunt shrugged. "They do not seem much interested. I'd like to work on the gas lighting, but not if I'm improving the place for the comfort of an encroaching slug."

Arnaud nodded thoughtfully. "And you think my great-aunt's diaries might lead us to a fortune?"

"Actually, no. If Grandmother Gabrielle knew how to find the earl's fortune, she wouldn't have sold her pearls. But I would like to understand her thinking in giving up her one valuable asset to preserve an isolated manor her children were unlikely to appreciate."

"You're enjoying the mystery," his cousin accused.

"I am. I hate helplessly rusticating. This gives me a challenge without ruining my knee. I understand if you prefer your own sort of work."

"My own work is out of reach. For a brief time in my youth, after

Napoleon's coup d'état, I owned a gallery in Paris. I was part of a community of artists. I hid my aristocratic heritage. For that brief moment, I was happy. But then, the Treaty of Amiens was broken, and I was old enough to be conscripted. I had to choose joining Napoleon's army or to oppose him. I chose to oppose. The British won, but I lost everything. There is nothing left for me. And now, we are at war again."

Hunt heard the desolation in his cousin's voice. "You did not lose. Napoleon was defeated and will be again. You were part of that first victory. Someday, it will be safe to return. Perhaps you can rebuild your reputation here. I'm not sure I can save the manor on my own."

Hunt hated admitting helplessness. He didn't know when he'd decided to keep the manor out of the bank's hands. He'd been telling himself it wasn't his concern. But it was. People were relying on him. He possessed knowledge others didn't. He doubted engineering was applicable, but if there were any chance. . . Or maybe, like Clare, he simply wanted to solve the mysteries.

Arnaud finished his coffee and wrinkled his brow. "You ask me to trade my warring French relations for your slightly mad English ones, an interesting exchange."

"I am family. Henri is family, and he appears to be willing to stay. None of these others are blood relations, but can't friends be family too?"

"I thought my artist friends were family. I don't know who to trust any longer. Perhaps, if I help you with your mystery, I will learn who here has the interests of all in mind and might be trusted. I can try uncovering the code in the painting if that might help."

"Only you can clean that artwork. That would be of tremendous help. What about the abominable oils in the foyer? Do you need to look at those too?"

"Perhaps all the paintings should be examined." Arnaud stood and pushed his chair in. "I believe your lady is already in the library." He left the room with a jaunty step.

His *lady.* Hunt didn't have a lady. He had a co-general with the instincts of a rat terrier.

He'd almost laughed aloud last night when the lady terrified of her own shadow tore after an armed interloper with a fire iron. Her swing would have bounced right off the man and probably got her shot. He doubted she'd given that an ounce of consideration. Her friend had come before her safety.

Hunt wagered Clare could be trusted. He just couldn't trust her to think the same way he did.

~

"YOUR GRANDMOTHER GABRIELLE DID HER BEST TO USE THE MAINTENANCE funds to provide for the village." Too aware that she was alone with a brooding, hulking beast, Clare set aside the volume she'd finished and reached for the next. "I suppose that is why the draperies are excellent, but the carpets are tattered or gone entirely. The village had seamstresses but no carpet weaver."

Last night had been a revelation. *The beast had helped Meera.* She knew now that the captain wasn't a danger, that he actually might be. . . Well, *helpful* was probably too strong a word. Allowing her to bury her face in his coat had not been useful, except to quell her panic. Adding his weight to her weapon had been presumptuous—but effective.

Refusing to sit on the library floor with her to move the diaries around in front of the fire, Hunt stretched his legs from a chair and waited for her to choose the next one. "Judging by these books, my grandmother was furious with the earl, to the point of inarticulate. I fancy she wasn't quite so parsimonious with words when speaking aloud. She seems a bit volatile." He sipped from his coffee cup that another new maid had delivered.

The servants were finding their way back. Clare left them to Mrs. Gaither to delegate. The surly housekeeper knew better what was needed.

"Do you think Lady Reid feared someone was reading her diaries?" she picked up the next one. "So, she only wrote what she didn't mind being read?"

"To what purpose? To justify her existence to people who didn't seem to care? You are looking for a way to give up on the diaries, aren't you?"

Clare pursed her lips and considered that. "You are right that if she knew where the jewels were, she'd have paid her debts and probably returned to London. I just can't help thinking she knew the answers to mysteries."

"That would probably mean starting at the beginning. What happened to send her to France?"

"She was only what? Not even twenty? A lover's tiff. I can imagine a great deal more, but people are basically simple. They aren't complicated melodramas."

"Last night wasn't melodrama? I suspect my hot-blooded grandmother would have approved of your dramatic friend. Your Mrs. Abrams hides a passionate nature behind her scientific mind."

Clare had spent the night consoling Meera until she'd finally slept. Such heartbreak ought to be avoided, she supposed. "It is human nature to wish to be loved. Not many of us enjoy loneliness. Complications set in, however, when we reach out and mix our lives with others." She gazed pensively at the slender book she'd opened. "Perhaps the viscountess came to the manor to sort out her complications."

"You're overthinking. She had run out of money. Her daughters were gone. Her relationships in London didn't appear to be any steadier than in her youth. She fled to her only remaining home, where her expenses were minimal. We may never know my grandmother's story. Some day, I'd like to hear Meera's, though."

"Well, it's hers to tell, not mine. But she's been a good friend since Oliver and I returned from Egypt to find my mother bedridden. I'm not sure how we would have fared without her." Clare chose the next volume and skimmed the entries. If nothing else, her meager French was improving.

"You were in Egypt?" He sounded impressed. "Is that how a lady learns to fight with fire irons?"

"We hardly needed fires there," she said dryly. "It was hotter than Hades. But when one lives alone, it's necessary to consider the weapons at hand. Thank goodness I've not needed them in London."

"Egypt is more interesting than my grandmother's histrionics. Tell me about Egypt." He actually picked up one of the earlier books and carried it to the library table to squint at through his lamp magnifier.

Clare shook her head, but if story-telling was what it took to hold his interest. . . "Egypt was hot and crowded. I played nanny for an infant while my sister and her husband robbed graves. Or tried to, I assume. I was only twenty and overwhelmed."

"I take it grave robbing did not pay off." He flipped pages slowly.

"No, it was deadly. Some madman blew up the bazaar and killed my sister and everyone around her. I only survived because I'd lingered to haggle over a shawl." A shawl she had burned because of the blood spatters. "My brother-in-law put Oliver and me on a ship and sent us home. Fortunately, as it turned out. He died of malaria and dysentery not long after."

Apparently hearing the pain in her voice, he gingerly set himself amid the books on the floor with her. "I am sorry. I should not have asked. No wonder you are so brave."

His solid presence allowed her to recall all the loneliness and fear of enduring those deaths. She vehemently shook her head. "I am not brave. I'm an utter coward who lives in constant fear. I came here hoping to find guardian angels or mighty knights to make me feel safe again."

She caught her breath on a sob, trying not to reveal the gaping emptiness that admission caused.

Siting beside her, Hunt drew her under his arm again. "And you found only a crippled soldier and a bookworm. I'm doubly sorry."

She laughed and sobbed into his broad shoulder. "A fierce dragon with one eye and an honest steward. I probably would have got Meera shot last night had you not been there."

She'd had nightmares every time she'd drifted off last night. She'd spent most of the night reassuring herself that Meera still breathed.

"You did not flee danger but armed yourself and ran to the rescue. You are a brave sorceress."

To her amazement, Hunt gathered her in his arms and proceeded to kiss away her protest.

TWENTY-THREE

Kissing was far more satisfying than squinting at musty, smelly pages of written histrionics, Hunt decided. Clare was obviously inexperienced but enthusiastic. Sitting amid books, holding her in his arms, he felt a hundred-ten percent better already. Perhaps it was the ancient sachet scenting the air and making him giddy as a horny adolescent.

Before he could do anything stupid that might scare her off, Oliver and the dog-mop slammed into the room, shouting and yapping excitedly.

"Carriages! Carriages on the drive!" They ran out again, hallooing and barking.

"Oh, my." Pushing away, blushing, Clare hastily straightened her gown. "I'd better make myself presentable."

Hunt could have told her that kiss-plumped lips and sparkling eyes made her beautiful, but she'd probably remember to slap him. He awkwardly pried himself off the floor using a chair as a crutch and held out his hand to assist her in standing.

"Carriages might mean family?" he asked, to drive away any tears.

"Consider which of them know the way here without asking." Cheeks pink, she raced out.

If it was the smirking banker, Hunt would meet him at the door with a musket. Hard to miss with a musket.

He had one loaded and concealed behind the lion statue in the entry by the time the carriages arrived.

To his utter astonishment, Gaither bumbled from his hiding place in the kitchen to open the door. He even wore a facsimile of a butler's uniform, although the shirt was rumpled and the tie askew. Was that a pistol underneath his shiny, tailed coat? Fine, let the butler answer the door.

Hunt retreated to his study, where he loaded a fowling piece.

Walker caught him doing it and raised a questioning brow. "Is this how you greet family?"

"You don't find it suspicious that they arrive, unannounced, after last night's drama?" Hunt added shells to the desk drawer.

Walker primed his pistol. "If cockroaches stick together, you may be right. But from all Meera has told me, last night's vermin is little more than a leech."

Interesting. Hunt didn't have time to ask what Walker had learned. The knocker sounded. The dog mop raced for the entry, yapping. Hunt took his seat behind the desk and wished it wasn't too early for whiskey.

Oliver crept in. "Gaither won't let them in," he whispered. "He says we're not at home."

"Oh, jolly fun, more melodrama." Walker said in a plummy fake British accent.

Hunt chuckled. "I'm beginning to enjoy the farce." He turned to Oliver. "Tell your aunt. Ask what we should do."

Oliver grinned. "She said to prepare your weapons and call for tea."

"That means she's taking the front lines?" Hunt didn't like the idea, but people in carriages generally did not shoot ladies.

Would butlers shoot ladies?

"Clare is saving us eccentric Americans for shock value," Walker concluded.

"Melodrama. Put a stack of ledgers on the desk as if we're actually working. Sometimes, one must lure the enemy out of their positions." He wasn't certain when unannounced visitors had become the enemy, but he was no longer green enough to believe anyone arrived without ulterior motives.

They heard Clare's crystal-clear, aristocratic tones—a good sign that she'd won the battle with Gaither. Unsurprisingly, she did not lead their guests into the study.

Smelling of cheap gin, Gaither arrived with the silver salver and a decidedly dour expression. Hunt studied the cards presented, then checked the tapestry. *Lady Lavinia*—Lavender's grandmother?

And *Lady Spalding*, his mother's sister, his Aunt Elaine! She was about to become more than a name in a diary.

He was not ready for this. He picked up the other two cards—the banker Benedict Bosworth Jr. and. . . Bosworth *Sr*. His father? The one too weak to ride out here? *Jolly fun* didn't cover it.

"Can we tell them I'm out riding the grounds and unavailable?" Hunt itched to tuck a pistol in his pocket before leaving the study but assumed that was uncivilized, not to mention dangerous to his private parts.

"I tried, sir," Gaither said mournfully. "They insist on waiting. Miss Knightley took them into the great hall."

Great hall. Hunt snorted. An enormous drafty two-story vault with scattered sofas, chairs, tables, and the world's ugliest landscapes. He should ask Arnaud to check for codes in those paintings as well. His cousin was probably hiding in the gallery to avoid their visitors. Where was Lavender?

He no longer needed a cane to push from his chair, but he debated carrying one anyway. Smacking ladies with it would probably be frowned upon, though, and the weaselly banker would no doubt flee if Hunt so much as snarled. He left the cane behind.

Walker chuckled and settled in with a good ledger. "I'll stay close and listen for screams."

Hunt flung a book at him—and missed.

The medieval hall was a freezing chamber where old furniture went to die. It had no rational purpose other than to chill the bones. Clare hadn't called for a fire, so he assumed she had reservations about their visitors. Strange how he understood the mind of his co-general, as if she were an officer who'd learned his tactics. She'd certainly learned his kisses.

That gave him a measure of satisfaction when he entered the chamber and the visitors studied his scarred visage with barely concealed horror.

Hunt had despised feeling inadequate in these sorts of encounters before Clare arrived. She had reminded him the British aristocracy was just as fallible as he was. He might be half blind and crippled, but he was still in charge. And a lovely, perceptive woman had enjoyed kissing him.

That understanding allowed him to appreciate the drama and study the visitors in return. Two elegant ladies still sensibly wrapped in fashionable coats and bonnets sat on a gold striped sofa. An elderly, fragile man with a ring of white hair and freckled head slumped in one of the delicate wing chairs. The smarmy banker stalked up and down, examining the artwork. Cockroach. He should have punched him out a window when he'd met him in Stratford last time. English fair, slightly paunchy, and not over-tall, the dandy wore a tailed coat that probably cost more than Hunt owned.

Clare had changed into one of her frilly gowns, one in blue to match her eyes, and curled a few blond ringlets at her temples. She'd taken a sofa with a shin-bumping table as shield instead of the comfortable chair beside the hearth. Battle lines drawn, Hunt concluded.

Lavender was conspicuously absent.

This was not his sort of battlefield, but he wielded the only weapons he had—knowledge and a complete disdain for titles. He bowed to the ladies. "Aunt Elaine, it is a pleasure to meet you at last." He assumed the middle-aged, matronly woman with faded blond hair and jowls to be his mother's marchioness sister, although they looked nothing alike. Had he lived, the viscount might have looked like his daughter.

"And Lady Lavinia—I assume my mother's aunt?" Slender, gray-haired, with a large mole on her upper lip, the baroness sat so erect, he had to assume her corset strings held her up.

Both women pursed their lips as if tasting something sour, but they didn't correct him.

Clare stepped in. "Ladies, may I present Captain Alistair Huntley, late of the U.S. Army, grandson of Lady Reid. He is responsible for reminding us of the existence of the family manor."

"Bosworth told us the place was a waste of coin and, with no male heir, only a burden." The marchioness frowned—at the world in general, presumably.

Hunt bowed again and took a sturdy wing chair near Clare's. "Did he now? Bosworth, what have you to say to that?"

"It is a burden and there is no male heir," the banker repeated, resentfully.

"That is not what the papers the estate solicitors sent me say. Perhaps you should have brought them with you," Hunt suggested with a smirk. Until he learned what this was about, he'd try not to antagonize—too badly.

One of the new maids carried in a tea tray. The contents rattled nervously as she set it down on a table before Clare—ah, so that was why she had chosen that position. She controlled the provisions.

"We are so very glad you are here." Clare didn't precisely purr, but the tone was nearly as false as his own. Hunt decided to let the ladies lead the front while he watched from behind the lines, prepared to order cannon as needed.

"We are on our way to London." His aunt, the marchioness, was a hefty woman he knew to be in her fifties. Hunt could imagine her in the towering wig and panniers of her youth. Her travel coat concealed her garments, but he assumed she would not fare as well in the current frail designs.

"Yes, the city will be filling up." Clare handed around the cups as if she were the marchioness. "I thought my nephew might prefer the country to the crowds, so we've leased our home for the Season."

"Your nephew?" the stiff Lady Lavinia abruptly aroused to the conversation. She had to be in her eighties, if Hunt recollected rightly—probably the same age as the elderly banker who seemed to have nodded off.

"Oliver Owen, my sister Beatrice's son. We lost her and her husband much too early. Our family has known its share of losses, has it not?"

"My son might have been earl if it had not been for the harlot." With the privilege of age, Lady Lavinia practically spat in her teacup, which trembled in her frail fingers. "I will not countenance her bastard living in my father's house!"

Clare's personal invitations had mentioned Lavender. Now he understood the reason for their visit. No luggage, so they obviously didn't intend an extended stay.

And he might not know all the rules, but he was fairly certain earldoms did not pass through the female line without special dispensation. His great aunt's wits might be to let. Was Bosworth taking advantage of her?

"You refer to your granddaughter, Lavender?" Still maintaining her coolest tones, Clare picked up a teacake with unconcern. "She's a lovely child, talented, quick-witted. I suppose sending her to a boarding school for young ladies was a waste though, if you didn't intend to acknowledge her. She's still young enough to learn a respectable trade."

Both women nearly hissed.

Deciding this wasn't melodrama but a catfight, Hunt focused on the pacing banker. "Would you gentlemen prefer to talk in my study?"

Bosworth bowed to the ladies. "Forgive him. As you can tell, he's an uncouth American. Would you prefer that we conduct our business elsewhere?"

Gaither appeared as if he'd been listening in the hall. The butler held open the door and bowed. "A fire has been laid in the study, sir."

Hunt hated leaving Clare with the old witches, but she seemed better prepared to handle them than he. He pushed himself out of his chair and gestured for the bankers to follow Gaither.

As soon as they stepped into the wide corridor, Gaither turned around, pistol in hand, and aimed at the younger Bosworth. "I'll not let the likes of you rob me and mine again."

Before Hunt could react, the weapon fired—and *Gaither* fell. Bosworth shrieked like a little girl.

161

TWENTY-FOUR

Serenity blasted by the echoing detonation in the midst of her polite tea party, Clare rushed to the door and swallowed her scream. She took in the shattered porcelain vase by the stairway and Gaither's flattened form and forced herself into Hunt's commanding officer mode.

As far as she could tell, no one was bleeding. That was a good start. What had happened? Someone had shot a vase. Had they shot the butler too? The pistol was in Gaither's hand, and there was no blood. This made no sense.

Under the captain's orders, the men carried an unconscious but still breathing Gaither to the back room with the trundle bed. Not needing prompting, Meera rushed to the kitchen cellar to find the housekeeper and prepare calming concoctions, which left Clare with hysterical ladies and vanishing maids.

Locating a terrified Lavender lurking in the family parlor, she enlisted her aid. "Pretend you're my younger sister, if you must, but I need your help. I'll settle the old tabbies in rooms upstairs, if you'll find a maid and order up hot water and tea and fires. You know what to do."

"Aye, aye, captain," Lavender said warily. "I'll make a good housekeeper someday."

"You can do better than that. Today, you're hostess of an earl's manor, and you're entertaining a marchioness and a baroness."

"A grandmother and a witch, understood." She sailed off to order about whichever maid could be found.

162

Leading the wide-eyed Lady Lavinia and Lady Spalding upstairs, Clare thought the loud men gathering in the study needed calming more than these stalwart old ladies.

She swallowed hard when she saw even Arnaud joining Hunt to face the justifiably shaken bankers. They all had weapons, it seemed, which terrified her beyond measure.

As she located clean rooms and deposited her guests in them, the shouting in the study below reached wall-shaking. She shivered in fear that more shooting would ensue. Instinct screamed to run but ushering family out of harm's way prevented hysterics.

After last night's episode with Jacob, she'd best learn to deal with firearms or retire to her room and never come out.

Why had Gaither shot the ugly vase with the branch bouquet? Meera had mentioned an apoplexy before she ran off to find Mrs. Gaither. Did apoplexies lead one to shoot vases?

Still, Clare had heard the butler's shout. What had he meant that he wouldn't *let the likes of you rob him again*? One assumed he meant the bankers?

Meera would find out what she could from the housekeeper. That left Clare to calm her nerves by confronting relations who had never acknowledged her existence. Her mother's toplofty aunts and cousins certainly hadn't been there for her funeral or to offer support when Clare and Oliver were left alone in the world.

The haughtily erect Lady Lavinia, the late earl's daughter, would be of an age with Gaither. She'd have the most knowledge. Arriving with smelling salts, plus a rosemary pomander to refresh the room where she'd deposited the baroness, Clare tapped at the door, then let herself in without waiting for an invitation.

Lavender must have found a maid. The slender, gray-haired old lady in a pompadour from another era was sitting upright in a chair by the fire, sipping tea. It appeared smelling salts were unnecessary.

This woman with the mole on her lip was her great aunt, her grandmother's older sister. Clare vaguely recalled that she'd married late in life. She'd like to believe, under the gruff exterior, the baroness might be a stiff but loving mother—except the baroness had thrown out her granddaughter as if she were an unwanted puppy.

"Do you have a maid or anyone nearby we can send for, my lady?" Clare laid the pomander on a table and threw a few pinecones on the fire to freshen the musty air of the unused room.

"We left them behind. We had only planned a brief visit." She lifted a gnarled hand in dismissal. "That girl who brought the tea is not your sister, is she?"

"Lavender?" Well, the lady was not stupid. The girl must have been curious or couldn't find a maid. "I'm thinking of adopting her as the little sister I've never had. As I said, she's clever, in her own way, and she does have all the family traits."

The haughty baroness scowled into her tea.

This might be her only chance to discover the manor's secrets. As long as she was pretending she was in charge, she may as well be bold. She took the chair across the hearth. "Did you ever live here?"

Surprised by that conversational leap, the baroness studied her over her cup. "This was the first earl's home, mid-sixteenth century, I believe. Drafty, old-fashioned place. By my father's generation, the estate had much more comfortable manors. We visited here as children, of course. I was only a little girl, but my brother was older and liked to hunt and fish. Reid died too young. As you said earlier, our family has more than our share of losses."

"Our family curiosity often does kill the cat, as was my sister's case. How did Lord Reid die? I know nothing of the family tales." Clare poked idly at the fire, stirring the flames, trying not to look too interested.

"Drowned, I was told. He was only four years older than me, but we were never close. Our father spoiled him, I suppose, so our mother spoiled us girls. Why do you ask?" The old lady looked weary.

Strange to think of Hunt's late grandfather as older than this woman had he lived. They'd been reading about the viscount in his youth, and he was young in her mind. Clare gestured carelessly. "I like a good mystery, and it seemed strange that this place was left abandoned. After all, Wycliffe lived here for quite a while, as well as Lady Reid. And then suddenly. . . no one. And now Gaither acting so strangely. . . I possess my fair share of the family curiosity."

Lady Lavinia narrowed her wrinkled eyes. "The only mystery is why an American impostor is inviting us to take on the burden of this horrible old hall."

"The captain is not an impostor. He makes no claim to be one of us, except by law. He is the one who has been forthright and honest, not the solicitors, not the bankers. I had my own solicitors read the earl's will, and they have concluded that it was written to include even Hunt as heir, since he is a legal descendent through marriage. Your father apparently had parliament pass a special dispensation to allow female descendants to inherit. That means the women of the family own a share of the property outright, not through husbands or a trust. *Ours.* I found it interesting that the solicitors kept us from knowing this all these years."

The old lady closed her eyes and leaned back in the chair. "I am tired. Have my driver go back for my maid and boxes. I don't think I can make that journey again today."

Clare stood and bobbed a curtsy, even though it couldn't be seen. "He may not be back by nightfall. I'll have Lavender look for nightclothes. A maid will come up later to ask your preference for dinner, although I fear our cook is currently distraught."

The baroness grimaced, so she heard. Clare slipped out to confront the next obstacle occupying the room next door. It was a good thing Mrs. Gaither kept these chambers clean.

Lavender peered anxiously from her room as Clare emerged. "What did she say?"

"Nothing of use. Even if she pretends otherwise, she knows who you are, though. We haven't fooled her." She listened for shouting, but it had died down. "Have the men killed each other? Do we need to look?"

"The bankers stormed out, vowing to call a magistrate. Will they put Gaither in gaol?" The girl emerged reluctantly, glancing at her grandmother's door as if Lady Lavinia might open it and breathe fire now that she knew her embarrassment of an illegitimate granddaughter was here.

"I cannot imagine any prison will wish to care for an unconscious man. Let us worry about the moment. The ladies are apparently staying. They'll need nightclothes. I need to send someone out to their driver and ask him to ride back for their boxes and maids, but he'll never return before tonight."

Clare glanced at the marchioness's door. "Although perhaps I need to see if Lady Spalding is in agreement. Perhaps she'll wish to go back with her driver."

"I have all the clothes I've found in my room. I'll sort through them. Communicating with the servants is difficult with no housekeeper or butler. I'll speak to the driver myself." Frowning, Lavender took off down the stairs.

Wondering if the child was auditioning to be housekeeper in Mrs. Gaither's place, Clare threw back her shoulders and dared the she-dragon's lair. As with Lady Lavinia, she merely knocked and let herself in. She was growing bolder by the minute. Rage did that, she was learning.

She hadn't realized she was angry until she confronted the actuality of a family who might have come to her aid over all the terrible years and hadn't.

Lady Lavinia was *her* great-aunt, too, and she assumed Lady Spalding was her mother's cousin.

She had a whole spectrum of relations who had disappeared because her father had dared to dabble in trade and finance.

The disagreeable marchioness, whose society debut may have bankrupted Lady Reid, was much broader than her elderly aunt. Her jowls and heavy lids hid much of her prior beauty, but her resemblance to the earl's family was clear.

The lady had divested herself of her traveling cloak to reveal a wide-skirted, gray traveling gown of good broadcloth but of some age. Like her aunt, she sat warming herself by the fire.

She glared at Clare. "What do you want?"

Clare had survived Hunt's much blacker, one-eyed glare without shriveling into dust. "Lady Lavinia has requested to stay the night. Before we send your driver back for maids and trunks, do you wish to return with him?"

The marchioness glanced at the darkening window. "I don't wish to kill the old lady. I'll stay. We'll have to share your maid."

The one she didn't have. With evil intent, Clare pulled a chair closer to the fire and sat down. "I have a few questions."

Lady Spalding's glare grew blacker. "Have you not caused enough trouble?"

"I wasn't the one who brought the bankers. Do you have any notion why Gaither would try to shoot one, which is what I assume happened?" Clare tugged her shawl tighter, shivering at her own temerity. "I am the stranger here. I did not even know you or this place existed until I received the captain's invitation."

"I don't know why my grandfather didn't sell it instead of his other much prettier properties." Turning away from Clare, Hunt's aunt set her feet closer to the fire. "Although I suppose leaving the Norfolk estate for my dowry was better than leaving me this moldering manse. I was told my parents lived here when I was very young, but I don't remember it."

"We've been studying the tapestry your mother created. You were only five when your father died, so I don't imagine you have many memories of him at all." Clare tried obliquely approaching the topic. "I was fifteen when my father died, and it was a horrible shock to learn one could lose a parent."

The marchioness made a moue of distaste. "I scarcely knew my father. My first memories are of my nanny and the London townhouse where I grew up, but he was seldom there. When he died, the house was draped all in black, and it was dismal until my mother returned." She gestured at the room. "This place, no. I was too young."

"Lady Lavinia says the viscount drowned. That sounds as if he must have been here when he died, unless he fell into the Thames. We're surrounded by so much tragedy. One wonders if the place might be haunted if the earl and your mother died here as well." Clare had never used her spoken words as she did her written ones, but spinning tales came naturally, she discovered.

"Which is why the place ought to be sold," the marchioness said dismissively. "I cannot imagine why it has not been."

"Because the earl gave it to *all* of his family, to be shared. We're not even sure how many of us there are. Captain Huntley has been attempting to find out, but he's not receiving much response." That sounded good, even to Clare. "It can't be sold without everyone's approval."

"Hmpf. I suppose that means the American wants to keep it. But the bastard chit isn't a legal heir. She doesn't have a vote. If we offer the American a sum, will he go away and let us sell it?" She reached down for a carpet bag and pulled out knitting needles.

"Oh, quite possibly. He only came because he smelled a rat, I think, and he'd been invalided by the war and could do nothing else until he healed." Clare needed to keep that firmly in mind when the dratted man spun her head in kisses. "That Gaither shot at the bankers worries me greatly. Now I wonder what is being hidden by the bankers and solicitors who did not tell us everything."

Lady Spalding turned her glare on the snarl of knitting. "My stepson, the current marquess, had his solicitors look into it. They say the will is unusual but verified that it's legal. Other than that, I know nothing. My mother was little more than a French doxie, not to be trusted, but she merely owned a life estate in this property. The London townhouse was put in trust for her since it was purchased with her dowry, as I understand it. She sold it and retired here after my sister married and sailed away. I never visited. For all I know, she had an affair with the bankers."

"Possibly the younger one," Clare said in amusement. "If I understand the family tree, she died fifteen years ago, at the age of fifty-four. Bosworth would have been what, in his thirties then? I suppose it's possible, but not likely."

The marchioness snorted. Ladies of her generation tended to speak more bluntly. Clare thought she might learn to like the older woman had she not wielded a chip on her shoulder so wide it would take Hercules to nudge it off.

Oh well, as long as she was poking her nose where it didn't belong. . . "We have counted over forty heirs so far. The information we're using is old, so I'm sure there are more. And the bank seems to believe there is a lien that must be paid should the manor be sold." Hunt hadn't told her that, but she could surmise it from his grumpiness. "I don't think that will leave much more than the maintenance trust to divide up. It seems a shame to give up a perfectly sturdy house for a miserly sum that will barely buy a Season's gowns."

"A lien?" Lady Spalding glowered. "That is ludicrous. My mother didn't have the right to borrow against it. My grandfather had more money than Croesus and didn't need to."

Clare rose and hid her smile. "This is the reason someone needs to pay attention to the property. It's been hidden from us since your mother's death. One must ask why?"

She departed, leaving the marchioness to stew.

A moment later, she was at the bottom of the stairs watching Betsy lift a small, rather filthy object from the debris of the broken vase.

～

"I CAN'T PROVIDE LUNCHEON, BUT I THOUGHT YOU MIGHT ENJOY A HEARTY TEA." Looking like an avenging angel, Clare sailed into the study bearing sandwiches.

Hunt wanted to hug her. The noon meal had gone by the wayside, and he was starving, but that wasn't the reason he wanted to hug her. Her sane approach to madness simply tilted the world back to its normal axis. She'd been placed under a strain that had grown men verging on histrionics. He had feared she might sensibly flee.

"We would most likely have begun gnawing on each other out of starvation if you had not arrived," he said, avoiding hugging by grabbing food and gesturing at Arnaud and Walker. "Have you settled in the old witches?"

"*And* interrogated them. Not that I learned much that we hadn't already surmised. How about you? Do we have any notion why Gaither did whatever he did?" She held the platter while Walker picked through her offering.

"Meera and Mrs. Gaither are taking turns at his side. We are hoping he may wake and talk." Walker sat back and crossed an ankle over a knee to balance the ledger he was working on while he ate. "The bankers fled after

Arnaud loomed and glowered. Apparently, a cripple and a servant aren't threatening enough. It takes a mad French artist wielding a paintbrush."

Hunt appreciated that Clare nearly doubled up in laughter. He hadn't found it funny at the time. He'd been prepared to rip off heads, except he was doing his damndest to be properly British polite after Gaither's insane— or drunken—behavior. His co-general was unusually cheerful after a hair-raising event. He narrowed his eyes and forgot his food.

Arnaud swiped the remaining sandwiches off the platter. "The Bosworths claim the *chien* Lord Reid signed the liens to cover gambling debts, and they come due in December, including all the interest that hasn't been paid in the last fifteen years. I could not sell enough paintings in a hundred years to pay off a sum so large."

"It's a fifty-year-old mortgage." Hunt leaned back in his chair. "The sum is nowhere as large as the worth of this place, as far as I am able to ascertain. But if we cannot pay it, the result is much the same. The place must be sold or given to the bank." He shrugged.

Setting down the tray, Clare rummaged in a hidden pocket and produced a filthy round object, leaving it on his desk. "Perhaps one of you gentlemen might know more about this than I."

While everyone leaned forward to look, Clare backed toward the door. Hunt realized there was nowhere for her to sit and not one of them had stood to offer her a seat. He started to do so, but she waved him down.

"The viscount died shortly after he signed this mortgage?" she asked. "Lady Lavinia believes he drowned. Perhaps he threw himself in the river. And we don't know what Gaither meant when he claimed the bankers had robbed him. Perhaps I should talk with Mrs. G."

"We have tried," Hunt admitted, his insides knotting a little when she stated it that way. "While the bankers were still here. She simply kept crying."

"So, our captain threw out the bankers instead of the cook," Walker added in amusement, picking up the dirty object to examine it. "I have a notion they didn't expect that."

Clare shook her pretty curls. "At least no weapons were involved, thank you. I do not think I will ever adjust to firearms in the house. I may start having the vapors if anyone else fires one. Stand forewarned." She sailed out with her empty platter, frail skirts picking up the wind of her hasty departure.

Hunt glanced at the holes in the ceiling. "The lady's sister was blown up by a bomb. We need to pretend we're civilized and not shoot anyone else." He should probably listen to himself.

"Post guards at the door and shoot the bankers outside," Walker suggested callously, handing the object to Arnaud. "I think the lady just handed us a diamond."

TWENTY-FIVE

THAT NIGHT, MEERA CARRIED UP A TRAY OF SOOTHING HERBAL TEA AND A HOT soup for the distraught housekeeper attending her husband. "You must take care of yourself. He will need you when he wakes."

"Better he should die," Mrs. Gaither said bitterly. "They will put him in prison to rot in misery."

"He didn't actually shoot anyone." Meera set the tray down and spread a napkin over the old woman's lap. Unlike Clare, she wasn't shy about stating her opinion. "If we could prove those nasty leeches were the real criminals, no one would think to press charges."

Mrs. Gaither sniffed pathetically. "It's all legal, I'm sure. He had a little too much of his medicine and shouldn't have done it. The rich have their ways that us poor folks can't understand."

Not with that attitude, but Meera understood helplessness. "Captain Huntley already suspects the Bosworths of dishonesty."

The cook didn't taste her soup, just clasped her cup and shook her head. "It's a dishonest world, it is. His lordship was bad, he was. Mr. Bosworth did what he could. If you'd all stayed home where you belong, we'd have been fine."

This was a very strange attitude. The cook's mind must be wandering. "We're young, Mrs. Gaither, and not completely poor. We can help. We just need to know what happened."

Mrs. Gaither leaned back in her chair and wearily closed her eyes. "There was lots of us way back in the day, a dressmaker and a butcher and a proper grocer and all. My William had his daddy's place. The old earl that was shouldn't have given it all to Lord Reid. He destroyed everything, he did."

Meera checked the patient's pulse and breathing and tried to interpret the rambling. "I believe the solicitors told the captain there have been no rents, and that is why the village is not maintained. Did Lord Reid raise the rents?"

The cook shook her gray head. "His lordship threw us all away. Mr. Bosworth picked up the pieces when the lady left."

Which lordship? The viscount? Mrs. G had known the viscount? She might be old enough. Then, she might be old enough to be talking about the elder Bosworth. "*Lord Reid* threw away his lady?"

The cook sipped her tea. "He was a bad one, right spoiled rotten, that one was. We was all young and foolish then, water under the bridge."

Interesting choice of words. "Is that what happened to the viscount? They say he drowned."

Mrs. Gaither kept shaking her head. "The river rises and wipes away the rot so we can start anew."

Meera thought maybe they'd better start reading the first diaries instead of the last.

∾

"I don't even know how groceries are ordered," Clare complained as she joined Lavender and Meera in the kitchen. Even if what they'd found was a real diamond, it wouldn't put food on the table today.

Lavender's companion, the ancient Mrs. Ingraham, had assembled Betsy, Marie, Ned, the new maid, Prudence, and an unidentified skinny boy who had showed up looking for work. The old lady was pointing out pots to be scrubbed and sorting through the pantry.

"The larder is full. We won't starve tonight." Meera stirred the soup on the ancient stove. "It's too late for anything elaborate. If everyone starts chopping vegetables, I'll make a crust, and we can have a pie with the soup."

"You'll need more than one pie," Clare observed. "I'm pretty certain each of the men could eat a whole one, and we still have the ladies upstairs to feed."

"There's a ham and some tatties," Mrs. Ingraham suggested. "Cut 'em up and with a bit of sauce. . ."

This was not at all how Clare had envisioned spending the next months. She'd never done serious cooking or cleaning in her life. She could prepare tea, change a bed, help with the laundry, but even her small household had a cook and maid. Decisions would have to be made—but not tonight. Tonight was about coping in the face of disaster.

Gaither had yet to recover consciousness, and the bankers had no doubt rode off to fetch the law. If only he'd wake and explain himself. . .

The men intelligently praised their offerings when they delivered trays to the dining chamber. The two old ladies merely sipped soup and nibbled bread in their rooms.

"There must have been elegant meals here once," Clare said as Walker and Arnaud offered to clear up afterward. "There's china, crystal, silver, and lovely tablecloths."

"Which I suspect the bankers mean to claim if we don't sell them first." Hunt picked up a lamp and gestured for Clare to precede him upstairs. Out of hearing of the servants he continued, "I'll have to take the diamond to a jeweler to determine it's worth. Even if it's genuine, I doubt it will pay the whole mortgage."

Upon Meera's advice, she carried the first dozen diaries, but she feared she was grasping at straws. "I cannot imagine why a diamond has been in that vase all these years. Three people have *died* here in the last half century. I am envisaging villains who kill off every obstacle in their path to wealth and land, but really, who would want this money sinkhole?"

"Bosworth Jr. I see avarice in his eyes every time he studies all this old stuff." He gestured at the hall.

"I can't feature how he means to pay the upkeep, if so. The maintenance trust would go to the heirs, surely?" Clare was acutely aware that they were alone as they entered the blue salon. Everyone had left on their own pursuits.

Hunt had *kissed* her. Did he plan to do so again? Did she intend to let him? She had enjoyed it much too much and feared kissing might be addictive.

Nervously, she set the diaries on her reading table and took her usual chair. He was American, she reminded herself. He would go home by summer's end. Look where seductive kisses had led sensible Meera.

"Maybe he believes the tales of hidden jewels." Hunt settled in the big chair across from her.

Lavender had sewed a new eye patch for him, one that hid only his eye and not half his face. His wounds had healed. The ragged scar marring his sturdy cheekbone to his temple showed how close he'd come to dying—and only made him more dashing.

Clare swallowed and glanced away. "If we found a single diamond, maybe Bosworth has *reason* to believe in more, not that he will tell us. The codes in the paintings must mean something." She opened the first diary that they had originally set aside.

"Pity the old earl didn't keep a journal explaining himself, if he is responsible for hidden jewels and codes. If Gaither is upset about losing his home, I'd like to hear if the diaries have anything to say about the state of the village when Lady Reid returned after being away for so long." He poked at the fire.

Clare wrinkled her nose and set aside the first volume to pick up the last one she'd read. "In this volume, when she returns to the manor, she only wonders why the village has deteriorated. Did she actually make inquiries? I wish I could read French faster, although she's using more English in these later years." She flipped the pages looking for references to the village or shops.

She read passages aloud that mentioned anything resembling the people who had once lived here, but thirty years ago, there had still been staff. The situation hadn't been so noticeable. It must have been after the viscountess died, and there was no work at all, that desperation had set in. It still didn't explain why poor Mr. Gaither thought he'd been robbed.

"So, Lady Reid was only vaguely aware that people were poor, and she could do little, since she wasn't rolling in wealth either." Clare studied the later volumes unhappily.

Lavender popped in looking less than her cheerful self. "I will not play ladies' maid for the old besom."

"No, of course not." Clare didn't wish to send Meera either. They helped each other dress because they were friends and equals, not servants. "We will have to promote Betsy for the evening. If I promise to pay her the value of her buttons, she shouldn't object."

Lavender grinned. "By the time she tears all their hooks and spills all their pins, they'll be sorry they asked." She dashed off.

"If we lose this place, I'll have to take Lavender home with me, but that won't help the village." Troubled, she was unwilling to start the diaries from the beginning at this hour. Hunt's presence stirred longings best repressed. "We should retire early. Tomorrow is likely to be a long day."

He rose when she did, then boldly brushed a loose tendril from her face. "You have been an excellent co-general today. Sometimes, diplomacy works better than warfare."

She shook her head. "Pure cowardice drives me. I cannot bear violence. I'd best check on our patient before retiring."

She would rather burrow into the captain's comforting strength, but she was much too old and wise for missishness.

"I think when I take the diamond into the jeweler, I'll stop and ask the solicitors for a copy of the mortgage agreement and for a verification of the signature. If we aren't to trust our banker, that develops a whole new set of concerns." Hunt placed a broad hand on her lower back to guide her out.

To her surprise, she enjoyed the sensation entirely too much. "That would be more practical than shooting vases for diamonds, admittedly. Perhaps I can discreetly question our guests some more. They may know the jeweler the family used."

Hunt ran his thumb up and down her spine as he spoke. "Should we show them the codes?"

A loud wail from below prevented any answer.

"They have killed him! They have killed my William!"

A howl of misery followed.

TWENTY-SIX

"At least no one blamed *me* for Gaither's death," Meera said wearily
Saturday morning as she helped Clare don her mourning gown.

"If you didn't poison Mrs. G after all that wailing, then no one would
believe you poisoned an unconscious man. You need to go to bed and rest all
day. That babe you carry should be your first concern." She didn't know
when she'd taken up Hunt's bad habit of calling the cook by her initial. Clare
pulled her own hair into a sober knot and capped it with black lace.

"If you don't mind me deserting you to your domineering family, I think
I will. I don't think I'm needed to watch over a body." Dark shadows marred
Meera's eyes.

Clare hugged her friend and sent her to bed. Next, she checked on Oliver.
He'd been asleep last night when the wailing started. That didn't mean he
had slept through the commotion.

"Mr. Gaither died last night," she told him when he looked up from his
book. He'd known enough death in his life for her to be frank. "We must be
quiet and respectful for Mrs. G's sake. She won't be preparing meals today. I
can find some bread and cheese and maybe some preserves, if you'd prefer
to stay in here."

He tilted his small head so a lock of fair hair fell into his eyes, then clam-
bered down from the window seat. "I can toast."

She didn't want him anywhere near a fire, but he had to learn sometime.

Even the men were solemn as they gathered in the kitchen to help Mrs.

Ingraham, and the rattled servants rummage through the pantry. Betsy flapped about in protest at their presence, until Clare sent her and Marie upstairs with tea and toast for the ladies and Meera.

"There's an ancient graveyard and crumbling mausoleum down the hill, fitting for a place called Gravesyde Priory, I suppose," Arnaud told them. "But it will take days before a vicar can attend. He will have tomorrow's services to handle first."

"I'll ask Mrs. Gaither what she wants. What happens to that poor woman if the bank forecloses?" Clare left Oliver toasting bread and the men slicing meat and cheese while she sent a tray up to the chamber where the cook kept watch over her husband's body.

By late morning, word had mysteriously spread to the surrounding countryside, and people began showing up at the kitchen door. Clare helped Mrs. Gaither down to her little sitting room to preside over her guests and left Prudence, the newest maid, at her beck and call.

"I didn't know so many people lived nearby," Clare whispered to Hunt as he donned his coat to go in search of the cemetery. Mrs. Gaither had admitted a preference for a quiet burial since they had not attended church in so long.

"They come from the farms about here, I imagine. While the women natter, I'll speak to the men, learn what I can. I'm leaving Arnaud and Walker to guard the front in case a magistrate arrives." He hugged her and hurried out.

Rattled by the familiarity of the hug, she told herself it came from working so closely these past weeks. She just shouldn't like it so well.

She tried not to be terrified of the looming disaster presented by a magistrate and the bankers if any more villagers felt as Mr. Gaither had. Shuddering at the possibility of more shooting, she conjured a vision of solemn, respectable visitors leaving their cards and going away again, as one should.

This wasn't London. Anyone appearing at the front door would most likely expect food and possibly bed. Which caused her to panic more when she heard wagon wheels on the drive shortly after noon. Mentally counting the number of empty beds in the main block and wondering what shape the linens were in, she peered out the massive gallery windows. *Henri!* She almost melted in relief.

Arnaud's brother leapt from the cart's seat, opened the back, and began handing out people. Clare gawked as he assisted a few sturdily dressed women, a tall man of middle age and considerable bulk, and a youth who resembled the older man in height if not weight. Henri gestured toward the back of the house while he unloaded baggage that might possibly be his.

He was entering the front as family.

Smiling for the first time that day, Clare joined Arnaud in greeting this new member of the household. She ought to be petrified of another man joining them, but nothing about Henri was intimidating. And gloomy Arnaud needed his cheerful brother.

"Welcome, welcome," she cried. "It has not been a happy day, but you have driven away the gathering clouds! We have a room prepared, but I fear we cannot offer much in the way of refreshment."

Arnaud hugged his brother, Walker shook his hand, but Clare held back. He might be Hunt's relation, but he was still a stranger. It was hard to fear his handsome smiling face, but Bea's warning always stayed with her —*pretty faces empty pockets*. And Henri's pockets were most decidedly empty.

"I have brought all your orders, including the button making equipment and the fabrics." Henri gestured at a crate. "If you are successful in producing as many as your pretty Betsy believes, I will enjoy spending fewer days on the road. I will help in whatever way I can."

Henri apparently didn't know about the mortgage. Clare didn't wish to be the one to dim his cheerful outlook. Instead, she took on the task of setting the new servants to work finding rooms in the attic.

~

RETURNING FROM TALKING WITH THE LOCAL FARMERS GATHERING FOR THE funeral, Hunt limped upstairs to change but followed voices instead. He discovered his aunt and great-aunt walking the upper gallery, examining the artwork. He'd seen their carriage arrive bearing boxes and maids shortly after Henri. Now appropriately attired, they had ventured from their lairs.

Conscious of his decidedly rough country apparel and scarred visage, he limped in to join them anyway. He'd traveled an ocean to meet family. He might as well be done with it.

He offered the best bow he could manage without toppling. It worked better when he wasn't drinking. "Ladies, I'm pleased you have chosen to extend your stay, but I'm sorry the circumstances are less than I'd hoped."

"You have the look of your mother." Lady Spalding sniffed, studying him with an old-fashioned lorgnette. "And presumably her father."

Hunt acknowledged that with a nod. "You have met my cousin, Arnaud Lavigne. His brother Henri has just arrived. They're the sons of Comte Lavigne, my uncle. He and my grandfather were lost in the revolution. I fear my cousins are much prettier than I am." That was the simplest explanation of his complicated family tree.

Lady Lavinia gave an unladylike snort. "If you like pretty Frenchmen. Were you raised in a log cabin? That neckcloth is a disgrace."

Since he wasn't attempting to do more than cover his neck, he dismissed the insult. "Unfortunately, the war has left me with little more than uniforms, but I was raised in a proper brick home outside of Philadelphia. My mother sends her greetings and good wishes and is eager to hear more of her family."

He offered his arm to the slender, elderly baroness who wore her mole like a beauty mark. "Perhaps you would introduce me to my relatives?" He indicated the family paintings.

"You will note we are all fair," his aunt, the stout marchioness said tartly, leading the way. "The earl is first, as a young student, then his siblings in order of age, and then his children."

Lady Spalding stopped in front of a young woman in a wig adorned in butterflies and wearing a diamond necklace interlaced with emeralds. Displayed prominently, the mole went uncovered by white cosmetics. "This is you, isn't it, ma'am?"

"I haven't seen that necklace since the portrait was made." Lady Lavinia squinted at it. "I believe Wycliffe was keeping it to give to my eldest son when he married."

"That would be Lavender's father?" Hunt asked, sorting through the family tree and pinning down the aging crone.

His great aunt sniffed and proceeded to the next painting without acknowledging his presumption. "This one is my sister, Eleanor. She only had girls, y'know. She wore the rubies and diamonds at her presentation, and then I believe Wycliffe broke up the set and gave pieces to her daughters. I'm not sure where the diamond pendant is."

Well, Hunt understood the source of the rumors of missing jewels now. "One assumes the earl sold the rest when he sold off everything else. Did he have a regular jeweler?"

"The same one my mother used," Lady Spalding acknowledged. "Don't think she didn't ask about the family jewels. They should have gone to my father and thus, to us—under normal circumstances. After my father's death, Wycliffe changed his will. It left everything to all of us equally, but by then, he'd disposed of everything except this place, as far as we are aware."

"And the jeweler?" Hunt returned her to the original question.

The earl's daughter squeezed his arm with her bony fingers. "The jeweler claimed to know nothing of these gems. We all inquired at one time or another. He even produced invoices back to the last century showing the work he did for Wycliffe. We could account for the pieces we all received but not the missing ones."

She pointed at the next portrait of the woman wearing pearls and sapphires. "That's my youngest sister, Clarice. Her daughter was Claudia. We tend to name our daughters after ourselves, but Mr. Knightley insisted his eldest daughter be named after his own mother. So, it was his younger daughter who received the family name."

Clare, named after her grandmother and mother, point taken. Clare was one of this aristocratic family. He was not. Hunt didn't care. "Miss Knightley mentioned that the family believes the jewels were hidden, but given the late earl's generosity, that does not seem reasonable."

Lady Spalding halted in front of the painting of her father, the viscount, as an infant on the earl's knee. "In my youth, I remember my mother and Wycliffe having frightful rows over the jewels, among other things. I know she was allowed the London townhouse because her dowry purchased it, and she received an allowance according to the marriage settlements. She had documents proving my father gave her the pearls, nothing more."

"Surely they did not cut *you* off." Hunt followed his aunt to the next portrait of Lord Reid as a young man. The viscount wore a jeweled watch fob and cravat pin. His hand rested on a small casket from which a length of pearls spilled.

"Mother claimed I should have inherited the whole, but the earl didn't want her to have access, so he was waiting until I married. Unfortunately, he made the new will and died before I was even presented. I had only my mother's pearls to wear." The marchioness touched the casket in the portrait. "Perhaps that was all that was left. I never saw anything else."

A furious knocking at the front door echoed through the gallery below. Hunt glanced out the windows but the angle wasn't sufficient to see the drive. The manor had more visitors today than in all the last fifteen years, he'd wager. Perhaps there was a reason the bridge over the river had never been built.

He bowed to the ladies. "If you will excuse me, ladies. Without a butler, we are at somewhat of a disadvantage. I must see who this is."

He limped off, hoping Walker and Arnaud had their pistols. He suspected from the fury of the knocking that this must be the banker returned with the magistrate.

TWENTY-SEVEN

AFTER THE KNOCKER SOUNDED, CLARE RUSHED FROM THE FAMILY PARLOR WHERE she'd been interviewing the new servants. In dismay, she watched Walker and Arnaud arm themselves with pistols. Terror froze her. . .

And then she straightened her spine. . . The manor was her *home*.

She was hiring servants and trying to establish civilization. *This was not a war zone.*

Gathering her shreds of courage, she lifted her skirt and raced ahead of the two big, armed men, stamped her foot, and pointed back down the hall. "*No weapons*. None. At all."

They halted but didn't disarm. The knocker thumped louder. She could hear Hunt limping toward the staircase. He probably carried a weapon too. The idea of towering soldiers firing pistols over her head spewed a medley of bloody mental images, but this time, she'd prepared.

"Quincy," she said loudly. "Please answer the door."

The bulky giant she'd just hired as butler emerged from the parlor, glanced quizzically at the gentlemen, and lumbered in the direction she pointed. He was still wearing an old suit from three decades ago, but his shirt was ironed and his cravat was straight, if worn thin.

"Quincy?" Walker asked skeptically.

"Apparently his ancestors were of a Puritan faith and some migrated to the Americas. His parents are proud of their relation to revolutionary war heroes." Clare flashed him a defiant smile. This was Walker, after all, not an

Egyptian mob. Her anxiety lowered a notch now that she was on firmer ground. "Even I know a little of your history."

Angry voices carried from the entrance. Quincy's rumbling mumble couldn't be interpreted. He emerged from the vestibule, threw a bolt across the hall door so their guests couldn't burst through, and held out the salver with the visiting cards. Ah, so that was the point of the vestibule. The earls must have had a lot of dangerous callers.

Hunt had reached the hall by the time they'd read the names.

"A magistrate and Bosworth Jr.," Walker reported, holding up the cards.

To Clare's surprise, the old ladies followed Hunt in their full glory, ancient petticoats billowing over their buckled slippers. Her family didn't appear to be much interested in modern fashion.

"Magistrate?" the late earl's daughter asked in her regal voice. "Wycliffe was magistrate here. Who dares take his role?"

Hunt took the cards and squinted at them. "A Mr. Ephraim? I am unfamiliar with the locals."

The ancient baroness sniffed haughtily. "Show them in. There is no Ephraim in this district."

Clare glanced at Hunt, who shrugged. Well, the ladies knew more about the family and the manor than they did. She was fully prepared to enjoy the entertainment—as long as no weapons were involved.

Hunt escorted the ladies into the chilly great hall. Clare nodded at the intimidating butler. Only a month ago, she would never have dreamed of hiring a man as large as Quincy. Gaither's behavior had made her think twice about hiring this one. But she was learning that not all men were irrationally violent—most of the time. "Show our guests in, please."

She settled the ladies near the fire Walker and Hunt were starting. The plump marchioness retrieved her knitting and the haughty baroness simply glared as the new butler opened the door. Two gentlemen in pristine white cravats, tall top hats, and tailored coats that hugged their narrow, sloping shoulders entered. As inhabitants of an earl's manor, Clare and the others were decidedly outmoded and ill-dressed in comparison.

Wealth did not make the man—or the woman. She'd take her eccentric family over Bosworth any day.

The banker took a step back at finding the elder family members still present. Holding his hat in gloved hands to reveal his fading blond hair, he bowed. "I had thought you would be on your way to London, my ladies. I hate presenting you with this hubble-bubble."

Clare studied him in the light of day. He wore his hair too long to discern his ear lobes, but there was something about his brow and hair line. . . But he had jowls instead of dimples.

If the ladies didn't see Bosworth's familiarity, then she must be allowing her imagination to run amuck, seeking villains everywhere.

The late earl's daughter waved Bosworth off and fixed her steely glare on the self-effacing little man calling himself magistrate. He was barely taller than Clare and quite dapper, wearing a soldier's fashionable sideburns and a stickpin. After glancing at Walker and Arnaud and dismissing them, the magistrate focused on Hunt, ignoring the lady's scowl.

"Captain, I understand there was attempted murder here yesterday." Mr. Ephraim remained standing, since no one had offered him a seat.

"Mr. Gaither objected to having his property stolen and shot a vase. Unfortunately, he died last evening of an apoplexy." Hunt didn't bother looking at the banker but leaned against the mantel, refusing to sit.

"I was *assaulted* in this household!" Bosworth protested. "Assaulted and shown the door!"

"Shut up, Bosworth," the earl's stiff-necked daughter ordered, shaking her beribboned walking stick. "You, sir." She pointed at Ephraim. "Tell us who you are and how you dare present yourself as magistrate."

The slender man looked taken aback. Clare hid a smile. That was an assault, if she'd ever heard one, only verbal and not physical. Maybe she could grow up to be like her great aunt.

"Abraham Ephraim, my lady, of Birmingham. As a solicitor, I was appointed to my position."

"Fah." Lady Lavinia tugged her shawl tighter around frail shoulders. "This is Gravesyde Priory. Birmingham has no jurisdiction here. If you knew your history, you'd know the priory is an exclave of Shropshire. I doubt seriously any magistrate has been appointed since Wycliffe died. Captain Huntley here," she pointed her walking stick at Hunt, "is the resident owner. If he didn't appoint you, then no one did."

Clare tried not to choke on astonishment.

Bosworth goggled. "My lady, you side with this impostor? He is no heir. I thought you understood that."

From beneath her lashes, Clare glanced at Hunt. Tall, his square shoulders filling his rough coat, his dirty waistcoat clinging to a broad chest, he lounged insouciantly, obviously not caring one way or another about how this argument ended. He was prepared to go home at any time.

Her romantic heart lurched dangerously, and she looked away.

"The captain is family. If he's good enough to be heir when you needed his signature, then I assume he is good enough to be magistrate. We'll ask the servants and villagers, shall we?" Lady Lavinia gestured at Clare. "There are mourners gathered in the kitchens, are there not? We can ascertain if they live within our boundaries. They can all have a vote."

"They don't own property here!" Bosworth protested. "No one owns property here except me. . ." His eyes widened, and he shut up.

The following silence was ominous.

~

WHAT? THE *BANKER* OWNED ALL THE LAND? HOW COULD THAT BE?

Fury escalating, Hunt straightened, prepared to snatch the stout dandy by his starched collar and propel him to the study.

His knee reminded him that he could barely propel himself. A pistol might be useful at moments like this, but Clare was burning holes through him with her blue glare. His pistol was in the study.

Before he could bellow for the heavyweight boxer she called a butler, Lavender entered with a tea tray and the dog-mop. Oliver proudly followed bearing a platter of burnt scones—a bloody battle scene wiped away by innocents. This was why Clare abjured weapons.

Hunt hauled in his temper and curtly gestured for the visitors to follow him. They appeared rightfully reluctant to do so.

Lavender set down teapot and cups. "Captain, they're ready to carry the coffin to the graveyard. Mrs. Gaither hopes you will say a few words." She bobbed a curtsy at the strangers. "Sorry, sirs, but this is a sad day. You are welcome to attend with the others."

The chit had very pretty manners, if no one else did.

"I wish to attend and pay my respects." Her lips set determinedly, Clare rose and took Hunt's arm. "It is the least the captain and I can do. Ladies, please, help yourselves to tea."

He'd enjoy her appropriation if he thought the delicate miss was looking to him for support, but he feared she thought she would prop him up on the rainy drive. Or perhaps she was throwing him out. The dainty fairy aspect masked a ferocious dragon.

The older ladies settled into their chairs, but his cousin and Walker accompanied him to the hall. The new butler actually waited with their outer garments. Bosworth and the magistrate followed in confusion.

Lavender pointed to the narrow side hall. "They're gathering in the stable yard."

Clare pulled a hood over her lacy black cap. Hunt donned the short-crowned top hat he'd purchased before sailing, feeling decidedly outdated beside the higher hat Arnaud slapped on. But his brim was wider and kept the rain off his face and that's all he asked. He was surprised when the banker and magistrate chose to accompany them.

They met Henri in the muddy stable yard. "The brook is rising over the drive. We'd better do this quickly or half the people here will be stranded."

The magistrate halted, looking uneasy. "I need to return home before evening. Perhaps we should leave this for a more appropriate moment. That will give me time to research districts."

Bosworth hesitated. Quite willing to shove the banker into a flood, Hunt prodded him. "I asked you for a copy of the mortgage document. I don't suppose you have brought it with you?"

After that slip about Bosworth owning the property. . . Hunt fought the nasty grinding in his gut. Realizing he clenched his fists, he forced them to relax. He could not punch anyone at a funeral. Half the inhabitants of the district had gathered, prepared to bury one of their elders. And he was the only adult male representative of the earl's family in residence. Not just propriety required he refrain from violence, but a good officer displayed leadership by setting aside personal animosity. He might not be an officer in the army any longer, but he could still be captain of this troop.

Bosworth wrestled with a document in the inside pocket of his tight coat, finally prying it free and handing it over. "It's all there, signed and sealed. I give you good day." He swung on his heel and strode toward the waiting carriage.

Hunt shoved the papers in his pocket, covered Clare's gloved hand with his own, and led her toward the waiting mourners. He'd attended more funerals than he cared to count. Every mortal soul deserved respect. He knew how to do this.

Henri hurried to help carry Gaither's coffin along with the other men Hunt had only just met. Getting to know the neighbors had never been part of his plan. He'd meant to hand the keys to family and sail away, not become involved with strangers. But these weathered men and women had once lived here, had known the earl and his family, had memories to tell. He'd only skimmed the edge of them this morning.

With Gaither's cry of robbery echoing in his ears and the damning document burning in his pocket, Hunt had a need to know the manor's history. If wrongs had been done, the family needed to right them. As an outsider, he might be the only person capable of acting on what he learned.

As if hearing his thoughts, Clare squeezed his arm.

Did he want to leave her behind when he sailed away? He would have to. He had nothing to offer, and everything she loved was here.

He clenched his molars and watched the mourners, looking for the ones he wished to question again. Gaither had felt strongly enough about Bosworth to shoot him. Why?

TWENTY-EIGHT

FEELING GUILTY THAT SHE HAD NAPPED THE WHOLE DAY WHILE CLARE DEALT with cantankerous old ladies and a funeral in a rainstorm, Meera took the opportunity offered by everyone's absence to tidy up the room where Gaither had been laid out. She wondered if it might once have been an infirmary of sorts. The cot and shelves indicated it had some utilitarian purpose. The ground floor did not contain any other bedroom.

She stripped the linens, then gathered teacups and water glasses to take down to the kitchen. Using a rag to wipe up spills on the bed table, she caught a whiff of a scent that shouldn't be in here.

She held the rag to her nose. Nightshade?

She'd have tasted the powder to be certain, but she had no idea what the poison would do to a babe, even in granular amounts. Had Gaither woke last evening and Helga given him a sleep potion? How well did the cook know herbs? Why had she not let anyone know he regained consciousness?

Uneasy, she carried the dishes down to the kitchen. The aroma of fresh bread scented the air. A sturdy, blond young woman she hadn't met turned a roast on the fire.

At Meera's arrival, she bobbed a curtsy. "The lady said I might try the position of assistant cook. I'm Lara Evans. I didn't know Mr. Gaither, so I thought it might be all right to stay and prepare a light supper."

"Excellent choice, Mrs. Evans," Meera agreed. "If it's still raining, we might need to set up tables in the stable for the mourners. I'm Meera Abrams, Miss Knightley's companion."

"Pleased to meet you." The young woman had an accent as educated as Meera's own. "Will young Ned know where to find tables? He stayed to mind the horses."

"I'll ask. Do you know if Mrs. Gaither keeps a cabinet of herbs?" She didn't think she needed to explain herself to the new cook.

Mrs. Evans tapped a small cabinet door. "It's locked. Only Mrs. Gaither is allowed to use the herbs and spices."

Meera wasn't in a position to argue this arrangement. It was possible the old cook had simply meant to ease her husband's sleep with a little belladonna.

But nightshade was the last thing an apoplexy victim needed. What good would it do anyone to tell her she may have killed her husband with kindness?

WHILE THE WOMEN HEADED BACK TO THE MANOR TO SET UP TABLES AND FOOD, Hunt lingered to watch the diggers shove in the last of the dirt over poor Gaither's corpse. He hadn't had time to read the mortgage document, but the stories he was hearing from the mourners hurt his head.

"The viscount *mortgaged* the village and all the farm acreage? I am not familiar with English law, but could he do that without Wycliffe's permission?" Hunt limped toward the house, accompanied by two middle-aged farmers whose families had tenant-farmed for the Wycliffes for generations but now worked as unskilled labor wherever they could.

A lanky yeoman shrugged. "The boy gambled and wenched and had debts. Mayhap the old lord thought he'd learned his lesson and made him pay with his inheritance. Ours ain't to understand our betters."

"But the village? The entire village?" Hunt thought perhaps he understood Gaither's last words. If he'd had a cottage and the viscount mortgaged it out from under him. . . But why shoot Bosworth? "And the bank has done nothing with any of it? If they called in the loan, why haven't they sold it?"

An older, more portly man replied. "Land's costly. People are poor from the war, their sons lost in battle. Way back when the lady was here, she rented land from the bank so some could keep working. But oncet she passed, the youngers didn't see no reason to stay."

"Do any of you know what happened to the viscount and his lady? They both seemed to die so young." They were nearly at the house. The question had met with silence anytime he'd asked. Perhaps he should have waited until he'd poured ale into these men, because they seemed reluctant to speak.

The older man shrugged. "I was just a lad when Lord Reid was pulled from the river and wasn't here when the lady died. There's no bonesetters here abouts, none but old wives to see to the sick."

Old wives, like Meera, whose unguents had helped his knee better than any surgeon. His grandmother may have died from neglect because there was no physician. Hunt could see that the manor was the heartbeat of the district, the reason for people to live here, the provider of necessities. The last of the land had died with her.

What the devil was Bosworth about letting the place rot like this? Or were the estate lawyers equally responsible? Hunt suspected distant lawyers had no interest in land or people, just the income from managing the trust.

With what income had his grandmother rented lands? The sale of her London home?

Drenched from another downpour, Clare handed her cloak to the brilliant Quincy and slid off her muddy pattens at the side entrance. "The ale barrel is empty, and it's almost dark. I believe the last of our guests will depart shortly."

Quincy nodded. "The ladies have dined and are in the small parlor, madam."

"And Mrs. Gaither? I sent her back to rest. She did not look herself at all." The housekeeper had barely been coherent. Prudence had steered her back to the house.

"She has taken to her bed." A hint of disapproval edged the butler's voice. "Mrs. Abrams and Miss Lavender have assigned duties to the new staff."

"I'll thank them." Holding her damp boots, she stood only at chest-level to the burly butler. "And yes, I know Mrs. Gaither should probably be pensioned off. Just not today."

"Of course, madam." He took her boots, presumably to be polished.

Clare ran upstairs to change into dry clothes. With the house all at sixes and sevens, she couldn't hope for hot tea unless she fetched it herself. A lady's maid wasn't in the budget unless they found entire vases full of diamonds and pearls. Perhaps she could set the men to shooting vases. Outdoors.

The manor had a *real* butler. She could scarcely believe it. Her dream of a welcoming staff and family had just become a little more real. She'd have to hug Henri.

She'd rather hug Hunt. She was an old maid with no delusions of her own grandeur. She needed to apply these fantasies to her manuscript. As soon as she checked on the old ladies and Meera and the staff and. . .

Oliver. Where was Oliver? She hurriedly donned her simplest warm gown and dry slippers and rushed out to check his room. He wasn't there, of course. He could scarcely come to harm in a house full of people, but she'd been his sole caretaker practically since birth. She couldn't completely assign him to others.

A footman, an actual footman, appeared noiselessly at the bottom of the stairs when she rushed down. She knew this was Quincy's son, Adam. They'd both been trained in the household of a baronet who'd died recently, leaving them unemployed. She didn't know how Henri had found them, but she was eminently grateful. Adam reported that Oliver had been last seen in the estate office with Walker.

Walker's dark skin hadn't been particularly welcomed by country people suspicious of foreigners, so he'd left the socializing to Hunt.

She hurried to the back of the grand corridor until she heard voices and slowed down. If she did not mistake, Walker seemed to be teaching her nephew to read. . . ledgers? She peeked around the corner of the doorway. They were sitting in chairs, side by side, poring over account books. She backed away.

Walker would make a superb tutor in mathematics. Probably not in history, geography, French, Latin, or all those other subjects Oliver must eventually pursue. She wondered if Henri knew how to find tutors. But Hunt's cousins could teach Oliver French! And now that she was recovering some portion of hers, she might help a little.

The funeral and Mrs. Gaither's absence had upset regular dining hours, but she was relieved to find a buffet set up in the formal dining parlor so no one would go hungry. She'd eaten with the mourners but helped herself to a roll.

Meera would hide below in her workshop as long as the family presided over the main floor. Where were the ladies? She had to consider herself hostess unless they claimed precedence. She did wonder at their lingering. Finishing her roll, she went in search of her great aunt and cousin. She assumed, as granddaughter of the earl, the plump Lady Spalding must be her second or third cousin.

To her amazement, she found the ladies in the family parlor with the diaries stacked on the floor between their chairs. They had a blazing fire and a supper tray and appeared as if they'd made themselves at home.

Lady Lavinia lifted her lorgnette at Clare's arrival. "My eyes are tired. Where has the harlot's chit got to? After the expense of her education, she should be able to read this."

Any acknowledgement from Lavender's grandmother as to her existence had to be a positive step, Clare decided optimistically. She wouldn't dampen the lady's opinion by telling her that Lavender claimed not to know French well. "The must and mold from the pages make her sneeze. I can be your eyes, if you will. My memory of French lessons has faded, but the diaries are helping to refresh it. Where did you start reading?"

She refrained from asking *why* they'd started reading. *Because they were nosy* wouldn't be the answer she'd receive.

Plump Lady Spalding dropped her tome beside her chair. "At the beginning, of course, My mother had the sense of a peagoose."

"At the beginning, she was only fifteen years old." Clare pulled a chair over next to the elderly Lady Lavinia. "At the end, she attempted to save the manor and your inheritance. Did she or your father leave you anything?"

Lady Spalding wrinkled her nose. "My father left debts. My mother had nothing of which I'm aware."

"You've read all the diaries?" Lavender's grandmother held up her lorgnette to find the page she'd been reading before handing it to Clare.

"There hasn't been time. We only just found them and have been drying them out. I started with her time in London but have recently skipped back to the early days of her marriage." She didn't mention they were hoping for jewels. All the pearls were gone?

"I cannot believe she spent so many hours scribbling scurrilities about my father." Hunt's aunt scowled at the page of the book she'd just opened. "They're simply excuses for what she did."

"I believe Captain Huntley was hoping to give his mother some explanation of her history. Have you found the books where she leaves for France?" Clare donned her spectacles to check the date on the diary the baroness handed her, but she'd already read that one.

"That would be in 1764. I was only two." Lady Spalding opened several books until she found the one she wanted. "This one is late 1763." She handed it to Clare and shifted her plump frame deeper into the cushioned wing chair. "My eyes are tired as well. Read aloud, please."

Clare had no idea how good her pronunciation was but no one complained as she stumbled through the spiky, faded writing. Without Hunt here to translate, she didn't comprehend everything, but his grandmother's dramatics leaped off the page. Of course, the poor thing was only recently married, scarcely as old as Lavender, and living in a foreign country with odd customs and strangers. Had she been brave or foolish to marry Reid?

"A mistress," the marchioness scoffed after Clare closed that book. "They were newly wed! If he had a mistress, then it was because she didn't try to please him."

"Or he didn't try to please her?" Clare suggested carefully. Her sister had explained the facts of life from her usual demanding perspective. "She was so very young and terrified."

Wearing dry clothes and carrying his brandy snifter, Hunt entered before an argument could ensue. His cousins and Walker followed. Clare looked anxiously for Oliver. He trotted in last, carrying biscuits in his fists, slipping behind the draperies as if they wouldn't notice.

"Excuse my interruption, ladies." Hunt limped over to the card table and laid down a thick document. "But Walker and I have been perusing the purported mortgage on the manor. If you don't mind, I'd like your opinion, as you are more familiar with the grounds than I am."

"Not likely." Lady Lavinia sniffed, causing her mole to bob. "I haven't visited since my youth, and I won't tell you how long ago that was."

"You knew about the exclave," Hunt reminded her. "I had no idea such a thing existed. I had to consult with the locals. So even if you are not familiar with the manor, you are familiar with customs that I am not."

Clare knew about exclaves—small geographical areas originally attached to one district but left behind as boundaries and politics changed. But she was from London. It would never have occurred to ask about the manor's district.

He tapped the paper. "This document is nearly half a century old. It's a copy, not the original, but it's been notarized by the estate solicitors as correct."

Lady Lavinia frowned. "There is something in the document that you believe is not correct? Shouldn't the solicitors have informed us?"

"To the solicitors, this is simply a formal document between Lord Reid and the bank. The terms are straightforward. If the debt is not paid by this year, it comes fully due. Walker has gone over the accounting. The ledgers, up until 1800, confirm the bank's figures. There has been no one here to make payments since, and the interest has brought the balance to a sum that we can't pay." Hunt accepted a chair that Henri shoved under him.

"Don't expect *us* to pay," Lady Spalding said. "We have no interest in this ramshackle abode."

Hunt waved his hand. "No, I did not mean to imply that at all. It would be a sad waste to throw the manor away for this paltry sum, but none of us have need of the place either. It's the villagers and farm folk who will suffer. But that's not my concern right now."

"How paltry is the sum?" Arnaud asked. "Could we. . . ?"

Hunt waved him away too. "First, let me explain my concern. Walker and I are trained surveyors. As far as I am aware, we use the same measurements and terms as England."

Clare couldn't argue with that. She hadn't a notion how surveyors worked. Apparently, none of the others did either. They waited expectantly.

Hunt handed over a page with numbers and odd symbols, letting the elderly baroness see it first. They passed it around but no one had any understanding. Clare tried to compare the numbers to the ones Arnaud had been uncovering in the painting, but she saw no similarity. Would bankers and lawyers understand surveying language?

Walker rolled out a drawing of the estate's lot lines, using diaries to hold down the corners.

Hunt gestured at it. "This map is what I've been using to determine the manor's boundaries. According to this, the manor grounds include the village to the south, the entire hill this structure sits atop, and fields on the east side across the stream."

"But it's an old map," Arnaud said. "Land could have been sold since."

"The locals tell me it has. I'll have to speak with the solicitors to verify the sale since they seemed unaware. My concern," Hunt tapped the map, "is the west side of the hill. It's forested, rocky, and good for little except hunting."

"I remember Wycliffe speaking of the park," Lady Lavinia said, looking a little less bored. "He and Reid would hunt and fish here every fall. Doesn't the stream flow into a river on that side?"

"The river is not on the map since it's not part of the property, but visually, I'd say yes. The lack of a bridge there is why the manor is so isolated. I assume your brother preferred the isolation for a hunting lodge?" Hunt glanced up to study his great aunt.

"He did. He said there wasn't enough arable ground beyond the park to justify buying the land at the bottom and building a bridge. He was wealthy and didn't need the rents, so he simply let the locals go on as they'd been doing and let the highway pass us by."

Hunt nodded in satisfaction, took back the page he'd passed around, and laid it on the map. "If my reading of the mortgage and this map is correct, then Reid mortgaged the hunting grounds, not the manor or any other part of the estate. If we let the mortgaged property go back to the bank, all they'll have is timber and rocks inaccessible to anyone unless they build a bridge. My grandfather might have been a drunkard and a gambler, but he was not entirely stupid."

TWENTY-NINE

SUNDAY MORNING, HUNT JOINED THE PRAYER SERVICE CLARE LED. OUT OF respect for the deceased, she wore a plain navy-blue gown, but the bodice was cut low and her scarf slipped enough to keep him entertained. Surely, he was at least allowed to admire.

The old ladies attended, and Mrs. Gaither dragged herself from her bed of grief to shepherd the new servants to the gallery. Hunt was a little startled when Clare chose one of the passages underlined by the viscountess about the evils of men and sinners.

Wondering if she had a purpose, he watched the participants. Several of the women nodded. The old housekeeper merely covered her face with a lace handkerchief and rocked back and forth. Not exactly revealing. He had a ridiculous wish that he and Clare might share their early hours alone to discuss the day ahead, but she rightfully avoided him.

Once the service ended, everyone scattered to their own devices. Hunt met Walker in the study, and they beat out a letter to the solicitors and the bank advising them that they would forfeit the hillside in lieu of paying the mortgage on it. Mrs. Gaither entered as Walker was reading the final draft aloud.

She seemed agitated and grew more so by the time Walker finished. "Will Mr. Bosworth and the magistrate be returning? Did they wish to speak to me?"

"They didn't mention it. I doubt they'll be returning on a Sunday, with the water so high. I'll ride out and inspect the stream and river after I'm done here." Hunt didn't like the notion of being stranded by high waters.

She wrung her hands and nodded. "Will the bank be taking the manor then?"

Hunt tried to reassure. "The bank will *not* be taking the manor. We don't yet know about the village, but you will always have a roof over your head as long as we are here."

Walker picked up the letters they'd been working on and silently departed to copy them out. Hunt waited for the cook to leave as well.

"My son said as he'd take care of us. He's a good boy, he is. Gaither didn't understand. They none of them rightly understood. But it will all come right in the end, as the good lord says, the meek shall inherit the earth. There's flooding in the old cellar, my lord. It will come into the kitchens if let be." She waited expectantly.

"Flooding? We can't let that happen. Show me where." Hunt rose, eager to do something active besides writing letters to damned banks and solicitors.

He didn't know what the cook rambled on about, but rising water, he understood.

~

AFTER SERVICES, CLARE RETURNED TO THE FAMILY PARLOR TO CONTINUE READING the diaries aloud to their guests. She finished the young viscountess's passage on losing her unborn infant, scrubbed at tears, and set the diary aside. The passage had been furious, grief-stricken, and scarcely coherent, but clear enough to understand that the viscount had knocked his young wife down in a drunken rage.

The older ladies sat silent for a change. Lavender had brought in a tea tray earlier and stubbornly taken up a position in a corner with her sewing, staying out of sight. She threw another log on the fire now while surreptitiously wiping her eyes.

"I didn't know my father at all," Lady Spalding said, knitting furiously. "I vaguely remember him as dashing but. . ." She gestured helplessly. "He was my father, and I was barely out of leading strings."

Lady Lavinia wrinkled her already wrinkled brow, her widow's peak disappearing into the furrows. "My father and I did not bump along on many things. Wycliffe was a generous man later in life, but. . . While my brother was alive, he could do no wrong. I doubt that Wycliffe realized Reid's temper had such violent outlets."

"The infant Lady Reid lost would have been the grandson the earl craved. To hit her so cruelly that she fell downstairs. . . Is that the act of a rational man?" Clare had to ask.

Wycliffes were known to be eccentric, but she'd never heard of this degree of irrationality. Just as she'd started to trust men, was she to believe even her own family was violent?

Lady Spalding sighed heavily. "It's the act of a drunken beefwit. He'd lost a wager. Wycliffe wouldn't pay it. He was frustrated, half-seas over, and she dared confront him with complaints from a maid. It happens in the best of houses, I fear. Most women learn to avoid confrontation."

"Not Lady Reid." Clare admired the lady's courage, if naught else. "She was barely seventeen, and she defended a helpless maid and stood up to the bully. Not intelligent, perhaps, but she had little experience to draw on. She loved him. She thought he'd listen."

"Read the next book," Lady Spalding insisted. "We know my mother didn't leave him then. What happened that could possibly have been *worse*? Or did she find a prince and run away?"

The diaries were almost as good as a novel, except they weren't fiction. Clare wanted to make notes on the viscountess's personality. She didn't think she could write a character quite so tempestuous. Despite her interest, she wasn't prepared to read about the lady's devastated grief. Just this one passage had her aching to hug her nephew.

The mention of the maid's name set off a whole set of new concerns. Reacting to a ridiculous frisson of fear, she set the book aside.

"Let us have a small break, ladies, please. I need to see to Oliver, and there are a few tasks I should attend. Perhaps you would care to stretch a bit and see what our resident artist is working on in the gallery?" She rose and helped Lady Lavinia to her feet, aware that Lavender watched wistfully. "Miss Lavender could accompany you. She understands what he's doing better than I."

Clare left them to fight it out. Lady Lavinia had no grandchildren other than Lavender. If she wanted to live a lonely life rather than acknowledge a baseborn child, Clare had no sympathy with the arrogant old woman.

Wanting to tell Hunt what they'd learned, she checked his study, but he wasn't there.

She continued to the back of the house where she found Oliver with Walker in the estate office. While Oliver practiced his letters and numbers on a slate, Walker appeared to be working on a new letter to the heirs. What would she do when this quiet man and his employer departed? Grieve, she feared, and then run back to London and safety.

The diaries had raised irrational fears. She had wanted a little reassurance that the world was sane. She hugged Oliver until he squirmed, but her fear did not subside. She had an illogical need to know everyone was safe. "Have you seen Meera? I'd like a word with her."

"In her workshop. Do you need her now?" Already on his feet, Walker looked eager for action.

"If you would, please. Do you know where Hunt is? We can meet in his study." She was being stupid, wanting to discuss what she'd read in a half-century-old book, but it was more than that. The house seemed hollow somehow, as if the heart had gone missing.

"Last I heard, Hunt was talking with Mrs. Gaither about the bank and flooding and having a roof over her head. That was hours ago. I assume he rode down to inspect the water." Walker didn't seem concerned. He left Oliver doing calculations and strode off in search of Meera.

Remembering the viscount had died by drowning, nerves already set on edge by shooting, death, magistrates, and the diaries, Clare went in search of Quincy. She found the butler polishing silver in the pantry. "Have you seen Captain Huntley?"

He stopped what he was doing to push his glasses up his nose. "Not since he left to check the stream."

Her foolish pulse escalated. If the blamed man had gone out and got himself killed. . . Before she traversed the entire manor again to find her cloak and check the stable, she stopped in the gallery to see if he might be there for some reason. The house was so blamed huge.

The ladies were there, as she'd suggested. With his easel set up near one of the enormous front windows, Arnaud silently worked, leaving the talking to his brother—and Lavender. They eagerly showed off the codes Arnaud was uncovering as he cleaned the artwork.

"Has anyone seen Hunt?" Clare interrupted, too anxious to be polite.

"He went exploring," Henri said, looking puzzled at her concern. "Shall I check the stable to see if he's returned?"

"If you wouldn't mind. If he's there, tell him I'd like a word." She'd like to send out search parties, but that was letting her imagination get the better of her. "I'll be in the study."

She set off, hoping Meera would already be there to calm her down and tell her she was being foolish. But puzzle pieces kept falling in place and something just felt *off*. . . Perhaps the funeral and Gaither's death had affected her more than she realized. But it wasn't as if Gaither had ever been much of a presence.

The scent of jasmine seemed to linger, and she feared the viscountess and her story was haunting her.

Meera wasn't in the study. Walker was, pacing. He looked up anxiously.

If Walker was anxious, something was wrong. "Meera's not in her workshop or the garden."

Surely, they both couldn't be missing. "Did you send a maid to see if she was lying down?" The way she ought to be, although Walker didn't know that.

He nodded. "Last anyone saw her, she was going outside to pick herbs. She's not there now."

"Maybe she and Hunt have gone off to look at—"

Henri stomped in, shaking moisture from his hat, his cloak still on. "Hunt's horse is here. He's not. He must have gone on foot."

Still running on terror, Clare tried to focus her spinning fears. "How badly is the stream flooded?"

Henri looked grim. "It could carry off a horse."

THIRTY

Looking for a leak, Hunt squished through a few centuries of mud beneath the crumbling stone arches holding up the gallery and great hall. If this was the crypt of the original priory, any graves were truly buried.

Mrs. G had shown him the hidden entrance on the western side of the manor in his first exploration. The shrubbery hadn't been tended in decades. This may once have been a dungeon for the original manor for all he knew.

It appeared the stone foundation seeped water from the saturated ground, but he saw nothing indicating imminent danger. He winced as the lantern light caught on the skeleton in a dry niche of an inside wall. He really should mention it to Lady Lavinia, at least. Perhaps she knew if the sixteenth-century cellar had once been used as a mausoleum. There didn't seem to be any connection between this space, and the manor's old kitchens where Meera worked now.

He examined the scraps of fabric still clinging to tiny bones, but they were barely more than wool threads, probably an infant's blanket.

He verified there was no wood rot from previous inundations. What had Mrs. G meant by needlessly sending him down here when he should be inspecting the stream?

That's when gut instinct twinged. Mrs. G hadn't exactly been coherent. Perhaps she thought she was saving him from the water that had drowned the viscount. Had her husband's death unhinged her?

Reassuring himself that the cook was too frail to cause much harm to herself or others, he mucked back to the cellar door. He'd left the old oak panel open, but it was closed now. Wind must be blowing harder than he realized. He didn't think this was the original door, just wood someone had installed to replace a rotted entrance. It swung out instead of in.

He shoved the oak. It didn't budge. Swollen from the rain, most likely. He applied his shoulder. It didn't give. Odd. The bolt hung down and couldn't fall in place on its own—although it did make him wonder why there was a bolt on the outside. Perhaps as magistrate, the earl had used this as a prison? Cruel, if so. The crypt might once have been grand, but centuries of flooding had taken its toll.

His bad knee didn't have much strength for kicking or standing. He tried bracing himself on the wall and slamming the door with his good leg. The angle didn't allow him to do more than scrape the wood with his boot heel. He'd have to find something sturdy to prop himself on. He thought there'd been an old shovel further back.

Cursing, wishing he'd told someone where he was going, he slogged back through the wet, swinging his lantern. He hoped the lamp had been filled last night. Being down here without any light at all would be like being buried alive.

Buried alive. Mrs. G had sent him down here. She knew he was here. Would she tell anyone?

What had that business been about her son? He'd not heard mention of a son before. At the time, he'd been relieved to know she had family. Where had her son been when they'd buried Gaither? He'd be thinking like Clare shortly.

Trying not to fret until he was in a position to question, he located the old shovel. It was too short for his height and wouldn't make a good prop but might suffice if he used it as a ram. The damp had his knee aching abominably by the time he reached the door again.

Gathering his strength, he wrapped both hands around the old handle and rammed it into the swollen panels. The sound of splintering had him ramming it again.

The door didn't move. The shovel handle split down the middle.

IN THE LIBRARY, THE MEN DIVIDED UP THE STREAM AND RIVER ON A MAP, choosing the most likely routes Hunt might have taken.

"If his horse is still here, might he not still be in the house?" Clare asked tentatively. "Perhaps he fell and hit his head and can't hear us calling?" Although if Meera were with him, she could hear, and they couldn't find her either.

Walker paced. "There are not too many places where his knee might give out. The front stairs are the only ones he takes."

"But the lady is correct. We should search the manor more thoroughly. If Hunt hurt himself and Meera is with him, they could be waiting for us to find them." Expressing Clare's hopes, Arnaud stalked toward the door. "The ladies and servants can organize that search. We still need to explore the grounds. He may have simply walked down the hill and slipped."

"If we find him, how do we let you know?" Feeling a little frantic, Clare clasped her hands in her skirt to keep from wringing them. She kept telling herself Meera and Hunt were sensible people and probably just fine, that her fear was as senseless as the one that had her ducking at loud noises, but if everyone else was equally worried. . .

"Ned has a pony. Send him after us. The rain seems to be letting up." Sounding like a commanding general, Arnaud walked out. Had he been an officer in the war? He and Hunt had been close-mouthed about his history.

The older ladies had retired to their rooms. Clare desperately wished she could join them or retreat to her writing desk and let this day pour through her pen.

But with the men busy and Meera missing, only Lavender remained to help organize a thorough search. Clare could write a book and pinch a ha' penny until it screamed, but. . . She'd never led an army. She couldn't expect Lavender to do what she could not.

Hunt and her best friend could be hurt, and the last hours of light were fading. Fighting her old anxiety and uncertainty, she had Lavender take the new servants to the attics to search, emphasizing stairwells. She ordered the chamber maids to search the second floor of the main block and both wings. She left Quincy and his son hunting through the sprawling ground floor chambers. Since they were unfamiliar with the manor, she had Oliver tag on their heels to direct them to concealed doors.

There could be dozens of hidden stairs they had yet to uncover.

Near the point of weeping, she conceded she needed the grieving house-keeper's aid to search the cellar. Overcoming her reluctance to breach etiquette, Clare marched down to the kitchens.

To her dismay and shock, she found Mrs. G sitting at the kitchen table, an array of herbs hacked to dust on the cutting board, chopping knife set aside, and gin bottle in hand.

Close to Clare's age and usually cheerful, Mrs. Evans, the new assistant cook, now wore a worried frown. At Clare's questioning look, she shook her short blond curls, shrugged, and continued stirring a pot on the stove.

Keeping an eye on the drunken housekeeper, Lavender's elderly companion chopped vegetables on the far end of the table.

Maybe she should enter the kitchen more often. Clare slipped onto a bench across from the grieving widow. "We need to look for Mrs. Abrams and Captain Huntley. We fear one of them may be hurt. If I send people to search down here, would you direct them to all the stairs?"

"He's gone to the river, like t'other. The river washes them clean, the good Lord says. She saved my baby, so I saved her, didn' I? And then she returned. She shouldna 'ave returned. None of this woulda happened. . ." She blinked blearily at Clare. "Go back where you belong."

"I think we need to tuck you into bed." In alarm at the woman's state, Clare stood. Finding Betsy wringing her hands in the pantry, she gestured for aid in helping the cook stand.

Before they could touch her, Mrs. G grabbed her chopping knife and slammed it into the cutting board. "I'm done here. I can' do it wit'out the old goat. My son needs to take his rightful place." She swung the knife at Clare. "Go home."

Everyone gasped. No one moved but Betsy. Twice Mrs. G's size and half her age, she caught the cook's arm from behind. The knife wavered. Clare grabbed a bony wrist and squeezed until the blade clattered to the stone floor.

The cook began to weep. "Fix the tea, then. If you won't go, fix the tea. Betsy, bring us some mugs."

"We don't have time for tea," Clare said gently. "Captain Hunt could be hurt." She glanced up at the wary kitchen staff. "I'm unfamiliar with the rooms down here or the servants' stairs. Have any of you seen the captain or Mrs. Abrams?"

They all shook their heads.

"Fix the tea!" Mrs. G ordered, pushing back from the table. "Men don't come back from the river. My boy will come."

At the old cook's agitation, Mrs. Evans poured hot water into a teapot, wrapped it in a cozy, and carried it to the table with the requested mugs. "Sit back down and rest, Mrs. Gaither."

Leaving the old lady with her tea and Mrs. Ingraham and the cook to soothe her, Clare gestured for Betsy, Marie, and the new scullery maid to join her by the pantry. She couldn't watch helplessly while the others searched.

"Sit. Drink!" Mrs. G shouted, pointing at the bench Clare had vacated.

"You sit with her, miss," Betsy whispered. "We'll look about."

Clare hated relaxing over a pot of tea, listening to a grieving old woman ramble, while Hunt or Meera might be in pain. But if this was the only way to keep her calm. . .

Mrs. G was mumbling and spilling herbs on the floor and pouring tea with a shaky hand. Perhaps she'd pass out shortly.

A bit of tea would certainly hit the spot. Clare took the mug shoved in her direction and tested the heat. It had been poured before it boiled properly. It tasted bitter but was cool enough to sip.

Before she'd drunk enough to ease her shattered nerves, Oliver raced down the stairs shouting. "Ghost in the gallery! Ghost in the gallery!"

Clare pushed away from the table, glad for any excuse to escape. "Betsy, please continue looking down here. I'll be back to let you know what's happening."

At her imminent departure, the cook shouted incoherently, looked about, then dived for the knife on the floor. Mrs. Ingraham stepped on the blade. Lavender's companion was a sturdy old woman and seemed to have the matter in hand.

Clare fled up the stairs before confronted with any more madness. Oliver ran ahead, small boots clattering. The corridor seemed an eternity long. What on earth would incite Oliver into believing in ghosts? Had Hunt and Meera been trapped in some missing passageway?

Instead of encountering a scene of panic in the gallery, she found. . . relative calm. The massive butler stood in the center of the long, windowed room, his balding head bent over a small leather notebook and pencil, scribbling. His son prowled the edges, tapping on walls. Clare skidded to a halt. Had madness infected the entire household?

Then she heard it, a rap, rap, rap coming from. . . the floor? Not the wall, where they'd heard Arnaud going up and down stairs.

Quincy held up a palm when she started to speak. His lips moved as he counted out the raps on his fingers, then jotted in his notebook.

Adam, his son, straightened and crossed the room, carrying a lamp. Evening gloom had set in.

"Code, miss," he whispered. "The ghost is speaking in code."

Madness. The whole household was entirely mad. Clare rubbed her temple. And here she thought she was imaginative.

A long string of taps followed. Quincy gave up counting on his fingers and started making hasty marks in his book.

"Hunt knows code," Oliver whispered.

"Then Walker knows code," Clare whispered back. "Fetch him. He's searching the yard." She might as well join the insanity. She wasn't accomplishing anything else. She absolutely, categorically refused to think in terms of a vital man like the captain as a ghost or she would be sobbing worse than Mrs. G.

The tapping paused and shifted to a different section of the gallery. It started again with only three short raps. Coordinating the search, Walker wouldn't be far, she prayed.

Clare's insides roiled and her head whirled. She wanted no more than to sit down with a decent hot tea, put her feet up. . . The rapping began again. Five, this time.

"He's repeating hisself," Quincy stated. "Three, five. . ." He counted the longer string. "Twelve."

Unable to take it any longer, Clare unceremoniously sat down on the nearest gilded chair. She held her head in her hands as the raps pounded another twelve times. Three, five, twelve, twelve. . . No, she could make no sense of it. But if he was actually repeating himself. . .

That was no ghost.

"Hunt." She sat up straight again. "Hunt is down there. How do we reach the cellar?"

Male boots clattered into the vestibule. The tapping continued. She clung to the chair arms to keep from falling out, but her stomach wanted to heave. She didn't have time to be ill. . .

Walker raced in, followed by Oliver. Clare pointed at Quincy and his notebook. "Code. Hunt's in the cellar."

Cellar. C—third letter of the alphabet. E—fifth letter. Two twelves. . .

Was he hurt? Why was he signaling? Was he trapped by rising water? Vague images of blue water rising, rising, washing over the walls. . .

As Walker rapped a reply on the wooden floor, Clare quit fighting the nausea and spinning and let go, toppling onto the floor.

MEERA STRUGGLED AGAINST THE ROPES SHE'D SPENT FOREVER LOOSENING. IF only she could reach the jackknife in her pocket, almost there. . .

The woodshed beside the stable was icy damp. She shivered uncontrollably, terrified she might be shaking the babe like gelatin. She'd heard horses riding out what seemed like an eternity ago. Did that mean the men had left? Why?

Fury kept her straining at her bonds. If Jacob had harmed the hair on the head of one single person inside that manor, she'd take an ax to his thick skull, chop off his hand at the wrist so he couldn't lift another weapon. . .

Her fingers finally wrapped around the folded handle of her herb knife. She wiggled it out and flipped it open, then began the arduous task of sawing the rope tying her hands. The rope was rotted. It frayed quickly. Stiff, aching, shaking with rage and cold, she broke free. The ax in the corner had held her fixated the entire time she'd been bound. She grabbed it now.

What was Jacob doing? Someone would have been out here if he'd been caught sneaking about. If he'd been hiding in the shed all this time, did he know their routines? Was it dinner time yet? If he knew everyone was occupied. . .

He couldn't possibly know where she'd hidden her book. He'd be hunting in her isolated workshop, where no one ever went—unless they were looking for her. If it was dinner time, Clare would be looking for her. Or Walker.

She swallowed her fear, barely able to hold the ax as she stumbled into the gray light of evening. She almost fell into Ned, the deaf mute. A slight, gangling youth of fifteen, he held the reins of his pony cart and startled at her appearance. She couldn't send a child after a madman.

She held a finger to her lips and gestured at the portico side entrance of the ground floor, then indicated she'd take the servants' stairs. She tried to imply urgency with a pointing finger. He ran for the manor. She clung to the ax and staggered for the stairs.

The babe inside her moved, or she thought it did. She was shivering so hard, she could be imagining it. Or maybe she was losing it—her mind or the child. She wasn't entirely certain as she traversed the old cellar stairs downward. Where was everyone? Shouldn't there be a clamor in the kitchen with dinner preparations?

Her workshop under the old manor had probably once been a root cellar, or perhaps a place to store the preserves no one made anymore. Shelves lined the walls, which was why she'd chosen it.

The half door was open. One glimpse inside revealed no Jacob, but his vengeance was complete. He'd ripped off shelves in search of a hiding place, strewing all her carefully labeled jars and tins across the floor. He had to have deliberately stomped on them for the destruction to be so thorough. He'd even torn her pages of notes.

She'd weep, but then she couldn't find the monster and kill him. She crept down the passage to the kitchen, past the laundry and ironing rooms, the plate storage, the servants' hall. Just as she feared Jacob had murdered them all, she heard Walker and nearly fainted in relief. Except he was shouting about Clare. Unbelievably, Jacob was shouting back, and Mrs. G shrieked like a banshee.

Feeling murderous, Meera burst into the chaos like an avenging ghost, with her hair loose and streaming down her back and her clothes filthy and in disarray. She didn't care. Lifting her ax, she focused on Jacob—holding a pistol on her friends. He had his back to her. One strike to the neck. . .

But she was a true physician after all. She couldn't do it. Instead, she swung the ax with the flat of the blade. Helga screamed and Jacob ducked. Meera staggered, off balance, straight into Walker's strong arms. He held her close, refusing to let her strike again.

Wielding a heavy iron skillet, the old cook walloped Jacob's weapon hand, blessedly sending the pistol skittering across the stone floor. Disarmed and outnumbered, the monster turned tail to flee past Meera and Walker.

Grabbing a meat cleaver, shrieking about the river and her son and the good Lord preserving them all, the cook continued her wild attack, chasing Jacob down the passage toward the exit.

While the rest of the staff broke into shocked babble, Meera collapsed, weeping, against the safe harbor of Walker's strong chest.

THIRTY-ONE

A̲t̲ ̲t̲h̲e̲ ̲c̲o̲d̲e̲d̲ ̲r̲a̲p̲p̲i̲n̲g̲ ̲a̲b̲o̲v̲e̲ ̲h̲i̲s̲ ̲h̲e̲a̲d̲, Hunt sighed in relief and leaned on his broken shovel. He'd been heard and understood. He'd feared the old stones were too thick and that everyone had left the gallery for dinner.

As soon as he had tools in hand, he was ripping off that damned door panel. Let all the creatures of the forest pour in the opening to live down here. No more dungeons.

He limped the length of the entire old hall or priory or whatever the hell this structure had once been. He wouldn't install any coal retorts until there were two exits, soundly built and with a bell pull to other sections of the manor. Given the solid wall between this crypt and the rest of the manor, he wasn't certain how he'd arrange that, so the retort might never be built.

His knee ached like hell, and he wanted nothing more than a hot bath and a brandy.

A little whisper in the back of his head said he'd rather have Clare hugging him, kissing his cheek, rubbing soothing warm cloths over his head. . . or other parts, as long as he was dreaming.

First, he had to work out what the devil had happened. Why had the demented cook sent him down here? How had the door been blocked? And why?

The door scraped open just as he reached it. It was dark outside, but he could hear Henri and Arnaud. Of course, Clare wouldn't be out there. She was all aristocratic female who, without lifting a finger, organized an army of servants to heat water and pour tea and light fires. Surprisingly, he thought he could live with that, if he could have her in his bed at night. Her kisses promised warmth under the prim demeanor.

She'd be returning to London by autumn. He didn't think he wanted to stay without her. That would put him right back in the black hole where he'd been a month ago. He needed to figure out how to engineer a relationship.

Did women expect declarations of love? Adoration? He didn't think he had the words.

When the panel flew off, Hunt staggered out and had to brace himself on Henri's shoulder. His cousin cursed as they climbed the stairs. Arnaud leaned in to grab him, half hauling him up. At the top, Henri pounded Hunt on the back, then ordered the new stable hands to rip off the door and bolt. His younger cousin might wield a golden tongue, but he grasped danger like a good soldier.

Someone had bolted him in. Hunt didn't care to think about that. He'd rather think about easing Clare's fears. Would she look happy at his return? Scold him? Be disgusted at his weakness? It was a lot to consider and far more vital than dungeons.

The main entrance was halfway down the front of the sprawling manor. Hunt stayed upright long enough to enter without falling on his face. He despised helplessness and dreaded being treated like an invalid.

Inside, women ran about with lamps and candles, weeping, railing. . . and completely ignoring him. He halted, bewildered that no one even acknowledged their entrance. Arnaud hauled him onward. It was a sign of his confusion that Hunt allowed it.

Not until he was in his study with brandy in hand did he gather his thoughts to speak. "Where's Clare?" were his first words, because nothing would make sense until he heard her pragmatic explanations. He'd even accept her flights of fancy about now.

"Drink." Arnaud pushed the brandy at him. "The servants are preparing hot water. Do you want to bathe down here or can you climb to your room?"

That's when he knew something was very wrong. Hunt shoved the decanter back across the desk. *"Where's Clare?"*

"The women are with her. There's nothing we can do. The kitchen should be sending up food. Get warm until we know what to do next." He started to walk out.

Hunt flung a book at him—and hit him square between the shoulders. His arm had improved, even if his aim hadn't. He'd been targeting his cousin's head. *"Where's Clare?"* he roared, rising from his chair because it was evident she wasn't coming to him. So, he'd go to her.

Fear gnawed at his gut. *He'd been locked in a cellar for a reason.* What had happened to Clare?

"The kitchen says our mad housekeeper has run off into the night with a monster. We don't know what's happening. Sit, drink. A demented old witch can't go far." He continued out the door.

To hell with brandy. Hunt grabbed a sturdy walking stick and limped back to the corridor. Arnaud outpaced him and vanished into the far reaches of the hall. Where the hell was Walker?

The women appeared to be rushing up and down the marble stairs, so he headed that way.

"You're filthy, boy!" His aunt, the stout marchioness grimaced at his condition and swept past in a rustle of silk, calling over her shoulder, "Bathe. You stink. Where have you been?"

"Where's Clare?" he demanded, continuing up while rapidly losing what remained of his patience.

"You can't see her in your condition! She's not your wife or even your housekeeper. Although maybe you ought to do something about the current housekeeper. She's quite mad." Lady Spalding sailed off on a mission of her own.

He'd be quite mad if someone didn't tell him what the hell was happening.

He discovered Oliver sitting forlornly in the hall outside the chamber Clare occupied. The boy scrambled up as soon as he saw Hunt. "Don't let her die," he whispered.

Die? Eyebrows soaring to his hairline, Hunt flung open the bedchamber door.

The scene resembled every sickroom scene he'd ever encountered, without the bloody bandages and hacksaw. A maid carried away a pan that smelled of vomit. Engulfed in an enormous white apron, a mobcap not restraining her loosened, wild, black hair, a weeping Meera replaced a wet cloth on the patient's sweating forehead. One of the new maids heated bricks on the fire. Well, the dog mop whining in the arms of the weeping adolescent in the corner wasn't normal.

Swallowing sheer terror, Hunt approached the bed. He was vaguely aware that Clare wore only a thin nightdress under the blankets, but it was her pale face that held his attention. Even when she'd scolded him like a prim miss, she'd had high color in her cheeks, and her lips had been rosy and plump. Her big blue eyes could pierce the hardest heart.

Her eyes were closed. Her face had no color. Her lips looked dry and etched with pain.

"What happened?" he roared, almost falling down on the bed when he tried to sit.

As if she heard him, she blinked, and her lips twitched in what might have been a smile, except it winked out again, and she returned to tossing her head and twisting in pain.

"She's been poisoned," Meera stated coldly.

Not certain he'd heard right, Hunt turned to the little apothecary. "What the *hell* is happening here?"

As if he hadn't spoken, Meera rubbed at a bruise forming on her cheek. "I've administered an emetic. She probably hasn't eaten most of the day, so the poison acted quickly. Have they caught Mrs. Gaither yet?"

A modicum of rationality began to filter into his befuddled brain. Mrs. G had sent him to the cellar. Locked him in? And then. . . He shook his head, still not comprehending.

"Mrs. Gaither? The housekeeper? Why would she poison Clare?" Hunt caught Clare's restless, pale hand and held it between his grubby ones. He was leaving mud all over the clean sheets and didn't care.

"I think she poisoned Gaither too. There was nightshade on his bedside table. After she ran off, I had Walker break open her herb cabinet. She has foxglove and belladonna and even poppy seeds." Meera lifted a liquid concoction to Clare's lips.

"Flower seeds in the herb cabinet? Doesn't laudanum come from poppy seeds?" Hunt sorted through his scrambled brain for what fragments of medicine he knew.

"They can all be used for medicinal purposes, if you know what you're doing. They're also deadly poisons. Nightshade would have slowed Gaither's blood, constricting what little flow he had to the brain. Foxglove affects the heart, but fortunately, Clare's is strong. She lost consciousness, but I think she'll come around if we got it out of her system. It takes more than a sip of tea to kill with foxglove, unless there's an underlying condition." Meera used a glass to listen to her patient's heartbeat.

The diminutive woman as physician was distracting enough. Meera looking as if she'd been through a war beneath the bulky apron. . . Where was Walker?

Focus required cutting through his terror to ask the right questions. "Why would Mrs. Gaither poison Clare?"

"Bosworth," Clare whispered, not opening her eyes.

"Bread and broth," Meera shouted. "Bring bread, broth, and a pot of hot tea."

Oliver shouted and pushed past Hunt to climb on the bed and hug his aunt. Clare's arms circled him instinctively, even though she still looked like a corpse. Hunt gulped air and forced himself to sit still and cypher facts before shouting bloody murder.

Lady Spalding halted in the doorway with a tray of tea. "Bosworth? Did she say Bosworth? The banker?"

"Diary," Clare whispered. "Read diaries."

"Bosworth poisoned you?" Hunt couldn't fathom that.

"Mrs. Gaither poisoned her, I told you." Meera took the tray and poured a small amount of tea in the cup, blowing on it to cool it down.

"Son." Clare caressed Oliver's head. "I think. Find Mrs. G."

"All right. I can do that." Wishing he were in Oliver's position, Hunt hauled himself up and almost tumbled again.

"Not you." His aunt smacked him with a napkin and pushed him back down. "You'd just topple down the stairs. You should take a bath."

Oliver hopped up and raced out, on a self-appointed mission. The mop dog leapt from Lavender's arms and ran after him. At least it didn't yap, much. Hunt was beginning to think he'd fallen and hit his head and was having nightmares.

"If the cook or a banker or anyone else poisoned Clare, then I'm finding them and pushing them through a meat grinder." Hunt rose again, but his knee caved, and he sank back to the bed.

He thought Clare giggled. Fear and hope chased in circles through his unsteady thoughts.

Before Hunt could make another attempt, Walker finally made an appearance, holding a wiggling Oliver by the collar and gesturing a protesting Lady Lavinia inside. "The pony cart is gone. We assume the cook or Jacob stole it."

"Jacob?" Hunt roared.

Meera practically growled. "I should have killed him."

Clare opened her eyes again, looking alarmed. "Your book?"

Meera gently soothed her brow with the cloth. "Locked in the hidden space where the diaries were, wrapped in oilcloth. It's safe."

Walker sent her a harried, worried look but continued, "Henri and Arnaud are riding after the cart. Adam and Quincy are guarding the ground floor entrances. Everyone stay in here until it's safe." He dropped Oliver in the room and shut the door after the irate baroness.

Leaning on her walking stick, the irate Lady Lavinia resembled an elderly preying mantis. "What is the meaning of this? Why can't I sit peacefully in my own chamber? Why must I be subject to. . ." Her glare encompassed a filthy Hunt as well as her granddaughter setting down the tea tray. "Sick-room smells and filth."

"Because an assassin is on the loose and it might be your maid," Lavender answered spitefully.

Meera emitted a strangled giggle.

If Meera was giggling, then the worst must be past. Or she was hysterical. *Jacob?*

Oliver produced one of the slender diaries from the back of his trouser band and shoved it at Lavender, distracting from any irate response.

Flouncing down in a corner with the diary and flipping through it, the girl glared. "It's in French. I can't read it."

"What do you mean, you can't read it?" Her grandmother's pompadour shook as she smacked the old book with her stick. "I spent a fortune on your schooling and *you can't read French?*"

Resigned, Hunt sat down again to watch Clare consume her tea. He was too weary to ask for explanations or even brandy. Walker could learn to keep an eye on the troops.

Maybe the book held answers to this madness. "I can't read unless you hold a lamp and a magnifier over the scrawl. Sound out the words, Lavender, and I'll translate." He turned to Oliver. "Why this volume?"

"Date." The boy settled on the window seat with a biscuit he'd nipped from his aunt's tray. The draperies were still open. Night had settled in.

"It's the next one from the stack Clare's been reading." Lavender flipped it open and held it to the lamp beside her chair. "July, 1764."

Clare struggled to sit up. Hunt assisted her, exchanging glares with Meera until the mob-capped chemist backed away to plump pillows. He needed to hold Clare, feel her warmth, assure himself that she was alive. He didn't want any more death on his watch. Her frame was far too slender.

He handed her a fresh teacup and helped her wrap her hands around it while Lavender stumbled over the opening page of the diary.

It became instantly apparent that the girl could barely read at all, much less pronounce foreign words. The frail Lady Lavinia snatched the volume in disgust and lifted her lorgnette to take up reading, while Lavender curled in her chair, sniveling.

Propped against her pillow, Clare coughed, handed her cup to Hunt, and tried to catch the lady's attention. Hunt simply stood, snatched the book from the old witch, and handed it to Clare.

She gave him a wan smile, then whispered hoarsely, "Lavender, come here, please."

With uneasy glances at her seething grandmother, the girl took a place on the other side of the bed.

"Read this." Clare held a trembling finger to the page.

She was obviously too weak to hold the book. Hunt wanted to take it away, but he wanted to hear what she had to say first. Lavender's pronunciation had been nonsense to him, and his French was decent.

Looking as if she'd rather be shot, Lavender leaned over and re-read the line. It still made no sense. Clare had her read the next line with the same result. She was stumbling over gibberish. Hunt leaned over to see the line, lifting his eyepatch in some self-destructive belief it might help. For a change, the lamplight didn't hurt. He could make out a few words that didn't resemble what Lavender was reading.

"My mother had this problem." Looking frail, Clare handed the book back. "She had to memorize the way words looked after someone sounded them out. She couldn't sound them out on her own. Words in an unknown language would make reading that way impossible."

"Your mother couldn't read?" Willing to be distracted from whatever was happening below, Hunt tried to fathom surviving without reading. Well, he'd have to, wouldn't he? His eyesight would never be whole again.

"She could read and write, but it was difficult, so she didn't often try. She mostly memorized her prayer book. Her spelling was appalling. I had to write letters for her. She wasn't stupid. Neither is Lavender. Their minds just don't function with the written word. It may be one of our lesser family traits." She gestured weakly at Lady Lavinia. "Let us hear what the diary says. I think it might explain Mrs. Gaither's actions."

Hunt had no idea why a viscountess might write about a cook, but he waited to hear what his grandmother's diary had to say. If he had to guess, he'd surmise Mrs. G might be of an age with his grandmother, had she lived.

Looking stunned and relieved, Lavender retired to her corner and her sewing. Applying her lorgnette, Lady Lavinia began reading a rant about the viscount's infidelities. She hmphed and skipped pages. Apparently finding something that caught her interest, she stopped and looked up. "Helga. She's speaking of a maid called Helga. Is that not. . . ?"

Mrs. Gaither's name was Helga.

THIRTY-TWO

LISTENING TO THE CROTCHETY BARONESS READ, CLARE NIBBLED A PIECE OF TOAST. The toast was cold, but no one was leaving the bedchamber for food until Mrs. Gaither and Jacob were found. She didn't have the strength, and the others were mesmerized by the late viscountess's grief and anger.

She really needed to add this level of pathos to her novels. It was riveting.

Or would be, except having Hunt's big body at her side was disturbing her muddled brain. Their hips practically touched. She could smell his earthy maleness beneath the stink of mud. He was crippled and in pain, and he still hovered protectively between her and the door, as if he'd hold off an army with a mighty sword. Or his stench. She tried not to giggle at that.

The reading stopped any further urge to laugh.

Helga says Reid wants to drown their son like an unwanted kitten. HIS SON! My husband is mad.

The baroness stopped reading and handed the book to Lady Spalding. "There are tears spotting the ink. I can't read anymore. Reid is your father. You decide whether to go on." Her voice quaking, Lady Lavinia amazingly accepted a cup of tea from her bastard granddaughter. Her wrinkles deepened beneath the gray pompadour, and her mole quivered as she sipped.

The younger marchioness hesitated over accepting the aging tome. "I don't know if I can. He was my father. I only remember him in polished perfection. I know men have affairs and children out of wedlock, but. . ." She didn't look at the pages.

Meera stood to take the book. "Helga poisoned Clare and Mr. Gaither and most likely locked Hunt in the cellar. She allowed Jacob to carry me off. I think she was trying to drive us all away. We need to know why and what she might do next. Is she likely to set the manor afire?"

She returned the book to Clare and brightened the lamp beside the bed. Clare stroked the cover, trying to think what Hunt's grandmother must have suffered. If her husband had wanted to drown an *infant* just because it was a bastard. . . The viscountess had a right to histrionics.

Hunt squeezed her hand encouragingly. "We need to know," he murmured.

She aligned the book beneath the light so it fell on the spiky handwriting. She translated aloud as she read and fell under the spell of the horrible story.

Her listeners sat silent after the last passage.

"Lady Reid was what, around seventeen?" Clare handed the diary to Hunt, who looked thunderstruck. "Her husband was the magistrate. She had no one to turn to."

"She did everything right," Lady Lavinia declared stiffly, rubbing at the mole on her lip—or a tear. "It's all any woman could have done. Showing her husband the blacksmith's stillborn infant to prove his baseborn son was dead, as he'd ordered, was brilliant. Reid didn't deserve to know that the child lived and went to a home that welcomed him."

Hunt squeezed the book in his filthy hand. "I think the stillborn infant may have been carried to the cellar. I don't think it was buried. If Helga did that, she may have been slightly mad even then."

Clare covered her mouth and tried not to gag. She glanced anxiously at Oliver, but he'd fallen asleep in the window seat, bored with what he couldn't understand.

Hunt brushed his muddy print off the diary's cover. "Assuming the Helga my grandmother writes about is the same one who tried to poison Clare, then she was Reid's lover, bore his son, and gave it up to a gentleman in *town.* Not the village. When she led me to the cellar, she kept referring to her son and how he would take care of her. Unless she's completely mad, she knows who he is."

"And she's gone to fetch him," Clare whispered. "She told me to go home. She said her son would take his rightful place. That wasn't all she said." She strained to recall the cook's exact phrasing.

Hunt rubbed her shoulder with his big hand, as if he could ease her. As warm and welcome as his touch was, he couldn't take away her fear and sorrow. The housekeeper who'd had command of the manor for decades was unhinged and running loose—and their presence may have driven her to it.

"If I'm remembering correctly. . ." Clare paused, gathering her weak wits. The poison and lack of food left her muzzy. "She told me Hunt had gone to the river, like *the other*. She said the river washes them clean. And then she rambled about someone saving her baby—that would be Lady Reid then, wouldn't it?"

"But I didn't go to the river. I went to the cellar." Hunt frowned at the puzzle.

"My father ended in the river," Lady Spalding said, looking appalled. "Do you think she. . ."

"*The river washes them clean,*" Clare murmured. "That's what she told me."

"She ranted something similar as she ran after Jacob," Meera said, appalled.

Hunt shook his head, starting to grasp the whole picture. "The viscount got drunk, went to the river for some reason, and she shoved him in, believing she'd sent him to his just rewards?"

"That would have been *years* later." Clare took back the diary. "This was written while the viscountess still lived here. She didn't flee until a year or more after this incident. The viscount was still alive for years after that. Lady Spalding was old enough to remember him visiting."

Clare rubbed her temple, trying to remember exact words. "Mrs. G said that she, Helga, saved *her*. Lady Reid? She later helped Lady Reid to escape?"

"We need the next books." Lavender stood up. "I'll fetch them."

"Wait." Clare tried to calm her churning insides. "Helga also said *she* shouldn't have returned, and she kept insisting that we leave and go back where we belong. I don't think she wants us here. When I refused to leave and insisted on searching for Hunt, she poisoned me."

"She may not have been trying to kill you, just drive you away? Or stop you from finding Hunt?" Meera asked.

"You think she may have killed my *grandmother* for returning?" Hunt stood, apparently grasping the implications. He appeared dangerously near murder himself.

"Look at the dates." Clare gestured at the diary. "If our conjectures are correct, Helga's son would have been born in 1763 and only about four when the viscount died. But by the time the earl died in 1781. . . I suppose there is no point in looking into Wycliffe's death now. . . Helga's son would have been a young man. Could she have been mad enough to believe the earl would leave the manor to his baseborn grandson? Did the earl even *know* about him?"

"Reid and his wife were given life estates in the manor," Hunt reminded her. "Helga had to know it belonged to Lady Reid for her lifetime. After his son's death, though, the earl left everything to his siblings, daughters, and *grandchildren.*"

He limped for the door. "If no one else claimed the manor, then Helga's son might have applied. Just as Lavender might apply to be listed as heir. By law, they can't, but Wycliffe did not specify legitimacy. They have a case. That means there may be another heir lurking in the shadows."

He stalked out, shouting for Quincy to find Walker.

Clare glanced at Lavender, who had frozen in place at learning she might have a claim. Both the old ladies appeared shocked, but that didn't prevent them from speaking.

"Baseborn children cannot inherit," Lady Lavinia stated unequivocally, pounding her stick. "It is unheard of, beyond the bounds of law and decency. Why, we'd have tinkers and blackamoors showing up at the door, claiming to be relations."

Clare coughed on any reply. Henri was close enough to a tinker. He was Hunt's relation. Hunt was actually no relation to the earl at all. And she rather thought Walker had more sense than to make any claim to a madhouse. But Mrs. Gaither's illegitimate son. . .

"Bosworth," Lady Spalding said out of the blue. "You said *Bosworth* earlier. The banker?"

Clare nodded, waiting to see if the marchioness had more to add to her wild speculation.

"Bosworth Sr. must be ninety, if he's a day. His wife died years ago, but she wasn't much younger. Bosworth Jr. is most likely in his fifties. It's not impossible that she had him late in life, but unlikely." Lady Spalding covered her mouth and widened her eyes as the possibility registered.

"Bosworth is the right age, has the hair and eye color. . . and thumb," Lady Lavinia admitted in resignation. "I saw it before he pulled on gloves and wondered. Oh, what a tangled web we weave. . ."

"I don't think the men understand the danger!" Clare shoved off her covers and attempted to swing out of bed, despite her spinning head.

Meera shoved her back. "They know. I'll remind them, then bring up food you might keep down."

THIRTY-THREE

HUNT STILL DIDN'T HAVE THE FULL STORY OF JACOB'S PRESENCE AND MEERA'S disheveled state. He wasn't being told everything. He only knew two dangerous killers lurked in the shadows.

If he weren't here. . . The manor might become a nest of thieves instead of a home for the homeless. He was starting to think like Clare. Maybe this wasn't all about him. Maybe he needed a woman to remind him.

As he reached the ground floor, Henri strode from the side entrance, looking damp and weary. Seeing Hunt, he grimaced and said with finality, "Your cook won't be poisoning anyone else."

Hunt felt the knife edge of guilt twist in his gut. He didn't want to be judge and jury over anyone, least of all, a woman—but that's what his position here might entail. "What happened?"

"The brook has become a muddy river filled with debris overflowing the bridge. We don't know exactly what happened, but the pony is on the far side of the bridge and the cart isn't." Henri scrubbed at his damp hair with a towel Quincy handed him. "Ned isn't precisely clear at the best of times, but he seems to be saying that Meera's husband was in the cart when it went into the stream, dead or alive, we don't know. By the time we arrived, any trace had washed away. Arnaud has gone into the village to find help in looking for bodies."

Hunt would have sent the mad old woman to assizes for her crimes, not ordered execution. Perhaps she preferred it this way. He ran his hand through his hair, trying to *think*. He wished he had the luxury of his grand-mother's histrionics to cover his confusion.

Thinking like an army man helped. He turned to Quincy and Adam. "Do we have anyone we can send to help search?"

If *Jacob* had been here. . . the cad could rot in hell if he'd hurt Meera, which he apparently had. The usually colorful, always neat chemist had strived to conceal it, but underneath the servants' garb, she looked as if she'd been through a mill.

Quincy nodded at his son. "Gather the stable hands, lad. Do what you can to show Mrs. Gaither respect."

A murderess didn't deserve respect, but Hunt saw no reason to destroy the reputation of a grief-driven old woman now that she was gone. His leg and his eye might be weak, but his shoulders were still strong. He'd carry that burden alone.

The kitchen servants watched with terrified solemnity when he took the stairs down. They had no notion of what was happening. Troops should never be left uncertain, especially on the eve of battle.

"I'm afraid Mrs. Gaither, in her grief, has lost her life trying to reach her son. The men are going to the river to bring her body back. They'll be needing a hearty hot meal when they return. Do any of you know her family?"

Wringing her hands, Betsy spoke up. "She didn't have naught but Mr. Gaither. We never knew about no son."

Lavender's gray-haired companion nodded. "She told us naught about family."

Hunt frowned. "If we can find no one else, we'll see her buried here. She's served the family all her life and deserves a proper service."

Whatever gossip they may have been whispering, the servants all nodded agreement to his command. Putting chaos into order was familiar territory and eased more of his confusion. "I think the ladies will be ready to dine shortly. Are you able to provide a meal under these circumstances?"

The young plump assistant cook, Mrs. Evans, spoke up. "We have lamb roasting and a vegetable soup, nothing fancy, but nourishing."

Mrs. Ingraham asked, "How is Miss Knightley?"

"Miss Knightley is recovering from a slight stomach ailment. I believe she'll need to eat lightly tonight, but she should be well by morning." He hoped and prayed. Her head was certainly working just fine. *Another bastard heir?* A male one.

"Does Miss Lavender need me?" the old lady Hunt suspected to be the girl's maternal grandmother asked anxiously. "I can help here if not."

"She's with Miss Knightley and fine. Have you seen Walker?" Growing impatient, Hunt returned to his purpose.

The new scullery maid led him through the warren of cellar rooms to Meera's workshop, where Walker cleaned up an unholy mess of tins and smelly weeds.

At Hunt's arrival, he glanced up in relief. "If they don't find Jacob's body, I'll have to hunt him down and kill him."

Hunt nodded wearily. "If the cook chased him out with a cleaver, we can't be sure he was alive when he left here. A body should wash up somewhere. When they dig the housekeeper's grave, we'll throw him in too."

"He destroyed her workshop, her library, and tried to kill her and their child." Walker spoke with disgust, as if he wanted to spit. "The man had freedom, education, and a secure position but wasn't satisfied."

"Petty minds need to control their little world. Meera escaped his control, and he couldn't allow that." Hunt had known abusive men. He'd never understand them.

Walker looked uncomfortable. "She's afraid she'll lose her babe."

Hunt hadn't known the little chemist was carrying a child. He ran his hand over his hair and studied Walker. He was pretty sure Walker was behaving like a man who worried over a woman to whom he was attached— as Hunt was fretting over Clare. They were no longer all just acquaintances.

Walker would be happier here, where he didn't have to fear men who would lock him in chains. This really wasn't all about Hunt and his injured sensibilities.

"The monster tried to kill his own child." Walker rubbed his temples in disbelief.

"As Lord Reid tried to kill his bastard. Apparently, life doesn't have meaning to some people. Does she think she'll keep it? She seems to be a pretty sound physician." Hunt hoped. He'd been relying on Meera to help Clare.

"I mixed the concoction she ordered, but she won't rest. That's all I know. We need a midwife." Walker returned to sweeping.

If they stayed here. . . a midwife was the least of what they needed.

First things first. . . were they staying? And if they did, should they hunt the cook's bastard—or was *he* hunting *them*?

∾

ON MONDAY, AFTER A GOOD NIGHT'S SLEEP, CLARE FELT A LITTLE EMPTY BUT strong enough to check on Meera.

The villagers had recovered the bodies of both Mrs. Gaither and Jacob. No one had mentioned whether or not Jacob had hatchet wounds.

Last night, Walker had insisted that they move Meera to the safety of the ground floor infirmary where he'd fixed up the cot for her. From the looks of the new infirmary's shelves, he had sorted the remains of her bottles and jars as well.

Clare found Meera cutting and drying herbs over a grate to replace the ones lost. Walker was a wise man. Meera could now sleep and work on the main floor and not risk the babe by going up and down so many stairs.

"Now that there is no fear of Jacob, do you still wish to stay in the country?" Clare asked.

Meera gestured wide. "With all this land for growing and replacing what it took me years to gather in the city? Of course, I want to stay."

Besides, Walker was here, at her beck and call. Clare hid her smile of relief and understanding. After yesterday, she was none too certain about returning to the city herself. She needed more time to understand how Hunt felt.

She sought him in his usual hiding places and located him in the library with his lamp and magnifying glass, sketching on a large drawing pad.

"You're avoiding me." When they'd first arrived, she'd wanted nothing more than to avoid him. In the past weeks, he'd become a necessary part of her life, almost as much as Meera and Oliver. She no longer feared this commanding officer. It was amazing how much lighter she felt having some of her anxiety removed.

Last night, the ladies had read the rest of the viscountess's diaries. The story of Lady Reid's escape to Paris—leaving her beloved daughter in Helga's care—had not been pretty. The diary verified the name of the man who had adopted the maid's son as the one who helped her escape—Bosworth Sr.

Helga was gone. Her son remained. She knew Hunt had been stewing over that revelation ever since.

Clare stood next to him at the table, studying his sketch. It seemed to be of a wide bridge with railing, one large enough for a carriage?

He glanced up. "I was waiting to see if you packed and fled."

"Why would I do that? The manor and the village need us. Unless you tell me that Bosworth has the best claim on the property, then I see no reason to leave." She'd thought about it, admittedly.

"For his ignorance in not having a professional read the deed, he owns no more than the rough side of the hill. I'll speak with him before we turn the matter over to attorneys." Hunt set down his pencil and brushed a straying curl from Clare's face. "I want to speak with you as well, but I don't know how."

Her insides bubbled in anticipation, but she understood his reluctance. "We don't know each other well enough, I understand. These past weeks have been. . ."

His expression softened. "Exactly. So let me be blunt, since that does not seem to scare you."

She almost laughed. "Aye, aye, captain. You lead, and I will follow."

He looked a bit surprised but continued carefully. "If we both stay here, I want to court you. If it's all right with you, I'll ask permission of your great aunt, but I fear that's only out of politeness. I won't listen to no."

The familiar terror cut briefly to her core, but this was Hunt, her steadfast captain, the man strong enough to accept her, fears and all. "I've never been courted," she whispered, feeling longing pushing away anxiety. "I think I would like that, if we do not kill each other in the process."

He laughed in relief and drew her into his arms. "I won't destroy books or shoot bats for your sake. It's a great sacrifice. I demand recompense." He leaned over and kissed her.

Courting seemed superfluous after that.

THIRTY-FOUR

AYE, AYE, CAPTAIN. HUNT HELD CLARE'S WHIMSICAL RESPONSE IN MIND AS HE gathered his troops on Tuesday morning. He knew she'd fight him if he took her obedience for granted, but her respect had given him a confidence he'd been lacking when he'd first arrived.

He'd thought himself a dried-up husk, good for nothing. Without his eye, he'd never be what he was. But she'd made him realize that he could offer more than most men when it came to this manor. . . and to Clare. For Clare, he might even become more than he was. It would take time, and the aid of a winsome lass who didn't appreciate how special she was.

At breakfast, the older ladies declared their intention of leaving for London the next day, after the cook's funeral. They offered to take Clare with them. To his utter relief, she refused.

They'd found the bodies of both the cook and Jacob caught in tree roots before they'd reached the river downstream. He'd sent word to the solicitors and Bosworth. He didn't know if they'd attend the interment today. With the help of his new family, Hunt was prepared, if they did.

Before the funeral, the rain stopped. Clouds still scuttled across the dawn as Walker picked out the men to carry Jacob to the graveyard. They'd dug the grave a distance from the small mausoleum where the viscount had been interred, next to Mr. Gaither's fresh one. Then they'd discreetly buried the cad beneath a layer of dirt and straw. There were no mourners.

The housekeeper was laid out in the community coffin. The grave diggers waited as the villagers carried her remains to the manor's cemetery. No one showed excessive amounts of grief. If there was gossip about her death, none spoke of it.

Bosworth showed up at the last minute to say a word for the woman he claimed to know only as a long-time housekeeper and caretaker. The solicitors he'd brought with him stayed in the manor.

By the time Mrs. G was laid to eternal rest, the day had turned sunny. Hunt provided a keg of cider for the mourners who had traveled a distance to pay their respects. The kitchen served up hearty soup and meat pies. Hunt offered the servants a half day off and left everyone to their gathering.

Having no idea if the banker knew they'd just laid his mother to rest, Hunt led him into a manor prepared for war. Shrugging off caped coats and top hats and handing them to the stalwart butler, they strode into the impressive, oak-paneled great hall where the solicitors waited with the ladies.

Clare was presiding over the tea tray as usual. His battle-axes of an aunt and great-aunt had taken strategic positions in the wing chairs by the fire, where they plied their needlework. Holding her dog in her lap, Lavender had defiantly taken a lady's place next to Clare on the sofa. Meera sat at a table, copying the notes from one of her torn notebooks into a fresh one. Hunt was learning to appreciate the stamina of the delicate sex.

Arnaud, Henri, and Walker arrived to take up stations on the perimeter. Their futures depended on the outcome of this meeting as much as his did. Hunt had debated inviting the domestics and the villagers but decided that while he might thrive on conflict, others might not.

Ignoring Hunt, Bosworth appropriated the largest chair and gestured at the eldest solicitor as if he were already lord of the manor. "Explain the details, please, Latham."

Like a good general, Hunt took a tactical position on the sofa on the other side of Clare. He rested his aching leg on a low stool while the mortgage documents he and Walker had pored over were read aloud. Latham was a decent man, a little long in the tooth and deficient in knowledge, but otherwise trustworthy. Hunt didn't interrupt him.

His cousins poured themselves brandy and took sentry positions at the windows to watch the drive.

Walker commanded a straight chair and perused an estate journal on the sidelines. The lawyers really ought to be paying attention to him. They wouldn't, of course. An African in a clerk's collar, unassuming Walker was Hunt's secret weapon.

When the solicitor was finished presenting his case that the estate was, indeed, in debt to Bosworth and his bank, that the heirs were liable for the debt, and that the trust account could not be used to pay it, Hunt set his foot down but did not rise.

"Most excellent summary, gentlemen, thank you. Would you care for a brandy? Quincy will be delighted to provide anything you need while we present our case." Hunt signaled Walker, who sat near the newly installed bellpull. Being new to staff, the butler had chosen to forego the funeral festivities to look after the company.

"There is no case," Bosworth objected. "Had you not insisted on coming here instead of signing the papers we sent you, you would not have wasted everyone's time. The earl refused to pay the debt. Lady Reid attempted to make payments. They were not enough. The bank owns the manor and the mortgages the locals took out to buy their lots when Reid sold them. You have no means of raising the funds to repay what is owed."

Quincy arrived bearing bottles and glasses. Latham and his associates accepted them. Still wearing his gloves, Bosworth waved him away.

"The mortgage document is quite legal, sir," Latham said mournfully, sipping his brandy. "The copy given to you is exact."

Hunt nodded and waved off the brandy as well. "Yes, we've examined it. I believe you were told that I'm a surveyor, as is Mr. Walker." He nodded at his friend, who didn't bother glancing up. "We have read the document and compared it to a map the earl had surveyors draw up. The reason the earl did not pay his son's debt is because the mortgaged land is worthless. You will find the particulars on the table over by the window. You are free to hire your own surveyors, of course."

Bosworth looked in danger of turning purple. "The estate is not worthless! Perhaps to its heirs but not to the bank."

Oddly, the sweet scent of jasmine seemed to waft from the walls—or perhaps all the diaries Clare had piled up. Bosworth wrinkled his nose with a puzzled expression, as if he smelled it too.

One of the solicitor's associates strolled to the window to examine the map and documents.

Ignoring ghostly perfumes, Hunt signaled Lavender, who'd been awaiting her moment. "Would you please show the gentleman the display you've created in the library?"

The dowager marchioness raised her stout frame from her chair. "I will go with you. I expect the proceedings to be noted in the estate files, Latham. I will have them sent to my stepson and his solicitors for verification."

Her stepson, the marquess. With the lady's permission, Hunt had apprised Spalding of the situation. The marquess was in London and not interested as more than his stepmother's agent since he didn't stand to inherit. The title sufficed as a threat for now.

Hunt stood and followed their grumbling guests into the library, where Lavender had created a neat display of the meager evidence they'd gathered: the bloody glove and prayer book, the dirty diamond, the shreds of an infant blanket, the estate journals, and the diaries, three of them opened to the most distressing pages.

Arnaud had also arranged a row of family portraits, newly cleaned.

Hunt let his aunt speak first.

The marchioness held up one of the diaries—and the perfume scent grew stronger. "As much as I hate to speak ill of the dead, and of my father, in particular, I have been made aware that he was a sot and a wastrel. My mother did all she could to save him, to save the staff, and to save the manor. The evidence is here, in her own writing."

"That was well before our time, my lady," Latham said gently. "All water under the bridge."

"Not entirely. Fifty-two years ago, my father did his best to destroy his legacy." She cradled the bloody glove. "My mother escaped his abuse, but before she left, she ensured that the earl's heirs need not suffer as she did. As the passages marked in her prayer book indicate, she did not think highly of men and did not trust them with her secrets."

One of the solicitors checked the passages. Bosworth did not.

Hunt picked up the second diary and handed it to the banker. "The viscount's abuse had already caused Lady Reid to lose one child. When she knew she was to bear another, she did everything possible to protect it. She was only nineteen, frightened, and alone. This book describes how she gathered as many of the family jewels as she could persuade the viscount to let her wear."

He indicated the family portraits with their ostentatious display of gems, then continued, "Rather than return the jewels to the bank vault, she claims to have hidden them on the premises so he could not pawn them. The diary does not name her hiding places."

"She had pearls. She sold them. How do we know she did not sell them all?" Bosworth scanned the hysterical passages of French and frowned. "What is that scent? It seems familiar."

"Jasmine, sir," Clare murmured. "The viscountess apparently enjoyed sachets."

She'd be declaring a ghost watched over them if Hunt did not intervene. "The pearls belonged to the viscountess, a gift upon marriage. That's been documented. She knew the other jewels were entailed. There would have been no mortgage if Reid could have sold them."

Hunt pointed out the small diamond from the vase Gaither shot. "We think my grandmother may have hidden some of the smaller jewels in the vase. We assume, since the viscount didn't use them to pay the mortgage, that the earl must have found them. This one escaped."

"That does not mean she didn't steal the rest. You said she was with child when she fled? Are you saying Lady Reid had a son we don't know about?" Bosworth looked incredulous.

Arnaud stepped forward. "No, she arrived in France with only her pearls. She lost the child she carried. Her family will attest to that. They are sending the diaries in their possession, but they have not yet arrived."

"Then this is all meaningless blather unless you produce a fortune in jewels to pay off the mortgages." Bosworth flung the diary back to the table.

The scent grew stronger.

"You have not been listening." Hunt lifted one of the estate journals and nodded at Clare as she entered. "Miss Knightley warned that ancient books and ledgers were excellent research documents. She was right. Once we read all the diaries and started searching, we found some answers in the half-century old ledgers that were on hand before the lady fled, others from the years of the earl's occupation."

He flipped ledger pages to reveal yellowing documents stuffed between them. "Besides her diaries, the viscountess warned her mother-in-law of what was happening before she fled. You will find her letters in here, as well as copies of the mortgage documents and so forth."

Bosworth's high color faded as he picked up the documents and read.

"We think she may have told Wycliffe or his countess where to find the jewels. We have found some correspondence hidden in the ledgers but not all. Lady Wycliffe died not too long after the loss of her son, so there are many gaps in our knowledge." Clare opened another of the enormous estate books, revealing more yellowing documents. "After the earl's death, when the lady returned, her diary mentions finding his notes but not the jewels. It's possible he sold them. After his son died and the entailment was broken, they were his to dispose of, of course."

Hunt added, "We only tell you this to show we are being completely and open and honest about our research."

Bosworth glared but studied the correspondence.

Hunt continued the story. "The earl built a fortune by paying attention to detail. My great-grandfather distributed the majority of his estate to those who most deserved it, but it appears he didn't wish to let Wycliffe Manor, his ancestral home, out of the family, even if the title died with him."

He produced a document and pointed at the coordinates. "All these deeds read just as the mortgage you showed me did. Now that I have a better understanding of exclaves and districts and property that has never been properly conveyed, I was able to see what he understood—that the coordinates of these deeds are not based on the manor's legal boundaries as shown by the properly surveyed and recorded map in the other room."

Bosworth snatched the yellowing document, found the coordinates, and marched back to the great hall where the map was laid out. The solicitors pored over the remaining papers, comparing them to their files and murmuring.

Hunt followed the angry banker. Clare hooked her arm through his, not bracing him but easing his tension.

"Explain," Bosworth shouted, pointing at the map. "I am not a surveyor."

"Oh, it's simple enough once it's explained," Lady Spalding said, taking up her knitting again. "My grandfather gave his son, my wastrel father, an old deed of the manor property, one based on an oak tree by the river and a rock by the old stone fence and whatnot. Given his lack of character, my father may even have known the deed was incorrect and that the mortgages he signed were fraudulent. As magistrate, he had to have known we were an exclave of Shropshire and not Worcestershire, as the documents say."

"Fraudulent? How can that be?" Pale, the banker turned and yelled, "Latham? What is this?"

The elder lawyer hastened in to examine the map, holding a yellowed document. "This is all before our time, sir. This was between our fathers. I cannot say exactly. . . I would need to research. . ."

While Clare drifted back to the sofa, Hunt leaned against the mantel, taking weight off his knee. "Basically, the viscount mortgaged property that did not exist. When the documents were drawn, they based the coordinates on property lines that were conveyed by handshakes and drawn up centuries ago. The map you're looking at is recent and properly surveyed, showing the correct district, ordered by Wycliffe during his latter years."

"But my f-father. . ." Bosworth stuttered to a halt. "He s-said. . ." The man who did not partake signaled for the decanter.

Hunt tried not to feel sorry for him. The sins of the fathers shouldn't fall on the sons. "Whoever added the property description to these half-century old mortgages must have used medieval documentation that described the creek and the river and places where no one can actually build. Or perhaps the creek and river changed banks over the centuries." He added the last to ease the possibility that a respected banker had been duped.

"To which father do you refer?" Clare asked sweetly, settling back on the sofa as if she hadn't dropped a bombshell.

THIRTY-FIVE

Clare knew Hunt intended to tell Bosworth he was a potential heir, but the dratted captain liked playing cat and mouse too well. As much as she admired Hunt, she could never be submissive to all his whims. She wanted to know just how much Bosworth had known from the first. Had his adopted father known his only son's birthright? Had he told him?

"Wh-which f-father?" Bosworth sat down abruptly. Arnaud handed him a snifter of brandy. It indicated the state of his mind when he accepted it.

Latham's head swiveled from the banker to Hunt, then he, too, refilled his glass and took a seat.

Clare considered taking notes for her novel as Lavender carried in the diaries and passed them around. The lady's exotic sachet faintly scented the books, but the perfume seemed stronger than usual. If she were writing her novel, she'd claim a ghost had returned to visit the boy she'd rescued.

She wouldn't say that in front of these dense men, who finally read the books aloud, although with disgust and amazement. Did they even understand what they were reading?

Would she ever be able to narrate the nuances of character when it came to men? They scoffed at the lady's emotion but delved into the legal import of her declarations. Really, it was tiresome.

Apparently, the elderly Lady Lavinia thought the same. She impatiently whacked her walking stick against the hearth. "Irrelevant, all of it. Latham, tell them a baseborn child has no legal standing. There is nothing to negotiate. If the deeds are fraudulent, then the land belongs to the estate, as my brother intended. There's an end on it. When is dinner?"

"We shall go and dress and leave the men to it, shall we?" Clare rose, shook out her skirts, and left the gentlemen to argue. She had all confidence that Hunt would set them all to the path he'd already decided on. They simply wouldn't do it in front of women.

Hunt smiled faintly and offered a small salute when she looked back. He'd tell her later.

Her heart still pounded that so handsome and intelligent a man even noticed her, much less respected her opinion and wished to *court* her. She blushed at just the thought.

When they came down later, the visitors had departed, and only their little family of gentlemen waited in the family parlor. The men hadn't taken time to change, but then, none of them exactly had dinner clothes anyway.

At her arrival, Hunt straightened and crossed the room, not limping as badly as he had been. He bowed over Clare's hand. "You look ravishing, as always, but it is your brilliance I most admire."

Clare did her best to behave as if she'd received such flattery all her life. "Fah, sir, you will turn my head."

"And flutter your heart?" He took her hand through his arm and led her away from the others so they could speak privately. "The money details are tedious and difficult. Reid borrowed that money. So did the villagers when they attempted to buy lots that didn't exist. The bank must be repaid in some manner, no matter what sleight of hand the earl pulled."

"A much better conversation than flattery. How did Bosworth take his new position? Or did he already know?"

"He contends he did not know. I am not inclined to believe him. He's shifty, that one. Like father, like son, perhaps."

Clare waved dismissively. "We need only find the missing jewels and voila, all is well." Would she be here when they were found?

"We can't count on the earl not having sold the jewels. One alternative is allowing Bosworth to move in and play lord of the manor. He left in a huff, but if the diaries are correct, he is morally as entitled as I am, even if not as legally." He leaned against the mantel and stroked her cheek with a finger. "May I state bluntly that I wish to stay and don't wish to drive you off?"

She tilted her head to admire the warmth in his one dark eye. "You are the one Bosworth will challenge. Are you prepared to stay and fight?"

"If Bosworth chooses to take us to court, we might not have an outcome soon." He shrugged. "I am accustomed to living rough and working hard. The village and farmers will need help to rebuild. If the court agrees that the village still belongs to the estate, then the trust can fund repairs, as well as a bridge and lighting. I will be well occupied. But we need a woman to manage us."

She laughed. "I daresay I might, if I can find a tutor for Oliver. Until the estate can earn an income, Bosworth must stay in town and earn his bread. Besides, I can't resist a treasure hunt."

"I've found my treasure. Jewels cannot compare." He lifted her hand and brushed it with his lips. "If we were alone, I'd kiss you now."

Shivering with excitement at his words and touch, Clare spoke loud enough for the others to hear. "Oh, captain, I believe I've found a mousehole. Will you take a look?"

With mischief, she led him away from their audience. Once they were out of sight, she entered the closed vestibule where even Quincy and Adam wouldn't see.

Her brilliant suitor knew better than to hunt mouseholes. With their ancestors glaring down from above and jasmine wrapping them in its heady scent, Hunt cradled Clare in his arms, where she wanted to be, and they practiced the intimacy they would need to carry them through these next months—and possibly years.

SEVERAL DAYS LATER, AFTER THE GROUND DRIED AND THE OLDER LADIES HAD LEFT for London, the household poured onto the drive at Hunt's direction. Adjusting her shawl, Mrs. Ingraham stood expectantly at Lavender's side. Even Meera emerged from her infirmary to join Clare and the servants. With the departure of Bosworth and the solicitors, Hunt had assumed the role of master of the manor.

Unlike the dismal night of their arrival, the bright sun beamed on woods ablaze with purple violets and bluebells. Primroses peeked from untrimmed shrubbery. Sunshine gleamed on the old golden stones of the manor's three-story façade. Even the orchards on the hillside had hints of flower buds. In another month or two, the old roses clinging to the walls and hedges would be a blaze of glory. Clare drank deeply of the spring air, delighted with her inheritance.

What came next. . . she didn't know. She'd hug Oliver, but he was chasing butterflies or squirrels. Instead, she hugged Meera, who briefly leaned her head against her shoulder. Friendship mattered as much as this old manor.

She wanted to hug Hunt, but he was at his officious best for the moment. Despite the rapture of stolen kisses, neither of them was ready to declare themselves. They were both too mature for infatuation or impetuosity. Too much remained uncertain.

This morning, the captain tilted his top hat to shade his eyes as he stood on the stairs, facing them. He was wearing his blue military coat without formal braid, and a pristine white waistcoat he must have saved for a special occasion. His trousers clung to legs as sturdy as tree trunks, even though she knew one of them ached. The small black eye patch was just part of him, like the dashing scar across his cheek. He'd shaved his usual scruff and someone had trimmed his dark hair so it no longer brushed his collar. He made an excellent image of officer. . . or lord of the manor.

The whispers of the servants silenced when Hunt cleared his throat.

"I have consulted with the solicitors and the bankers. As of the moment, I am now in charge of restoring the estate. My friends and family and I will be needing all manner of workers, so notify your friends and families. The earl's trust will provide wages and housing. We will attempt to establish a button and toy factory to provide income while we rebuild. If the estate earns a profit, we will expand. I cannot make more promises than that. The future will depend on all the people employed here. If you are not comfortable working in this non-traditional setting, you are free to hire out elsewhere. We hope you will stay."

He paused as someone cheered and applause broke out. The cheering grew as it sank in that they might come home again. A few of the stable hands threw their caps in the air.

For a soldier, Hunt was doing quite well. Clare beamed at him. He sent her one of his secret smiles that fluttered her heart. When the clamor died down, he continued. "Today, we celebrate new beginnings. After the dark days that have just passed, we need to welcome the light. I have asked my cousins to fetch food and ale and set up tables on the lawns. We've also brought in a dressmaker, if you'll take turns in the library to be measured for proper uniforms. The day is yours. Enjoy!"

He stepped down, heading straight for Clare.

Perhaps all the manor's secrets had not been uncovered, but their future looked much brighter, indeed.

ACKNOWLEDGMENTS

When I realized I'd created a protagonist called Huntley and an antagonist called Headley, I screamed in frustration, then called for help. My valiant *Rice's Magical Reads* group on Facebook came to my rescue with such amazingly creative villainous names, I am saving them for future use.

Which is only one example of how it takes a community to write a book. Besides my wonderful readers, the hardworking writers at Book View Café are a large part of that community. They are always there to produce the correct answer when I whine about the arbitrariness of commas. They research, edit, and gently remind me of production timelines when my memory fails. Running both a bookstore and publishing company from time zones around the world, Book View Café members perform astonishing feats on a daily basis, and I am grateful for them.

And then there is my amazing cover designer, Kim Killion at the Killion Group. Anyone who can translate my rambling descriptions into the magical covers she produces needs a standing ovation. Take a bow, Kim.

And the usual suspects—the Cauldron and Word Wenches for brainstorming and support, and my family and friends for their kind understanding of my eccentricities.

Over forty years and more than eighty books, I still cannot thank everyone enough. I am always grateful for their ever-lasting support and for not killing me.

CHARACTERS

Captain Alistair Huntley—engineer, US Army
Daniel Walker—Hunt's accountant, secretary
Benedict Bosworth Jr.—banker for Wycliffe Manor Trust
George Reid, Earl of Wycliffe—deceased 1781
Viscount Nicholas Reid—Hunt's grandfather in name only; deceased 1767
Viscountess Gabrielle Reid—Hunt's maternal grandmother; deceased 1800
Frances Reid Huntley—Hunt's mother; Gabrielle's youngest daughter
Elaine, Lady Spalding— marchioness of Spalding, Hunt's aunt; Gabrielle's eldest daughter;
Clarissa (Clare) Knightley—spinster; great-granddaughter of Earl of Wycliffe
Beatrice Knightly Owen—Clare's deceased sister
Oliver Knightley Owen—Clare's seven-year-old nephew
Meera Abrams—druggist/apothecary; Clare's best friend
Miss Lavender Marlowe—granddaughter of Lady Lavinia Marlowe
Mrs. Ingraham—Lavender's maternal grandmother
Lady Lavinia Marlowe—baroness, Wycliffe's daughter; Lavender's paternal grandmother
Henri Lavigne—Hunt's cousin, son of Comte Lavigne, and great-nephew of Lady Reid
Arnaud Lavigne—artist brother of Henri

Jacob—Meera's lover
Helga Gaither—Wycliffe housekeeper
William Gaither— Wycliffe butler

GRAVESYDE PRIORY MYSTERY

The Mystery of the Missing Heiress
Book #2

Wycliffe Manor, a magnet for murder...

On a long-delayed errand to remote Wycliffe Manor, ex-Lieutenant Jack de Sackville stumbles across the murdered body of London dandy, Basil Culpepper, in the hedgerow, a long way from his usual haunts. To Jack's dismay, he discovers the earl's daughter Culpepper ruined hiding in Wycliffe's kitchen.

Disguised as a lowly cook, Lady Elspeth Villiers may have liked to shoot Culpepper for ruining her life, but she dropped out of sight for more immediate reasons than an old scandal—her wealth has become the focus of greedy men. The arrival of Jack, the man she's adored since childhood, along with Culpepper's corpse, mean her hiding place is no longer safe.

But once Lady Elsa reveals herself to the unconventional inhabitants of Wycliffe Manor, they become the protective family she has never known.

Outraged to learn the beautiful woman he once loved and lost has become a target of greed, Jack joins the investigation into Culpepper's death.

With a murderer on the loose, the amateur sleuths must unravel a deadly tangle of kidnappers and counterfeiters or the Manor's eccentric inhabitants will be in as much danger as their cook.

Buy The Mystery of the Missing Heiress

The Secrets of Wycliffe Manor
Patricia Rice

Copyright © 2023 Patricia Rice
Cover design © 2023 Killion Group
First digital edition Book View Café July 11, 2023
ISBN: 978-1-63632-153-0 ebook
ISBN: 978-1-63632-158-5 print

Published by Rice Enterprises, Dana Point, CA, an affiliate of Book View Café Publishing Cooperative.

Book View Café
304 S. Jones Blvd. Suite #2906
Las Vegas NV 89107

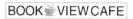

ALSO BY PATRICIA RICE

THE WEDDING QUESTION

THE WEDDING SURPRISE

School of Magic

LESSONS IN ENCHANTMENT

A BEWITCHING GOVERNESS

AN ILLUSION OF LOVE

THE LIBRARIAN'S SPELL

ENTRANCING THE EARL

CAPTIVATING THE COUNTESS

Psychic Solutions

THE INDIGO SOLUTION

THE GOLDEN PLAN

THE CRYSTAL KEY

THE RAINBOW RECIPE

THE AURA ANSWER

THE PRISM EFFECT

Historical Romance:

American Dream Series

MOON DREAMS

REBEL DREAMS

The Rebellious Sons

WICKED WYCKERLY

DEVILISH MONTAGUE

NOTORIOUS ATHERTON

FORMIDABLE LORD QUENTIN

The Regency Nobles Series

THE GENUINE ARTICLE

THE MARQUESS

ENGLISH HEIRESS

IRISH DUCHESS

Regency Love and Laughter Series

CROSSED IN LOVE

TWISTED GENIUS

Tales of Love and Mystery

BLUE CLOUDS

GARDEN OF DREAMS

NOBODY'S ANGEL

VOLCANO

CALIFORNIA GIRL

Historical Mysteries

Graneside Priory Series

THE SECRETS OF WYCLIFFE MANOR

Urban Fantasies

Writing as Jamie Quaid

Saturn's Daughters

BOYFRIEND FROM HELL

DAMN HIM TO HELL

GIVING HIM HELL

ABOUT BOOK VIEW CAFÉ

 *Book View Café* Publishing Cooperative (BVC) is an author-owned cooperative of professional writers, publishing in a variety of genres including fantasy, romance, mystery, and science fiction — with 90% of the proceeds going to the authors. Since its debut in 2008, BVC has gained a reputation for producing high-quality ebooks.

BVC's ebooks are DRM-free and are distributed around the world. The cooperative is now bringing that same quality to its print editions.

BVC authors include New York Times and USA Today bestsellers as well as winners and nominees of many prestigious awards.